BROKEN WINGS

BROKEN WINGS

TERRI CICCARINI

COPYRIGHT © 2010 BY TEREZA S. CICCARINI.

LIBRARY OF CONGRESS CONTROL NUMBER:		2010905685
ISBN:	HARDCOVER	978-1-4500-7935-8
	SOFTCOVER	978-1-4500-7934-1
	E-BOOK	978-1-4500-7936-5

This is a work of fiction. Names, characters, places and incidents either are the product of the author's imagination or are used fictitiously, and any resemblance to any actual persons, living or dead, events, or locales is entirely coincidental.

This book was printed in the United States of America.

To order additional copies of this book, contact:
Xlibris Corporation
1-888-795-4274
www.Xlibris.com
Orders@Xlibris.com
75695

CONTENTS

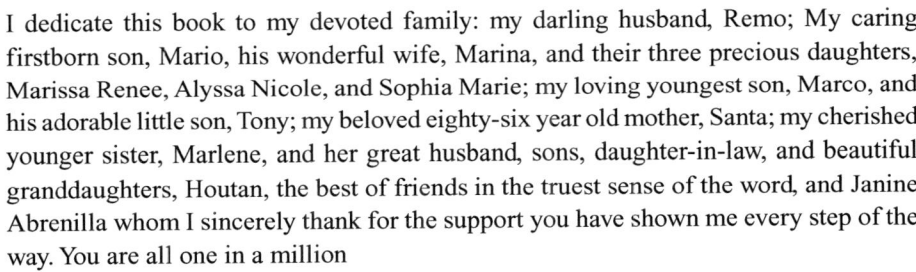

I dedicate this book to my devoted family: my darling husband, Remo; My caring firstborn son, Mario, his wonderful wife, Marina, and their three precious daughters, Marissa Renee, Alyssa Nicole, and Sophia Marie; my loving youngest son, Marco, and his adorable little son, Tony; my beloved eighty-six year old mother, Santa; my cherished younger sister, Marlene, and her great husband, sons, daughter-in-law, and beautiful granddaughters, Houtan, the best of friends in the truest sense of the word, and Janine Abrenilla whom I sincerely thank for the support you have shown me every step of the way. You are all one in a million

The love and respect that I feel for each and every one of you is something that I carry deep within my heart and soul!

LITTLE BIRD

Fly, little bird, fly . . .
Soar across the vast blue sky,
Where the sun is warm and bright;
Freedom is yours when up so high,
Out of reach, but still in my sight,
Wings spread out, so regal and wide,
Filled with power while gentle and light.
Don't look back and don't ask me why,
Forget your problems when gliding by.
Harm won't reach you if up in flight.
Though deeply hurt, you did not die,
And watching you makes everything right.
So leave your problems behind and fly
Little bird of mine . . . Just fly, fly, fly . . .

Written by Tereza S. Ciccarini

INTRODUCTION

The sleek maroon sedan sped through the dark, deserted streets of Derby, Connecticut. The wary driver, Drew Millner, could not take his eyes off the road in front of him, not even for a split second. The only visible sign of how nervous he truly felt was his white-knuckled hands gripping the steering wheel for dear life. Beside him, his wife, Jill, moaned as another strong contraction threatened to split her lower abdomen and pelvis in two. Drew wished that he could do something, anything, to help her, but he felt at a complete loss as to what or how. If he could only manage to peel his right hand off the wheel just long enough to touch the side of Jill's face, he knew that it would be of great comfort to her. He had done that same loving gesture hundreds of times before, but, God forgive him, he simply could not at the moment. Jill's breathing suddenly quickened and became even shallower, alarming her worried husband even more than he already was. "Hang on, babe, we are almost there," he said, trying to sound far more confident than he really felt, but the truth was quite the opposite. He was terrified that they would not make it to the hospital in time and that something could go terribly wrong with his wife, his baby or, worse yet, with them both. Silently, he prayed that all remaining traffic lights stayed green just long enough for him to drive right through without having to stop as he instinctively pressed down on the accelerator with increasing force. Just as he was about to lose his composure altogether, the large illuminated sign indicating the entrance to the emergency room at Griffin Hospital appeared to his right. "We are here, honey," he said in a relieved voice, exhaling the breath he had been holding for the last two blocks. As he pulled the key from the ignition, a yellow taxi slowly came up the wide driveway and parked right next to the Millners' car. In a second, Drew was at his wife's side, bending down to carefully help Jill to her feet. Just then, a pregnant young woman got out of the taxi and reached into the backseat, from where she retrieved a small overnight bag. As she was about to start walking, a contraction suddenly gripped her pelvis and back, but she did not utter a sound. She automatically flinched, her grimace momentarily distorting the beauty of her delicate features. Her green eyes, a pool of unshed tears she tried hard to control, reflected only a hint of the discomfort she was feeling at the time. Glancing over at Jill, she nodded in empathy, the pain finally subsiding to a more tolerable level. As they clumsily made their way toward the double glass doors of the hospital, the young girl slowed her pace considerably, thus allowing the couple to enter the facility ahead of her. By then, a soft mist had started to gently fall, covering the ground with a glossy sheen that reflected all the lights around with distorted brightness. The midspring night was a mild one, a precursor to the warm months yet to come. New England was, without a doubt, one of the most beautiful areas of the United States, and the differences between each of the four seasons presented a charm that was uniquely their own. Inside the ER, they were met with an unexpected combination of bright lights and loud noises, making them all feel momentarily overwhelmed. The chaotic pace they encountered stood in stark contrast to the quiet dimness of the outside world they had just left behind. The atmosphere in the large waiting room was one of human suffering and need. For many, relief would soon come as they eventually received the help they were looking for, but for some, no amount of support would suffice, a striking reminder that blessed are those who at least had their health. The sigh of gratitude and relief expressed by the ones that could be helped blended with the crying of those who could not, an undeniable yet necessary reminder that life was indeed precious. How ironic it was that many only realized that fact after it was already too late to clearly drive that point across. That harsh reality was a costly reminder that nothing in this world was ever 100 percent guaranteed, especially when referring to the health, and in some cases, the unfortunate lack of it, of all living creatures.

CHAPTER 1

The ER remained incredibly busy even though it was well past midnight by the time Drew, Jill, and Amy made their way to one of the admissions desks. Jill was quickly wheeled directly into the labor and delivery Unit, while Drew stayed behind in order to provide the pertinent information necessary for his wife's admission. Since she had arrived at the hospital alone, the other expectant mother had to personally provide the information needed on her own. The sympathetic clerk, realizing how uncomfortable the young woman was, apologized for the delay, but Amy was way beyond caring by then. Her pain level was so elevated that it prevented her from assimilating much around, blocking her ability to think or express herself clearly. Everything took a great deal of effort on her part, and the only thing she wanted to do was to simply be allowed to go in and have her baby. Finally, a relieved Amy was wheeled into the labor and delivery unit as well and given the room next to where Jill had been placed. Since both women were already so far along into their labors, the large unit, which until then had been relatively quiet, suddenly sprung to life. The nurses' station became a flurry of activity and precisely issued commands as several staff members paraded in and out of the two rooms. Each expectant mother was assigned her own medical team, which would assist during and after the birthing process. Each team included many well-trained nurses and several other support personnel, all in order to ensure the safety of both the patients and their respective newborns. Dr. Christina Sommers, the obstetrician who had cared for Jill since she was two months along, would be delivering the Millners' baby. Amy's baby, on the other hand, would be delivered by Dr. Nathan Harris, one of the clinic's OB/GYN doctors. Fortunately for her Dr. Harris, who happened to be the physician on call that night, was well-acquainted with her case, since he had been following the young woman's pregnancy for the last six months of her gestation. Both labors progressed without any unexpected complications, and soon the patients were moved to adjacent delivery rooms located at the end of a long and wide corridor on the west side of the large ward.

Drew found great comfort in finally being able to help his wife during the arduous process, especially during the final stages of the delivery. With great tenderness, he gently wiped her sweaty face with a cool cloth, whispering words of pride and encouragement as the birth became more imminent. With his fears and concerns at ease now that she was in capable hands, he was glad to concentrate on Jill, his own emotions on the back burner for the time being. Next door, Amy clutched the sides of the mattress as her labor intensified as well. She tried to stay focused on a small dark spot on one of the dropped ceiling tiles, which she had noticed while being wheeled into the delivery room. She fought hard not to scream every time another intense labor pain assailed her weak and tired body. The nurses were amazed at the way she handled herself, especially for one as young as she appeared to be.

She endured what they knew to be extremely severe pain without crying out. Having assisted in literally thousands of births, many commented how unusually strong her self-control was—a rare thing indeed during the hardest stage of any delivery. With tears running down her pale face, Amy continued to focus on the dark spot above her head, redirecting her attention from the excruciating pain she was going through to that abstract small stain, which became a substitute birthing coach. The nurses had seen firsthand how labor pains had the power to reduce even the most stoic of women into screaming masses of suffering, and yet this young woman held her own with unflinching courage and dignity. Pain, however, was only one aspect of the complex delivery process, since raging hormones usually took center stage, often creating havoc with the soon-to-be mother's emotionally and physically compromised status. Add to the mix the anxiety brought on by knowing that, after nine long months, they were just about to meet their child for the very first time, their minds embarked on a literal rollercoaster of great joy and overwhelming fear. More than likely, the tears that were freely running down Amy's face as her child was about to finally be delivered were from a combination of all those factors, give or take a few more personal ones. And so it was that, on an early Tuesday morning, on May 14, 1974, at exactly 3:45:18 a.m., at the very same time, down to the very same minute and second, both infants entered the world. A healthy baby boy was born to Drew James Millner and the former Jillian Elizabeth Chandler, and a beautiful little girl was born to Amy Brennan. Within seconds, the familiar sound of newborns crying reverberated up and down the hallways outside the delivery rooms, the sweet sound of life's renewal at its ultimate best bringing an instantaneous smile to anyone who was privileged enough to hear them. The cycle of life had come full circle, resulting in something so special that it never failed to touch the hearts and souls of those involved. How could one miniscule egg and a tiny sperm work so perfectly and diligently at creating the truest miracle that was a human life?

The ecstatic new parents were allowed to hold their precious infants right after they were cleaned up. Soon they were doing what most fathers and mothers had been doing for centuries before them, rich and poor alike. Gently but very thoroughly, they meticulously began to check their precious little ones, marveling at how utterly perfect and beautiful they really were. Tiny fingers and toes were counted, fragile little heads and faces caressed, and kisses were rained on soft, warm cheeks. For some reason, babies seemed to always smell like nothing else in the world, perhaps a simple combination of fresh little bodies and innocent little hearts. In spite of everything they had to go through in order to be born, they still managed to somehow smell like nothing else could. Smiles quickly replaced the painful grimaces and the worried frowns of not that long before. Hugs went hand in hand with utter relief that everything turned out so well for the mothers and their adorable newborns. The intense pain that was so difficult to endure in the hours preceding the actual birth was immediately forgotten the second they were able to hold their babies in their anxious arms. There was nothing more rewarding for the members of the labor and delivery unit than the trouble-free birth of a healthy baby, which was what they strived for but never took for granted. They were very aware of the fact that unforeseeable complications could arise at any minute during the birth, even when the pregnancy had progressed problem-free for all nine months. All the medical personnel who worked in that field had seen more than their share of tragedy, and there were many instances when the outcomes were far from the happy ones usually associated with the arrival of a baby. Thank God those episodes constituted only a small percentage of all the births in the USA, but they always left a lasting impression and tremendous sadness among the staff and everyone else involved. Especially difficult for the staff to handle were the cases in which those tragic outcomes could've been prevented, such as the babies who were born to drug-addicted mothers, thus addicted themselves, or those with fetal alcohol syndrome who possibly faced a life of physical and intellectual delays. To the health team, the look of love, pride, and gratitude they saw reflected on the new parents' faces was the reward they basked on and of detrimental value to their overall sense of emotional well-being, their inspiration to continue with their daily duties day after day. And ultimately, those were the only thanks they needed in order to go from birth to birth, regardless of the tragic circumstances they had to sometimes handle and learn to overcome so that they could go on helping other families to welcome a new child into the world.

Drew could not stop staring at his son, still unable to believe that he was actually there, silent tears making their way down his intent face. He felt suddenly overwhelmed by the depth of the love that he felt for his child, causing his heart to swell with pride and passion. Images of pockets full of squiggly worms, of frogs being squeezed by chubby dirty little hands, and of cuddling by the fireplace with his child snuggly asleep on his lap quickly filled his mind. They joyously competed with those of little league baseball games, scraped knees that needed to be kissed, bedtime stories being read to a pajama-clad sleepy little boy, and much more that he was already looking forward to. He could almost swear that he could hear his son saying "I love you this much, Daddy" as his child wrapped his small arms tightly around his father's neck, his fierce hug embracing both his heart and his soul. A smile spread slowly across his face as he watched his wife breast-feed their little boy, more than ready for this new and exciting chapter in their love story. This was the wondrous point in their lives when one plus one magically made three.

After a while, both newborns were whisked away to the neonatal unit, where they would be further examined and fully evaluated, bathed, diapered, and snugly wrapped in a hospital blanket, a tiny hat covering their little heads in order to preserve their precious body heat. As their babies were being cared for, the new mothers were undergoing a thorough evaluation of their own, their personal hygiene deferred to until all of the necessary postpartum care was expediently carried out in order to minimize the chance of any avoidable complication from the delivery. It was only after that aspect of the birthing process was completed that their much-desired personal needs were finally tended to. They were then transferred to the maternity ward, which was located right around the corner from the nursery where their infants were by then fast asleep. Upon arriving at the ward, they were both wheeled into the same room; Amy was placed in the bed by the window, and Jill was given the one by the door. Drew soon arrived with a massive bouquet of yellow roses, Jill's absolute favorite, and a huge smile to go with the beautiful flowers. After lovingly kissing his wife on the lips, he promptly informed her that, in spite of the very early hour, he had already called her parents, as well as his mom and dad. Beyond ecstatic that everything went so well, they had promised to call the rest of the family and close friends in order to share the excellent news. In her bed, Amy had a faraway look on her young face. Lost in her thoughts, she appeared to be totally unaware of her surroundings, her expression a mixture of sheer happiness and deep longing. For a second, a touch of sadness crossed her amazingly beautiful emerald green eyes, giving her delicate features a hardness that was not there before, but it quickly faded away as she relaxed once more.

Drew remained with his wife a while longer before telling her that he would soon be heading home for a much-needed shower and some sleep, in that precise order. His voice was laden with emotion as he murmured to her how proud he was of her and their child, his right hand tenderly caressing the left side of her face. With that intimate and affectionate gesture, he was able to instantly put a radiant smile on both of their tired but contented faces. As he bent down to give her a gentle good-bye kiss, he whispered in her ear how much he loved her, promising that he would be back soon, by early afternoon at the latest. Before leaving the hospital though, he made another stop by the nursery, where the sight of his precious little son instantly filled his eyes with joyous tears. He felt beyond relieved and extremely grateful that everything had gone so well for all of them. "My son," he whispered, loving the way the words sounded when spoken. "Our son," he quickly corrected himself, chuckling at his temporary lack in judgment. By the time he finally left the hospital, it was a little past seven o'clock in the morning. He could not contain his enthusiasm at being a father and found himself singing all the way home, images of his wife and child occupying his mind and warming his heart. "What a lucky man I am," he said out loud, between off-key lyrics of songs he did not recall even knowing. Before he realized it, he was pulling into their driveway. Upon entering their home, he was struck by how empty it felt already without Jill and their baby in it. Heading straight to the nursery, he opened the wall-to-wall closet from where he retrieved a light brown teddy bear with big padded paws and a smiling face.

He had fallen in love with the stuffed animal the minute he saw it because it reminded him of his very own Mister Boogles, which his mother had bought when she found out she was pregnant with him. Kissing the top of the bear's soft head, he lovingly placed it on the right upper corner of the crib. "Our son's first teddy bear, Jill," he whispered, picturing his little boy asleep in the crib that patiently waited for its precious occupant to arrive. "Very soon. He'll be home real, real soon," Drew added, his heart overflowing with happiness and pride.

Unfortunately, although they were both beyond exhaustion from the long and intense ordeal they had just gone through, neither young mother was given a chance to get any sleep right away. Several staff members continually paraded in and out of the room, a common occurrence in every hospital setting, as the night shift came to an end and another day shift got underway. It was nearly nine o'clock when Amy and Jill were finally able to get some well deserved rest. Before long, they were both blissfully asleep.

Drew was pleasantly surprised when he got back to the hospital at around 2:00 p.m. and encountered his parents waiting by the elevators. Deborah and Raymond Millner could not contain their enthusiasm at the prospect of seeing their new grandson, the first one that they would be able to thoroughly enjoy as he grew up. Drew was the youngest of their three children, but his siblings had moved to California several years before along with their spouses, so they were not around when the grandkids started to arrive. Jill's family, on the other hand, all lived within thirty miles of one another. The youngest child of William and Sophia Chandler, she had two brothers, one sister, and several nieces and nephews.

Since only two visitors were allowed at a time, Drew escorted his parents to the waiting lounge before heading in to see his wife. Her Mom and Dad were sitting on her bed talking with their daughter when he entered the room. Getting up to congratulate their son-in-law, their broad smiles made their eyes appear like two half almonds on their happy faces. After kissing Jill, Drew proceeded to boast about his big boy, pride written all over his overjoyed face. After several trips to the nursery, both sets of grandparents decided it was time to get going, heading out at the same time. The remainder of the day was filled with a stream of visitors as Jill's siblings and their spouses stopped by to welcome their brand-new little nephew into the family. Even Marissa, who had been Jill's best friend since their first day of kindergarten, managed to sneak in, eager to see the baby. Drew spent the rest of the afternoon and evening alternating between being by his wife's side and running back to the nursery, excited to show off his little one to every visitor who came by, whether he knew the person or not. Before long, Jill's side of the room was overflowing with all kinds of colorful flower arrangements. Congratulatory cards soon filled the large metal card holder that hung on the wall, facing her bed.

On the other side of the partially pulled curtain, Amy lovingly stared at her precious little angel, slowly taking in her tiny round face, her pink heart-shaped mouth and button nose, and the soft and shiny dark hair covering her little head. She felt so utterly blessed that she began to weep tears of pure happiness, her sweet baby daughter cradled snugly against her chest, peacefully asleep. The rhythmic sound of her breathing filled Amy with such a sense of peace and joy that it caused her to instantly go from weeping to smiling, no further traces of sadness to be found in her tear-filled emerald eyes. She tried hard to block out the fact that she had no visitors while her lucky roommate had more than her share. She was not jealous, not really. She just wished that a certain someone was there with them, especially during such a special time, that was all. There was no one to show off her little girl to, to brag about how truly amazing she was. She made believe that it didn't matter anyway as long as she had her baby in her arms, but it did. Deep down she was willing to acknowledge how much it really hurt, but she wasn't going to let it get her down, not now that she had her daughter right there, next to her heart. Before long, she had fallen asleep as well, all worries about their future put aside for the time being, a wonderful respite even if it would only last for a short while. When she was sleeping, she was blessedly spared from the pain that lurked just beneath the surface, one that she hid so well from everyone but herself. Buried deep within her soul, she couldn't get rid of it anymore than she could her own shadow on a sunny day, regardless of how hard she tried to. Longing was such a sad and unforgiving emotion, taking over hearts and minds with indiscriminating hunger. Thank God Amy had her little angel now, a bright ray of sunshine in her life from that moment on. It would be enough to help her get through anything life might have in store for her, she was sure of it. An angel of her own, her daughter and now her world, the grandest gift of all . . .

By the second day, Jill and Amy began to exchange a few details about their personal lives, which often happened when people were confined together in a small hospital room. Jill, clearly the more talkative of the two, was more than willing to share quite a bit of information about her life. Amy, who had a tendency to be much more reserved, was quite the opposite, preferring to listen instead of talking. Their personalities forged a perfectly harmonized atmosphere between the two of them from the get go, they soon realized. Amy was glad to hear all that Jill had to say and was actually grateful for the temporary reprieve and distraction from her own thoughts. Her emotions had been all over the place lately, an odd mixture of joy and sadness, of longing and belonging, of hope and fear, all rolled up into a silent heartache. At times, her sadness managed to overshadow all of her other emotions except where her daughter was concerned. She loved the fact that she was a mother and could not imagine life without her little girl.

Jill proceeded to tell her roommate how she first met Drew, when she was just a sophomore and he a senior at Sacred Heart University in nearby Fairfield. They were both taking classes geared toward respective careers in the educational field. It was definitely a case of love at first sight, she confided, and their engagement, a year after they had started dating, came as no surprise to anyone who knew them. Being wise beyond their years and clearly more mature than most people their age, they had both agreed that their wedding should wait until Drew had the chance to complete his master's degree program, a decision that proved to be the best they could have ever made, since it provided them with a more secure financial base to build upon.

The wedding ceremony, which took place on a sunny Saturday morning, on September 19, 1972, was "like a fairy tale," Jill recalled in a dreamy soft voice. "Tell me all about your gown," Amy interjected. She certainly didn't look like someone who just had a baby the day before but more like a curious teenager. With her chin propped up on both hands and her legs crossed under her slender body, she eyed Jill with genuine interest, her long dark hair framing a heart-shaped face that radiated nothing but friendliness. "Well," Jill answered, "the dress was the same one my mom wore when she married my dad thirty-five years ago. Since we are both very similar in height and weight, it ended up only needing some minor alterations. The gown was made of satin, with a high collar and long slim sleeves. The top was fitted, and I asked a seamstress to bead it with tiny crystals and small pearls. The bottom part of the gown started out fitted as well, but it cleverly flared out from the hips down. There were literally a hundred little satin-covered buttons running from my neck to my lower back, at which point a multiple pleated design hid quite a bit of material. That little trick gave me plenty of room to walk and dance comfortably in. And Drew, I'm sure, simply had a great deal of fun undoing all those buttons afterwards," she added with a mischievous grin. She went on to reveal that she bought the full length veil a few weeks prior to the happy day. "How about your bouquet, Jill?" Amy asked, her eyes glued to the other woman's glowing face. "It was all white and consisted of small roses surrounded by pompom carnations. A simply stunning white orchid was placed in the center of the bouquet. And the bridesmaids, they looked absolutely gorgeous in their off-the-shoulder deep purple gowns, their flowing full skirts gently swaying in the mild September breeze when they walked. They later confessed how scared they were that I would choose one of those hideous dresses we have all laughed about but were pleasantly surprised that I ended up picking such a lovely style. The groomsmen all wore double breasted black tuxedoes with black vests and bowties. Drew, however, was simply dashing, wearing the same style tuxedo but with a silvery-gray vest and bowtie as did his adorable five-year-old nephew. Justin looked like a little man. When I close my eyes, I can still picture both of them, blond hair and all."

Loving to elaborate on every minute detail, Jill went on to say that Justin looked just like a mini-Drew, giving her an insight as to what their child could look like should it be a boy, and she had loved what she saw. She admitted that she went totally overboard with the final number of attendants they ended up with, saying that she simply wanted to be surrounded by as many of their loved ones and friends as she could. It was, after all, the most special day in a woman's life. The wedding party consisted of ten pairs, including her precious little niece, Emily, as the flower girl, and Justin as the ring bearer. Her sister, Tara, was her maid of honor, and Drew's brother, Phillip, his best man.

"Where did you go on your honeymoon, Jill?" Amy asked, her chin still propped up on her hands and a look of deep interest on her young face. She seemed to be living her own dream through her roommate's romantic descriptions. "Well, we both decided to go to Italy, a place we had heard so much about and truly wanted to see. We landed in Milan, an extremely metropolitan city and the capital of Italy's renowned fashion industry, and stayed there for two full days before moving on. We tried to visit as many cities as we could during our two-week stay, but we could have used an extra one for there was so much to see, so much history everywhere. Still we managed to see Venice and the famous Piazza San Marco and even took a trip to Murano, where handmade glass is made. The color of the final product is controlled by the artisans making it, depending on how long they blow into it. And yes, we did go on a romantic gondola ride. You can't go to Venezia and not do that; it would be a sin! From there we visited Pisa, and let me tell you, the darn tower looks like it's about to fall! The incline is so blatant that it really scares you. We climbed hundreds of small steps that went around and around until we reached the massive bell. What a view! We then proceeded to Genova, Firenze or Florence, Bologna, Napoli or Naples, the Island of Capri, Pompeii, and Rome. In the Island of Capri, we visited the Blue Grotto, and let me tell you, I have never seen water so transparent and blue in my life! Venice was absolutely the most romantic place on earth, I swear, but Rome," she gushed, "Roma, as the Italians call it, was the icing on the cake." On a roll now, she went on to tell Amy that she was the youngest of four children and had two brothers, Daniel and Nicholas, and one sister, Tara. She further told a totally fascinated Amy that Drew had one older brother, Phillip, and a sister, Hannah.

All of a sudden, Jill stopped talking altogether, a frown appearing on her forehead for some reason. "Wow! I never realized how much I love to talk until just now," she said. "Your poor ears must be hurting like crazy after listening to my babbling for so long," she added with an apologetic look on her face, which had guilt written all over it. She took a deep breath before continuing in a contrite tone of voice, "No wonder my mother-in-law often calls me her little chatter box!" The self-reprimanding in her seemingly repentant voice caused Amy to burst out laughing for the first time since they started sharing the same hospital room. The sound of her laughter, so warm and spontaneous, brought a genuinely satisfied smile to Jill's face as well as giving her the go ahead she hardly needed to continue talking. "I can't help it, I swear. I can't change who I am even though I have tried, I really have," she added, suddenly serious and in a reflective mood. "Then don't," Amy was quick to reply, "not on my account anyway! Truth be told, I wish that I could be more like you, but I'm not. You can't change who you truly are anymore than I can change who I am, Jill. Besides, I happen to think that you are fine just the way you are. Please, don't change." Her reassurance seemed so warm and sincere that it caused Jill to wink at her roommate, a mischievous glint in her crystal blue eyes. Her mouth, bless her huge heart, was already all set to get going all over again.

As she so candidly admitted to Jill, Amy had always been far more comfortable listening than talking. She didn't reveal much about her life or herself other than the fact that she was from out of state and had moved to Connecticut just a little over two years before. She also admitted that she chose to name her daughter Samantha, a name she had loved ever since she was a small child. Surprising herself with how much she had revealed already, she further added that she was very relieved that she had a little girl instead of a boy. Noticing the quizzical frown that suddenly formed on Jill's forehead, she was quick to explain the reason why. "I am really ashamed to admit this, but I never considered the fact that the baby I was carrying was anything but a girl. That is why the thought of having to chose a boy's name just in case never even crossed my mind." Upon hearing her candid admission, Jill started to laugh hysterically, causing an equally questioning frown to appear again but on Amy's forehead this time around. "You want to know something? I'm guilty of the exact same thing, only in reverse," Jill said in a conspiratorial tone of voice. "I never entertained the notion of giving birth to anything but a little boy. I would certainly be in the proverbial creek without a paddle if my son turned out to be a daughter after all." As she said that, Jill looked from side to side a few times as if she was afraid that someone had overheard her confession. As they stared at each other, the puzzled look on their faces was so utterly pathetic that they were suddenly overcome by peals of laughter. With tears streaming down their faces, they continued to laugh until their sides literally hurt from laughing so hard and for so long. Here they were, two first-time young mothers who were practically strangers but who happened to share a unique and genuine bond. Developed during an exceptionally sentimental time in their lives, they felt like old friends already. A truly comforting feeling all around, it had an extra special meaning for Amy, who was in dire need of a friend during such an important time in her life. Simultaneously taking a deep breath, they found themselves laughing all over again at their shared faux pas, clutching their sides in hilarious agony after minutes of actual silly behavior. It took them quite a while before they were able to resume talking without breaking up all over again, the air in their small room one of camaraderie and solidarity. Their uncanny ability to get along so well was a blessing in disguise for Amy. She really needed to laugh like she just had for reasons so painful that she could not bring herself to talk about them, not even with someone as kind and as understanding as Jill. Some things, erroneously so, seemed to hurt a tad less if not acknowledged or talked about, not until the person who was hurting was ready to finally face the pain. The level of her aching loneliness, as well as its ultimate meaning and hidden ramifications, were something that Amy was not up to dealing with, not just yet. Let her simply enjoy being Samantha's mother a little while longer. Besides, the very real possibility that she probably would never be able to deal with her pain was always there, in her heart and soul.

Jill turned out to be more than friendly and talkative, for she soon realized the stark contrast between the two sides of the small room. It was obvious that Amy did not have any visitors, but there could be many reasons why, she reasoned, not wanting to jump to any conclusions. Jill felt great empathy for her young roommate, knowing that Amy had been in Connecticut for only a short while, therefore she probably didn't have many friends in the immediate area. The total lack of phone calls really concerned her, but it was the fact that the baby's father never came around to see them that bothered her the most. Could he be away? Was he in the military, perhaps? And why had Amy never mentioned him or his name? There were no flowers or congratulatory cards on her side of the room either. Jill actually felt guilty at having so much adulation from so many people while Amy had none. She could only imagine how lonely her roommate must be feeling, seemingly all alone during such a special time in her life. She quietly asked her kind husband to buy some special flowers for Amy and her baby, and within an hour, an absolutely gorgeous bouquet of two dozen long-stemmed red roses with a delicate white rose in the center for the baby was promptly delivered. The flowers were artfully arranged among bunches of pink and white baby's breath and placed in a lovely pink, yellow, and white ceramic vase in the shape of a baby's bootie. "Good job, sweetheart," Jill whispered upon seeing the exquisite flowers. *I could not have done a better job myself,* she gladly conceded, truly pleased with Drew for his obvious generosity and good taste. The attached card, written in Drew's long and lean handwriting, stated: *Dear Amy, from now on you will never be alone again. With our best wishes and sincere affection always. Drew, Jill, and Drew Jr.* Caught totally by surprise, Amy had to read the card a few times before the sentiment and meaning of the words finally sank in. She couldn't believe the act of friendship and thoughtfulness that they were extending to her and little Samantha, especially given the fact that they barely knew each other at all. With determination, she fought hard to swallow the stubborn lump that had formed in her throat as she read the card once more. The beauty of the massive bouquet that now graced her otherwise bare night stand was indeed incredible, something she had only seen in movies and magazines, but what it ultimately represented to her was something that money could never buy. She blinked a few times in order to keep the tears that filled her eyes from making their way down her face. She had hardly cried since Sam's birth, and she knew that if she did so now, she might never stop. After a few minutes, she slowly walked to where Jill stood with a radiant smile on her lips. In a smooth movement, Amy gathered her roommate gently in her trembling arms, giving her a hug that came straight from the heart. She was clearly touched by the young couple's extremely kindness and loving gesture. No words were necessary as Jill caught the shimmer of tears pooling in the corner of Amy's eyes. There were moments when equally shared and understood silence spoke much louder than any words ever could. And this was, without a doubt, one of those moments. The absence of the baby's father was never mentioned.

A couple of days later, both new mothers were eager and more than ready to be discharged. Drew pulled Amy aside and offered to drive her and little Samantha home, but she politely declined the kind offer. She explained that a friend was already on her way to pick them up. Although she put on a good front, Drew could see right through her brave façade. He was sure that Amy wasn't telling him the truth but decided to go along with it. He could easily understand why she found it necessary to tell such a harmless lie. Wise beyond his years, he knew that there were many times in a person's life when pride was probably the only thing that held them together, that motivated and compelled them to forge ahead and not look back, the special glue that prevented them to fall completely apart. He also understood how much courage it ultimately took to accomplish that. It would certainly be much easier to simply cave in and give up, to get immersed and totally lost in self-pity, and to feel sorry for their situation since no one else seemed to. When you added necessity to that pride, as he suspected it was in

Amy's case, the structure upon which that person stood upon was a fragile one to say the least. That foundation would only get stronger if the person was able to hold on, if their need not to fail was stronger than their need to simply continue to survive. It was important to be aware that to move one step forward, you had to make sure that you did not move ten steps backward. Even a slight crack on any of the thin walls they erected around themselves for protection and survival could turn into a crater capable of causing those same walls to come crumbling down, burying them under all the rubble. If the structure managed to remain intact, the person then had a chance to start over again, gaining inspiration and momentum from their strength and will to live. But should it all fall to pieces, the process of rebuilding a new foundation would be a hundred times more difficult the second time around. Amy got herself to the hospital by taxi, Drew remembered well, and he was almost certain that she would get herself and her daughter home the same way. He truly admired her courage and tenacity, especially for someone as young as she appeared to be, so he decided to keep his suspicions all to himself, not wanting to add to her already heavy burden. She had most likely been hurt enough thus far, he realized, the obvious absence of her daughter's father foremost on his mind. Besides that, he didn't want to worry Jill either. He knew his wife well and was sure that she would be quite upset if she found out what was really going on. After all was said and done, it was Amy's decision and nobody else's he finally acknowledged. He had every intention of honoring her wishes, even though it pained him to be aware of the truth. It would be so easy for him to take them home, he sadly admitted, his conscience killing him. It was not only a question of it being a real simple thing to do but, most importantly, the right thing to do as well, especially for someone as sweet and humble as Amy. It was, however, not up to him to question her decision, regardless of how much he wanted to help her and her child. Without being noticed, he slipped ten twenty-dollar bills into Amy's bag, praying that the young woman would manage to get wherever she was headed safely. He also prayed that somewhere in her life there was at least one person that would make sure that they remained that way, for Amy and her baby deserved at least that. Again he was reminded of how truly fortunate he really was to have the love of his life by his side, to share everything with, the good and the not so good. And now they had their son, their beautiful and healthy little son, the most precious gift they could have given to each other.

Amy and Jill took their time saying good-bye and then proceeded to kiss the babies, trying hard not to cry as they got ready to leave. Soon the Millners, with their little infant carefully all bundled up, were finally led out the door. Jill tried hard not to turn around and look at Amy one more time; she knew that she would break down and cry if she did.

*   *   *

This time around, the car ride was quite different than the one they had taken just a few days earlier. Drew, feeling totally relaxed, proudly looked from his cherished wife to his adorable little boy lying safely and snuggly in his car seat. The soft sounds that the baby made while he slept captivated Drew's heart, especially the soft sighs that escaped his little lips in slumber. He still couldn't believe how lucky he was and how deeply he loved his wife and little son. He often managed to stroke the side of Jill's face with the back of his right hand. That simple and yet very personal and intimate gesture always managed to put them in a happy mood as proven by their radiant smiles; this time, though, those smiles stayed on their faces all the way home. They saw the large bunch of blue and white balloons tied to their mailbox as soon as they turned from Mohegan Road to Rydell Drive. The banner across their front porch, written in huge bright blue letters, proudly announced the arrival of the newest addition to the Millner household as it read: "It's a boy! Welcome home, little Drew Jr.!"

CHAPTER 2

Entering their spacious and comfortable home, Jill headed directly to the nursery, which was conveniently located right next to the master bedroom on the right side of the ranch style house. She gently placed her still-sleeping son in his crib and covered him with a soft yellow blanket. She then proceeded to leisurely look around, taking the extra time to truly admire and appreciate the beautiful room she had so lovingly decorated during her pregnancy. The pride and care she obviously took in carrying out the painstaking work was evident in every minute detail. Her patience and creativity had earned her high praise from everyone who had a chance to see the room after all the work was completed. A masterpiece, her pleasantly surprised husband called it when he saw it for the first time. He was totally impressed with her meticulousness and great ability as a decorator, hugging his wife's very round body within the safety of his strong arms. As if on cue, their soon-to-be-born child chose that instant to start one of his famous kicking workouts as if in total agreement with the perfection of what would soon be his very own sanctuary. Indeed she managed to do an excellent job, she now conceded, still reticent to give herself too much credit for something that came so naturally to her and her motherly heart. The walls were painted two-thirds of the way up in a soothing shade of sage green with a soft buttery-yellow color the rest of the way up to the antique-white ceiling. The two pretty pastel colors were joined together by a lovely twelve-inch-wide border, depicting adorable smiling frogs resting on top of lily pads. Several tiny dragonflies, snails, turtles, ladybugs, bees, and butterflies completed the tranquil pond scene. The same theme was repeated on the small lamp placed on top of the changing table, on the ruffled window valance topping the creamy white chiffon curtains, and on the mobile and linens adorning the dark oak crib. A few quilted and framed pictures, repeating many of the key scenes from the border, complemented the utterly charming décor. *A little piece of paradise for our little gift from Heaven*, Jill whispered with infinite gratitude. She felt completely pleased and peaceful at the moment, her soul flooded with happiness while her heart simply overflowed with renewed hope for the future. She blew a kiss in her sleeping child's direction and, with a contented sigh and a smile, proceeded to join her husband in the family room. The inviting fire crackling in the massive red-brick fireplace–probably one of the last of the season–did wonders at chasing away the mid-May chill from the large room. At Drew's request, she stretched on the comfortable oversized recliner by the fireplace. Both sides of the family, their loving, generous, and closely knit family, thoughtfully decided that visits to the new baby could very well wait until the following day, thus giving the new parents some much deserved time alone. Their first night at home as a newly formed family was a relatively quiet one, much to the Millners' relief. The baby woke up every three to four hours for a quick diaper change and a feeding and then fell asleep with not much of a fuss to speak of. Jill was glad to be back in her own bed and with Drew's arm around her waist, something he had not been able to do for the last three months of her pregnancy. She was also glad that their son had arrived, that he was healthy, and that he now slept peacefully only a few feet away from where they laid, in the comfort and security of his own large crib.

The following day started at 6:00 a.m. for the sleepy parents, with the baby's wake up hunger cries replacing their faithful alarm clock. Drew awkwardly fought with his son's diaper before handing him to Jill for the breast-feeding. It was a tough battle for the new father, this diaper duty stuff, but he soon got the hang of it, sort of anyway. The first phone call they received was from Phillip, Drew's older brother, who had moved to California right after marrying his high school sweetheart, Kelly, in 1968. Their boys, Justin and Jonathan, six and four now, kept on interrupting their dad in their eagerness to talk to the new baby, which caused everyone to burst out laughing. Drew missed his brother terribly and was thrilled to hear his voice. Now that he was a father himself, he was sorry for not having a bigger role in his little nephews' lives. The last time he had seen them was at his wedding. Drew's sister, Hannah, was the next to call, again from California, where they had also relocated after her husband's firm transferred there in 1971. Hannah and Josh were the parents of twins, Jordan and Rachel, fourteen months old. Unfortunately, he had only seen the twins in pictures and was really looking forward to meeting the adorable pair in person, the sooner the better.

For a while, the phone was actually silent, giving the doorbell a chance to wake the baby as family member after family member marched in to see the little one. Soon the house was brimming with activity, and children were laughing as they ran everywhere. Besides both sets of grandparents, Jill's siblings began to appear as well, their little troops not far behind. First to arrive was Tara, her older sister, who had married her husband, Paul, the year before and was now expecting her first child in less than four months. Next to show up was Daniel, her oldest brother, along with his wife, Kristen, and their three kids–Kathleen, eight, Gabriel, six, and Vanessa, three. The last to arrive was Nicholas, her middle brother, with his wife, Simone, and their two little girls, Denise, five, and Melissa, two. Everyone wanted to hold the baby; the kids wanted attention; Drew wanted to show off his son; and Jill wanted peace and quiet. As glad as she was to have such a devoted family and as happy as she was they had come over to see the baby, she just wished that they hadn't all shown up at the same time. It was true that when it rained, it poured, she chuckled, causing her mother, Sophia, as laidback as a naturally laidback person truly was, to give her a questioning mystified look. Jill was simply beyond plain relieved when, after what to her seemed more like over a week's stay, they all decided to leave at once. The amount of noise inside the packed house, having reached the all-time highest volume for sure, blessedly returned to a more tolerable level once again. She was in bed by 7:00 p.m. and didn't wake up until midnight, when Drew had no choice but to bring the baby to her to feed. He was an accomplished diaper-changing pro by then, but he would never be able to breast-feed DJ. The equipment needed to carry out the crucial task was something that only Jill was in charge of!

Drew reluctantly returned to his teaching job the following Monday and grunted when he heard the baby wake up, as usual, at six that morning. He truly loved being a seventh grade math and science teacher, and Park Ridge Elementary School, where he had worked since he had finished his master's degree, was like a second home to him. His true affection for Jackson Brooks, who was the principal, was an added bonus, for he really enjoyed spending time with his friend, who is as dedicated to all of their students as he also was. Conveniently located just a little over a mile from where they lived, Drew could actually walk there if he wished to. Right now though, all he wanted to do was to stay home for a few more days, but his duties couldn't wait. He continued to literally grunt the entire way there. With the end of the current school year in about five weeks' time, he could hardly contain his enthusiasm at the thought of being able to spend the summer months with his little one morning, noon, and night.

Jill, on the other hand, who worked as a guidance counselor at the same school, was still on maternity leave. Luckily for her, she didn't have to resume her position until the beginning of the following school year. She actually basked and glowed in the knowledge that she would be able to remain at home with their son for at least the next three months, thank God, during which time she would continue to breast-feed him. She knew that she had to get the baby used to the bottle at some point, so she wisely began to introduce it to him at the start of his second month, thus giving Drew the pleasure of further bonding with the ever-changing little boy. She pumped her own breast milk about three times a day, storing the milk already in their bottles, all set to go inside the refrigerator. The routine she devised for the three of them was a genius-worthy simplistic one. It made it much easier to assimilate their transition from a newly formed couple as well as passionate lovers to that of a newly formed couple and passionate lovers fully integrated with that of brand-new parents of a much-loved baby, their precious little DJ. Bless his wife's huge heart, Drew acknowledged, his own swelling a million times over with awe, admiration, and unabashed pride. Being married to Jill was by far the easiest "gig" he ever had. No need to get paid, honest!

* * *

It was during the third trimester of her pregnancy that Jill and Drew began to talk at length about who they should choose as the soon-to-arrive baby's godparents. They came to the same conclusion three weeks before the actual birth. Ever since she was a little girl herself, Jill had felt extremely close to one girl in particular, and their friendship had only grown stronger as the years flew by. Because Marissa had been her best friend from kindergarten on, she chose her to be her first child's godmother. Drew, on the other hand, did not meet his best friend, Eric, until his first day of high school, but they soon became more like brothers than friends. He couldn't remember the number of times Eric was more than happy to eat leftovers at his house before crashing on the living room couch for the night and vice versa. He was sure that Eric would be the perfect choice as the baby's godfather. When asked, they both felt beyond honored at being even considered, telling Drew and Jill that they would take their role in the little boy's life very seriously and would continue to be there for them through thick and thin.

Jill and Marissa, who often referred to themselves as the proverbial two peas in a pod, couldn't be more different if they tried, yet they became literally joined at the hip from the moment they met. Extremely extrovert Jill and extremely shy Marissa. Book-smart Jill and book-phobic Marissa. Blonde-haired, blue-eyed Jill and dark-haired, brown-eyed Marissa. Petite and lean Jill and tall and curvy Marissa. They could well pass for The Odd Couple all right but were more like Lucy and Ethel in their antics, nurturing their special friendship through twenty long years, and becoming even closer during their turbulent teen period.

A product of the sixties, they sure had their fair share of close calls and told each other things they wouldn't dare tell anyone else! They did indeed smoked pot a few times but didn't like the way it made them feel afterwards. Alcohol, so available back then, posed a problem for Marissa, who felt her inhibitions dissipate after a few drinks. Jill didn't buy into the feeble excuse that alcohol and cigarettes were not drugs simply because it was not illegal to buy them; anything you felt dependent on to get through the day was indeed a drug, legal or not. She helped her friend through many drinking binges, mostly between the ages of fifteen and seventeen. She often covered up for Marissa, never allowing her to drive when she was drunk, and having her friend sleep over her house so that her parents would not see their daughter when she had a hangover. Jill's tireless and diligent loyalty to her best friend and confidante was inspiring, and she simply refused to entertain the thought that Marissa needed professional help; fortunate for both, she had been right. By the time they graduated from high school, Marissa had stopped drinking altogether, thanks to the good Lord and her good friend Jill. Hard drugs were never "their thing" though because they were too afraid of the many consequences associated with them and didn't want to risk becoming addicted to them. They were too smart to risk the problems often associated with the tendency to only increase their use the long you stayed on them. It was a well-proven fact among addicts that the longer you "used" them, the more drugs your system needed to feel the same effect. Even Drew didn't know about these little secrets, and if he shared any with Eric, he didn't tell her about them either. They had a tremendous amount of respect for each other for their unwavering loyalty to their best friends and vice versa.

"It's really amazing, you know?" she told her husband one day as they were having one of their heart-to-heart talks. "A best friend can mean more to a person than many blood relatives. There are times when they mean even more than immediate family ever could, isn't it true?" Drew, who totally understood what she was trying to say, simply nodded his head, for he felt exactly the same way. You didn't get the choice of picking any of your blood relatives; you were simply born into a family that was formed already, with many great people and a few not-so-great ones, if you were completely honest with yourself. Friends, however, were a totally different story, for with them you had the chance to choose or not, depending on what you were looking for. With best friends, it was even a more selective mystery, since you were simply drawn to them and often for totally odd reasons that might fail to make any sense whatsoever to anyone but those directly involved.

Drew and Eric, as a matter of fact, were a perfect example of one such especially odd relationship. Meeting during a very difficult time in a young man's life, the turbulent midteen years, they were able to continue to build onto their friendship well into adulthood. Often going on double dates before and even after Drew met Jill, Marissa was the logical choice to make. Drew was literally floored when Eric confided in him that he was beginning to fall for Marissa but even more surprised when Jill told him that her best friend felt the same way about Eric. After they had been dating for a year, Eric finally proposed to his unsuspecting girlfriend on Super Bowl Sunday 1973. He intentionally bypassed Christmas and New Year's Eve, two very popular dates for marriage proposals, in order to really surprise his bride-to-be. Besides, he added in a conspiratorial tone of voice, there was no way he could ever forget his engagement date. It was, after all, Super Bowl Sunday for goodness sake! Upon hearing his real reason for picking that particular day, Drew busted out laughing at his incredible common sense and ingenuity. Congratulating the young man on his engagement, he praised him for his fail-proof plan. Their well-anticipated wedding was set to take place on July 27, 1974, two weeks after the Millners' baby's baptism. Jill would be happy to assist Marissa as her matron of honor, proud to be standing by the friend she thought of as a sister, if not by blood ties, certainly by the strings of their hearts. Their friendship, created in innocence and nurtured by kindness and loyalty, had been cemented by plenty of love. Drew would serve as Eric's best man, his buddy and confidant for so many years now, the friend who made his own brother's absence a little more tolerable. Soon Marissa Renee Spencer and Eric Thomas Mason would become husband and wife, and Drew and Jill couldn't be happier for the pair. Lucky were those who knew the joy of having a true best friend like she had Marissa and Drew had Eric, and now their friendship was embarking on a wonderful new journey, taking them from young adults and friends to members of their own newly created little families.

The baby's christening took place on a sunny morning on July 14, 1974, at Saint Lawrence Church, located in downtown Huntington, which was a picturesque section of

Shelton. The truly majestic and impressive tan brick structure, with a few intercalated red bricks here and there for added character, was at the center of a sizable compound. It was the tallest of the many buildings there, with each providing their own set of services to their community and surrounding towns. Beside the church, it included a state-of-the-art daycare facility, a large elementary school, a very popular sports center, and a football field. Saint Lawrence had been the Chandlers' parish for over forty years now. It was where William and Sophia had been married in 1938 and where all of their four children had been baptized as well. The Chandler sisters had also been married there in 1972 and 1973 respectively. All the ceremonies were performed by the same priest, Father Anthony Mancini, who was by now considered a member of the family. After the beautiful ceremony, the clergyman generously presented the newly baptized infant with a blessed yellow gold medal of Saint Anthony of Padova, his patron saint. The medal, encased in a delicately etched crystal case, was an heirloom that had been in the Mancini family for several generations, going all the way back to the late eighteenth century. The crystal case was quite old as well and had belonged to his ancestors back in San Clemente, a small farming village that was nestled in the hills of the Abruzzi region of Italy, a place that had remained practically unchanged over the centuries. The people that continued to live there were younger generations of families that never left the village, and they knew each other so well that they almost felt like they were actually all related. Father Mancini was one of the few that had left and never came back, for he knew that his calling took him out of San Clement for a reason he hadn't felt any need to question. There are occasions in a person's life when getting an answer was not as crucial or as important as not having the need to ask the question to begin with. Father Mancini was such a person, and San Clemente the question that needed not be asked, regardless of what the answer would eventually turn out to be.

Father Mancini often delighted Drew and Jill with stories from his hometown and the family members he still had there. According to the elderly priest, the Abruzzi area had the most beautiful seacoast of all of Italy, with miles and miles of clear blue-green water and sugar white sanded beaches. Pescara, the most famous of the several equally spectacular ones, was considered by many of the northern Italians to be the Saint Tropez of Italy and was often referred to as the Riviera. A large city, it was located right across the Adriatic Sea from Yugoslavia, and it was indeed a magnificent place. In the summer months, especially in July and August, its population quadrupled as the high summer season welcomed many families from up north such as Milan and Torino as well as people from Spain, France, Germany, and Belgium, to name a few, most of which usually traveled by train. Extremely proud of his heritage, Father Mancini was deeply touched when Drew and Jill made a point of visiting San Clemente during their honeymoon trip to Italy. Now, the aging priest was glad to be able to pass along the beautiful gold medal and crystal case to the newest member of his extended adoptive family, who he continued to cherish and grow close to with each passing day.

Soon the Millners' lives took on a comfortable and peaceful routine. In the fall, when they both resumed their positions, Drew's mother, Deborah, gladly offered to care for her grandson while his parents were busy at work. Her house, located in the nearby town of Trumbull, was a quick and easy ten-minute car ride from their own home. Drew would drop the baby off in the morning before heading to Park Ridge Elementary School, and Jill would pick him up after leaving work—a schedule that seemed to work well for all of them. By that time of the afternoon, the baby would be changed and fed already, giving Jill the freedom to concentrate on getting dinner ready while Drew played with their little son. Drew William Millner Jr.—DJ for short—turned out to be a very content child, who cried mostly if he was overly tired, dirty, or hungry. The baby, to everyone's amazement, started to sleep through the night by the time he was just about eight weeks old. To his parents delight and relief, he went to bed right after his last feeding of the day, which was usually at around 11:00 p.m., hardly making much of a fuss unless he was not feeling well. The adorable baby was sitting up by himself by the age of five months and beginning to crawl by six. His proud paternal grandmother found his first little tooth when he was days shy of turning seven months old, and he took his tentative first steps shortly before he was eleven months of age. And, of course, every milestone, great or small, was cheered by the entire Millner-Chandler clan and their close friends, who shamelessly doted on the blond, blue-eyed charismatic child with the face of a little angel. It was a face that clearly reflected a perfect combination of the best features between his proud father and outgoing mother, but he also had some that were definitely and undeniably his very own. The two round dimples that charmingly appeared in the middle of his rosy cheeks were certainly a pleasant surprise, and the contagiously congenial personality he demonstrated more than a few times was undoubtedly his and his alone!

DJ's first birthday was celebrated with a huge springtime picnic in his parents' backyard. The truly joyous event was attended by all of their relatives and friends. Drew and Jill realized that they went a bit too far with the preparations but couldn't help it. This was after all their firstborn, they said as if they felt the need to explain their motives to anyone. They felt a little guilty over what might be perceived by some of those present as a case of overindulgence on their part, which was not far from the truth. "I'm sure that by the time the fourth one arrives, he or she will be lucky to get a cupcake," Drew added, laughing, causing everyone to laugh as well. Their little boy was their world, and they were not afraid to show it. Colorful blue and white balloons added to the truly festive mood of the special occasion, and an old-fashioned popcorn cart became a focal point of interest for both children and adults alike. One of Jill's cousins, Jessica, was kept busy, creatively painting small flowers and tiny creatures on eager children's cheeks. The most popular seemed to be ladybugs and butterflies by far, but little dragonflies were no far behind! Cinnamon, the clown, made whimsical animals out of extremely long and thin balloons, delighting all with his crazy antics as he went from child to child with clearly exaggerated pomposity and flair. It was a well-know fact that everyone loved a clown, and Cinnamon was no exception. His huge purple shoes, red pompom nose, and bright orange wig made every child from one to ninety-one squeal with unrestrained delight. DJ even managed to blow out his birthday candle without any help at all, even if it took him more than a few tries before he was finally able to get the job done. He literally dove into his cake without hesitation, a fork or spoon totally useless at a time like that, licking his chubby little fingers with gusto, a huge smile never leaving his adorable face, and turning his eyes into thin slivers of clear blue happiness.

Life couldn't be any happier for the Millners, who often thanked the good Lord for their many blessings. They felt that they were very blessed and beyond being simply lucky; they had each other and little DJ, their lovingly growing families, and a slew of friends. A few of those special friends were so dear to them that they were absolutely proud to refer to each as more than family. Everyone seemed to be in excellent health and doing extremely well. A happy DJ continued to thrive and grow, and his presence was a gift that was thoroughly enjoyed each second of everyday. He was nearly two years old when Drew and Jill decided the time was just perfect to start trying for another baby. Whether they gave their son a little brother or sister didn't matter at all, they agreed, as long was the baby was born healthy. They often teased each other about how much fun they were having just trying to conceive. If practice indeed made it perfect, then this second child of theirs was going to be something to write about. They loved to "practice" almost as much as they loved "doing it." And then, without warning, tragedy struck.

CHAPTER 3

As he did every morning during the week, Drew was on his way to drop DJ off at his mother's house. The giggly and chatty little boy was happily singing the "Itsy Bitsy Spider" song, by far his favorite, intently looking at his little hands with great concentration. His little fingers, not able to imitate the itsy, bitsy spider going up the water spout quite yet, moved clumsily from side to side, but he continued to sing anyway, not to be deterred by something as unimportant as that. Securely strapped in his car seat, which was placed directly behind that of his father's, DJ, in the innocence bestowed upon every child, seemed not to have a single care in his world. It had poured all night long, the kind of steady rain that fed newly blooming flowers and trees from the ground up. That type of rainfall also had the magical power to lull tired bodies into a state of relaxed and peaceful sleep like no other sound could. Warm and snuggled under the comfort of soft flannel sheets, and with the security of knowing that there was a solid roof overhead, one could almost forget that there was a world outside their bed, at least until it was time to get out of it again.

Father and son were traveling on Daniels Farm Road, an area Drew had known practically all his life. Suddenly, he hit a large puddle, momentarily losing control of the car, which unexpectedly crossed the double yellow lines in the middle of the two-way road in a blink of a eye. The oncoming driver never saw him coming and, in a split second, they collided head-on, in a crash so violent that it sent both cars flying in opposite directions. Drew's car rolled over twice before landing on its roof with a profoundly reverberating thud. The other car spun around a few times, all tires screeching, before coming to rest at the bottom of a slight hill. The incredibly loud bang caused by the impact was instantly drowned by the eerie silence that followed the horrific collision. That silence was broken only by the cruel noise of the overturned car's spinning tires in their furious attempt to continue a journey that had just ended. A child's faint cry could barely be heard above the utterly sickening sound of the still-rotating wheels. By the time the stunned witnesses had recovered enough to come to the victims' aid, loud sirens announced the imminent arrival of rescue vehicles as they sped toward the accident scene without a minute to spare.

A Trumbull fire engine was the first to show up, along with the fire marshal's official car. By then, a small crowd of horrified people had already surrounded both cars in a frantic attempt to help the occupants as best as they could, given their shocked states of mind; some were openly crying. Also responding to at least a half-dozen desperate calls to 911, a large crew of paramedics sprung from several ambulances that had followed the fire department's arrival. The accident scene was so devastating that they were afraid of what they were going to find once they reached the victims. That fear, however, evaporated the second a rush of pure adrenalin kicked in, their extensive training mandating that they do whatever needed to be done to assist and save the injured. Sadly though, there was absolutely nothing they could do for Drew, who was killed instantly when he was partially ejected from the vehicle. Unfortunately his chest had been crushed under tons of twisted metal as were both of his hips. His face, both arms, and lower legs however, were clearly visible as they peeked from under the overturned car. One look at him was all that took for the paramedics to know that he was already gone. The other driver, who was extricated for his mangled vehicle still alive, sadly died on his way to the hospital as a result of massive internal injuries. Although the paramedics worked feverishly to revive him, he had been critically wounded on impact and never regained consciousness. He appeared to be so young that the rescuer who had worked so hard to bring him back simply dropped his sweaty face on both of his hands and simply sobbed like a small child himself. Another unfortunate accident had just happened, another young life was forever taken, another family member was eagerly waiting somewhere for someone who would never come home again.

DJ, still strapped in his car seat, hung upside down, held only by the belt that crossed his little chest, from his left shoulder to his right hip and then across his lap. The child, dizzy from being in such an unnatural position and totally scared by what had just happened, pitifully cried out for his daddy. The little thing looked like a small human marionette, his bruised arms and legs jerking around in every direction possible. The firefighters and paramedics who had been through more than their share of tragedy came very close to becoming totally unhinged by the plight of the totally helpless and frightened little boy. After a quick assessment of the toddler's overall condition, they began to carefully put together a plan of action, concentrating mainly on the safest way possible to free him from the precarious position he was in. The fact that the mangled mess that had once been an automobile was now on its roof made matters that much worse for the victim and his anxious rescuers. Utilizing all the resources available to them, they started by using what they refer to as the "jaws of life," the tool used to cut away at all the twisted metal in order to safely and expediently get to any trapped victim. With the child's safety foremost on their minds, they paid close attention to the delicate task they were about to carry out. Not knowing how much internal injury the little boy had suffered already, they worried that if they made even a single miscalculated move, it could be enough to place his very life at risk. Trying with all their expertise to free the toddler as soon they could, they decided to work in pairs in order to avoid inadvertently adding to his injuries. Crouched inside extremely cramped quarters and with shaky hands and worried hearts, they began to work diligently and with meticulous precision, all the while talking to the child. By constantly reassuring the frightened little boy, they were trying to keep him as calm as they could under the heart-wrenching circumstances. In a carefully orchestrated maneuver, they managed to place a collar around DJ's neck in order to prevent further damage to his spine, should he have any. Since the little boy was precariously held upside down by the straps of his car seat, one false move could result to the child coming crashing down on his head, and none of the rescuers were willing to risk that. "Think twice before taking one action" had always been the motto they went by. One of the paramedics inside of what was left of the backseat tenderly but firmly placed both hands over DJ's shaking shoulders, cupping them as securely as he could, the look of utter concentration and determination never leaving his face. He was trying to block out the overwhelmingly sad sight of the little boy's dead father lying only inches away from them but found it to be impossible and very disturbing to say the least. Not able to understand why his daddy was not answering his calls, since he was right there, DJ stopped calling out to him and started to call his mommy, deeply affecting those who were trying so hard to help him. Upon hearing the child's pitiful cries, they doubled their efforts to free him, their hearts crushed by the sadness of it all.

The second paramedic, crouched inside the same cramped space but having entered the car from the opposite side, positioned himself in a way that provided him with the surest way to catch the child in a safe manner once the seatbelt holding him was finally cut by a third rescuer, the firefighter who was crouching right next to the mangled wreck. Taking collective deep breaths, they all said a quick prayer. The two rescuers inside the car then gave the final go ahead to the third one to cut through the thick belt, which he did with unflinching speed and precision. A loud round of applause erupted from the worried crowd as the little boy was safely lifted from the wreckage. He was quickly rushed to the hospital by ambulance, sirens blaring as it sped away from the gruesome scene of twisted metal and broken dreams, the scene where two young men had so tragically lost their lives.

After being carefully assessed and thoroughly examined by the ER physician, the toddler was found to have suffered only minor scrapes and bruises as incredible as it sounded. To everyone's astonishment and utter relief, he had not broken a single bone anywhere. No one could explain how that could possibly be, given the seriousness of the accident. That and the fact that the car in which he had been traveling had flipped over twice before finally coming to a stop, and upside-down to boot, should have done much more damage to his fragile body than it had. It was nothing short of a miracle, they agreed. The backseat was a mangled mess of metal, and the upholstery had been practically shredded to pieces, and yet DJ had escaped with only minimal injuries. His father, Drew James Millner, was pronounced dead at the same hospital at 8:30 a.m. on April 26, 1976, at the tender age of twenty-nine.

*   *   *

School had just started when Jill received a message that the principal, Jackson Brooks, wanted to speak with her. In her position as one of two guidance counselors who worked at Park Ridge Elementary School, that was a common enough occurrence–these impromptu meetings between the two of them. As soon as she saw Jack though, she simply came to a complete halt. His eyes were downcast as he attempted to hide the tears that were quickly forming there. His shoulders, always so erect, now sagged as if the weight of the world rested squarely upon them. Her instincts immediately told her that something had happened, something very serious, for the school principal and her close friend to act so shaken up and subdued. A police officer slowly entered the room, and her suspicions were instantly confirmed. One look at his somber face and her heart began to race out of control, pounding against her ribcage with such violent force that it caused her breathing to become quick and shallow. "Jack . . . ," she said but couldn't go any further. She had heard several emergency vehicles, their sirens blasting, going by while she was getting ready for work that morning. She couldn't help but worry about Drew and DJ, who had left the house fifteen minutes earlier but quickly dismissed her thoughts as being unreasonable and downright silly. Just a natural human reaction, she told herself. And now, that same human reaction threatened to suffocate her. Her head spinning, she tried to remain calm, but it was of no use. Her heart had painfully lodged itself in her constricted throat, bile rising rapidly to meet it there. Inside, she was silently begging the officer not to say what she wasn't prepared to hear, but he went ahead and did it anyway. The room began spinning around her by the time he got the words out. He had barely finished telling her of the accident and of her husband's death when she fell in a heap on the cold floor, her world gone dark, her legs nonexistent. The poor man didn't even get the chance to let her know that her son was still alive and all right. "Sometimes I really hate my job," Patrolman Andrew Sullivan said in a choked-up voice that was barely above a whisper, tears stinging his downcast eyes. His statement, although said in a very low tone of voice, resonated inside the painfully quiet room as if he had spoken into a megaphone, bouncing off the walls like a wounded bird that had lost its sense of direction and ability to fly. He wished with all his heart that, at this exact moment, he could simply be someone else, somewhere else, doing something else. Times like this reinforced what he had known all along, although far too many people didn't still, either due to ignorance, inability to, or plain indifference; there was nothing in this sometimes wonderful and many times crazy world that we all lived in more important or irreplaceable than the sanctity of a human life. And many times, it took a tragedy like the one now painfully unfolding right in front of his eyes to reinforce the veracity of such simple but often overlooked reality. If we could only turn back the hands of time.

Jill didn't remember the trip to the hospital in the squad car. She didn't remember how Jack had to put his arms around her shaking shoulders either in order to keep her from simply crumpling on the seat if he didn't hold her upright. His heart was going out to this poor young woman, one he considered to be a good friend as well as a valued colleague. And Drew, his friend for so many years now. Why had this terrible tragedy happen to these wonderful people? Why did it have to happen at all? Jill didn't even remember the worried look on the policeman's kind face as he kept checking on her through the rearview mirror, fearing that such shock could very easily push the young woman over the edge. Her first recollection was of seeing DJ, who was being held in a nurse's arms, just beyond the crowded emergency room waiting area. He cried out for her the minute he saw his mother, and she literally ran to him, tears rolling down her colorless face. In her shock and pain over Drew's death, she had forgotten all about their precious little boy. She hugged him tightly against her chest, unable to control herself any longer. She went on sobbing until she ran out of tears or so she erroneously thought.

William and Sophia arrived at the hospital shortly after their daughter. Still in a state of shock, they walked like robots, not certain where they should go once they reached the ER. Upon seeing the confused look on their faces, a nurse kindly led them to where Jill sat, rocking her son with a blank expression, distorting her otherwise beautiful features. She ran to them the minute she spotted them, just like she used to do when she was a little girl and had gotten hurt. This time, however, she knew that their kisses wouldn't make the hurt go away like they had always managed to before. This, unfortunately, was not a case of a bruised ego or of a scraped knee. She felt completely and utterly numb and empty inside. Her in-laws arrived a few minutes later, and the raw pain she saw so clearly etched on their pale, stricken faces brought her quickly back to reality. Their anguish unleashed a torrent of newly formed tears she thought had all dried up; she was so wrong. Deborah and Raymond embraced Jill and DJ, their bodies trembling with sobs so excruciatingly painful that they managed to rip the hearts right out of William and Sophia's chests. *What a horrible tragedy for our or daughter and grandson; and poor Debbie and Ray*, they silently mourned, hoping that their true feelings did not betray them as they attempted to remain composed on the outside while falling apart on the inside. But it was a task easier said than done. They knew that they had to stay strong for all of them, but they wished that they didn't have to put up such a brave façade. What they preferred do, if only they could, was to let their guard down and simply cry as hard as their darling daughter and Drew's parents were doing at the moment, for there was great comfort in allowing tears to simply flow freely at a time like that. Such a devastating loss had the power to crush everyone involved by the sheer enormity of its desolation and pain. How were Raymond and Deborah going to survive and overcome a tragedy of such proportion and magnitude? What could be worse than having to bury your own child? Nothing. Their forlorn and devastated expressions said far more than words ever could. There was no need for talking then, for hearts were often better able to express what overburdened minds often could not. What William and Sophia hoped more than anything else during the difficult days, weeks, and months ahead was that they stayed strong as their child leaned on them for support, be it physical, emotional, or spiritual. They were certain that she would need them far more than she had ever needed them before.

*   *   *

Drew's wake passed in a haze of grief and tranquilizers. Even the funeral mass at Saint Lawrence failed to elicit any reaction from Jill, who sat very quietly and still, flanked by her crying mother and father. With Sophia's arm lovingly and protectively wrapped around her thin shoulders and her hands loosely clasped on her lap, she seemed beyond unable to believe that this was anything more than a horrible nightmare from which she was going to wake up any minute now. Father Mancini, his own heart crushed by sadness and shock, delivered a touching and personal eulogy during the mass and had to stop talking several times in order to compose himself, finding it increasingly hard not to openly cry. At the gravesite service, however, his resolve disintegrated the minute he saw the open hole beneath the casket. The finality of his friend's time here on earth hit him really hard then, and tears just sprouted from his eyes and silently ran down his cheeks. Having to say good-bye to the young man he had gotten to know so well, the kind and gentle friend he grew to love with all his heart, was more than the elderly priest could handle. For the first time, during his four decades of officiating at funeral masses for all his parishioners who had passed away, young and old alike, Father Mancini finally broke down and cried as he sprinkled holly water over his friend's casket for the last time. He cried for Drew, for Jill, for little DJ, for the Millners and the Chandlers, for their friends and loved ones, and, yes, he also cried for himself.

The sight of Drew's seventh grade students as they huddled together like a herd of lost little lambs was indeed a powerful one. Still unable to believe that their beloved teacher was really gone, they simply held onto each other for support, shocked and beyond desolate, openly crying in each other's arms. Their wonderful Mr. Millner would not be back at school, ever, and that was the hardest thing for them to deal with; they had loved him so. Those in attendance who had managed not to weep until then, simply broke down before the emotional scene, unable to hold their tears any longer. The overwhelming grief was more than anyone could handle, and there was not a single dry eye among the hundreds of mourners who sadly approached the dark mahogany casket in order to say their final good-byes to the handsome young man with captivating blue eyes and a heart made of gold. It was a good-bye no one saw coming or would ever be remotely ready for.

Jill, who until then had not uttered a sound, became inconsolable, calling out her husband's name between heart-wrenching sobs. As she placed a single yellow rose on his casket, her legs gave out and she collapsed to her knees, saying that she would not leave the cemetery without him. She kissed his casket several times, imploring Drew to please come back to her and to their son. In a flood of tears themselves, her parents begged Jill to please come with them, but she appeared unable to hear their pleas, let alone heed them, for it was something she truly was not able to accept. As she had done so many times in the past, albeit in far less tragic circumstances, Marissa quickly came to her best friend's rescue. Seven months pregnant with her first child, she slowly kneeled beside her dearest friend and put her arms lovingly around her trembling thin shoulders. In a low, soothing voice that only Jill could hear, she tried to console the distraught and grieving young woman. She had consistently and sincerely loved Jill with all her heart for over twenty-two years now, this friend whom she considered a sister in the truest meaning of the word. At first, the desolate young widow adamantly refused to even listen to Marissa's words, but exhaustion ultimately prevailed and a worn-out Jill finally gave up and, against her will, slowly acquiesced. Barely listening to anyone, she simply allowed them to take her away as they kept on telling her over and over again how much her little boy needed her, now even more than he ever did before. *I know that DJ needs me. And I need my Drew,* she silently thought, immense sadness taking hold of her heart and soul. An ever growing hole was now where her heart used to be, a sickening feeling of emptiness that had been created when she was told that her cherished husband had been killed. "Oh, Drew! How do we go on without you? How do I, my love, go on without you? How do I go on without you with me, in my life, and by my side? I truly doubt that I will be able or that I even want to," she murmured very low so that no one could hear, but Marissa did. Taking her hand, she gave it three little squeezes, their special signal that they would always be there for each other. Although very grateful, Jill simply didn't have it in her to acknowledge her best friend's comforting gesture. An icy hand was now squeezing whatever was left of her hopes, her mind, her dreams. One by one they disintegrated into thousands of little pieces, fragments of a fairytale love story forever taken away from her, forever gone. Death had to be, by far, the most devastating blow a person could ever receive, endure, then try to overcome. Many people never completely recovered from the overwhelming sense of longing that absence had a way of creating, and which often followed a crushing blow such as the one Jill had just received. Life without her husband was something she never thought about or considered. Life without her Drew, how could that ever possibly be? *DJ needs me. And I need my Drew . . .*

The house was filled with well-meaning people as relatives and friends tried to offer the bereaved family their love and support. The only thing that Jill wanted and needed at the moment, though, was to be with her son. She slowly headed to the nursery, finding the little boy peacefully asleep in the safety of his crib, his arms protectively wrapped around Charlie, the teddy bear that his father had given to him when he was born. *But who was protecting who,* Jill wondered, her heart twisted into a painful knot at the sight of the two of them embraced like that, so small and innocent. That teddy bear meant as much to DJ as it did to Jill, and it had meant even more to Drew, especially on the day that his son finally reached for it before falling asleep. Gently touching the silky softness of his blond curls, her eyes instantly filled with sorrowful tears. Bending over the side rail, she tenderly placed a kiss on his pink warm cheek and another on his half-open lips. His sweet, warm breath fanned her nose, so she just stood still for a little while, breathing in the peacefulness of his sleep. She placed a kiss on Charlie's ear as well before she left the room.

Unable to face anyone just yet, she quietly asked her mother to please make the necessary excuses for her and retired to the spare bedroom. Once more, she collapsed on the bed, her tears quickly soaking the soft pillow underneath her head. Feeling as if the entire universe had suddenly opened up and swallowed her whole, she eventually fell into a fretful and torturous sleep, tossing and turning in her desperation as Drew's lifeless face penetrated the darkness that had taken hold of her decimated mind. Sleep was the only reprieve left for her at this unrelentingly sad time. But the unforgiving grasp of pain and grief that became her permanent companion, however, didn't seem to care much about her feelings or to respect her need for forgetfulness from the reality of the cold truth. Even when she was asleep, the respite that she was in dire need of still managed to evade her. It offered absolutely no relieve for the overwhelming sadness that had taken hold of her entire being—body, mind, and soul. Drew, who possessed the uncanny ability to somehow know what she was thinking before she even had the chance to formulate a particular thought; Drew, who was able to actually verbalize that very same thought when words would not come to her; Drew, who often came up with just the right answer to questions she didn't even get the chance to ask; Drew, who was capable of still loving her in spite of her shortcomings and, on many occasions, because of them, her Drew was gone. It couldn't be. It shouldn't be. But it was.

For those who read about the accident on the newspaper and didn't know him at all, even for those who attended his wake and funeral but didn't know him that well, Drew's death was an unfortunate incident that momentarily saddened most of them. Not only was the nature of his loss a truly senseless one, but the fact that he was still so young served as a reminder that life was indeed a gift to be lived and enjoyed. And that gift could very well be taken away at any time and under a multitude of unforeseen circumstances. For those who knew him well, though, the feelings and emotions they were left to ultimately deal with were absolutely devastating—a long and arduous process of heartbreak and, hopefully, eventual healing, which could take years to achieve. For Jill, embedded deep within the fibers of her spirit and her soul, that same process would undoubtedly be far more complicated in nature due to her difficulty in getting over her loss. She would be sent spiraling into the depths of despair and often taunted with glimpses of the love they had so deeply shared but no longer could. In the end though, she would have no choice but to come to terms with Drew's death and prepare to face life without him, although she now fought that thought tooth and nail. She had yet to realize that she was her own worst enemy because she allowed herself to get stuck in the past. Drew had been, after all, her lifetime soul mate and lover, her confidant and best friend, the only man to make her weak at the knees while taking her breath away. He was, and would forever remain, the father of their precious DJ, the fruit of their physical and emotional passion. Her darling husband, he had been the center of her world, where desire, want, and need finally met, where fire ignited destiny, which then led to a thing called fate. And Drew had definitely been and would continue to be her precious partner and ultimate fate until the time came when they could be joined again as they had vowed on their wedding day. *Till death us do part,* Father Mancini had said then. She had no idea then how soon that day would arrive.

The weeks following Drew's death were extremely difficult for his loved ones, but for Jill, they were absolutely excruciating. She found herself wandering aimlessly from room to room, her heart a crumbling mass of longing. She consciously avoided going into the master bedroom, unable to handle the fact that her husband would never again sleep on his side of their bed. It pained her to know that she would never feel his passionate touch on her willing body or hold him in her now achingly empty arms, make love to him, kiss him good night before falling asleep next to his warm and virile body. If it weren't for her son's daily needs and their families' support, she was certain that she would lose her mind altogether. Gate of Heaven Cemetery, where Drew had been buried, was located within walking distance from their house, and Jill went to his grave every single day. She sat on the newly growing grass as she lovingly talked to him, painfully aware that he was no longer able to answer her. She would never hear his cherished voice again except in her dreams. "Oh, Drew," she sighed often, emptiness and loneliness causing her thin frame to sway back and forth with the pain of losing him. "Here you are, my love, so close to me and yet so far," she whispered on more than one occasion. The cruel reality of what had happened was something she wished she could erase altogether so that she could start rewriting their love story all over again but with a completely different ending. Every day, she came to the cemetery alone, and every day she left alone, no matter how often she begged God to bring Drew back to her. She knew that she would never get what she asked for, and yet, she continued to ask for it anyway, hoping that God would eventually grow tired of listening and grant her wish just to shut her up.

CHAPTER 4

FALL OF 1976

Daily life had the merciful ability of moving things along, and time had the uncanny ability to heal even the deepest of wounds, even when the wounded person was nowhere near ready or willing to start the healing process anyway. They both possessed the wisdom not to stop unfolding, of always forging ahead, often without the knowledge or permission of the people who were in deep mourning still. The ache in Jill's heart was far from over, but she was now able to think about Drew without automatically falling apart, which had been the case in the weeks and months following his death. DJ asked about his daddy all the time and wanted to know why he never came home anymore. He was thankfully too young to understand what had happened, even though Jill tried, on numerous occasions, to explain the facts to him as simply and as truthfully as she could, mindful not to further scare the already frightened little boy. Still, he was not capable yet to grasp the concept of death and dying and why his daddy was no longer there. There were times when Jill truly envied his innocence, for it buffered him from the sadness and pain she continued to experience. To him, everything remained the same except for the fact that his father was away, and he was still not able to figure out why.

Drew had managed their finances very wisely, thus making sure that his wife and any future children they had would be well-provided for should anything happen to him. He had taken out two different life insurance policies instead of the conventional one. Besides that, he had taken an additional insurance policy on their bank loan when they first bought their house, which would pay off the balance on their mortgage in case anything happened to him so that the house would be free and clear of any debt. That, plus the settlement she received from the automobile accident, gave Jill the added peace of mind to be able to quit her job in order to care for DJ full time without having to worry about how she was going to pay the bills. From then on, her son became her number one priority and her main reason for living as she proceeded to dedicate her life to him and his needs. With his golden-colored hair and blue eyes, DJ resembled his father more than he did his mother, and she could not imagine loving anyone as much as she loved him. He was the only tangible part of Drew she still had, and she considered his existence a miracle in itself, never to be taken for granted. Drew continued to live through their child and that single thought brought much needed peace to Jill's forever altered life. She clung to it like the survivors of the Titanic had hung onto any piece of debris they could find after the sinking of the majestic ship. Slowly, a feeling of gratitude began to fill the huge void that her husband's death had left deep within her soul, but the longing was there still. Drew was never absent from her thoughts.

As the weeks continued to pass by, Jill's prior position as guidance counselor and her extensive background in psychology were of great help to her. She understood that the healing process was a trifold one. First, you had to acknowledge your loss, which was a critical step toward recovery. You then had to grieve for your loss, and Jill had plenty of tears she had shed when she least expected. Finally, you had to accept your loss, but she was not there yet and probably would not be for quite some time to come. Only then could the long road back to true healing begin, with one baby step at a time, and from the inside out. Jill was willing to do whatever was necessary, desperate to find the peace of mind she was in such dire need of. DJ deserved that much from her, but just as importantly, she deserved that much from herself. Drew would not have wanted it any other way and had told her that on many occasions while he was alive. "You have so much love to give, honey," he had said, his usually relaxed face taking on a serious expression, "and I don't want you to be alone, sweetheart. Life is to be lived and not to be overlooked or, worse yet, acknowledged. Promise me that you will keep your heart open to love again because by not doing so, you will ultimately only hurt yourself, and thus hurt DJ in the process. I truly adore you, and seeing you happy makes me even happier," Drew had whispered before taking her in his arms and kissing her with all the passion he felt for his darling better half. The last time they had this conversation was coincidently three days before he was killed.

*   *   *

Wanting to spend as much time as possible with her little one, Jill decided not to place him in nursery school. There was nothing they could teach him there that she could not manage herself. She was, after all, an educator, and quite capable of teaching her son what he needed to learn. Besides, she knew him better than anyone else and was aware of how far she could push him without crossing the line between his abilities and her expectations. The two of them often went to the neighborhood playground where DJ could play with kids his age. She was aware of how detrimental it was for his emotional development to learn how to interact with other children. An excited DJ quickly joined in the fun, running from the swing to the slide and back to the swing again. His innocent laughter eventually began to work its magic, slowly chipping away at the block of rock-hard sadness that had encased his mother's broken heart, one small pebble at a time. He seemed to get along well with the other kids in the park, happily following them around and often joining them in their games when invited to. It was very important for Jill to see her little boy so content, she realized one day as she watched him totally immersed in playing in a nearby sandbox. "Someday I hope that I can be as happy as he seems to be right now," she whispered, a wistful smile crossing her sad face. She promised to try to find her way back to being able to laugh again, even if she knew how much it would hurt not to have Drew there to share it with. She realized that it would take a great deal of effort on her part, time and patience the best tools she could use to assist her, but she had determination on her side, a trait that her husband was very proud to point out. He had told her that many times, often saying that she had more than enough of it for both of them and "especially for such a wimp like you," he would tease with a wide grin. To a certain extent, she was willing to admit that she would have to accept Drew's death and prayed that she would find the strength to achieve that someday. It was by far the most essential hurdle to overcome in order to ensure an emotionally healthy path to follow in the months and years to come. It was up to her, and only her, to seek and grasp at the chance to be happy again; she could almost hear Drew telling her, but that was something that was much easier said than followed. Although deeply wounded, she acknowledged the reality that she needed to be made whole again. At the moment, however, she knew she was far from it, and her conscience wouldn't allow her to cheat DJ out of having a whole mother again, not merely a shadow of what she had once been. DJ had lost his daddy already, and it wouldn't be fair for him not to have his mommy as well. Deep down she knew that she could never, and would never, do that to her little boy, *their* little boy.

*   *   *

Marissa, who gave birth to a little girl in June, continued to be a rock for Jill to lean on, as loyal and dependable as ever. She made a point of visiting her best friend at least once a week, her precious daughter, Amanda, always in tow. Jill simply loved to hold the baby, having forgotten how tiny an infant really was, for DJ, nearly two-and a half by then, was a giant by comparison. It tore Marissa's heart to ask Jill to be the baby's godmother, for both she and Eric knew that Drew would have been the godfather if he had not been killed. Jill immediately accepted the honor, but the unmistakable look of longing instantly filled her sad eyes even though she held back her tears for Marissa's sake. During their visits, they would keep their conversations on the light side, often reminiscing about their growing up years, which had more than their share of drama. Every once in a while, Marissa even got Jill to actually laugh at some of their crazy antics, especially during their teen years. As the months went by, however, Marissa began to delve into more serious and personal subjects, trying to pull Jill out of the cocoon she had weaved around herself since Drew's death. She soon realized that there were many layers to get through and that was why she wisely decided to back off a little, at least momentarily. She needed to proceed slowly if she were to gain any ground with her still-grieving best friend, or she would risk souring their friendship forever by being too persistent. Marissa had to remind herself of the fact that, during a painful period such as the one Jill had been going through, one mini step in the right direction could mean a giant step in the long run. Mini steps would become her specialty!

Father Mancini, still having a hard time dealing with his young friend's death, made sure to have dinner with Jill and DJ every Thursday evening. He would then linger around, sometimes playing a board game or watching TV with the two of them or sharing a cup of coffee with Jill alone. Slowly she began to discuss the car accident and how she truly felt, and the older priest simply listened, which was exactly what the young widow needed then. She even confided to him that there were numerous times when she felt angry with God for not preventing the accident from happening in the first place or for not sparing Drew's life if the crash could not be avoided. In time, she started to ask for his advice, always open to anything he had to say. Before they knew it, they found themselves helping each other to heal, without even realizing that they were doing so. She shared with him how odd it was that her siblings always seemed to be "just in the neighborhood" as they took turns keeping an eye on her even though Daniel lived and worked in Wallingford by then, which was a good forty-five-minute ride from her house, while Tara and Nicholas lived in Cheshire, which was almost as far away. Father Mancini had a hardy laugh over that one, telling her that they did so only because they loved her and their little nephew so much and were truly worried about their well-being. Jill simply nodded, patting the priest's right hand as it held her left one. With the passing of time, more and more laughter was again heard in the Millners' household as sadness gave way to resignation.

Although she started out slowly at first, Jill was also able to find small and simple ways to help her cope with losing Drew—what she affectionately referred to as her very own "first-aid kit." The kit consisted of things that were probably taken for granted by most but that meant the world to her such as the pleasure of feeling the warmth of the sun on her face after a cool spring night. Or the sight of birds busily building a nest, their mates always nearby, fluttering their wings or chirping away nonstop, followed by the joyous sound of newly hatched eggs a few weeks later. Another one was the sound of crickets and frogs as the summer nights turned warmer and more humid, lulling her to sleep with their hypnotizing serenades. One of her favorite, though, was the vast repertoire of beautiful melodies that hundreds of birds sung happily early in the mornings, way before she was ready to get out of bed. She loved to just lie there, listening to their carefree little tunes whether it was raining outside or the sun was shining brightly already. The sight of a cloudless autumn sky was special to her, the richness of the blue color so intense that it almost appeared to have been painted that particular shade after a great deal of thought had gone into selecting it, and by very skilled hands, the hands of a brilliant artist! And then there was Chloe . . .

Chloe was the small mallard who had decided to claim one of Jill's gardens as her own nesting ground. Jill woke up one day to simply find the beautiful wild creature comfortably nestled right in the middle of a massive bush of Bleeding Hearts, located near her back door. Chloe took off the minute she saw the intruder, exposing her carefully built nest and the nine eggs she had laid there, their coloring a beautiful shade of pale blue. She did not fly too far though, suspiciously eying the stranger with her small but very bright eyes, which seemed to miss nothing at all around her. The minute Jill went back inside the house, she returned to the nest, carefully sitting on all of the newly laid eggs with a gentleness that amazed Jill. Because there was a large bow window right above the garden, she was able to watch the whole thing without being seen, from inside her own kitchen. Jill built a good size makeshift tent over the duck's "home" in order to keep both the sun and the rain from bothering her or any of her future offspring. She also started to bring Chloe fresh water daily, along with some food, talking to her in a soft tone of voice while she tentatively approached the wild duck, mindful not to come too close too fast. From the get go, Chloe seemed to trust Jill for some odd reason, one dedicated mother to another, and just remained sitting very still while her water and food were being changed, and that became their daily routine. About three weeks later, Jill was delighted to find a tiny little head peeking out from under the duck's fluffy body. Upon closer inspection, she was pleased to see several little webbed feet sticking out as well. With tear-filled eyes, she congratulated Chloe upon the safe hatching of all nine eggs. By then, the duck seemed to really trust her, never fretting or getting upset when Jill came around. One day, she woke up to an empty nest, several sets of footprints clearly silhouetted across the cover of the inground pool, which usually had a thin layer moisture from the dew that lingered in the air during the very early morning hours. The footprints were clearly going in the same direction, one set of large prints followed by several sets of small ones, all headed to the backyard and directly to the small brook that ran at the very end of the property, where it formed a tranquil pond. Approaching the water's edge, she was happy and relieved to see Chloe surrounded by nine tiny caramel–and brown-colored ducklings calmly gliding around the secluded spot. As she got closer, she called out the duck's name and, to her absolute astonishment, Chloe swam closer to where Jill stood as if she was proudly showing off all of her little ones. "Good job, girl!" Jill exclaimed, her eyes brimming with happy tears. From that first spring on, Chloe always came back to the exact same plant every single year, usually appearing by the first week in May. Her trust in Jill continued to grow with each subsequent nesting season, the number of eggs hatched varying anywhere between nine and fourteen. She never saw the duck's partner, only Chloe. Same duck, same time, same spot, gifting Jill with what she needed the most and that was the fact that life could be truly amazing, as beautiful as nature was itself, and that trust and respect were earned, not given. Chloe's undeterred dedication in bringing forth new life year after year became, by far, the most helpful and important item in Jill's very own "first aid kit," one she tried to use whenever the situation called for a little extra push. And counting on something to look forward to, fully believing that it would happen again and again, the sometimes mundane repetition of a particular routine had the power to calm even the most frazzled of nerves and the saddest of thoughts. It was in the simplicity of a thing called life's renewal that the key to healing was ultimately found, especially for the mind and soul of someone who had been thrown through the revolving doors of tragedy and pain without any warning. Knowing what to expect, especially when you had been forced to face the unacceptable, could be the most effective and comforting feeling of all, after the trauma of losing one as dear as a spouse, a child, a parent, a sibling, a best friend . . . So many people were touched by Drew's premature death, with so much potential denied, so many ties severed, a loss that simply defied logic for all those left behind to mourn. Then along came Chloe, with her determination to continue to carry out the cycle of life year after year, gifting Jill with an inside view of her tenacity. The odds were stacked high against her little ones, for the ducklings were easy prey for all kinds of scavengers, especially the red-tailed hawks that were often seen gliding by in search of a meal. That reality would not deter Chloe, for having multiple ducklings on a yearly basis was what she did. She continued to lay her eggs and then quietly sat on them for weeks at a time, not going anywhere, and only changing her position every so often, in order to make sure that they all got the same amount of her body heat so that they would all develop and hatch. Who would ever guess that a wild creature had the power of comforting a human being by simply existing and for doing what came so natural to them? Jill was deeply grateful that Chloe had chosen her to share the miracle of birth with, along with a mother's unstoppable determination to carry it through. And she was twice as glad that she had taken the time to accept the gift that nature had so kindly presented her with in the form of a wild duck she named Chloe.

CHAPTER 5

DJ's terrible twos didn't arrive until he was nearly three years old. As he grew, so did his vocabulary, with the words "no," "I want," and "I don't want to" apparently his favorites to shout. Taking this new phase in stride, Jill continued to concentrate on her son's safety and well-being, choosing not to pay much attention to his temper tantrums and negative behavior. She knew very well that he was testing her to see how much he could get away with. She took him to the park almost daily during the week so that he could spend some of his endless energy in the company of other kids. While at the park, he would almost forget his tantrums, although they still occurred sometimes, even there.

"Wanna play with me?" Upon hearing the question, DJ looked up to find a little girl staring at him. "Sure," he answered as he turned back around and ran off with the true refined manners of a four-year old boy. The girl had no choice but to run after him, her long dark hair bouncing up and down as she ran. Catching him by one of the slides, she proceeded to climb the steps right behind him. They went down the slide quite a few times before running off to the seesaw. "What's your name?" she asked, her large emerald green eyes dominating her small face, which was a perfect match to her petite frame. "DJ," he answered, smiling at her. "What kind of name is that?" she went on, an inquisitive expression taking over her delicate features. "It's what everybody calls me, that's all. What's yours?" he countered back. "Sam," she said in a very sweet voice. "Sam? That's a boy's name," he fired back, as if offended. "It's just what everybody calls me, that's all," was her innocent reply. "How old are you?" she went on with an intent look in his direction. "Four," he said. "Me too," she squealed. "When's your birthday?" Sam continued, not quite finished with her inquisition yet. "May 14. When's yours?" DJ asked in return after thinking about it for a bit. "Mine too! We have the same birthday. That's really funny," she giggled, covering her eyes with her hands, really surprised at the coincidence. "I guess so," he grumbled back before he was up and running again. DJ and Sam played together for the next couple of hours, one never far from the other

48

until her grandmother approached the little girl and told her it was time to go home. Sam waved good-bye to DJ as she was being strapped in her car seat. Within minutes, all he could see was the back of the dark blue Voyager as it made a right turn onto a main road, taking Sam away from him.

"You met a new friend today, huh, DJ?" "Yep," came the one word reply. All of a sudden he seemed to be totally engrossed in inspecting every inch of his small dirty hands. "What was her name?" Jill asked, trying to engage him. "I don't know," DJ answered, not really wanting to talk about the girl he liked a little too much already. "How old was she?" Jill went on, to his utter consternation. "I don't know" was the now standard reply as he proceeded to slowly wipe his right hand on his pants' leg. If his mother was going to continue questioning him, vagueness was his only escape. A look of either annoyance or plain embarrassment took over his smudged face, but Jill was not quite sure which. Perhaps it was a case of equal doses of both. A hint of comprehension slipped into Jill's loving eyes as she tried to think and behave like a four-year-old again. "You don't know much about your new friend, do you, DJ?" she ventured. "Huh, hum," he grunted, her only clue that he had actually heard her. Total silence soon filled the confined quarters, and Jill decided to let her son off the hook once and for all. Enough teasing already, she laughed inwardly. His feelings would remain his own and his alone. Or at least until he chose to share them with her, which he probably would not. Jill didn't press him any further. Would his nice new friend be at the park again the following day, DJ silently wondered? Soon, he had fallen into a peaceful sleep, the face of a pixie little girl with huge green eyes temporarily erased from his thoughts.

*   *   *

DJ's first day of kindergarten arrived far sooner than Jill had anticipated, and she found it harder than her child to let go. He looked suddenly so grown up, she marveled, as he proudly marched up the wide walkway leading to the school, G.I. Joe backpack slung over his slender shoulders and a huge smile on his little face. He had chosen the adorable Smurfs lunchbox all on his own without any help from his mother, the colorful one with the likeness of Papa Smurf on the front and of Smurfette on the back, which was all the rage among kids his age. He was unusually quiet during breakfast earlier that morning, quite the opposite of the chatterbox he had been the night before, when he seriously announced that he was just too excited to sleep. As Jill read him his favorite bedtime story, *Good Night, Moon,* he finally closed his eyes and dozed off, much to his mother's relief. He remained on the quiet side during the short car ride to his new school, the same one where both she and Drew had worked at until the day he died. DJ was about to enter his assigned classroom when he suddenly turned around and, in a split second, ran back to where his mother remained standing, an unreadable expression on her beautiful face. With tear-filled eyes, he reminded his mother not to forget to be there when school ended "at exactly at 2:45 in the afternoon," he emphasized in a shaky voice that caused his lower lip to quiver in a precious way. He repeated his request a few more times before he was finally satisfied with her reassurances, kissing his mother on the cheek and bravely following the other children into their room. He gave her one last look before disappearing among the crowd of five-year-olds. *My poor, innocent little boy,* Jill lamented, her heart overflowing with sympathy and understanding. That he would even think she could forget to pick him up from wherever it was she was supposed to stirred in her a series of emotions, the most prevalent being those of profound tenderness and great sadness for her little boy. *Unfortunately,* she admitted, the stubborn lump that refused to dislodge from her throat perfectly matching the heavy knot that was tying her motherly heart, *I know exactly why you found it necessary to remind me so many times to be here when you get out of school. After all, your Daddy went away one day and you never saw him again and that has you scared, hasn't it?* "Don't worry, my love. I'll be right here, waiting for you when you get out, that much I will promise you, today, tomorrow, and every day. As long as the good Lord allows me, I can guarantee you that I will always be here for you no matter what, my love. I will never give you any reason to doubt that, son," she said to herself in a low, husky voice as she slowly walked back to her car. She found it very difficult not to breakdown and openly weep, for DJ, for Drew, and for herself, his fears breaking her heart in two. *I wish that I had that elusive magic wand so many seek but no one ever claims to have found, the one that grants all kinds of wishes to all the good little boys and girls. I could then use its power to bring your daddy back, thus being able to simply erase the hurt and pain you have gone through in your young life already, sweetheart. Unfortunately though, I can't, but you have me for life, my love; that much I can promise you with every ounce of strength in my body.* On the drive back home, she reflected on how difficult it was to be separated from her son, even if it was just for a few hours. This was the first time she was away from him since the day his father had died. She was determined to make every second they had together really count, for life was indeed very short. Jill was extremely sad and heartbroken for having found out so personally how truly short life could actually be.

CHAPTER 6

As the years passed, Marissa tried to encourage Jill to start thinking about dating again, telling her that she was still too young to remain alone. She also reminded her that she was more than sure that Drew wouldn't want it that way for her either. Kindly but firmly, Jill told her that she was not ready to meet anyone yet and probably never would be. She added that she still missed her husband like crazy and that the thought of going out with another man simply nauseated her. "Besides, I'm not really alone, am I? I have our little son. He is more than enough for me right now," she retorted. "But is it enough for DJ?" Marissa shot back. "Don't you realize how much pressure you are placing on him by making him your entire world? He could very well grow to resent you later, honey, and with reason. Give him back the freedom to be more than simply your son or a fill-in for Drew's absence, please! He needs to return to be just a child again," she said, trying to warn her dearest friend. A mother of two by then, she was deeply worried about the fact that Jill relied mainly on her son for companionship and emotional comfort, which was not healthy for either one of them. Afraid for her best friend and her godson, and because she cared so much about Jill's future, Marissa kept a certain amount of pressure on until she finally agreed to give dating at least one chance.

Brian Sanders was a thirty-four-year-old bachelor, who had been good friends with Eric for a very long time. At Marissa's request, Eric invited Brian on a double date with his wife and her best friend. Brian made it a point to stay away from blind dates, but Eric was so persistent that he finally caved in just to shut his buddy up. As the coach of the Shelton High School football team, he hardly lacked female attention wherever he went, but the most obvious ones were the frisky students at Shelton High, many of them Farrah Fawcett wannabes, with their manes of platinum blonde locks and an overinflated ego. A few of the younger female teachers there had also shown interest in the handsome and extremely fit coach, but he made it a point never to mix business with pleasure, knowing that it never worked out in the end. Tired of the bar scene of his twenties, he had spent the last four years going on meaningless dates, often with women that had everything going for them on the outside but very little content on the inside. He was ready for a serious relationship; the problem was that he hadn't found anyone with the same wish. Although he was leery of blind dates, he only agreed to this one because it was Eric who had asked him, and he trusted his friend not to set him up with another airhead. Besides, Marissa would be there to keep the conversation flowing should things not work out for him and his date, and he really liked Marissa. Why had Eric found her before he had a chance to, he would often tease his friend with. "She would pick me over you in a nanosecond, you big oaf, and you know it!" Besides being very fond of Marissa, he got to know her well after she married Eric. Besides being a kind and sweet friend, she was a loving and dedicated wife and an excellent mother.

As a matter of fact, it was Marissa who suggested that they should go out to a night of dinner and dancing, a far less intimidating prospect than having to sit through an entire movie next to someone you just realized you shared no common interests with. Having a band around could actually work in his favor; he could always say that he didn't know how to dance too well, which was simply not true, thus giving him the opportunity to dance if he felt he had to but purely for politeness's sake.

On the evening of the blind date, Jill was a pile of nerves even before she dropped DJ off at her parents' house for the night. Although she said nothing, Sophia was glad that Marissa had been able to talk her daughter into giving dating a shot; it was about time already. Jill purposely arrived at Marissa's house at least a half hour before schedule, hoping to be able to beg her best friend to let her off the hook, but it didn't work quite like that. When Eric opened the door, he couldn't help but stare at the beautiful woman in front of him, for Jill was wearing a fitted deep-blue dress that accentuated her incredibly slim but curvy figure. The color of it did wonders at making her skin glow, and her eyes looked bluer than ever. Her long, honey-colored hair was smooth and shiny and was kept off her face by a delicate golden filigree barrette with a deep blue stone in the center. With hardly any makeup on, she looked young and fresh. Well-chosen and applied lipstick could really complement any face, he thought, especially one as pretty as Jill's. Very little else was needed after that. Even Marissa was pleasantly surprised with her friend's polished and elegant look. When the door bell rang again, a tall man patiently stood just outside. At about 6'3" tall, Brian was indeed a man not to go unnoticed by any female with half a brain in her head. He wore a well-tailored dark gray suit, which did wonders for his great physique, his well-toned body noticeable even when he was formally dressed. His deep blue tie matched Jill's dress to perfection, and they all had a good laugh about it when Eric introduced the two of them and made a point of saying so. That little episode managed to quickly break the ice, and the atmosphere became much lighter among the four of them. Because she knew how nervous Jill was, Marissa suggested that they all use Eric's car instead of going in separate ones. She didn't miss the look of relief in Jill's face when the guys agreed.

Eric had made eight o'clock reservations for four at La Petite Parisienne, a popular French Restaurant in Southport, a posh area of Fairfield, as famous for its cuisine as it was for its live Saturday night music. Brian tried not to stare at Jill but found it increasingly hard. Not only was she absolutely beautiful, but she seemed to be also very friendly and smart, he noticed from the little conversation they had during the car ride. Jill was also impressed by her date—a man who appeared to be easygoing and relaxed besides being extremely good-looking. She tried hard not to stare at him but found it hard, a fact that disconcerted her. She had been prepared to dislike him right off the bat but had not. Quite the contrary, if she dared to admit the truth.

The meal was excellent but the band was even better. As Brian danced with Jill, he simply loved the feel of her slim body as it fit perfectly within his arms. They managed to talk a little while they danced but preferred to simply enjoy the music and the moment much better. From their table, Marissa and Eric watched the pair, beyond happy that they seemed to get along so well. Before they knew it, it was midnight, and the band announced their last song for the night—a popular romantic ballad that got practically everyone on the dance floor. Brian deeply regretted that the evening was coming to an end, for he knew that he would not be able to be alone again with Jill once the song was over, since they had all come in the same car. Following his heart, he asked her if he could call her again, and to his delight and her surprise, she said yes.

Alone in her bed that night, Jill tossed and turned, her head and heart clashing with all kinds of thoughts and emotions going through her mind all at once. Her head told her Marissa was right, that indeed it was time to go on with her personal life. Her heart, instead, screamed that it still belonged to Drew, and only Drew, and that there was no room for Brian or any other man in it. Brian, alone in his bed, couldn't stop thinking about Jill, the first woman in a very long time to really catch his attention. He couldn't wait to call her again even though they hadn't even exchanged a good-night kiss when they dropped her off; how could he kiss her anyway with Eric and Marissa watching them like two hawks on night patrol? He would have to address the vigilance problem with his dear friends later on, he thought with an almost amused smile on his face. How deeply he regretted not having driven his own car that evening, the big oaf!

Jill's phone rang later in the afternoon the next day. Without hesitation, Brian told her how much he had enjoyed their date, which caused her heart to immediately jump. He asked her if he could see her again, and before she had a chance to reconsider, she said yes. They both agreed that he would take her out to dinner the following Friday night, with more dancing afterwards, if she liked the idea. When he arrived promptly at seven-thirty, he carried a lovely bouquet of pink roses in his hand. The smile on his face told her that he really liked her, and she found herself returning the pleasant feeling. She again looked as beautiful as he remembered, if not more so. He also looked very handsome, his navy suit as dashing as the gray one. They had a relaxed meal, with the conversation flowing back and forth with ease until they began to dance. Again, Brian felt a connection to her that caught him totally by surprise, reluctant to let her go once each song ended. Jill found herself enjoying the evening just as much, and she even told him a little about her son, which she had no intention of doing yet. As he drove her home, she began to get nervous again, for she knew he would most certainly try to kiss her that night, and she didn't know how she should respond. At her door, he gently took her in his arms as she instinctively turned her head in his direction, an anxious look on her lovely face. With great tenderness he began to kiss her, savoring the warm taste of her mouth as it met his. They kissed for quite a while, for Brian seemed unwilling to let her go. Softly, Jill told him how much she enjoyed their time together before she gave him a final good-night kiss and entered her house. Brian smiled all the way home, eager to call her the following day to see when they could go out again. He was extremely attracted to the pretty young woman, he couldn't deny that, and was more than ready and willing to make it work between the two of them.

Jill headed to the kitchen once she closed the door behind her, the taste of Brian's kiss still on her lips. She looked at the gorgeous pink roses and took a deep breath; they smelled wonderfully. With great gentleness, she touched one of them, a soft petal between her thumb and index fingers. The sigh of regret that escaped her lips came as no surprise by then. The beautiful roses were not yellow, and Brian was definitely not Drew. Her heart had been right all along, for it still belonged to her darling husband. Although he was a very nice man, there was no room in her heart for Brian or any other man. Not yet or in the near future anyway.

CHAPTER 7

LATE SUMMER 1981

In the years that followed their son's death, Raymond and Deborah Millner became an infinite source of solace and support for their daughter-in-law and little grandson. Even though their own hearts were crushed by the death of their youngest child, for no parent should ever have to go through the heart-wrenching grief of having to bury a child, they often placed their own pain aside in order to be there for Jill and DJ. After all, they still had each other to confide in and cry with, a union of kindred spirits besides their long union as husband and wife and were of great comfort to each other in their hour of sorrow and need. They, however, did worry constantly about their exceptionally loving Jill. She had lost her partner and soul mate, yet she still tried to maintain her emotions, and many times, her raw anger and resentment at losing Drew, under control, for their little boy's sake. The bond between the four of them, which had always been very strong to start with, had only grown deeper after Drew's death, a bond that literally became a lifeline for Jill as she fought so bravely to find her way back from the depths of desolation and desperation in which she was so cruelly thrown into. She counted on her in-law's support more than she ever thought that she would, and slowly that dependency turned into something else altogether. And as her sorrow slowly began to abate, her affection for the best in-laws ever created multiplied tenfold. Gratitude became loyalty, and need turned to genuine awe and respect.

From the beginning, Jill had always made sure that both she and DJ spent as much time as possible with Drew's parents. On weekends, she made it a point to always visit both sets of grandparents, and that routine, in its simplicity and predictability, became the first paving stones she used to build the path that finally would lead her back to emotional healing. It was during one of those visits that Jill noticed that her in-laws seemed to be unduly quiet and subdued. The sunny Saturday morning had started bright and early as mother and son went out for breakfast. McDonald's had become little DJ's favorite place to eat, along with about every other child in America, or so it seemed. After an unhurried meal, they headed to Raymond and

Deborah's house, just as they had been doing for quite a few years now. With DJ happily watching cartoons in the family room, her in-laws asked Jill to join them in the kitchen for an extra cup of coffee, which had become their own little routine. It was during those times that the grown-ups caught up on what happened during the week, and Jill always looked forward to their heart-to-heart talks. It seemed almost impossible, but it had been well over five long and hard years since Drew's accident already, and yet, at times like those, it somehow felt even longer than that. Clearly bothered by whatever weighed heavy on their minds, they started by first telling the young mother how much they truly loved both her and DJ and how much they had always meant to them and to the rest of the family. With eyes filled with tears of recognition and with tenderness and sincerity in her voice, Jill told them that the feelings were mutual and that she could not have survived without their unending love and support over the years. Finally, and with a lot of encouragement from their kind daughter-in-law, they took a deep breath as they proceeded to tell her that they had decided to sell their home in Trumbull and move to California so that they could be nearer their remaining two children. Phillip and Lisa had a total of four children by then—three sons, Jason, Sean, and Jeffrey, and an infant daughter, Abigail. After years of struggle to build his architectural firm, it was finally doing very well and had just landed a contract to build a thirty-three-floor building on Wilshire Boulevard in Beverly Hills. They had absolutely no plans of ever moving back to Connecticut. Ditto for Hannah and Josh. The twins, Jordan and Rachel, were doing fine, and their third child, a little girl, was due in less than two months. Hannah's job, as a neonatal nurse at Mount Sinai Hospital, also in Beverly Hills, was secure and her salary was finally catching up to where it should have been. Their chances of moving back east anytime soon were practically zero to none. Neither of their children, they were quick to add, ever hinted or pressured them to make the move. They knew how close their parents were to their sister-in-law and little nephew, who looked so much like their late brother Drew. They offered their help only after their mom and dad had already made the final decision to move, they assured her.

Ray and Deborah also told Jill why they decided to ultimately keep her out of the discussions at least until the final decision had been made. The last thing they wanted to do was to add any further stress to her burdened life. Once they made up their minds, though, they found it excruciatingly difficult to tell her about their plans, debating as to when the best time would be to do so. But the time never seemed right, they added with great effort, and they came to realize that no time would ever be right. They were afraid to hurt her, knowing how sad the news would make her, they continued, their voices faltering with each word they uttered because it saddened them as well. The truth, however, was that they were not getting any younger, and Drew's death had naturally greatly contributed to the decline in their overall health on a physical but mostly emotional level. If they were to make such a drastic change in their lives, the time to do it was then, while they were still relatively young enough to handle a major move like that.

Jill, for once, didn't say anything except to place both of her hands affectionately over each of her in-laws' cold ones as they revealed how they spent many sleepless nights tossing and turning, not knowing how they would find the courage to broach the difficult subject with her. First on their mind was the reality that they would be leaving her and their grandson behind besides the fact that they were, in a sense, leaving Drew behind as well, and that weighed very heavy on their hearts and conscience. Second, there was the question of where in California to relocate to once their mind was made up. They considered and discarded many areas in their search for the ideal spot, if there was such a thing. After a lot of back and forth suggestions, they finally decided to settle in Santa Monica, not far from the famous Santa Monica Pier for a very specific reason, and that was for its convenient location. Aside from the fact that it was truly a beautiful place, with its miles of clear blue waters and white-sanded beaches, it was also located halfway between Phillip and his growing family in Brentwood, and Hannah and her expanding family in Marina Del Ray.

Jill continued to just listen to them, which, for a recognizable chatterbox such as herself was more than a little unusual. When the initial shock had finally subsided, a stunned Jill managed to find her voice again, telling Deborah and Raymond how happy she was that they would once more be able to be close to their children and loved ones as it should always be anyway. She truly meant what she said even though her heart was breaking, but as a mother, she totally understood where they are coming from and why they decided to move closer to their remaining kids. DJ, however, was desolate, taking the sad news of his grandparents imminent departure with eyes filled with tears, which rolled down his face nonstop and which he tried to wipe with the palms of his little hands. No matter how much they hugged and kissed him, the young boy was inconsolable and, as a result, the three adults just gave up and simply cried along with him for quite awhile. He managed to stop crying only after his grandma and grandpa promised to come out east at least once a year. His mother also promised to take the little boy to California during his summer vacation months, which did wonders at lifting everyone's spirits, if only for the time being. It was not until DJ was safely tucked in bed and fast asleep later on that Jill finally let her guard down, tears quickly soaking her cheeks and sweater. Her in-laws had not left yet, but she could already feel the void they were going to leave in the wake of their departure. Things proceeded at an incredibly fast pace from that point on, especially for Jill and DJ, as days and weeks simply flew by, bringing them all closer to their scheduled leaving date and all the changes it would invariably bring to them all as a result.

*   *   *

It was on a cloudy, raw, and rainy Sunday morning in mid-September 1981, that a pensive Jill drove her equally pensive father–and mother-in-law to Bradley International Airport in Hartford, Connecticut. No one said much during the two-hour trip, each lost in their own feelings and thoughts. Looking in the rearview mirror, the sight of DJ as he laid his small head on his grandmother's left shoulder filled Jill with great sadness, which was further compounded by the look misery clearly reflected on Deborah's drawn face. She gently held her grandson's little hand in her trembling one, simply massaging his left arm absentmindedly but with infinite tenderness. Raymond chose to handle the situation by concentrating on the scenery quickly passing by outside his window, something he had seen at least a dozen times before. Anything to keep his mind from what was about to happen, for he would soon have to face the sadness of saying good-bye to the two people he loved the most in the world besides his own children. He didn't remember ever telling her so, but he was extremely proud of his amazing daughter-in-law for the way in which she handled herself in the face of tragedy and for how well she always cared for his son and grandson. Her undeterred courage, dignity, determination, and loyalty were admirable ever since that horrible day when his middle son was so tragically killed in that horrific car crash as well as in the years preceding and following his death. Without even realizing that he was doing it, Raymond took hold of Jill's right hand with his left one and brought it to his lips, pressing three tender kisses on the back of it before gently squeezing it between his shaky ones. He then returned her hand back to the steering wheel. Jill's eyes instantly turned into a pool of tears because her father-in-law, who had never been so open with his emotions, had never done that before, although he never hid how much he cared about her and DJ. Their affinity for each other started back on the day they had first met, at the beginning of her relationship with Drew. Without taking her eyes off the road, she brought her right hand up and softly touched his left cheek as his son had done to her so many times when he was alive. She made believe that she didn't see the tears that suddenly sprung from his bright blue eyes, as blue as his late son's, her heart skipping several beats as she stole a furtive glance at his beloved face. With enormous effort, she managed to keep her own tears at bay, at least for the time being.

Parking the car in the reserved garage, the foursome headed straight to the departure terminal, their heavy steps matching the heaviness in their hearts. Upon arriving at the check-in counter, the elder Millners expediently provided the documents needed for them to get their boarding tickets. After that part of the embarking process was done, they proceeded to dispatch their numerous pieces of luggage, which cost them quite a bit of money, since passengers were allowed only one suitcase per person. They remained on the common area of the airport instead of passing through the scanner that would give them access to the restricted area reserved for traveling passengers only. That was where all the departure gates were also located. They were simply not willing to leave Jill and DJ any sooner than was absolutely necessary. All of a sudden, they heard the boarding call for American Airlines flight 1228, from Bradley to LAX International Airport in Los Angeles, their final destination after a brief stop in Cincinnati, Ohio. Upon hearing the announcement, they reluctantly began to hug one another as kisses were rained on tear-soaked cheeks, their eyes speaking volumes without a single word having to be exchanged. With one last glance in their direction, Raymond and Deborah, with sad faces and slumped shoulders, blew them one last kiss before they finally disappeared from sight.

For quite a while, Jill and DJ just stood there, eyes fixed where they had last seen them. They did not move a muscle, as if by remaining still they could, somehow, convince her in-laws to change their minds and stay. Jill reflected on how ironic it was that the same event could have such opposite outcomes depending on which side of the country the persons involved lived. Here they were, crying so hard because they had to say good-bye to Drew's beloved parents, and in California, Phillip, Hannah and their families would probably cry just as hard upon seeing their parents and grandparents again after such a long and undoubtedly hard separation. It was often said that the exact same thing had the power of either adding to or taking from something and that it was simply a matter of time and place. Continuously heavy rain in areas that were already under several feet of water was viewed as an added hardship, while the very same amount of rain in water starved parts of the African Savannah were considered a huge blessing. The sun that worked its magic so that seedlings were able to sprout and grow into whatever plant they were meant to be was no different than sun that caused nothing but destruction, banishing any kind of life from arid desert land all around the globe. Happiness and sorrow were indeed simply two different sides of the same coin—which side would come up had already been predetermined by something called destiny. Raymond and Deborah's tears of sadness at moving away from Jill and DJ were the exact same tears of joy they would shed when they arrived in California, for they would be finally able to remain closer to their remaining children and grandchildren. The plane had probably already reached flying altitude when Jill, tenderly grabbing her son's little hand in her numb one, admitted that as hard as it was, the time had come for them to go. She turned around and, on legs that seemed to be made of rubber, slowly proceeded to leave the airport and finally headed back home.

During the long trip, Jill had plenty of time to reflect on her life until that point. Deborah and Raymond had just left, yet the longing she was already feeling was only the beginning of the changes to come. A new chapter had started in all of their lives and hopefully for the better all around. Having Drew's parents in her daily life was like having a huge part of him still, but their leaving meant that she had to learn to lean on herself more, and that could be a positive step. She would grieve for Drew for the rest of her life, but there were different levels of grieving, she began to accept. Taking a slow, deep breath, she tried to concentrate on the road ahead, but the memories kept up with how fast her car was going. Looking through the rearview mirror, she was glad to see that DJ had fallen asleep, grateful for his ability to forget at least for a while his sadness at seeing his grandparents go. The events of the day, combined with the sound of the rain that had steadily began to fall since they left Hartford, had the effect of lulling him to sleep, and that was a good thing. His head, as it bowed forward chin to chest, bounced slightly from side to side with the movements of the car. His arms were totally relaxed next to his body, and his legs were sprawled at a truly odd and comical angle, causing her to actually laugh. The rain began to fall much faster, as if the skies were trying to cleanse the world around her and in the process, trying to clear her crowded mind as well. It would take some effort, but they would be all right, she believed, as she took a quick peek at DJ's sleeping face once more.

*　　　*　　　*

The first holiday season after her in-laws had moved away turned out to be pleasantly much happier than Jill had first anticipated or had reason to hope for. Christmas morning began on a joyful note as DJ, getting closer to his eighth birthday, woke up bright-eyed and bushy-tailed before 6:00 a.m. He quickly raced to the beautifully lit and decorated tree to find a dog bed nestled among the rest of the neatly wrapped presents, the colorful holiday wrapping paper a feast for every child's wondrous eyes. Just as he was about to open his mouth to ask his mother about the bed, a feisty ball of energy ran into the room and straight into DJ's arms, where it was soon happily covering the little boy's cheeks with wet kisses, all given with a tiny pink tongue as its tail wagged frantically out of control. The look of surprise and amazement on her son's precious face was one of those moments that would be forever imprinted in her mind, frozen in time. Needless to say, DJ didn't get to open any of his other gifts until much later that evening. He was totally mesmerized by the little puppy, a thirteen-week-old female red dachshund that Jill had picked up at the Shelton Animal Shelter the week before Christmas. She had kept the dog at her parent's house until that very morning, and her dad had promptly delivered her at 5:00 a.m. as planned. The teacup-sized creature, weighing no more than a pound, had enough energy to knock DJ flat on his back, taking advantage of the opportunity to jump all over him, digging her little snout playfully through his tousled blond hair and ears. She then proceeded to lick his eyes and nose until he finally shielded his face with his small hands, the enthusiastic tiny creature causing him to laugh so hard that he literally ran out of breath.

DJ decided to name her Pepper–Peppy for short–and both dog and child became inseparable from that point on. "Why do they call Peppy a red dachshund, Mommy?" he asked his mother as they ate breakfast one morning, a puzzled look on his preciously innocent face. "She is not really red, you know? She is more like a funny brown or cinnamon or something," he added with a frown on his forehead, making it look like he had spent a lot of time thinking about the subject. "You really got me on that one, sport! I really don't have the slightest clue," she answered him in a quizzical tone, as if she had been wondering the very same thing herself, a smile hidden in her bright blue eyes. "You don't always need to find an answer for everything, DJ. Sometimes things are simply the way they are, that's all. Besides, Peppy is yours, isn't she? Then you, my boy, can call her anything your little heart desires, right?" "That's okay, Mom. Red is good if you think about it. She is a red Pepper. Get it? Red Pepper. Yes, red Pepper," he repeated a few more times, cracking up at his own joke. His laughter was so pure and contagious that Jill couldn't help but join in, and soon they were both laughing so hard that they dropped to the floor, their sides starting to hurt. All the while, an ecstatic Pepper kept on jumping from mother to son, happily licking their faces and hands, tail moving faster than a hummingbird's tiny wings. Jill could almost swear that the little dog was laughing with them, but perhaps she was actually laughing at them, the little traitor. Tousling his wheat-color hair, she addressed her son in a mockingly serious tone, "Promise me just one thing, DJ. Promise me that you will not be in any great hurry to grow up too fast, my love." Caught off guard, he suddenly became very quiet for a few moments, seeming to think real hard about what his mother had just asked of him before finally speaking again. "I'll try, Mom, but my body sometimes does not listen to my head," he answered in a tone so contrite that caused Jill to start laughing all over again.

The house was always too quiet when DJ was not around, and Pepper appeared to feel his absence more than anyone else. The tiny dog didn't follow Jill around like she usually did with DJ, preferring instead to lie on the rug by the front door until he got home from school, which was usually by midafternoon. When he did, however, the house seemed to wake up all of a sudden the second he dashed through the door, bringing with him that burst of energy that kids seemed to have an endless supply of. That energy was quickly passed on to his dog, who could not contain her enthusiasm at seeing her buddy again, acting as if she had not seen him in several days instead of just a few hours. It brought Jill enormous joy to see the strong bond that so quickly developed between DJ and Peppy. The little creature was, without a doubt, the best therapy for her son, and she doted on both with unabashed pride. And the dog did a wonderful job at lifting her spirits as well, her love and devotion so contagious that it soon rubbed off on Jill before she had a chance to realize it. Animals had a way of giving much more than they ever got, she soon admitted, always happy to see their companion regardless of the situation at hand. They really didn't care if a person was in a good mood or in a bad one, rested or exhausted, calm or irritable; all they cared about was that the person was there, loving them almost as much as they were loved by them. And they also seemed to possess the uncanny ability to recognize when someone was sad or not feeling well, doubling their efforts to get the person to feel better again. And they did not give up until they were completely satisfied with the results of their overdose of canine tender loving care. Their needs were very basic and had much more to do with their owners' than with their own, for all they wanted was to be loved, period!

Weekends were, by far, their favorite part of the week, as they happily tried to catch up with the rest of Jill's large family and still managed to take Pepper to the park, either on Saturdays or Sundays. If they were really lucky, they got to do it on both days, when the three of them would play together, basking in all the fresh air as well as the loads of exercise and fun they found along the way. Visiting his maternal grandparents was always a treat for DJ, especially now that Drew's parents had moved so far away. Sophia and William unashamedly doted on the little boy, much to the little rascals' delight, and he took full advantage of that. "That is why God, in His infinite wisdom, created grandparents for, Jill. Haven't you realized that fact yet?" they kindly reminded their daughter when she tried to point out how much they let him get away with it. "You are both creating a monster, that's what you are doing. Have you no shame at all?" she protested, laughing.

"I would not go that far," Sophia interjected, laughing as well. "Your job is to love and discipline him. Our job, my dear, is to simply love him. We did our disciplining with you and your brothers and sister. A little spoiling goes with the territory, doesn't it?" her mother added as they teased back and forth. "Thanks a lot, you guys. I have just one question though–do you have to be so darned good at it?" she protested, amusement softening her "reprimanding" voice. Truth be told, she was well aware and more than grateful for the endless supply of love and support that both sides of the family had so generously showered on them. From her devoted parents to her siblings and families to Marissa and Eric, who were now expecting their third child, they had all pulled together in order to help them during their time of need and ever since. And even from California, Drew's parents and siblings continued to be a detrimental source of comfort, with their frequent phone calls and occasional visits. Trying to pick up the pieces after Drew's death had been a monumental task all around, and at times, it was still a work in progress even though they realized that they had come a very long way already. Jill also knew that without their unfailing guidance and constant support, true healing would have been an impossible task to handle, much less accomplish. Should she live to be a hundred years old, which she doubted very much that she would, she would not be able to repay even a fraction of all they had given her and her son already and continued to give still!

Marissa, who continued to insist that Jill was just too young to simply close her heart to another romantic relationship, did not hide her disappointment about the fact that she had not given Brian a fair chance. She knew how Brian felt about her, going as far as telling Eric that he was actually heartbroken when Jill didn't agree to go out with him again the few times he had tried to convince her to give it another try. Loving her too much to simply mince words, Marissa always told her exactly how she felt. During one of their more heated conversations, Marissa literally lost her cool, at one point even yelling at Jill, telling her that her martyr routine was beginning to get old fast, which caught her best friend totally by surprise. Even though she apologized for it as soon as she said it, her words wounded Jill deeply, but they also caused her to spend a lot of time reflecting about what Marissa had said afterwards. Was it true that she played the martyr without realizing that she was doing it? She had been so in love with Drew when he died that she couldn't get over it long enough to allow the deeper wounds to finish healing. Being honest with herself, she admitted, for once, that a part of her did indeed want to go on and find love again, while another part of her refused to let go of the love she had found with Drew. She felt trapped between unfound feelings and unfinished ones, a sort of limbo that could very well have turned her into a martyr. She still felt a great deal of resentment over the fact that her husband had been taken from her when she loved and needed him the most, but she finally admitted that she would get nowhere if she did not let go of that anger. After much soul-searching, Jill ultimately decided to put any love life she might have in the future in God's capable hands. If and when the right person came along, she would be ready. But she knew that that person unfortunately wasn't Brian, so why hurt him any further? For the time being, though, she wanted to savor whatever life had to offer instead of worrying about what was yet to be.

CHAPTER 8

The deep bond that quickly developed between DJ and Pepper was incredible–a genuine gift to and from each other. DJ, who had told his mother that he wanted to be a veterinarian when he grew up, started to show an amazing capacity to connect with all kinds of animals. He seemed to have an uncanny ability to find those who were in trouble or in need of help. The sweet child demonstrated a natural fondness for all living creatures, the smaller and defenseless ones in particular. Jill often thought that DJ probably identified with them because he had also been small and defenseless when he was trapped inside the overturned car that had caused his father's death. Perhaps that was his way of dealing with the accident, she suspected.

Jill had lost count of the endless number of times when a clearly upset DJ had brought home an injured animal, usually little birds or butterflies, for his mother to "fix," to take care of "like you always take care of me when I am sick." "Please, Mom, you gotta help them, please," he would always plead, his quavering voice a mixture of sadness, hope, and fear. He would then gingerly hand her the hurt little creature, a small bird or butterfly, often with its tiny wings broken or, at times, completely gone. Their plight never failed to touch a caring and deep chord in Jill's compassionate soul. She would help her equally concerned son minister to the animals' needs, often working well into the nightly hours, after an exhausted DJ finally agreed to go to bed, in order to try to give them a chance to recover. More often than not though, no matter how diligently she cared for the poor little things, most did not survive, and ultimately succumbed due to the seriousness of their injuries. She could count on the fingers of one hand how many times one of them made it, yet DJ never gave up. She absolutely dreaded the forlorn look of utter desolation she always saw reflected in his eyes every time she had to tell her eager son that one of his little friends had not made it, knowing how much he wanted them to be well again. And every time, with tears streaming from his sweet but sad eyes, he ended up having to ask his mother to help him bury yet another unfortunate creature. He looked for and managed to always find a special little container that was big enough to fit the dead animal comfortably in. Carefully lining the bottom of the box with several layers of soft tissue paper, he covered them with the same tissue paper as well, making sure to always leave its little head free of any coverings, so that it "could still breathe." For a child his age, his ritual probably made perfect sense, even though Jill had explained to him on numerous occasions that dead animals didn't feel any more pain and could no longer breathe. She believed, therefore, that DJ's continuous need to ensure the creature's ability to breathe was a symbolic one, his own personal way of keeping the creatures alive in his heart and mind. He would patiently fashion a miniature cross out of twigs that he gathered in their yard, which he then tenderly and respectfully placed on top of each little grave. With his right hand firmly over his heart, he would vow to never forget his little friend. "Cross my heart and hope to die," he always added with a muffled sob before seeking refuge in his mother's warm and safe embrace. This same ritual was repeated every single time there was another small animal that needed to be tended to, no matter how hard their deaths were for her sensitive son to handle afterwards. Jill didn't say anything to discourage him from his rescue missions because she knew the reason behind them. She had once overheard him say, as he sat by a very ill little sparrow, words that sent an arrow right through her heart, especially when they were coming from a sad seven-year-old boy. "I know that you are scared," he told the injured bird, "but I don't want you to be, okay? I'll take care of you, I promise. I really hope that you get well real fast, but if you die, I promise that I'll bury you in a nice safe place just like they did with my daddy when he also died." Astounded, Jill just wanted to run and quickly gather her child in her arms, but she could not. She didn't want him to know that she had heard what was supposed to be a very private conversation between him and the little bird. *That's why he feels the need to rescue all those injured creatures and give them a proper resting place,* she had agonized at the time, the words "just like they did with my daddy" resonating in her mind like a faintly disappearing echo. She was sure that DJ recalled much more about the accident than he ever talked about. Did he feel scared still, remembering the horrifying long time it took for him to get rescued back then? Did he feel guilty that he had survived the accident when his daddy had not? Kids were such sensitive little beings, filled with curiosity about everything, often speculating when they didn't know or understand how something worked. Jill promised that she would try hard to get him to talk, but she also realized that she would have to proceed carefully, mindful of the fact that she had to follow his pace instead of her own, for he was very young still. "Cross my heart and hope to die," she had said at the time, just like her son did so often. And she was, indeed, very proud of him, as much as her heart ached for what he had gone through. She was proud but also very worried, for she didn't know what toll all those animal deaths could eventually take on her little boy.

*　　*　　*

Mothers around the world were all alike in one aspect and that was the fact that they would do whatever they could in order to ensure the safety and well-being of their children, no matter what. Keeping their offspring free from any harm was every mother's goal, even when conditions beyond their reach dictated that it wouldn't always be so. Jill wished that she could weave a protective cocoon around her son in order to keep him safe when she was not around, but she was painfully aware that she simply could not. DJ's unusual display of sensitivity could indeed come with a very high price, one that she was not willing to have him pay, but how could she circumvent it? Her experience as an elementary school guidance counselor, unfortunately, filled her with genuine concern, since she had seen firsthand how cruel children could be to one another. If some of the kids sensed any sign of weakness in their schoolmates, whether such weakness was real or merely perceived as being so, they would see nothing wrong with picking on them. Bullies often used intimidation tactics on those they viewed as weaker, often in order to cover up their own sense of low self-esteem. Her son's soft heart could very easily be misinterpreted as such a weakness, making her fears for his safety that much more real, especially with middle school right around the corner. But how could a mother prevent her child from being the victim of bullying, since the problem was a widespread one and could easily be found in practically every school setting around the country and most probably around the world?

Jill indeed wished that she could weave a protective shield around DJ in order to deflect the cruel taunts and deeds she was certain would come his way. Such repetitious abuse had the potential of causing great harm to those who were targeted and often with dire results. She mulled over all of those facts in her head, especially in the quiet of the evening hours, after her son was already asleep. She pondered as to how she could best go about assisting DJ to find a healthy way of dealing with his peers' insensitivity and, at times, downright cruelty. If she could only help him to develop his own set of coping mechanisms, the so called "thicker skin" that many inferred to but very few could truly say they had "grown," she knew that it would eventually better enable him to fend for himself. The first thing that came to mind was that if she could her work with her son in becoming emotionally stronger, he would then be more inclined to let things slide off his back instead of taking them personally, something he had been prone to do until then. She remembered how her mother-in-law wisely said that small kids had small problems while big kids had big problems. She wanted to avoid having a big kid with big problems, but his formative years were well in progress already, and that was why she wanted to guide her son as best as she could while his character was still being developed. She hoped that by reinforcing his fragile ego, she would be helping him to build a much stronger sense of well-being and self-esteem. Her ultimate goal, though, was to make it less traumatic for DJ to endure and overcome the taunts and teasing he would most likely encounter as he grew older, thus greatly reducing the damage she knew could occur as a result of constantly being picked on. Bullying was indeed a serious problem and a well know fact among school-aged children. It crossed all lines, affecting youngsters of any gender, ethnicity, sexual inclination, cultural aptitude, or financial status. If not held accountable for their actions, young bullies grew up to become adult ones, with the vicious cycle starting all over again. No child was immune to this insidious, deprecating, hurtful, harmful, and ultimately destructive behavior. Armed with all that disconcerting knowledge, Jill tried hard to never let her guard down, always alert and on the lookout for any possible hidden danger. As far as her son was concerned, she was a very protective and vigilant parent, and she couldn't afford not to. She was, after all, the one and only parent that her son had since he was two.

CHAPTER 9

DJ was nine years old and in good physical health when he started to come home from school complaining of a headache on a daily basis. At first Jill was only slightly concerned, dismissing them as simply an annoying fact of prepubescence, a time when oscillating hormone surges could often cause a diversity of problems in many preadolescent children like her son. When his headaches, however, continued well into a second week, she began to really worry and immediately brought a listless DJ to the pediatrician. Dr. Jonathan Stewart, who had been her son's doctor since his birth, knew the child very well, feeling especially closer to the boy who had lost his dad so tragically. He remembered well how ecstatic Drew Millner had been when his son was born; unfortunately his pride at being a father lasted less than two years. At first, Dr. Stewart didn't appear all that concerned either, but when DJ complained that he often felt "kinda dizzy sometimes," his expression changed ever so slightly. "Oh yeah," the boy added as an afterthought, "my eyes get kinda blurry too when I look at the blackboard or when I'm watching TV." Upon hearing that, an expression of concern suddenly appeared in Dr. Stewart's eyes, a momentary look that thankfully went unnoticed by Jill or DJ. A chilling suspicion, however, had began to form in his head, causing his spine to stiffen just thinking about it. Not wanting to alarm her unnecessarily, he calmly instructed Jill to bring the child to the hospital for some testing, "just to be on the safe side," he cleverly added, speaking as clearly and steadily as he could. Dr. Stewart quickly went on to reassure the visibly worried young mother that there was probably nothing to fret about, not as far as he could tell from the examination he had just completed, but he could easily tell that she did anyway. His friendly tone of voice, however calm it appeared to be, in truth masked a myriad of thoughts, and none of them were even remotely pleasant. Doubts began to take root in his mind for reasons he was not willing to face unless he absolutely had to, but he started to worry nevertheless, although he carefully kept his fears to himself for the time being. Hopefully, he prayed, this will turn out to be only a minor problem, nothing more serious than the annoying headache that plagued everyone from time to time. Earlier that same week, he had become very concerned about another child's symptoms, none of them related to DJ's though, and had been relieved when they turned out to be nothing serious after all, but a minor health problem that was easily taken care of. He hoped with all his heart that DJ's case had the a similar outcome, but for reasons he couldn't quite pinpoint, he wasn't so sure this time around, and that fact had him deeply disconcerted. From the privacy of his office, he promptly placed a call to the emergency room at Griffin Hospital and ordered a stat CAT scan of the child's head, along with a series of blood tests. "And please, call me as quickly as possible after the scan is read. A verbal reading will do," he politely asked the ER physician before hanging up the phone and returning to his other patients for the day. DJ's symptoms, however, remained on his mind throughout the afternoon, their possible significance something he was never ready to contemplate.

*   *   *

The tumor in DJ's brain was impossible to miss due to its massive size. Appearing to originate right in the center of the brain, where the two hemispheres connected to each other, the mass extended extensively into the right and left sides, and downward as well, coming perilously close to the brain stem, where the medulla oblongata was located. Being absolutely the most vital part of the entire brain, the medulla oblongata was where both the cardiac and the respiratory centers were found. Any injury or disease to this essential area, unfortunately, often proved to be fatal in nature. Because his condition turned out to be so serious, DJ was promptly transferred by ambulance from Griffin Hospital, where he had been first admitted, to Yale New Haven Hospital, which was credited with having the most up-to-date pediatric unit in the state. Because Yale had an entire wing dedicated solely to pediatric oncology, should the tumor turn out to be a cancerous one, this was the wisest and most logic route to take. Dr. Patrick Wilson, a well-known and respected neurosurgeon and long time colleague of Dr. Stewart, was called in urgent consultation to evaluate the results of the head scan and to perform the much-needed biopsy that would follow. In pins and needles, Jill paced the halls before she was able to gather enough strength to lock her worries away for the time being. She was well aware of how easy it would be to give in to her fears and completely fall apart, which was simply out of the question for her at a time like that. She knew that she had to maintain a calm exterior when she was with her son in order not to frighten the little boy any more than he was already. All she wanted to do though, was to wail at the top of her lungs, her fears for him so overwhelming that they threatened to reduce her to nothing more than a pile of dust. The last thing she wanted was for DJ to notice how scared his mother really was and had been ever since she was told of the tumor in his head. She knew that she needed to put on the performance of her life and remain calm but, at the same time, strong enough for both of them, which was the only thing she could do for her precious little boy at the moment.

The results of the biopsy though, confirmed what Dr. Wilson had suspected all along–Glioblastoma Multiforme, a rapidly growing malignant tumor of the brain that was seen mostly in young children. A second urgent consultation was placed to Dr. Vincent Romano, a pediatric oncologist who specialized mostly in the treatment of solid tumors. The two dedicated specialists discussed at length their options but, unfortunately, ended up coming to the same conclusion, and the outcome was poor at best. A concurrent combination of radiation and chemotherapy was their only alternative, they ultimately concluded. The chemo medication, to be delivered directly into the little boy's brain, had to be given via a small apparatus. Called an Ommaya reservoir, this device would be surgically implanted in the child's head, right beneath the scalp. It was the only option available to them in order to try to shrink the tumor's size to a certain extent, thus helping to alleviate some of the symptoms that were afflicting DJ. The same could be said about radiation treatments, given Monday through Friday for two consecutive weeks. Without treatment, the boy's symptoms would quickly progress, becoming worse and far more incapacitating as more brain tissue, and therefore more brain functions, became involved. It was with great sadness that the physicians all arrived at that very difficult conclusion but not before having exhausted all other means and alternatives. These treatment modalities would be used for comfort measures only, for even after they were all completed, the tumor would still be too large to be safely excised. Even if they tried to carefully remove the mass, the child would not come out of surgery alive, and that was the only fact that they knew with certainty. DJ, they all concurred with profound sadness, was going to ultimately die, no matter how much they wished otherwise, and there was not a darned thing in the world they could do to prevent it from happening. That was exactly what they regretfully reported to a concerned and equally devastated Dr. Stewart a few minutes later. The three seasoned professionals were not even able to look at each other in the eyes as they talked; so great was their frustration and disappointment. Further compounded by their sense of hopelessness and helplessness at DJ's predicament, all those feelings translated into an immensely devastating heartache for every single one of them. Although each physician was well-recognized for his expertise in their respective field, they couldn't help but feel like minute specks of sand in a universe of magnanimous suffering and injustice. Their collective careers amounted to nearly sixty-seven years of experience, and yet they felt like their knowledge was minimal at best, especially when faced with a tragedy such as the one they were dealing with. The life of this child, whom they had grown to know and care about on such a deep level, was literally in their hands, and there was no damned thing they could do to save it! So much for the notion that health care professionals, especially doctors and nurses, should always try to keep themselves from becoming much too involved with their patients and their families, which was one of the first thing they were taught in medical school. Too late for that already. This little boy was the symbol of why they had become doctors and nurses to begin with. All life was indeed precious, human or otherwise, although far too many people took them for granted or at least until they had reason to actually taste the veracity of that sad fact. It was extremely difficult for the three physicians to see any human life, and in this case a very young life, coming to an end no matter how much they wished it weren't so. For DJ, the battle had begun, with life eventually the loser and death untimely and ultimately the winner.

*   *   *

For a physician, having to face the fact that he wasn't going to be able to help his patient get well again was just about the hardest thing to have to accept, and Dr. Stewart struggled hard with this senseless and harsh reality. How did one tell a hopeful mother that her beloved child was going to die? That in spite of all the progress and advancements in the field of modern medicine, some diseases were still totally out of anyone's capability to understand, let alone control or cure? For once, the usually composed doctor allowed his personal feelings to overshadow his professional demeanor, his heart filled with such sadness and a profound dose of frustration. The pediatric oncology unit had to be the hardest place in the entire hospital to work in, except perhaps for the burn unit. Because of the age of the patients and the nature of their illnesses, it offered little respite to all the loving and caring staff members who had dedicated their lives to caring for sick children in need, many of whom never got a chance to leave the hospital alive. These special people, who had to handle one sad situation after another, day in and day out, gave a lot and often got very little in return. Their main comfort came from knowing that they were indeed able to make a difference in someone's life or death, be it with their little patients or their loved ones, during a time when everyone involved could use a large dose of kindness and support. The parents, especially, truly needed a supportive and understanding shoulder to cry on, then more than ever in their entire lives. Losing a child was like having your heart pulled out of your chest by hands that had icicles for fingers. The hollow feeling left behind made robots out of even the strongest and happiest of people, and they only thought and breathed because they could not stop themselves from doing so.

Sitting alone in the total darkness of the conference room, Dr. Stewart tried to summon the courage he knew he would need in order to carry out the extraordinarily difficult task at hand. The fact that the patient was only nine years old made that task a thousand times harder to handle let alone accept it, if one was ever able to, and he certainly was not one of them. Until a couple of weeks before, DJ had been a happy-go-lucky little boy, full of enthusiasm and life, and now here he was, death coming closer with every breath he took. With four seemingly healthy little ones at home, the compassionate physician couldn't bring himself to fathom being the recipient of the news he was about to deliver. *It could happen to anyone and at any given time,* he sadly admitted, unchecked primal fear momentarily paralyzing him. He literally dreaded the prospect of having to face the hopeful mother, shuddering with the knowledge of the havoc his words would create within the unsuspecting mother's heart and mind. She had already lost her husband at a very young age and now her son . . . Why was life so cruel sometimes? Cold sweat chilled him to the core. No matter how experienced a doctor was, moments like these were never easy nor should they ever be. He was fully aware that Jill was counting on him and his expertise to cure her son, which he would do in a second if only he could. "Damned disease," he hissed, pounding his clenched fist on the large table in front of him, causing the objects on top of it to literally shake, his frustration level reaching an all-time high. Jill had placed all of her hope and trust in his hands, the same ones that now shook with the force of his anger and grief. He would have done whatever was necessary in order to ensure that DJ got well again. Unfortunately, he had been beaten back even before he could begin to fight for his patient. "If only I could have helped you, DJ", he whispered to the empty room. "If only I could have . . ."

The kind-hearted physician found a visibly exhausted Jill sitting by her son's bed, gently reading to him in a voice he recognized from experience to be trained to always remain calm under the most stressful of circumstances. *Very much like my own*, Dr. Stewart acknowledged, remembering how many times he had used the same well-controlled voice in the past and was about to use it again now. He was certain that under all of her outer calmness, Jill felt just like he did inside. He wished that he could scream his sadness and disillusion away at the top of his lungs from the hospital's rooftop until he no longer could speak. He couldn't help but truly admire the young widow and mother, who had handled herself with more dignity than he would have had he been in her place and gone through what she did and continued to. Slowly, she put the book aside and immediately turned her attention to him as he silently entered the room, taking a slow, deep breath, which she held for a few seconds before letting it out. Dr. Stewart motioned for her to follow him, which she did promptly right after placing a loving kiss on top of her son's partially shaved blond head. As soon as the door to the conference room closed behind them, she eagerly turned around to face Dr. Stewart but found that he wasn't looking directly at her, which caused her heart to skip a beat as it dropped to her abdomen. For some reason, he chose instead to focus on an abstract painting hanging on the wall behind her, slightly above her head. Although he started by speaking the carefully measured words in a slow and clear tone, his voice soon began to waver, for Jill appeared to be having a great deal of difficulty comprehending what he was saying. He more than understood why, his heart going out to this desperate mother who wished, more than anything else in the world, to be told that her little boy was going to be all right, when the truth was essentially the opposite. "Unfortunately, Mrs. Millner, your son will not get any better as I had so hoped and prayed that he would. I have consulted with the best specialists in the field, I assure you, but the tumor in his head is just too big to be removed. Radiation and chemotherapy will help a little, at least with the headaches, the dizziness, and the blurred vision, but we currently have no existing treatment to cure it; we cannot even risk removing it because he would not survive the surgery. You cannot imagine how sorry I truly am to have to tell you this, but the fact is that your son is going to die," he managed to say, no longer able to keep on looking at the painting regardless of how hard he tried. As he forced his gaze back in her direction, he was struck by the sheer terror he saw reflected in her wide eyes, her face devoid of any color, her entire body convulsing uncontrollably. Her agony struck him right in the chest, causing him to take a step back. *It is at times like this that I sincerely wish that I was a plastic surgeon instead of a pediatrician*, he reflected, devastated, his own eyes cloudy with the film of the tears he tried hard to control. "You mean to simply stand there and tell me that there is nothing you or anyone else in this world can do to save my little boy," she half-asked, half-shouted. "No, no, no, a million times no! How can you even suggest a horrible thing like that? I cannot and I will never believe that. There has to be something that someone, somewhere can do to help him, and one way or another, I will find it even if I have to go to hell and back to accomplish what I must," she vowed, spitting the words out as if they burned her tongue. "He is much more than my child; he is my world, my reason for living, for getting up every morning. I can't accept that, I will not accept that, I won't . . ." she began to wail, staring at the doctor in terrified disbelief. She hoped against hope that he would suddenly change his mind and assure her that it had all been a terrible mistake, that her DJ was going to be all right, and that everything was going to turn out okay after all. "I simply refuse to believe that I'm going to lose my son. I will never accept that, do you hear me? I will never accept that! Never . . . ," she repeated, her voice trailing off to a whisper. Looking at the doctor's drawn face and noticing the pooling of unshed tears in his eyes, Jill had to finally let go of the last shreds of hope she had been so desperately clinging to, allowing the unforgiving cold truth of his words to obliterate her heart and soul. Shards of her broken being were quickly piercing whatever was left of her decimated mind, killing her from the inside out, her pain so devastatingly deep that it blocked out everything else within and around her. Slowly and silently, she turned her back on Dr. Stewart and, defeated, walked out of the room and out of the hospital, not caring where she was headed or why. The only thing she was sure of was that she needed to get as far away as she possibly could from everyone and everything, especially from Dr. Stewart. But what she was ultimately running away from was the unforgiving truth that was about to destroy her.

She didn't know how she got there, but somehow she found herself in front of a church she had never seen before. Opening the heavy wooden door, she was struck by the glorious light cast inside the otherwise dark place as the late afternoon sun streamed through the multiple brightly colored stained glass windows lining the walls on both sides of the small parish. The place happened to be totally empty, and for that she was truly grateful. She started to bargain with God even before she reached the altar. She slid into the first pew and dropped to her knees, her eyes fixed on the sad, slim figure that was painfully nailed to the large cross high up in front of her. She felt humbled by the human suffering she saw so clearly reflected in the statue's features. "Dear God," she began talking, her low, husky voice laden with the weight of her desolation, "I kneel here, head bowed and with the weight of my child's illness heavy on my mind. My desperation knows no bounds, and his ultimate fate is something that I can't accept. You, more than anyone else, know exactly what I am going through right now–the pain of losing a child. Please, dear Lord, I beg you, spare my son's life. He is only nine years old and has just begun to live. I beg you, my Lord, my heart in my hands as I sadly stare at the face of your own fallen son, please, take me instead. I have already lived much longer than he has. Please, please, please, I beg you a thousand times please, take me instead, do whatever you must as long as my little boy is allowed to live." Her tears were flowing freely by then, rapidly soaking the shaky hands that were firmly clasped together in prayer. Her thoughts, totally of their own volition, darted from the wonderful day when DJ was born to the tragic day in which Drew had been killed, in a dizzying succession of images scrambled together as if they were part of a fast-forward movie reel. Moments of intense joy and immense sorrow alternated with flashes of happy smiles and gut-wrenching sobs. Images of her darling husband's handsome and ecstatic face on their wedding day intermingled with images of his lifeless body as he laid in his casket, the charming smile gone, so cold and pale, and so still. Glimpses of Drew's brilliant blue eyes forever closed in eternal sleep, and of his mouth, nothing but a pair of closed lips that had been forever silenced, came rushing in, reminding her of all that she had and was so suddenly taken away from her in a matter of mere seconds! The bouquet of beautiful yellow roses that her husband gave her on the day of their baby boy's birth were suddenly replaced by the image of the single yellow rose she had so sadly kissed before placing it on top of his casket, her body shaking with loud, heart-piercing sobs. Their magical wedding day, the birth of their child, the empty space on his side of their bed after the horrible car accident, his agonizing wake and funeral, all flooded her head at once. All the anguish and pain she had felt then, she experienced once more, causing the old wound to instantly reopen and crush her heart all over again as if it had just happened. She reflected on all she had lost already and was about to lose still, the weight of her despair threatening to destroy her in a blink of an eye. Suddenly, without warning, her desperate prayers turned into untamed fury, into a powerful and violent rage she never knew she was capable of until it was upon her, overpowering and empowering her, causing her to begin to shake with the sheer force of its strength and ferociousness. "What's the matter with you?" she shouted in anger, unable to stop herself or the newly released beast called a mother's desperation. She was instantly flooded with a sense of utter hopelessness and helplessness, its destructive power pushing her to go on, and pulling her into a furious and wrathful circle of indignation and rage. "When will enough be enough for you? Don't you realize how much I have suffered already, or is it that you just don't care? You have already taken my husband, the love of my life, away from me, but that alone has not satisfied you yet has it? For here you are, ready to take away from me again my very reason for living, for getting up every morning." Her fury gaining momentum, she charged ahead, totally out of her mind with the depth of her sorrow. "You know perfectly well that DJ is the most precious thing in my world, *that he is my entire world*, but that is of little concern to you, isn't that so? It is of little consequence to you that I can't bear the mere thought of losing DJ, for here you are, getting ready to take him away from me as well. *My only son! My son . . . How dare you?*" she shouted at the top of her lungs, continuing to shake to the core with the sheer depth of her pain. "What have I ever done to you to deserve this, but more importantly, what has DJ ever done to you? He is only a child. *A small child, do you hear me*? Here you are, believed by all the people who have worshiped you for as long as anyone can remember to be this merciful God, but what kind of mercy are you showing us now, especially to an innocent little boy like my DJ?" she screamed, her irate hands pounding on the hardwood pew she was sitting on. "You have always been referred to as our Heavenly Father, but what kind of father would allow such pain and suffering to befall his children, for whom you are supposed to ultimately be their protector and savior? You might have chosen to forsake your own son, but I won't forsake mine. You might have chosen to let your son die nailed to a cross, but I'll be damned if I let mine. I am a million times the parent you never were, do you hear me?" she went on, unable to stop. As her ranting spiraled totally out of control, any and all reasonable thinking was completely obliterated by the enormity of her suffering and frustration. Her overwhelming terror at the thought of losing DJ suppressed all other thoughts and feelings, reasonable or not. "What kind of God are you anyway? Guess what, you really don't need to answer that because I already figured it out on my own. You are the kind of God that I want nothing to do with. So much arrogance and self-importance! It is really pitiful, you know, that you would think so highly of yourself. Guess what! I absolutely don't care anymore! I know that you have no intention of helping us, of saving my son. So, to hell with you! Damn you and damn your sick and twisted church. If this is what believing in you is all about, I want no part of it." With her shoulders suddenly lifted by her newfound indignation, she turned her back to the altar she until so recently revered and stormed out, needing to get away from it all, from what she now believed were nothing but false promises of hope, incredible pomposity, and a bunch of lies. She quickly descended the steps without stopping once, to the freedom of the street below and the anonymity that it would offer her betrayed soul.

*   *   *

She was almost running now, adrenaline fueled by fury urging her on without a single glance back. With her eyes riveted on the pavement that was immediately in front of her feet, she failed to notice the person coming the opposite way, straight toward her, and they collided into each other. Startled, she looked at the man standing a few inches from her. His face was on the young side and strikingly handsome, with a perfectly shaped nose and chiseled cheek bones and chin. His lips were full and sensual, and his eyes were an amazing shade of silvery-gray. Gallantly putting his arms out to catch her should she lose her balance, he politely asked her if she is all right, but before she even had a chance to acknowledge his question, let alone answer it, he promptly addressed her again. "I know exactly what it is that has you so preoccupied and distracted, young lady. Your son is literally dying as we speak, is he not?" he stated in an unnervingly smooth and detached voice, one that lacked any warmth whatsoever. "How can you possibly know that?" she immediately questioned him, her already highly charged anger quickly escalating to a boiling point. "It matters not" was his curt reply, his nonchalant tone grating on her already frazzled nerves. "It might not matter to you, but it certainly matters to me," she answered in an equally curt manner, not at all intimidated by his open aggressiveness and confrontational attitude, for it was of her child that they were talking about. Smiling, he went on as if he hadn't even heard her, his arrogance reaching an even higher level. "Let me get straight to the point. What are you willing to do in order to save DJ's life?" he continued, the ever-present smile never quite reaching his piercing, cold, and calculating eyes. Taken back by the fact that he even knew her little boy's nickname, she became momentarily flustered and thrown off track. Albeit she found herself starting to pay more attention to this enigmatic stranger, his "I am superior" stance reinforced her resolve to fight for her child tooth and nail, regardless of the possible outcome. What did she have to lose besides what she was losing already anyway? "What kind of question is that? And how do you know my child's name?" she responded, staring him right in the eyes, her demeanor still as defiant as her tone of voice. "Just answer the question. What are you willing to do to save your son's life?" he repeated the question with a detachment in his voice that lingered heavy in the air as he continued to hold her attention with the power of his cold, unnerving stare. "Anything," she whispered, suddenly listening to his words much closer now, even though it went totally against her better judgment to be doing so. "I would do anything, just about anything in the world that I could, in order to save my little boy's life," she repeated, louder and with much more conviction in her answer this time, not taking her eyes off of his handsome but impassive face for a second. She wouldn't have been able to do so anyway even if she tried, but she had no way of knowing that fact yet. "Well, then," he slowly continued, the cocky tone in his voice enhancing the coldness of his precisely spoken and well-calculated words, the cynical smile never leaving his arrogant lips as if they were molded that way. "I have a proposition for you. You can take it or you can leave it. It makes absolutely no difference to me. It is your decision, not mine, and never forget that," he slowly drawled out the words, carefully emphasizing their ultimate meaning, staring at her without blinking at all. "I have never been accused of forcing anyone into doing anything that had not crossed their minds already, and I am not about to start doing it now. I am but a humble facilitator, a messenger if you will," he added, a sarcastic laugh following the pseudo self-depreciating and clearly false statement. "Give me the name of another child, any child will do, to take your son's place, and I shall in turn spare his life." *Spare his life?* Her mind registered in a split second, *how can he possibly do that? Does it really matter?* Her mind shouted back, as if chastising her for her indecision. *But even if he does have the power to deliver on what he says he is capable of, how would I ever be able to choose? It wouldn't be right,* she reasoned, clearly torn between what she should do and what she knew she desperately wanted to. Her son's life was at stake and ultimately, when all was said and done, she knew that she absolutely couldn't afford to make a hasty decision, one that could very well turn out to be the absolute worst she could ever make. The dire consequences should her choice turn out to be the wrong one, was something that her little boy couldn't afford to be subjected to. The full weight of her conscience threatened to throw her over the edge of a steep and treacherous precipice, one she knew she would never be able to climb out of once she found herself at the very bottom of it. *How can I provide him with the name of an innocent child, knowing that by doing so I will be sacrificing the life of someone else's child in order to save mine?* she struggled. "It wouldn't be right," she stammered, a great deal of torment clearly detected in her voice once more, as her words revealed what was going through her mind loud and clear. "And who decides what is right and what is wrong? You?" he taunted, clearly enjoying the injury he was so expertly inflicting upon his vulnerable prey. "Are you telling me that it is right for your son to die, then?" he went on, further taunting her, clearly savoring the moment. Never blinking or taking his eyes off her face, he continued to scrutinize every nuance of her tormented features, not missing the slightest change, and reading her like the open book that she was. "No, it is not . . . ," she sadly acknowledged, knowing that he had her cornered. "Then stop wasting my valuable time. I am, after all, a very busy man. *This might be your only way out.* I will not give either one of you another chance like this. Take it or leave it, but do it quickly, if you will," he continued, his unforgiving eyes burning huge holes on her crumbling façade. "My only way *out,* or your only way *in*?" she retorted, aware that he watched her like a hawk, looking for further signs of weakness in her demeanor and expression so that he could pounce on her once more. "You seem to be a fairly intelligent person, I'll grant you that! So do not play word games with me. *Out, in*, it is only a matter of interpretation, is it not? Do not bore me with your inconsequential babbling, my dear. And never again try to match wits with me. Never! Are we clear on that? I always come out ahead, I can promise you that!" Scared now, she realized that she had to act fast in order to save DJ. All the children she could think of, however, she knew on a personal basis and could never pick. Either they were the sons and daughters of her immediately family, of her extended relatives, the children of one of her friends, or they were one of DJ's school or neighborhood mates. *How can I possibly pick one? It would be unconscionable, and I simply cannot bring myself to do it.* She was beyond desperation now, unable to think straight. *But if I don't, my son is going to die and I cannot let that happen either, not when there is even the slightest possibility of preventing it*, she admitted, her heart a twisted mess of conflicting emotions, none of which made her decision any less complicated. With her tortured mind unraveling at a catastrophically high speed by then, she frantically tried to come up with a plausible solution to her tragic dilemma, hitting a dead end with every possible idea she came up with. She vividly recalled the day her precious little boy was born and the heartfelt promise she had made then to always love him, care for him, and above all else, protect him from all harm, real or perceived. How could she not honor such a loving and honestly made promise now, especially when his very life depended on it? Lost in her reverie, she was not aware that a long-forgotten face had quietly slipped into her mind, insidiously permeating her thoughts without any conscious prompting, and for reasons that she was totally oblivious to. It was the face of a young woman with amazingly beautiful emerald green eyes. They had shared a room way back at Griffin Hospital when she gave birth to her son nine years before. She had seldom thought about her for quite some time, especially in the aftermath of Drew's devastating car accident and subsequent death. Amy was her name, she remembered well. Amy Brennan, if her memory served her correctly. Amy Brennan and her daughter, Samantha. *That's it,* her insanely stressed and totally overwhelmed mind silently shouted, causing her head to spin with the vehemence of its insistence. *I don't know Samantha, not really,* she reasoned, trying to justify what she realized she was about to do. It was her only answer but, more importantly, DJ's one and only chance at staying alive. "I know someone," she blurted out quickly, afraid that she would lose whatever little courage she still possessed if she stopped long enough to think about what she was about to do; she knew very well that she couldn't afford to, not if she wanted to save her son. With eyes downcast once more, in shame and self-disgust, she rushed on, forcing herself to remain calm and to speak in a loud and clear voice so that she wouldn't have to repeat any of it ever again. "On the same day that my son was born, at the same hospital, and at precisely the same time, down to the exact same hour, minute, and second, another child was also born, a little girl. Her name was Samantha, and her mother's name was Amy. Amy Brennan," she added in a whisper, still intently staring at her feet in order to be able to continue. With a deep breath, she paused for a second, trying to gather enough courage to go on. Tentatively, she slowly raised her eyes, totally expecting to find a triumphant smile on her tormentor's despicably smug face but was surprised to discover that the young and handsome stranger was no longer there and that no detectable sign of his presence could be found anywhere.

*   *   *

Her head spinning from all of the events of the last few hours, a dazed Jill wasn't even sure if the encounter with the mysterious young man had really happened or if it was simply a product of her exhausted and beaten mind. She looked around, a stunned expression on her pale and frightened face, trying to find someone who could confirm that the stranger had indeed been there, but the street was totally void of people except for her own presence. With a knot in her stomach, she started the long journey back, her steps small and unsure at first but quickly picking up speed as she came closer and closer to the hospital. Jill approached the building with a mixture of apprehension and hope, fear coming perilously close to bringing her to a virtual standstill by the time she pressed the elevator button on her way up to the sixth floor. She stopped briefly outside her son's room, trying to collect her thoughts and gather the courage she needed in order to go in and face what she feared might greet her once she finally opened the door. With a sigh and a shake of her achy shoulders, she slowly stepped forward, hoping for the best but preparing herself for the worst. Her little boy was sitting up, looking so small, vulnerable, and frail in the middle of the oversized bed. As soon as she saw him, however, all her doubts immediately dissipated, disappearing beyond the appallingly thin form anxiously looking at her. His face, pale and sallow ever since he had been first admitted to the hospital a few days before, showed the faintest hint of color on his sunken cheeks. Her breath got caught in her throat for a few excruciatingly long minutes that felt more like hours before she was actually able to painfully exhale again. But it was his eyes, his big, beautiful, and expressive blue eyes, however, that actually captured her attention the most. To her amazement, they once again reflected a light that had been extinguished and that she had feared she would never see again, the light of life, of living, of healing. With two giant steps, she found herself instantly by her son's side, gathering him in her trembling and aching arms, holding her precious child with a fierceness that managed to scare them both but for totally different reasons. Without realizing what she was doing, she hugged her boy's small body tightly against her, her heart threatening to jump right out of her thin rib cage as it began to pound wildly inside her chest. Caught by surprise, DJ didn't know what to make of the overwhelming show of emotion coming from his usually more restrained mother. After what seemed virtually like an eternity to a bewildered DJ, Jill finally released her grip on him. Puzzled by his mother's sudden outburst of enthusiasm, he had absolutely no idea of what had gotten into her. Feigning an embarrassment he didn't really feel, he gently pushed her away, a weak smile brightening his adorable little face. He would never know why his mother was acting "so weird" all of a sudden, but he enjoyed her hug more than he was willing to let on. His mother's seemingly endless supply of love for him was what he needed the most, if he allowed himself to admit so, especially since the day he had been admitted to the hospital for what, in his child's mind, had to be many, many months before. For some reason that he couldn't quite figure out, he did feel a little better that day though. Maybe it was his mother's squeezing hug after all, he reasoned, feeling a little bad for having pushed her away after she finally let go of him. Dr. Stewart and the rest of the staff on the pediatric oncology ward immediately noticed the amazing change in the little boy's demeanor and spirits as well. A new CAT scan the following morning showed a slight but noticeable decrease in the size of his brain tumor. No one could offer any plausible explanation as to how or why, but repeated scans showed a continually shrinking tumor in the days that followed until, after about two week's time, no mass whatsoever could be further detected in any of the films. In all of their collective professional careers, neither Dr. Stewart or Dr. Wilson or Dr. Romano had ever seen a case such as the one before them, especially with a tumor as aggressive and of such a large size as this particular one had been. Dr. Stewart, especially, was simply mystified by the sudden and totally unbelievable turn of events, albeit very glad and relieved as well. As hard as they tried to come up with a plausible explanation as to how or why the neoplasm would vanish like that, they were simply unable to. Invariably they came up empty-handed regardless of how thoroughly they reexamined all the MRIs and CAT scan films, reanalyzed the results of the biopsy, or dissected the outcome of the totally unbelievable turn of events. Soon the word "miracle" became associated with the baffling case whenever DJ's name was mentioned, making believers out of even the most cynical and skeptical of nonbelievers, for nothing else could satisfactorily explain what had just occurred. To everyone's surprise and delight, a completely healthy and overjoyed DJ was discharged from Yale New Haven Hospital on a warm and sunny Saturday afternoon in late June 1983, after no further traces of the tumor's existence or presence were noted in any of the subsequent head scans. On that magical day, during which her son received a clean bill of health from all of his caregivers and found to be well enough to finally go home, Jill made a solemn promise to him and to herself that she vowed to maintain until the day she died. She would lock the memory of her encounter with the mysterious young man deep within the recesses of her heart and mind and forever "throw away the key," closing the door on a very traumatic and difficult chapter in both of their lives. By doing so, she would be ending the devastating experience on an extremely happy note, for her little boy had been given a second lease on life. She had needed to do just about anything and everything within her power to try and save her son's life and had been undeterred in her determination to accomplish that. Her resolve not to fail him had been much stronger than the price she would eventually have to personally pay for the bargain she had made, in a time of unimaginable horror and desperation for the devastated young mother. Her fate had been sealed on the day she had "accidently" bumped into the young stranger, and she had simply done nothing but whatever she had to in order to save her innocent child. That was all that mattered to her in the end. After all was said and done, she was DJ's ultimate protector, and it was her responsibility to ensure that he was well cared for, at least as long as there was any life left in her body. She was sure that she did precisely what any other mother would have done in her place, given the exact same set of circumstances. She would take her secret and shame to the grave, vowing never to look back regardless of the circumstances. And when her time in this life finally came to an end, she would answer for her sins with courage and dignity. No regrets, even though she knew that guilt would, more than likely, stare her in the face from time to time, especially during each one of DJ's birthdays from that point on, birthdays that he would've never had a chance to celebrate if she had not done what she did. But they would also be birthdays that another child would unfortunately never get a chance to see again because of a decision she had been forced to make. Her son was well again, and she tried to hold onto that thought for plain survival, especially during the times when life, every now and then, threw the proverbial unexpected curveball her way. DJ was, by far, Jill's most cherished treasure, above and beyond anything else in her life. Her darling son, the most important person in the world for her, was finally well again, and that was the only thing that really mattered to her, bar none.

*   *   *

Back home after his long three-week stay at Yale, a beaming DJ soon resumed the carefree life he knew before he got sick. The little boy, however, seemed to have developed a new perspective on the preciousness and beauty of life and have gained the ability to enjoy himself with renewed enthusiasm. He appeared to be having fun with even the most mundane of situations, living every moment with unrestrained fervor. His joy was so sincere and contagious that it quickly disseminated, spreading among those around him in an array of positive ways. Their routine soon returned to normal, and an ecstatic Jill couldn't contain her joy and gratitude at having her son back where he belonged, healthy and safe. Life was good, she chanted to herself over and over again. Life was really good! She felt whole again.

CHAPTER 10

OCTOBER 1983

The changes in Pepper started gradually and were quite subtle at first. Upon returning home from the hospital, DJ was enthusiastically greeted by the little dog, who was by then slightly over two years of age. Peppy returned to her normal ritual of following every step he took, delighted to have her buddy home again. In no time at all she was his shadow again, just like she had always been before he became ill. The two munchkins resumed their inseparable routine in no time at all. Within a few weeks though, Jill began to notice that Pepper no longer waited by the front door for DJ to come home from school, preferring instead to lie quietly under the family room sofa. Even with Jill's gentle coaxing, the little dog remained in her new hiding place, looking at her with what she could swear were very sad eyes. She still eagerly ran to DJ when he got home in the afternoon, her tail wagging back and forth as usual, but after only a few minutes, she again resumed her new favorite spot under the couch, with only her sweet face barely visible from her hiding place. There were times when Jill could swear that she heard the dog whimper for no apparent reason. She asked DJ if he knew why Peppy cried out like that, but he simply shrugged his shoulders, a totally puzzled expression crossing his handsome little face.

A visit to the vet proved unfruitful, as the experienced veterinarian couldn't find anything questionable with the seemingly healthy dog—no rashes, no broken or bruised bones, nothing at all in her blood work that could justify her obvious discomfort. According to Jill, Pepper continued to eat her food and drink her water as she had always done before and had no problems urinating or moving her bowels. But she also seemed to be very withdrawn and much quieter than before, even when DJ was around, a cause of added concern to her. Although she was no longer a puppy, the friendly dog who used to be so full of energy and spunk was indeed behaving in an unusual way, and Jill was confused and more than a little apprehensive by it. Soon Peppy began to limp when she walked and seemed to favor her right hind leg as well besides the continuous whimpering. The limp became increasingly more pronounced, prompting Jill to bring her to the vet twice more in less than one month. Nothing appeared to be physically wrong with the poor creature, Dr. Miller reassured Jill once more, but much to her consternation, the odd behavior didn't go away or improved.

Jill was in the kitchen preparing dinner one afternoon, when she thought she heard the dog growl. Both Pepper and DJ were in the family room at the time, and Jill was not sure if she had heard right. A few minutes later, however, she heard the dog growl again, followed by the sound of DJ crying out in pain. She ran to the family room to find her son gripping his right hand with his left one, a little bit of blood trickling between his fingers. "What's going on in here, DJ? Why did Peppy bite you?" she questioned him as she examined the wound. Pepper was again quietly lying under the couch by then. "I don't know. I was just playing on the rug with my toy truck when she just turned around and bit me." Because the incident was so totally out of character for the always gentle dog, Jill asked her son if he unwillingly or unknowingly somehow did anything at all to provoke the dog into biting him, but he vehemently denied it. He added that he wasn't even playing with her at the time, tears pooling in his eyes at being accused of something he would never do, and Jill felt guilty for even thinking that he could. Because she knew the little dog so well, she was finally convinced that something was definitely going on with the poor creature. And Pepper appeared to be growing progressively unhappier with each passing day. Alarmed, she immediately called Dr. Miller again and was surprised to hear that sometimes, for reasons no one could be sure of let alone explain, brain defects could develop, possibly causing great changes in a pet's overall behavior and personality. These changes, he added, could occur practically overnight and cause the afflicted animal to also suddenly and unexpectedly turn on the very people they loved the most, those who have cared for them all their lives. Another reason for such drastic change in her, he explained, could be the fact that a lot of dogs, especially those bought from pet shops, were born in breeding farms or "puppy mills," as they were often called. In these farms, unfortunately, female dogs were mated much more often than deemed safe, to the detriment of the dogs and their puppies. Besides that, mating between fathers and daughters, mothers and sons, brothers and sisters were common practice. "This inbreeding can often cause the enhancement of certain negative characteristics and traits in the puppies that result from such mating, a type of gene mutation, if you will. I regret to tell you, Mrs. Millner, that once these gene mutations occur, those poor puppies are capable of practically all kinds of strange behavior as they grow older. These behaviors can manifest themselves in a multitude of ways, with the degree and severity of the changes varying from mild to very serious ones and everything in between. Once that happens," he concluded, "there is nothing that can be done to reverse the process due to the fact that the problem is a physiological one as opposed to a learned behavior. Since Pepper was adopted from the animal shelter, it will be close to impossible to find out where she was born or came from."

Jill hung up the phone with a heavy heart, knowing full well that she would have to explain to her son, as difficult as she knew it would be on both of them, why it was no longer safe to keep Pepper around since she could turn against anyone at any given time.

Putting her to sleep was the only alternative left for them. Refusing to even listen to her, a heartbroken DJ begged his mother "not to kill my dog, please, Mom." The decision, however, had already been taken out of her hands the minute Peppy bit her son. It was the kindest, most loving thing they could do for her, she patiently tried to explain to a distraught DJ, but he was simply not ready to hear what his mother was trying to tell him. After he locked himself in his room, she heard him crying until he mercifully fell asleep. Jill decided to leave him alone with his grief, knowing that after he had some time to think about it on his own, he would come to the same conclusion that she had. She let him sleep through supper, and he only woke up the following morning. Although neither one of them wanted to lose Peppy, it was the kindest and most loving thing they could do for her, and she deserved to be treated with the utmost care, dignity, and respect, she emphasized. "We owe her at least that much, son," Jill finally told a calmer DJ after breakfast as she lovingly looked at the dog's little face. Pepper remained under the couch, just looking back at her friend with big sad brown eyes.

The difficult and painful responsibility of bringing Pepper to the vet to ultimately be put to sleep fell on Jill's shoulders—a fact she acknowledged with a mixture of resignation and anxiety but which she was determined to see through herself, as it should be. When she arrived at the Fairview Animal Hospital, she asked Dr. Miller to be allowed to remain with her beloved pet during the procedure. Knowing how devoted she was to the little creature, the understanding veterinarian was more than glad to grant her wish without hesitation. With trembling hands and a knot in her stomach, she placed Pepper on the examination table, which had been covered with a crisp white flannel sheet folded twice-over. She tenderly caressed the little animal, trying to control her shaking hands, telling Peppy how much she loved her and how much DJ loved her as she covered her sweet little face with tear-soaked soft kisses. Pepper remained unusually calm, eyes wide open, quietly laying there. She rested her head on her front legs and did not move all. She didn't even try to turn around to look at Jill, comforted simply by the loving hand that touched her long back. As Dr. Miller used a small needle to inject some medication into a vein on Peppy's right front paw, Jill silently started to weep as she continued to caress the sweet creature, trying hard not to fall apart. Within seconds, the little dog was gone even though her eyes remained open. Jill began to sob loudly then as she gently closed her beloved companion's eyes, apologizing over and over again for what she had been forced to do. Gathering the body of the small dog close to her chest, snuggly wrapped in the soft blue, green, and white blanket that she had so lovingly knitted in the weeks following her adoption, a distraught Jill started to pace back and forth inside the small room. She proceeded to rock the motionless and suddenly much heavier dog just as she had done so often with DJ when he was an infant or whenever he did not feel well as a baby. Her heartfelt sobs reverberated throughout the confined space and quickly permeated through the thin walls around her. They carried her desperation out into the reception desk and waiting area, piercing the hearts of the veterinarians, receptionists, and dog owners alike as all of them empathized with the poor woman's grief. To true pet lovers or those who had been through it, the loss of a beloved pet equaled the loss of a loved one. There were often times when a pet was the only family a loving owner had, and losing them was an extremely difficult and pain-riddled ordeal, the grieving as raw as it would be with the death of someone's life companion. But lucky were those who were privileged to experience the joy of truly loving and being loved by a pet, even if the anguish over someday losing them was something they tried not to think about until they unfortunately had to.

November 11, 1983, which had started out as a cloudy and utterly dismal day, was sadly a perfect match for the deep and achy emptiness in Jill's heart, from the moment she had gotten out of bed earlier that morning and culminating with the death of her beloved little friend. She stepped out of the Animal Hospital, cradling Pepper's still warm body close to her chest, her somber and morose mood far surpassing the darkness of the somber and morose day. Her death would become the source of numerous tears for the Millner and Chandler families, all of whom had simply fallen in love with the fluffy ball of energy with captivating and expressive big brown eyes back on Christmas day in 1981. Sitting inside the car, she continued to hug Peppy, allowing herself to cry for as long as she felt the need to, not in any hurry to let go. When she was finally able to compose herself a bit, she lovingly placed the lifeless dog, still wrapped in her blanket, gently on the passenger seat for what would be their very last trip together.

Although she cried all the way home, Jill valiantly tried to keep her tears under control by the time she finally entered the house. Calmly, she asked her son to help her bury Peppy next to all the little graves that now occupied a good portion of the west side of their yard. "It will be the perfect spot for her," she said in a very low voice, "because the sun usually shines brightly until late in the afternoon. Peppy will like that." Staring at his mother with a miserable look in his eyes, DJ began to speak in a voice so low that she could hardly hear what he was saying above the sound of his sobs. "She always hated the cold, you know? She always buried herself under her blanket every chance she got. I want the sun to keep her warm," he went on, his hands tucked deeply inside the pockets of his heavy parka. "She will love that, I'm sure," Jill whispered, trying to hold back a flood of tears of her own. The simple twig cross placed on Pepper's grave had a handmade red heart dangling from it, with the dog's name written on it in DJ's shaky handwriting. Jill managed to collect a bouquet of wild flowers that she was still able to find in her gardens, which she tied with a pretty pink ribbon before placing it at the base of the cross. She had gently placed Peppy, still snugly wrapped in her wool blanket, inside a sturdy plastic container she had purchased the day before she was euthanized specifically for the sad occasion. On the sides of the box, she had tucked the dog's red water and food bowls, all of her chewing toys, her balls, her bright pink collar, and her ID tags. She had then placed Pepper's small red stocking, which had been lavishly decorated with lots of gold glitter by a happy DJ during their very first Christmas together, on top of the other items before she closed the container. On the lid, Jill had written a heartfelt message, thanking the precious dog for all the loyalty, companionship, dedication, and love she had so generously showered them with. After signing her name on the lid, she had given the permanent marker to DJ, who added his name next to his mother's. With shaky hands, he had drawn tiny red hearts around both names and on all four corners of the lid as thick tears quickly fell on the newly written words, testimony to a child's sorrow at the loss of his playmate and best friend.

DJ refused to visit the grave after that terribly sad day, explaining that it was just too painful for him to go there. Jill respected his feelings even though she caught him often just staring at the grave through one of his bedroom's windows. "I just can't do it, Mom. I can't handle it," he cried in her arms a few days after the burial. She, however, could often be found kneeling by the small grave, spreading the cool but still soft dirt with her bare hands as if by doing so she could still touch the little dog buried there. She couldn't help but get emotional every time she thought of the day she went to the mall to purchase the container in which Pepper's body now laid, on the afternoon before she was put to sleep. She simply couldn't forget how empty inside and utterly devastated she had felt then, her overpowered conscience shouting at her that the poor animal was still very much alive and there she was, buying a plastic box that would become Pepper's final resting place. She also painfully thought of the trip back from the mall, the detested container hidden in the trunk of her car, where she had left it until the very last possible second. She felt extremely guilty for letting Pepper down and betraying the trust the gentle dog had placed in her ever since their very first encounter, when Peppy had been a tiny little puppy that Jill had adopted from the animal shelter as a surprise Christmas gift for her son.

Being always the reasonable one sucked big time, Jill came to realize, but she also had to be realistic, and the reality was that there was nothing she could have done to help Pepper except to put her down. That, however, was of little comfort to her or DJ, but as much as it had hurt her to do so, she saw it through to the very end. It had been, once more, up to her to get the job done, which she barely managed to do. Life could be so cruel sometimes, she admitted, especially when in the privacy of her bedroom, from where she was sure that DJ wouldn't be able to hear her crying. She tried to spare her son from any added pain for he had suffered enough already. It was what mothers everywhere were supposed to do from dawn to dusk and every second in between, wasn't it?

The weeks following Pepper's death were indeed very sad for Jill, for DJ, and for their immediate family. She found herself spending a lot of time simply looking at the many candid pictures of the little dog that were framed and scattered around the house. She gained great comfort in seeing how happy Peppy seemed to be in all of them, some with an even happier DJ right next to her. What she valued the most though, were the countless memories of their time together as a family, the love she felt for their precious pet safely tucked away for keeps. They would last a lifetime, this cherished collection of feelings and emotions that developed during their time with her. The beauty of memories was that they couldn't be taken away as long as they remained alive in one's heart and mind. They could not be erased by the passing of time either, merely preserved, regardless of how many years elapsed between the here and now and the day when everyone would finally be reunited once more, pets and people together as it should always be.

As a matter of fact, a few days after Pepper was euthanized, Jill received a wonderful short story called *The Rainbow Bridge* from her veterinarian and his dedicated staff. The amazing story was beautifully written by someone who truly understood the deep love that often bonded pets to their owners and vice versa. It touchingly described the emotional reunion between a dog and his beloved owner after they had both passed away, the dog's death preceding that of its owner. The inspiring words were read many times over as the days following Peppy's death turned into weeks, their healing power a source of great comfort that never ceased to lighten Jill's load. She could actually recite the entire story word for beautiful word. The meaning contained in that one page became a pivotal point in getting the much-needed healing process back on the right track. The treasured and irreplaceable story was now safely encased in a delicate white frame and placed on the wall right in front of the door that lead to the garage. And that was exactly where Jill planned to keep it so that it was the last thing she saw when she left the house and the very first thing she saw upon her return. The bright hues of the rainbow that spread from the top of the page all the way to the bottom, along with the beautiful light blue background the words were written on, never failed to exert their soothing effect upon her craving soul. She missed Pepper so.

CHAPTER 11

DJ's elementary school years went by quickly. After Pepper's death, Jill encouraged her son to join the local little league baseball team. After the tryouts, DJ proudly became a member of the Green Hornet family, and his green and black uniform was his favorite thing to wear. He was a really good player, and Jill was glad to see him out of the house more. Before long, she found herself looking forward to their weekly practice and games. Getting to know the other parents on the league was an added bonus. In most aspects, those years as a baseball player went by relatively smooth for DJ as he progressed from boy to teenager. The occasional summons to the principal's office went parallel with minor playground fights and homework not being handed in on time. Those episodes, however, were to be expected, especially given the fact that an insurgence of male hormones were suddenly assaulting his rapidly growing body, their oscillating levels a source of increasing mood swing episodes. Jill's deep fears that her son's overly sensitive heart could become a major source of heartache for him never quite materialized and were only a minor problem until he fell ill during the third grade. Losing Pepper had actually toughen him up a little, but his love for animals continued to guide him to many more wounded little creatures in need of help. DJ was halfway into fifth grade when scholastic problems began to surface, but once they did, they were more than hard to control.

In the scheme of things though, Jill considered herself to be very lucky still, especially where DJ was concerned. Her son was never known to smoke by his classmates, who prided themselves in knowing just about everything about everyone, or so they thought. Many of them admitted to smoking behind their parents' backs, and pot remained the recreational pastime of many, perhaps a leftover from the free-spirited, peace-loving, long-haired, and hippie-based 1960s. As far as she knew, DJ didn't touch alcoholic beverages either as quite a few of his friends got into the habit of doing on a regular basis. Weekends were always a problem when it came to alcohol consumption, with the teens getting together at a particular hangout or another. Somehow, in spite of all the talks about the dangers associated with drinking alcohol and drunk driving, someone always managed to produce a bottle or two of the heavy duty stuff just "to keep the fun going." No one ever mentioned any other type of recreational drugs, and Jill had no reason to suspect that her son was into any of them either, at least not that early in the game anyway. Before long, and to Jill's relief, graduation day finally arrived. Her biggest worry was that DJ would not be allowed to graduate with his class, mainly because of his dismal grades. Once all As and Bs, they had gotten lower and lower especially for the last three of his elementary school years. No matter how many talks she had with her son and all of his teachers, she was never able to accomplish much in getting him to improve them, which she was sure he could if he only applied himself a little more. To her bewilderment and frustration, they remained barely above passing all the way through the eighth grade, but he still managed to graduate with his classmates nonetheless, and for that she was deeply grateful. She simply didn't want her son to suffer the humiliation of being the only kid left behind during the graduation ceremony.

Right after DJ began the eighth grade, Jill started to think about where she should send her son after the current school year was over with. Her choices were Shelton High, where the majority of his classmates were undoubtedly headed, and Saint Joseph's High, a private school in the nearby town of Trumbull. She was well aware that her son wanted to follow his friends to Shelton High, for he had told her so in clear and less-than-pleasant words every time the subject came up. Her main objective though, was to provide DJ with the best education possible, especially given the fact that his grades had been so poor until then and showed no indication of improving. She spent many sleepless nights just tossing and turning, not wanting to make a mistake that could negatively affect her child for the rest of his life. His deplorable grades were indeed a major point of consideration, and unless he did a 180 degree turn, he was in for a bumpy road ahead, scholastically speaking. Things were so much simpler when DJ was little, Jill thought with a deep sense of nostalgia! Parenting was hard even under the best of circumstances, and not having a partner to share the responsibilities with made the already difficult job that much harder to handle. "I didn't realize how right my mother-in-law has always been until now," she told her mother one day, her level of frustration at an all-time high and clearly reflected on her tone of voice. "Small kids, small problems, big kids, big problems, she was very fond of saying. And DJ is not even trying to make this a little easier on either one of us," she added with a sigh. Sophia just smiled, nodding her head and patting her daughter's hand in sympathy. *Try multiplying that by four*, she wanted to say but refrained from it. She was well aware that all her daughter was looking for was a friendly shoulder to cry on and not a lecture, a great deal of understanding causing her to sigh as well. She was lucky enough to have been able to share all her parental decisions with her husband, whereas Jill had been deprived of the same privilege, and for that Sophia was really sorry. She squeezed her daughter's hand as she placed a gentle kiss on the same cheek she had kissed a thousand times before, while her youngest child was growing up and going through almost the same thing that DJ was now experiencing, only she hadn't realized it yet. No parent ever did while dealing with a teenager.

Jill had great hopes and expectations about Saint Joseph's, and high on her list was the probability that a new school setting would provide her son with the crucial change in environment that she thought he was in dire need of. New school, new friends, and perhaps a new beginning for him, she prayed. She also kept in mind the reality of important career choices for him even if he was too young to think about that aspect of his future yet and so far head. She was aware of his great potential, but he needed to apply himself to his studies a lot more than he had until then. Intelligence alone would only take him so far without a proper education to back it up, she told him on more than a few occasions, causing him to cringe inside, his need to rebel increasing with every word she uttered. Those discussions invariably ended with him rolling his eyes at her when he thought she was not looking, which, in turn, made her furious with him. To complicate matters, she was also aware of how difficult it would be for a teenager, any teenager for a fact, to have to go to a new school and have to try and make new friends all over again. She was not a wicked stepmother, for Pete's sake, and knew full well that the only thing her son wanted to do was to stay close to the friends he already had and was simply petrified to be separated from them. The security and sense of belonging that familiarity ultimately provided was something she knew a thing or two about only too well after all. How could she blame DJ for wanting the same thing?

After weeks of back and forth deliberating, vacillating, comparing, and, above all, worrying, Jill finally came to the conclusion that Saint Joseph's would be a better fit for her son's needs, much to his chagrin and consternation. DJ was not shy about letting his feelings be known, whether she wanted to hear it or not. As she had already anticipated, he didn't react well to the "verdict," as he called it, which precipitated the beginning of a very turbulent period between the two of them. Trying to give him the benefit of the benevolent doubt, she attributed the drastic changes in DJ's personality and the driving force behind his open hostility toward her to her final decision to send him to Saint Joseph's and not directed at her personally. The tension between them, however, was difficult to withstand to say the least. She had, after all, decided to separate him from all the kids he had known since kindergarten, and that was a bitter pill to swallow. That was the reason why she very wisely chose to take some of his rebellion in stride and not nitpick. "A rebel without a cause," she found herself calling him when he managed to really get to her. Being a guidance counselor was a huge help but not the answer to everything. Sometimes she wondered if a little smack across his smug mouth wouldn't be a better tool than all her psychological expertise, but she knew better than to give into her impulses regardless of how much she sometimes wanted to. The overstuffed pillow that graced the equally overstuffed couch in the family room had seen a not particularly flattering side of her personality, but she always felt better afterwards.

Avoiding a major confrontation with an increasingly defiant DJ became part of her daily little ritual, although there were many times when the arguments simply wouldn't be denied. The fact that she felt partially responsible for a great deal of his resentment toward her didn't lighten his outbursts or mitigate their outcomes. It made for a very unpleasant atmosphere at home, with invariably DJ slamming the front door shut behind him in his eagerness to get away from her, causing every light fixture to sway and rattle as a result of the power of his sheer anger. Although she knew that she wasn't the only mother going through a rough period with a teenaged child, it certainly felt like it at times. Given the fact that she didn't have a spouse to share her frustrations with made an already difficult job that much harder to manage. On the occasions when she felt her unending patience with her son on the brink of extinction, her urge to ground him for the rest of his life became a very soothing fantasy to nurture, if only in her head.

Jackson Brooks was proud of the fact that he remained a positive presence in Jill's life over the years. On more than just a few occasions, he became a source of great comfort to her during the entirety of DJ's trouble-riddled eight grade. Jill found herself leaning on Jack more and more as the school year progressed along. She always made sure to conduct those one-on-one meetings in his office and during business hours. As the weeks sped by, they changed their routine a bit, but she couldn't attest for certain as to the reason why. They started to meet every Wednesday for breakfast at a quaint diner in Monroe. Sitting across from each other, they often locked eyes when discussing one particular issue or another, and it felt so good being in his friendly company. When was it that their relationship began to change? she wondered. Was it when she noticed that he held onto her hands a little longer than necessary, often encasing both of her small ones within the protective shield of his much bigger ones, as if by doing so he could protect her as well? Was it when she finally realized how deeply blue his expressive eyes really were, those always curious and inquisitive eyes of his that seemed to reach right into your soul? Or was it when she noticed that his lips curved upward when he smiled? His sensual lips were indeed made for kissing, she thought with a touch of remorse one day, remorse for having those thoughts to begin with when she was still in love with Drew. The dimples that appeared at the center of his smooth cheeks when he laughed were endearing, making him look several years younger than his chronological age. His slightly receding hairline didn't affect his appeal at all, and the few gray hairs that now graced his temples only served to complement his polished and distinguished look. One day, he was simply kind and dependable Jack, a very dear friend and confidant; the next day he was dashing Jack, a good-looking and self-assured man that any woman would be proud to claim as her own. The way he looked at her, his hungry eyes speaking louder and louder with each passing day, made Jill's heart often jump with excitement and anticipation. There were times when she thought that she would simply melt under his intense stare, begin to slide down the caramel-colored vinyl–covered booth and run onto the gray linoleum floor. Breakfasts at the diner soon became dinners and a movie, and before long, their little secret was out.

For good old Jack, the journey had been a hard one but worth the heartaches and disappointments he at times went through. He had been the principal at Park Ridge Elementary School when Drew was killed and had witnessed Jill's pain front and center. Although he had gotten several very lucrative offers to move elsewhere, he decided to stay where he was for the time being and was still the principal there twelve years later. It was a decision he never regretted though, for it had kept him in a school he simply loved, doing a job that he was born to do, and more importantly, close to the woman he simply adored. He had loved Jill for so long that he couldn't remember what his life had been like before she had come into it. He had fallen in love with her the first time he saw her lovely face; he didn't even know her name then. The fact that she was married had stopped him dead in his tracks though. Getting to know her husband, who went on to become a very dear friend, further extinguished any minute cinders of hope he might have still harbored, especially after Drew Millner was so tragically killed back in 1976. There were many times since that horrible day that he came very close to telling Jill how much he had always loved her, but he was ultimately afraid to risk the certainty of their true friendship for the possibility of something more. Because he had too much to lose should she become uncomfortable with his feelings for her, he never told her how he really felt toward her for the entirety of their friendship, which was fast inching toward the two-decade mark. The price tag was simply too steep for him to even consider and not worth the risk in the long run. The truth of the matter was that it was much better to remain in her life as a friend than not being in her life at all. But it had all worked itself out in the end, and he couldn't be happier if he tried.

Things between them proceeded slowly, and Jill would've not wanted it any other way. Drew had been gone twelve long years, and Jill was surprised at how ready for romance she was once again, much more so than she thought she would ever be. She couldn't proclaim to be head over heels in love with Jack, but she certainly loved him. Not to be denied was the fact that she was also quite attracted to him, and the wonderful combination of love and physical attraction were two major points in their favor. Jill suspected that Jack had indeed fallen in love with her and was careful not to cheat him out of anything he was entitled to. He deserved no less from her.

To DJ's consternation, his school principal and his mother became an item, which he viewed as "a plot against him" if he ever saw one! He fought hard against it at first, but Jack's sensible attitude and the way he related to the teen finally won him over. Not to be denied was the fact that DJ held onto the hope that with Jack in the picture, the focus of his mother's attention would shift a little. It could be just enough to give him a break from her constant vigilance, which was more than suffocating at times. He often felt as if she was literally living her life through him, and that was way too heavy for him to deal with. By making him the center of her world, Jill had placed an enormous burden on her son ever since the day his father had died. It was a fact that Marissa had tried without success to point out to her best friend on numerous occasions when DJ was still a little boy. Many times he just wanted to scream at his mother, letting her know just how much she was hurting him. He wished that he could go even further by asking her to cut him some slack and get the hell off his back, but he never found the nerve to tell her so. Rebelling against the oppression he felt he was always under was much simpler than telling her how he truly felt. Leashing out at her before she had the chance to say anything was the way to go about it, he reasoned. DJ knew that he couldn't very well force his mother to send him to Shelton High, especially after her mind had been made out already, but he could certainly retaliate though, and retaliation was better than nothing. Plus it would give her a healthy dose of her own medicine, he gloated. There was very little that he felt he could do to regain control of his life, and not being in control sucked big time no matter how young or old a person was. His grades though, were a different story altogether! He decided to let them slide even lower during his last year at Park Ridge school, thus pissing his mother to no end. The fact that he was risking not being able to graduate with his class never entered his mind; so intent was he on upsetting Jill. She could have it in with the principal or talk with his teachers all she wanted; this one battle was his to win, come hell or high water!

The summer of 1988 found a still defiant and verbally confrontational DJ trying to break free from what he perceived to be his mother's controlling ways. Good thing that Jack was there to diffuse some of the more volatile situations, he soon came to appreciate. The troubled relationship between mother and son was riddled with problems that were clearly the by-product of human-related character flaws, a string of unchecked emotions, a slew of untapped coping mechanisms, and a series of ill-devised choices on both sides. On one hand, there was this dedicated mother's need to feel needed, her sometimes irrational fears for a child left fatherless at the age of two rending her blind to her own needs in the process. On the other, there was this teenage boy with a natural need for a certain amount of independence from his sometimes over-worried and strong-willed mother. Added to the mix was their inability to give and take, the need for her to see beyond the gate to her heart and fears, and for him to see beyond his ever-expanding need for freedom; he should be allowed to evolve and mature as he ought to, after all! As a result, both mother and son clashed over the most insignificant and mundane issues, while serious ones failed to be addressed properly, if they were ever addressed at all.

As Jill had predicted, the vast majority of DJ's friends did indeed transition directly from Park Ridge Elementary to Shelton High, save for four students besides her son, two of whom had moved to another state altogether. DJ's first day of high school caused him a great deal of anxiety even though he chose not to share his misgivings with his mother. He tried but couldn't eat any of his breakfast, which he left untouched on top of the kitchen counter. The thought of saying anything to his mother never occurred to him, but even if it had he would've not followed through with it verbally anyway. Although the thought of asking her son what was weighing heavy on his mind was very tempting, unfortunately for both of them Jill didn't follow through with it verbally either. A stalemate, that's what they had. Too bad neither one was willing to admit to, not even to themselves, the first step toward getting the lines of communication reopened and free-flowing again. As it was, DJ hardly shared anything with his mother, which was something he didn't have much of a problem with in the past, but he wasn't about to start confiding in her again anytime soon. He would never tell her just how nervous he was that morning and for a variety of reasons, most of which she probably wouldn't understand anyway. Either that or she just didn't give a shit, he reasoned! Why was she doing this to him? Why couldn't he go on to Shelton High like all of his friends did? He knew why. They didn't have Jillian Elizabeth Millner for a mother, and they hadn't survived a car crash that had killed their dad right in front of their eyes either, that's why! He didn't have a clue as to whether those two things could ever be separated or dealt with in a proper way, he thought with a large dose of anger-infused resentment and frustration. With an exasperated sigh, he exited the house with a quick good-bye and a grunt. He wasn't going to complain, he swore under his breath, and he wasn't about to let his mother know just how pissed with her he really was. He would never give her the satisfaction of knowing how truly miserable she had finally managed to make him. Why DJ chose to leave the house without even looking in her direction was beyond her, Jill thought with sadness. Didn't he realize how concerned she was for him on his first day at a new school? Didn't he understand that she only had his best interest at heart and how truly miserable she felt at having separated him from all of his former classmates and friends? "It wasn't an easy decision to make, son," she said to the empty kitchen, an exasperated sigh escaping her clenched mouth and overtaxed mind.

DJ said very little when he got home that afternoon even though he was well aware of the fact that his mother would probably love to hear just about everything that happened during the course of his first day at Saint Joseph's. How predictable she was, he scoffed, and a real pain in the ass to boot, he thought. The bitterness he felt toward his mother gaining momentum the more he thought about it. He answered only the questions she posed and nothing else, unwilling to volunteer any more information than he really had to. DJ knew that he could be a real pain in the neck, but he couldn't help it though. Not when his mother acted as if his wishes didn't deserve even a small amount of consideration on her part. It was his life anyway, wasn't it? Why was she so hell-bent on ruining it then? Didn't she have better things to do with her time? Like concentrating a little more on Jack, perhaps?

*   *   *

A teenager now, DJ had grown quite tall and lean, a few scattered pimples marring his otherwise strikingly handsome face. His hair had turned from pale blond to a sandier color as he got older, but his big and expressive eyes remained as blue as the sky. Being what Jill considered a typical teen, he seemed to be going through an extended period of rebellion. She hoped that it wouldn't last much longer than it already had, but she literally didn't know what to expect from one minute to the next. His behavior had been quite unpredictable for a couple of years now, to say the least, and Jill was at a loss as to how she should handle the uncomfortable situation at home. Quieter than his mother, he preferred to spend most of his time in the privacy of his own room, listening to music or playing with his computer. As far as she could tell, he had not started to date yet, which was not that uncommon for such an introverted young man. She noticed how often girls eyed her clueless son, openly flirting with the handsome teen without the benefit of even being noticed. He continued to play baseball, adding football to his roster during his sophomore year, which gave him more than enough opportunities to mingle with his colleagues outside a classroom setting. Time was definitely on his side, and being young and healthy gave him plenty of leeway as far as dating was concerned, Jill reasoned. There was certainly no reason to rush into something he might not be ready for just because others were doing it, and she was glad that he seemed to be his own person in that respect. Hopefully he wouldn't allow himself to be overinfluenced by his peers, as many teens around his age appeared to, their ultimate wish to fit in often clouding a significant portion of their better judgment. The need to be part of the crowd, to belong, often placed teens on a collision course with the very same values they had grown up with and which they often found themselves clashing with. It was often said that youth was wasted on the young, and Jill could now understand why, not until her problems with DJ had escalated to an all-time high. She wished she had the mentality she now possessed when she was her son's age so that she had the added wisdom to make the right decisions when the time came. But that would be totally against what being a teenager was all about, wouldn't it? Because they acted mostly on pure instinct, a teenager's resilience was often put to the test throughout the years, in final preparation for the grown-up time that would soon follow. Thankfully, most survived this turbulent period with nothing more serious than a few battle scars and a great measure of insight into which direction they could expect their future to lead, but there were always the ones that miserably failed to. The window of time during which emotions overruled all else was a short one indeed, the prelude to the rest of everyone's life, if they were lucky enough to have a long one. Every teenager dreamed of becoming an adult way too soon, not realizing what they were leaving behind once they became one. This total lack of appreciation and understanding as to how truly special the teen years really were was the real meaning behind the proverb that youth was wasted on the young. What teens had no idea of then was the truthful fact that, along with the enviable title of adult, they would be forced to face a new and foreign set of rules altogether. It came with the territory and with the complicated transition from childhood to adulthood. Responsibilities that they were spared from as teens, would eventually take hold, front and center. Commitment, along with several other key words, would take on a new significance and become of increasing use in their expanding grown-up vocabulary. Yes, youth was indeed wasted on the young.

Since they had always enjoyed an open and friendly relationship while her son was growing up, Jill tried to remain optimistic enough for both of them. She hoped that, once he realized that she only had his best interest at heart, DJ would relent a little and reconsider his position as his mother's self-appointed adversary. There was absolutely no reason why they couldn't try to be on the same page as opposed to butting heads over every single issue that came up, or so it seemed. And there was no reason why they couldn't find their way back to a truce once more, to more solid and common ground to again plant their feet upon. That, however, would take quite a bit of effort on both parts, and DJ appeared to be unwilling to go the extra mile. *I might very well be deceiving myself, son, but I believe in you and me. I can't understand why you won't believe in us too,* she thought sadly.

Jill often found herself confiding more and more in Jack, especially as things got really tough, and they certainly did on several occasions thereafter. Thankfully Jack had an infinite gift of wisdom and objectivity, especially when hers were at a record-breaking low. Since she had been the one who ultimately made the decision not to send DJ to Shelton High, she seemed to be the one walking away from their endless arguments as well, but that was simply the better of two evils. She opted to give him the time and space she thought he needed in order to cool off his heels and use some of the common sense she knew he was more than capable of. Instead of wasting precious energy worrying too much about his behavior, she chose to focus her attention on all the education opportunities and possibilities he would be exposed to. Both could be of great value to him later on in his academic career, even if he couldn't see it quite that way yet. Education was extremely important, for it would eventually give DJ the tools that he needed in order to get a solid head start in his chosen career. Because she was his only parent, Jill felt that it was up to her to see that he got every opportunity available to him, even if he failed to understand that fact himself. She missed Drew more than she could ever express but it was during certain specific times that her husband's absence morphed from truly hard to strikingly difficult. The reality that Jill fully understood the importance a proper high school preparation would be for a more secure future while DJ did not was one of those times, for she knew how crucial those years would be as a precursor for the rest of his life. The impact that Drew's death had on them multiplied tenfold every time she was confronted with another major issue, most of which involved their child. Securing DJ's future was indeed a huge one for her, perhaps the biggest of all, second only to his health and well-being.

Jack's opinion became increasingly more important to her, not only as a man and an educator but also as a man and a father himself, and an excellent one at that. Not wanting to shortchange him, Jill made sure to always be direct and honest with her gentle giant, mindful not to cross the fine line between profound honesty and obscured sensitivity. Not even close to insensitivity, something that Jill was very mindful of, obscured sensitivity came with its own set of hidden trappings. The line that separated the two was very fine indeed and could become easily blurred at times, especially when issues were not fully thought out before words were finally spoken because once said, they could never be taken back. And yes, lies hurt as much as the truth did, only for different reasons. She considered herself to be very open-minded and fair, yet Jill was always mindful not to rush into conclusions when having one of her many long conversations with Jack. Grateful for his input, she was careful to consider his advice well before forming an opinion, knowing that he only meant to help mend her broken relationship with her challenging son. She never wanted to take Jack for granted either, and that was the reason she tried to always be kind in her honesty with him. He needed to know where he stood and deserved to be treated a certain way. He had become a pivotal and intricate part of her life, and she wanted to make sure that he knew exactly how she felt about him, not only because of his positive influence on her son, but also because of the impact his presence had on her life. She was really thankful for all his help with DJ, for she knew that his wisdom had been of great value, and she felt a sudden need to let him know just how appreciative she truly was. Although Jack asked for little in return, Jill was so sensitive to his wants and needs that she had no problem meeting them, for they were indeed quite basic in nature. She tried hard never cross that line between obscure sensitivity and insensitivity. Heck, she tried hard to avoid getting too close to the first, and she fought as hard as she could to never be within sight of the second.

Jill missed the pillow talks she had shared with Drew, the dreams they had created, the plans they had made. Those plans were simple yet grandiose in their simplicity, for they were mostly about the little boy who slept so peacefully in his crib in the next room, among smiling frogs on top of lily pads and snails and butterflies and dragonflies. She knew that Drew had been wiser beyond his years and that his input could ultimately mean the difference between making the right choices versus making a colossal mistake. Priding herself on being an objective and conscientious parent wasn't good enough, and making the wrong decision was not an option, not as far as their son's future was concerned. After mulling it over and over in her head, she finally came to the conclusion that she was being way too hard on herself. What parent hadn't ever come to regret a particular decision in the process of raising a child, regardless of whether they were doing the parenting alone or with the help of a mate? After everything was said and done, analyzed, dissected, pieced together, and finally over with, DJ was still a teenager, and being a teenager was difficult under the best of circumstances. He was going through what every other teenager like himself had gone through for decades. The insecurities, fears, confusion, self-doubts were all real, and the frustration, anger, and lashing out were simply the end result. Add to that mix a surge of hormones, rapidly changing body images, fluctuating moods, and the concept of an evolving teenager was mapped, clearly developed, and ultimately formed, but with plenty of room for improvement. And a lot of the misgivings that had plagued young people for as long as the world was created were very basic in nature, such as the need to fit in and be accepted, with the few distinct differences between each subsequent generation nothing more than a reflection of the times and nothing else. On one hand, teenagers were no longer viewed as children once they hit thirteen years of age, while at the very same time, they were far from being considered adults quite yet either, a double whammy from every angle possible. It was a state of floating limbo that started when you were considered old enough to speak your mind but too young to make your voice heard. In DJ's case, he believed that his mother, who had put his well-being ahead of all else for years, had simply refused to listen in a matter that meant more to him than anything else in his confused life, a fact that ultimately brought equal doses of anger, resentment, and frustration to complicate things. What good was it to voice your opinion if you're not going to be given the chance to speak or be fairly heard? Patience was her most useful tool as far as DJ was concerned and the unconditional love she felt for her child, her ultimate gift to him, only he didn't know it yet.

True to his word, Jack was there every step of the way, advising Jill to never give in or give up when trying to reach her son, and clear, calm, and reasonable thinking was the surest way to accomplish that. "You know that you can catch many more flies with honey than with vinegar, Jill. Try not to forget that, sweetheart, even though I understand how you wish you could just grab him by the shoulders and literally shake some sense into his stubborn head sometimes. And also try to remember what it was like to be DJ's age, my love. It wasn't that long ago, right?" he reminded her, noticing the deep crease that had formed in her forehead, a foolproof indication of how stressed out she really was by the whole miserable ordeal.

Remembering Jack's wise words, Jill worked hard at trying to approach her son from a different angle, one that had much more to do with the productive and much less with the argumentative side of things. They could agree to disagree as long as they kept on talking, she told him during one of their more enlightened arguments. She wanted to make DJ understand that her motives were derived from her wish to help and protect him, not from her need to control him as he had so often screamed at her on more than one occasion. He had accused his mother of that far too many times, which invariably led to many angry outbursts and mean-spirited verbal exchanges on both parts, regardless of how sincerely she had tried to avoid falling into the same useless trap. She once more tried to reinforce the fact that she truly believed that the education he was receiving at Saint Joseph's was going to help him tremendously in the long run. It would come in very handy, she reiterated by the hundredth time, especially when he was ready to pick the university of his choice, which was usually a very stressful time in the lives of most collegebound young people. Why was it so difficult for the clearly bright DJ to understand that, she often wondered.

*　　*　　*

In the years following her husband's shocking death, Jill was very grateful that her wonderful father, William, and older brothers, Daniel and Nicholas, took time off of their own busy schedules to be a constant presence in little DJ's life. They took their sense of responsibility as role models to the fatherless toddler to heart, making sure to include the boy in almost every one of their outings as a family. But as DJ began to transition from a child to a teenager, they found him to be much less receptive of their genuine efforts and much more defiant and increasingly more resistant to their company and guidance. They never let on how much his change in behavior hurt them, deciding instead to concentrate on the boy's needs, not willing to be manipulated by his negative attitude as time went by. How could DJ doubt that they only had his best interest and well-being at heart? Jill counted on her father and siblings to help them through many of the challenges facing them, not feeling afraid or guilty about leaning on them for support. DJ, like all children, needed good male role models in their lives, especially during their intellectually formative years. Who was better qualified than her father and brothers to provide such to the grandson and nephew they loved so deeply? There were many things that she had gladly sacrificed in her quest to assist and guide her son, but being a masculine role model for him was definitely not one she could count on. Often times she had needed her late husband's sound advice, his wise solution to whatever the matter at hand happened to be always right on target, but unable to get it from him, she had turned to Jack, her dad and two brothers for help. She had always been able to count on Drew before his death, but the voice of reason in the face of turmoil had been forever silenced, she acknowledged sadly. His deep sense of honesty had been a wonderful change of pace from the standard answer some would give to many of life's complicated problems. He had possessed the uncanny ability to take everything in stride and had been more than objective and fair in spite of what the situation at hand happened to be. What she wanted more than anything else at the moment, she realized with a jolt to her heart, was to have Drew by her side, if only for a few minutes. With his support, along with all the help his endless supply of wisdom and patience could provide, she would be able to finally get a grip on what was happening between her and DJ. This was one of a handful of instances when she allowed her needs for her husband's guidance to supersede DJ's needs for the father he lost before his second birthday. This catastrophic void in his life was never far from Jill's thoughts and ultimately guided most of her actions as far as DJ and his needs were concerned. Her loved ones tried to warn her that this way of thinking could have a negative impact on both of them and turn into one huge headache as DJ grew older, but she failed to see any other option at the time. How could she not try to make up to him for his devastating loss as she worked so hard at being both a father and a mother to their darling boy? Easier said than done, she thought bitterly when her guard abandoned her, leaving her an easy prey to be pick on, a virtual sea of self-pity. Being self-centered was hardly part of her character, for she always found herself placing DJ's needs ahead of her own, but this once, she found herself thinking about her own emotional needs, a truth she was ashamed to acknowledge to anyone else, even to Jack. "Have I earned the right to be this self-serving now?" she questioned the smiling picture of Drew encased in a delicate filigree silver frame, a wedding gift from her mother-in-law. And no matter how much she stared at his bright blue eyes and full mouth, asking him for some sort of guidance, both remained still. There was nothing more final than death, she had to sadly admit. And for those left behind to pick up the pieces, nothing could ever come close to its undeniable cruelty either.

Jill was again reminded, perhaps for the millionth time, that Drew was never coming back, and it caused her heart to start bleeding all over once more as it had done so many times in the past since the horrible day when he was taken away. She was truly grateful for their son, by far the most valued and valuable asset in her life. This fact would never change no matter what, even if she were to live much longer than she could hope to. Redoubling her efforts to reach out to the child she loved with her heart and soul, she tried once more to reason with him. She reassured DJ how positive she was that, even though he failed to recognize and accept the fact quite yet, the difficult period he was undoubtedly going through would ultimately translate into a huge advantage on his behalf. It would eventually pay off big time, especially when he was ready to make the often difficult transition from high school to college. It was indeed a time that could be very exciting for some but very traumatic for most. DJ seemed to accept her reasoning to a certain degree, but his rebellious stage lingered on much longer than Jill had hoped it would. She truly missed all the chats they used to get involved in, all the feelings they used to share, she and this child who was the reason she had bravely endured so much pain and heartbreak, and all with unfaltering dignity and grace. But she still felt reenergized whenever she caught a glimpse at DJ's handsome face—by far the best legacy that Drew could have left behind when he had so suddenly died.

*   *   *

By his junior year, DJ finally seemed to have settled and become much more comfortable with his surroundings. He had developed a large group of friends, and young girls besieged him with attention and open interest. He was indeed the best-looking young man around according to his horde of female admirers, and being the quarterback on the football team didn't hurt either. When he turned seventeen, his mother decided to reward his much improved grades and attitude by enrolling her strapping son in Driver's Ed. A quick learner, he simply aced his test, proudly showing his brand new driver's license to all of his friends. Since she didn't know anything about cars, Jill enlisted Jack's help in finding a used car for her son, one that would be mechanically sound for at least a few years to come. They both fell in love with a Chevrolet Chevette with a crisp and clean light gray-colored interior and an impeccably shiny black exterior. The fact that it had always been garaged and that it had only thirty-six thousand miles cinched the deal. As a late gift for DJ's birthday, Jack had red sport stripes expertly painted on both sides of the car and a sporty-looking tail placed right above the edge of the trunk. Beyond ecstatic, DJ cared for his suped-up Chevy as if it was a brand-new red Corvette, which was by far every teenage boy's dream car.

With his mother's encouragement, DJ applied for and was hired as a security guard at the Milford Mall, which was a popular teen hangout. Working weekdays from 6:00 to 10:00 p.m., it was relatively easy for him to manage both school and work with a few minor adjustments on his part. He even worked an occasional Saturday or Sunday, when someone called out sick. Because he got paid every Friday night, this new financial independence brought on a major change in his mood swings. He seemed to really enjoy having his own money to do with as he pleased, and buying "cool" clothes soon became a new hobby to the no-longer-surly young stud. He was indeed much happier since he got his own wheels and income, a fact that brought immense relief to his mother's besieged heart. His grades eventually got back to the A and B+ range, which was more like the old DJ. His last year at Saint Joseph's turned out to be a very good one all around, and that translated into a much more relaxed atmosphere both at home and at school.

*   *   *

Everyone marveled at how extremely polite and respectful DJ turned out to be after all, especially given the fact that he went through such a prolonged turbulent period earlier on. He still held on to his security job at the mall, seeming to even enjoy his duties most of the time. He soon began hanging out with a handful of friends from school and work, and his weekends were filled with a combination of cruising around town and youth parties that he liked to refer to as "some simple and clean fun." "Nothing heavy at all, Mom, don't worry! You taught me better than that, remember?" he often said as he left the house for the evening. And he hardly broke curfew, which was 11:00 p.m. on weekdays and 1:00 a.m. on weekends.

As graduation date approached, DJ asked a classmate, a pretty green-eyed brunette named Alyssa, to the prom and was ecstatic when she said yes. "They make such a striking couple," Jill told Jack during one of their quiet evenings at home as they watched one of her favorite love stories of all times, the classic *An Officer and a Gentleman*. Her eyes were shining with happiness, and Jack couldn't help but gather her petite frame in his large one and kiss her with all the tenderness he felt for this remarkable woman, both in looks and in spirit. *How much luckier could a middle-aged man like myself get*, he wondered as the scent of her freshly washed skin pleasantly reached him, enveloping his entire being with a combination of mild soap and femininity. It made him forget everything but the woman kissing him back, her breath ragged and her mouth tasting like a freshly picked strawberry.

Alyssa was indeed a beauty, her shiny dark hair reaching just above her tiny waist. DJ's tall and lean golden looks was the perfect contrast to Alyssa's petite and trim frame and creamy olive complexion. They indeed made a striking couple, Jill realized, as she snapped picture after picture of the happy pair when prom day finally arrived. Both Jill and Alyssa laughed at how awkward DJ appeared to be trying to pin the white orchid corsage to his date's seafoam green gown. He was careful not to touch her perky and round breasts, which were clearly free of the protection of a bra due to the thin spaghetti straps holding the snug top in place. DJ could curse the two red dots that appeared on his cheeks, but what was the use of doing so? He was sure that they had suspected how uncomfortable he was by then, so the best thing to do was to laugh with them, which he did. Her son looked absolutely dashing in his black tuxedo, his cummerbund and bowtie in the same shade of green as his date's dress, and he literally beamed for the camera. His smile, however, didn't quite lighten his captivating eyes like it usually did, and Jill wondered why. *Prom jitters*, she figured, giving her son a kiss on the forehead before the young couple left for the evening, the energy and magical scent of youth lingering in the air for quite some time after they were gone. Jack arrived a few minutes later, a bottle of red wine in the crock of his left arm and a heavenly scented eggplant and olive pizza on the right hand. "I asked for it just the way you love it, darling, with lots of extra cheese," he quickly added. In the side pocket of his jacket, she saw a video cassette of *Pretty Woman*, another one of Jill's all-time favorites. "A man after my own heart," she laughed, tiptoeing to plant a soft kiss on his equally soft lips as he closed the door behind their embraced silhouettes.

Getting into Quinnipiac, a well-know and prestigious university in Hamden, Connecticut, turned out to be less complicated than DJ had first anticipated. His desire to become a veterinarian was stronger than ever, so he chose courses that were geared toward that. Since two of the classes had an added lab portion, he would end up getting four credits instead of three, raising his total to eighteen credits per semester instead of the maximum of sixteen. He met with the dean of students once he made his selections and was reminded that the extra credits he was about to sign up for would make his workload too heavy to handle. DJ reassured him that he was more than ready for the challenge, adding that he wanted to get as many credits as he could for the cost of his tuition. His days were spent at school and his evenings at his job at the mall, making for a very tight schedule from Mondays to Fridays, but he didn't seem to mind it one bit. He travelled back and forth to school and work in his little Chevette, which was beginning to show its age no matter how well he had cared for it. With his nineteenth birthday in less than two weeks, Jill knew exactly what to buy for her son, especially given the fact that he had managed to get his life back on the right track again. No mother could ask for a kinder, more respectful and loving son, and Jill was proud to claim the charming young man as her own.

A brand new electric blue Pontiac Grand Am sat in the driveway, spotless and all shiny. A massive red bow was attached to its roof, the ends of the ribbons flowing around in the gentle May breeze, the bright blue hue on the sky above complementing the brightness of the car's color. With a mug of coffee in his right hand, DJ casually wandered into the dining room and stopped dead in his tracks. His eyes became as big as saucers as he spotted the car, looking from the driveway to his mother with a look of utter disbelieve stamped on his face. With a satisfied smile, Jill quietly watched as his disbelief quickly turned into surprise, all clearly detected on her son's simply astonished expression. It reminded her that she had seen that same expression only once before, and that was when he saw Pepper for the very first time on Christmas day 1981. Speechless, he blinked a few times, trying to believe that he was really seeing what he thought he was and not just imagining the whole thing. With a shaky hand, DJ placed his coffee mug on top of the wide windowsill, spilling some of the contents on the floor. In two giant steps he had Jill in his arms, effortlessly lifting his petite mother in his strong arms, twirling her around as if she was no heavier than a small child. Kissing her loudly on both cheeks, he finally returned a very dizzy Jill to her unsteady feet, holding onto her until she was able to find her balance again. Way beyond ecstatic, DJ grabbed the car keys that his mother was now dangling from her outstretched right hand, the unmistakable look of pure adoration reflected in her absolutely beautiful eyes as blue as his own.

*   *   *

DJ was nearly twenty years old when he began to show increased interest in his social life, going as far as mentioning the names of several female friends during his conversations with his mother. Since he had never shared anything remotely related to his love life with her before, this new side of their close relationship pleased her to no end. This new development was of great significance to Jill, who thought that it was about time for DJ to start thinking about his future, and dating should certainly be a major part of it. Having learned from her past mistakes, she tried not to feel entitled to DJ's every thought and feeling simply because she was his mother, recognizing that he needed his own space in order to continue to mature and grow as the adult he now was. Keeping the lines of communication open remained of fundamental importance in this new phase they were both embarking on, and Jill felt very secure in the knowledge that her son trusted and valued her opinion again, for he hadn't done so in far too long a time by then.

DJ would talk about one particular girl or another for a period of time, giving Jill the impression that they were more than just friends, but he never brought any of them home for his mother to meet. When she mentioned that to him, he simply shrugged his shoulders as if the thought never even crossed his mind. With a shy smile, he simply explained that his life was far too busy at the time for him to get involved in anything more serious than an occasional romance. "Don't worry, Mom. When my career is more defined and I have a better job, I will find a girl to date seriously and eventually settle down with, I promise you. In the mean time, things are fine just as they are. It is only a matter of priorities for me right now, that's all. But when it happens though, you will be the first to know. Cross my heart and hope to die," he added, sounding just like he did when he was growing up and making a promise he had every intention of keeping. He sounded so sincere that she felt totally satisfied with his sensible way of thinking, which brought a smile to her face and peace of mind to her motherly heart. She never brought the subject up again, secure in the knowledge that her son seemed to know exactly where he was headed and how he was going to get there. *Oh, Drew! What a wonderful son we have created, sweetheart. Anyone would be proud to call him their child, but none more than myself, I can guarantee you, darling. He turned out to be everything a parent would ever hope for and then some.*

Even Jack conceded to Jill that there was a time when he came very close to giving up on DJ, not at all sure that he would develop into such a respectful, polite, and responsible young man. "And he has your incredible looks and kind soul to boot! He is certainly quite a catch, that son of yours, sweetheart," he added, almost as proud of DJ as Jill was, secretly wishing that he was their son together instead of hers alone. With three daughters and one son of his own, all a little older than DJ, there was more than enough room in his heart to love one more, which he already did and had ever since he found out about his good friend Drew's sudden death. It was soon after that horrible day that Jack took to heart the responsibility of keeping his eye on the little toddler and his grieving mother. He had been extra careful then not to be too obvious in his concerns over the two of them, lest his motives be questioned or misinterpreted by the young widow and her loved ones. And after all these years, Jack was glad to finally be able to let his feelings show, no longer afraid to open his heart and reveal how much he cared about them and had for over twenty years now. He was glad that his commitment and tenacity had paid off in the end, for it had allowed him to hang on when hard times forced him to reevaluate his position in the scheme of things. Life without Jill was something he had a hell of a hard time imagining, let alone lead.

CHAPTER 12

MAY 1994

"This new breaking story has just reached our station," the anchorwoman reported in a voice barely able to conceal her shock and anger. Jill, who was watching the local six o'clock news literally shook as she heard the facts of the case. According to the police, the body of a young girl had been found earlier that same afternoon in the town of Hamden. The twenty-one year old victim, whose name was being withheld pending notification to her next of kin, had been raped and strangled to death the previous night, according to preliminary reports. "Oh no! This can't be happening again," she whispered, unable to believe what was being said. This would make it the fourth murder of a young woman in a period of less than two years. According to the broadcaster, this latest victim had been killed by the same person who had killed the other three, as confirmed by the forensic experts who had investigated all of the three previous scenes. Perplexed, Jill walked from the kitchen to the family room couch and quickly turned on the TV set there. As she slowly sat down, her eyes remained glued to the TV screen. She couldn't bring herself to believe that the bastard had hit again. As the voice of the reporter resonated in the background, Jill's thoughts went back to the first time he had struck, the details still as vivid in her mind as they had been then.

July 1992 was a very hot month, with temperatures in the high 90s for days on end. It was during one of those hot and humid days that the body of first victim had been discovered, according to the six o'clock news anchorwoman. The pretty eighteen-year-old was found raped and strangled, her lifeless body callously thrown into a ditch alongside the southbound lane of Interstate 95 in Norwalk, a town about twenty-five minutes away from the Millners' house. The Fairfield University freshman had been reported missing by her distraught parents when she failed to return home from school two evenings before, which precipitated a county-wide search for her whereabouts. Unfortunately, that search culminated with the discovery of her beaten body two days later. Jill, who hadn't even been aware of the girl's disappearance, stared in disbelief as details of the tragic event were further disclosed. "How awful," she whispered, bringing her hand to her mouth, her heart rate nearly doubling at the sickening news. "You poor little thing," she empathized, her eyes instantly filling with tears. "And your poor family. What a terrible thing to go through," she went on talking to herself, feeling deeply sorry for the young girl and her loved ones. "As of now, there are no witnesses and no suspects," the reporter continued, his matter-of-fact tone grating on Jill's already raw nerves. DJ was the same age as the dead girl, and Jill found herself shaking at the thought that something like that could ever happen to him. She knew that reporters had to maintain a certain level of distance from the stories they reported, since objectivity and professional demeanor were crucial in their line of work. But some of them seemed to carry that need to an extreme, she lamented, often giving the impression that they had become desensitized to the depths of human suffering that was often involved. Their robotic description of a particular story they were reporting was a sad reflection of that fact. She hoped that she was wrong, not only for the sake of the people affected by those crimes, but for their own sake as well. Particularly sensitive when there was a death involved, Jill couldn't help but feel deep resentment at the manner in which the news was sometimes presented. Harder to accept still were the cases where the victims had been robbed of their lives at such a young age, for they barely had the chance to start living to begin with. "Son of a bitch," she hissed, her thoughts quickly switching from his latest victim to the perpetrator.

"I sincerely hope that the authorities catch the monster responsible for this horrible crime right away," she told her son when he got home from work later on. "You and me both, Mom," he answered, bending his head down to plant a soft kiss on his mother's equally soft cheek. "To die so young and in such a violent manner is hard to accept. Everybody at work was talking about the case, and I found myself being asked to please escort several women, young and old, to their cars tonight. I'm glad that I was at least able to do that much to ensure their safety," he said, a great deal of sadness detected in his concerned voice. "I can't help but identify with the dead girl, Mom. After all, we were the same age, you know?" he concluded. "Right now I'm really relieved that I don't have any daughters, DJ. I know that I can be overly optimistic at times, and perhaps I'm just fooling myself in my distorted view of seeing things, but I'm glad that you are a man. I might be totally wrong on this, but I truly believe that boys have a better chance at defending themselves simply because they are physically stronger, and that is the honest truth. That fact alone makes them less vulnerable than girls," she went on, a pained expression on her face as she thought of how much the poor girl must've have suffered at the hands of her heartless attacker. "How can one human being inflict such horror and pain upon another," she wondered out loud, shaking her head in disbelief. "And why should anyone have to be subjected to so much suffering and cruelty? I thought that we were much more civilized than that," Jill pondered, unable to comprehend the motives behind such atrocious behavior. "Unfortunately, Mom, we all live in a very violent world, one that seems to grow even more violent as we speak, in spite of the so-called progress we thought we had made since the caveman era of so many centuries ago. It seems like the further we try to forge ahead, the more we walk backward. That old saying that the more things change, the more they remain the same is many times truer than we hoped it would ever be." There was a lot of truth in what DJ had just said, and his candor and wise words hit Jill like a ton of bricks. She had to stop to gather her scattered thoughts before she could say another word.

Sensing his mother's need to unburden herself, DJ sat down right next to her and gave her his undivided attention, his arm protectively wrapped around her thin shoulders. "I hope that her family will be able to find the strength it will need in order to endure the difficulty of the days ahead. There is absolutely nothing worse for a parent than to have to bury a child. It is not in the order in which life is supposed to proceed. I went through such intense pain when I had to bury your father that there were many times when I believed that I was going to literally lose my mind. Fortunately, I had you to take care of, and your needs kept me going from one day to the next when all I wanted to do was to crawl into a ball and simply die, to join my husband and hurt no more. Giving in to my unbearable pain, however, was not an option for me, for I had someone else besides myself to think about. That, and the support I received from my parents, your dad's parents, and the rest of our family and close friends was what ultimately began to pull me through slowly out of my desolation and grief. As devastating as losing your father was though, I am sure that it would have been even harder if it were you I had to say good-bye to. Unfortunately, my love, death spares no one, regardless of any possible mitigating circumstances. It seeks nothing in particular and cares nothing about the suffering and devastation that always follows closely behind. In the end, my love, death simply is."

In a soul searching mood, Jill began to reflect on how the concept of death had so many meanings, depending on the time and circumstances surrounding it. Although sorrow was the first adjective that came to mind when the word was spoken, it wasn't always necessarily so. Natural was the one most of us prayed for because it came at the end of a very long life and because the human body was simply worn out after decades of living. Hopefully, the life that came to an end was a happy and fulfilled one, but unfortunately, that can't be hardly guaranteed even when the deceased person more than earned and deserved thus much. Relief was another, the well-appointed synonym that reflected the atmosphere surrounding many death passages, especially if the person went through a lot of suffering as they valiantly fought but couldn't get better from their noncurable diseases. It meant relief from the onslaught of terminal-illness-related physical or emotional pain, not only for the ill person but also for their loved ones. It was so devastating to witness a dear one struggle and suffer day in and day out, that death was not only a relief to all but welcomed as well. Salvation, for those who erroneously thought that death would solve what they perceived to be insurmountable problems. Unfortunately, what they failed to realize was that, for those left behind to deal with the aftermath of a suicide, no salvation or relief would ever be found, for guilt and self-doubt were incredibly powerful adversaries to face. Anger, for those who were told that nothing else could be done to help them, when all they wanted was to be allowed to live, if only a little while longer. Denial, for all those daredevils who took unnecessary risks with their lives in exchange for scattered moments of exhilaration, glory, and thrills. What were they really looking for, one was left to wonder. Panic, for the victims like the young girl that had just been found dead, who realized only too late that they were about to be robbed of what was most important in their life and that was life itself. Oblivion, for the unfortunate ones like Drew, who never saw it coming, thus denying them the chance to even say good-bye to their loved ones. And the list went on.

"And then, there are the children, all those poor and innocent children . . ." Jill thought, not realizing that she had spoken her thoughts out loud until she felt DJ's arm tighten around her slim frame, pulling his mother closer. "I know, Mom, I know. I can only imagine what you went through after Dad died like he did, so devastatingly and so needlessly. And with him being so young still, so vital and full of life . . . ," he said as he kissed the top of her bent head. His voice, low and comforting, sounded suddenly more mature and tired than she had ever heard before. Her son had been forced to grow up more quickly because he was the man of the house, she acknowledged, a mixture of pride and regret causing her eyes to tear up in an instant.

Fortunately for him, DJ did never realized how close his mother had come to losing him as well when he was only nine years old, and for that she was deeply grateful. He had gone through enough already in his young life, and he would never find it out, she vowed, even as old memories threatened to break free from their secret hiding place to no avail. Not as long as she had any breath left in her motherly soul, she vowed. She would stop at absolutely nothing in her determination to keep her only child safeguarded and protected as she had done from the minute he was conceived. Feeling extremely safe by the security of his protective arms around, Jill began to relax, resting her head on his chest, basking in the wonderful comfort the sound of his rhythmic heartbeat provided, as lost in her thoughts as DJ appeared to be lost in his. They remained like that, sitting side by side in silence for quite some time afterwards. Neither seemed in a hurry to spoil the magical moment, unwilling to break the spell that united their two souls but who shared only one unified heart.

*   *   *

The discovery of two more murdered young women conjured up the speculation of a possible serial killer on the loose, stalking the streets of Fairfield County and surrounding towns. Every major broadcaster reported at length each time a new victim was found, the identity of the person responsible for the crimes still unknown, yet the manner of the attacks and killings almost identical to one another. People everywhere commented on the cases, and reporters strongly urged their listeners to exercise extreme caution when going about their daily activities. They also encouraged every woman, young or old, to always carry some kind of defensive weapon with them, such as a can of mace or even a loud whistle. They emphasized that these items could be of great importance should they get accosted by anyone they were not familiar with or who looked or acted suspiciously to them. Even their car keys, or any other any key for that matter, could become a valuable tool if handled properly. They went on to demonstrate in great detail how the key should be held, the bigger the key, the more effective it would be in fending off possible attackers, but even smaller ones would do. Held flat in the palm of the dominant hand, and with the long end of the key extending forward between the index and the middle fingers, it became a stabbing tool once the hand was closed into a tight fist. It should then be quickly and forcefully jammed into an eye or an ear, rendering the startled attacker momentarily incapacitated by the great deal of pain it would cause. This would give the victim a lifesaving opportunity to run from the attacker and seek help. Because it could mean the difference between getting away or probably being killed, the maneuver was shown repeatedly, demonstrating how any key could be used effectively in an emergency situation, regardless of the size of the intended victim or the perpetrator.

To warn the viewers without creating widespread panic was quite tricky, but every news reporter was adamant about getting the message across. As they covered every detail of the violent crimes at length, they tried to remain focused on the task at hand, although some of them were barely able to mask their own fears. Their sole objective, they made sure to reiterate on a regular basis, was not to scare anyone, but simply to help keep everyone as safe as possible under the clearly dangerous circumstances. But the truth was that they were also afraid for every female member within their circle of family and friends.

The second victim, age twenty, was a petite strawberry blonde girl found a little over six months after the first one. She was described by those who knew her as being a friendly and easygoing person, one that was very popular with her peers and coworkers. She was well-liked at her job as a waitress at a popular restaurant in Newtown, a job she held for more than three years. She had been found in Cheshire by an early morning jogger, in a park adjacent to the local high school, raped and strangled in practically the same manner as the first one. Her partially naked body was severely battered and bruised, an indication that she fought fiercely for her life before succumbing to her assailant's brutal attack. Her body had been discovered nearly completely hidden behind a large rhododendron bush alongside a seldom used running trail, known mostly to avid runners. She had been killed the prior evening, according to the preliminary reports being released. As the details of the crime were being broadcasted, her photograph filled the television screen. It was the face of a radiant young woman with a captivating smile that enhanced her delicate features and cascades of wavy hair framing the stunning beauty of her light blue eyes. The few freckles across the bridge of her nose further accentuated how very young she was. She had just celebrated her twentieth birthday the week before at the restaurant where she worked. No one had been apprehended thus far and the police still had no concrete leads on either one of the cases, the reporter added with a clearly concerned look on his somber face. He reminded all listeners to continue to be extra careful when going about their daily activities, urging anyone with any clues whatsoever to please contact the authorities immediately, regardless of how insignificant they thought their information might be. As he was relating the news, a telephone number flashed across the bottom of the television screen, which had been set up specifically for that purpose. The identity of the caller and any information provided would remain strictly confidential, he assured the listeners. It was an easy number to remember, since it spelled 1-800-VICTIMS (1-800-842-8467). The newscaster went on to emphasize how crucial it was for the public at large to come forward and report anything and everything that they found to be of a suspicious nature to the authorities. He also added that those seemingly insignificant incidents could very well be linked to the crimes in one way or another but couldn't be followed unless they were reported. The authorities investigating the cases hoped that collectively they would to be able to stop the degenerate before he had a chance to kill someone else. They all felt that he would most probably strike again but refrained from voicing their fears in order not to further scare the public at large, who were more than frightened already. Fear led to panic, and that was the worst thing that could happen in as dire a circumstance as this was, with full blown panic only serving to interfere with the investigation; that was something they tried to avoid whenever possible.

A few months went by without incident, but on August of 1993, he struck again. This time the victim was a nineteen-year-old redhead, who was an honor student at Albertus Magnus College in New Haven. Her body was found in the town of Orange by an elderly man who was taking his dog for their routine daily walk. It was very early, a little before six, on a cloudy, hot, and very humid Tuesday morning. Because the sky looked so threatening, with dark and ominous clouds hanging close to the ground, the old man, named Frank, decided that the prudent thing to do was to simply turn around and head back home. He was not at all prepared to handle the downpour that appeared to be fast approaching, since he had chosen that particular day to be more stubborn than usual and not to heed his wife's advice to take an umbrella along. Damned be his thick skull, he thought with an exasperated sigh. After more than fifty years of being married to "the world's most nagging woman" though, he had learned a long time ago that the secret to a happy marriage was to simply train his mind to tune her out whenever he needed to. Now he regretted not giving her the benefit of the doubt once in a while as a picture of the darned umbrella, which remained safely inside the hallway closet, invaded his head. Cursing his luck, or in this case his total lack of judgment, he picked up his pace as the clouds overhead moved fast and furious, confirming his prediction that a deluge was just around the corner. The long-time Orange resident urged his small beagle, called Cocoa, to hurry up and do her business, all the while mumbling under his breath what a nuisance she was becoming as she got older. "You are getting as senile as me, old girl," he said in a gruff voice, trying to sound more annoyed than he really was, for the truth was that the dog, now eleven years old, was probably his best friend and companion. And she certainly didn't nag him the way his pain in the ass wife sometimes did, that's for sure! Suddenly, Cocoa started to bark, pulling on her leash with much more strength and determination that he had seen in years. She headed toward a dumpster that was placed on one side of a narrow and dark alleyway he had never even noticed before. When he got closer to the dumpster, which was disgustingly overflowing with all kinds of trash and old cardboard containers, he was startled to see a small human foot protruding from one of the overturned and filthy boxes. Not really believing what he was seeing, he rubbed his eyes with the palms of his hands, Cocoa's leash wrapped around his right wrist so that she couldn't get away. When he reopened his eyes, he saw that the foot was still there, and not simply a product of his grumpy imagination. He approached the box with a sick feeling at the pit of his stomach and, with trembling hands, carefully lifted the cardboard, yelling at the still barking dog to "shut the hell up for once." Moving the box to one side, he was horrified to see the lifeless body of a very young woman, bent and twisted like a broken rag doll. Her skin was extremely pale, and her lips were blue. The poor thing was completely soaked by the fine rain that had drizzled during the previous night. Unable to think straight, Frank simply stood there, frozen in place by the gruesome scene in front of him, looking at the dead girl through eyes that refused to accept what he was seeing. Her eyes were open even though they were no longer able to see, and her fixed stare was glazed over by the filmy curtain of death. Her lips were slightly ajar, as if a terrified scream had tried to escape her now forever voiceless mouth. It appeared like her body had been carelessly discarded by the heartless and evil son of a bitch that had killed her, as if she was nothing more than useless waste and of no more value than someone's day-old garbage. Frank felt a wave of nausea wash over him, cursing the bastard that had done that to the poor girl. For all his rough façade, he was more of a teddy than a grizzly bear, his heart bigger than anyone could ever guess just by looking at him. Even Cocoa, acting as if she knew that something terrible had happened, simply sat on the wet pavement, her small head resting on her front paws. She started to whimper pitifully as she looked from her owner to the dead girl, then back to her owner again. Her infuriating barking of a mere couple of minutes before was replaced by her crying, as if she was grieving for the dead girl, a mystified look on her questioning face.

After a while, he was able to get his wits about him enough to grab his cell phone, his shaky fingers making an almost insurmountable effort to dial 911. Stumbling over his own words as if he was heavily drunk, he tried to relate the facts to the person who answered the call as best as he could. He had one hell of a time making any sense to the perplexed woman, partly because he still couldn't believe it himself and partly because the words simply didn't seem to come out right. Somehow though, he managed to convince the skeptical operator that he was indeed telling the truth, even if his tale sounded farfetched even to his own ears.

In less than fifteen minutes, at least a dozen police cruisers had the alley closed off, and several yards of yellow tape were being crisscrossed in a back and forth fashion at the entrance and exit of the narrow passageway. The emergency lights on the patrol cars blinked nonstop from various locations surrounding the entire block, creating a surreal atmosphere around the usually quiet neighborhood. Loud sirens could be heard in the near distance as more emergency vehicles responded to the 911 call. A barrage of commands continued to be issued by those in charge as police officers moved quickly and efficiently into action in the process of securing the crime scene. A group of them were already busy combing through every inch of the alley and adjacent area in a chaotic and yet very organized flurry of activity. Mercifully, someone had the presence of mind to cover the poor girl's exposed body with a large white sheet, thus shielding her remains from the scrutiny of several pairs of curious eyes. It never failed to amaze Captain Douglas Wilkins, the officer in charge of the police force at the scene, how fascinated so many people were with the prospect of getting a glimpse of a dead body. It was a truly disturbing phenomenon that he never understood but one that was true in every single case he had ever worked during his thirty-two-year career. So much for living in a truly modern and civilized society, he thought. His feelings about those who acted in such disgusting ways, and which he shared only with his wife, were an odd combination of pity, disgust, and sarcasm, and with more than a pinch of intolerance for good measure.

Frank sat on the back of a fire department emergency vehicle, trying to answer the questions posed to him as truthfully as he could recall. No longer mindful of the heavy rain pouring from the darkened skies, he hugged Cocoa with a sense of need that frightened him. He was truly grateful to have the loyal dog to hold on to but even more grateful to know that his wife was safe and sound and waiting for him to finally walk through the door. When was the last time that he told her how much he loved her, their children and grandchildren, their modest but cozy and comfortable house, and the life they had built together? He couldn't wait to get back and tell her exactly that.

The shaken reporter who was sent to cover the unfolding story had to stop several times during the televised transmission in order to reign in his emotions. At one point, he became so physically ill that he had to excuse himself and literally run to a corner of the alley, the contents of his stomach lost all over a large portion of the crumbling brick wall and cracked pavement. Images of his own teenaged daughter's face kept on invading his mind and flashing in front of his misty eyes. His obvious stress over the case was slightly alleviated by the knowledge that she was safe and secure at home, along with his wife and the rest of their children. Finally able to compose himself, he resumed the reporting with barely controlled objectivity, telling the viewers that the murdered girl's parents had not been aware that their daughter was missing until two policemen showed up at their door. What he would never mention was that the officers didn't even have to say a word before the couple realized that something horrible had happened to someone they loved. It was only a matter of whom by then.

The policemen's posture and the fact that they were holding their hats with shaky hands spoke volumes to the frightened parents, but it was the look of sympathy, sadness, and utter discomfort on their faces that delivered the final blow. When they asked the shaken couple when was the last time they had seen their middle child, the anguished pair dissolved into tears, their sobs growing louder as they fell into each other's arms. In one swift move and with deadly force, their hearts dropped from their chest to their feet, leaving a trail of pain that would be with them for a long time to come. When they attempted to speak, their voices were completely muffled by the sound of their enormous grief. Upon hearing that her body had been found earlier that morning, they began to wail, their sobs so anguish-laden that soon both policemen were tearing up as well.

As the front door closed behind them, the two officers quietly returned to their squad car, which they had kindly parked on a side street and not on the victim's driveway. Although the small colonial house looked no different from the outside, they knew that things were forever altered for the poor family living inside. "No parent should have to bury a child," one of the officers said to the other, his hands absently squeezing his hat so fiercely that it resembled nothing more than a twisted dark blue rag. Both policemen remained unusually silent during the never-ending trip back to the precinct. Lost in their own personal thoughts, the stress of the day that had barely started had already taken a heavy toll on their broken spirits. Although their hearts were filled with sympathy and empathy for the murdered young girl and her distraught family, their emotions had embarked on a rollercoaster of their own. In the secrecy of their minds, they couldn't help but be grateful and relieved that such tragedy happened to someone else's child and not their own. Those feelings brought on a great amount of guilt for even thinking that way, but they couldn't help feeling like they did. As heartless as their thinking could be viewed, just because they were cops didn't negate the fact that they were also human, thus subjected to the same emotions as those they vowed to serve. That knowledge, however, was of minimal comfort to them, but as sick and as selfish as it made them feel, it was also the truth and a bottomless source of fatherly gratitude. They would hug their wives and daughters a little longer and a lot tighter when they got home that night.

No further details were made available at the time due to the sensitive nature of the ongoing investigation, Captain Wilkins explained during a news conference that same evening. He was quick to point out that they needed all the help they could get in order to stop the individual responsible for all three killings from striking again. "No lead will be overlooked, and no stone will be left unturned until we arrest the person responsible for these heinous acts of violence. I and my men and women will not rest until the perpetrator is caught! That much I can promise you," he concluded, proceeding to field numerous questions from members of the media, all eager for more information than they were getting. Captain Wilkins also told everyone present, as well as the public at large, that the police force assigned to the murders had been doubled. He also added that detectives were working on the cases 24/7 and would continue to do so as long as necessary. "We want to make sure that the sick bastard responsible for striking so much fear in the hearts of so many young women is no longer free to continue his brutal rampage of terror and violence. No one wants to see this individual behind bars more than I do," he vowed, pounding his fist on the podium, making it shake with the vehemence of his conviction. It wasn't until sometime later on that day that a small bag was found, tossed in a curbside trash container a couple of blocks away from the murder scene. Wiped clean of any fingerprints, the black leather purse contained only a handful of unused tissues and some spearmint chewing gum, and was later identified as belonging to the third victim.

A spokesperson for the police department for Fairfield and New Haven counties was assigned to keep the media and the rest of the residents of Connecticut updated as to what was going on every step of the way in an attempt to minimize speculation on either part. A cop for twenty years, Melanie Albright had spent the last eight working as a detective with the Special Victims Unit, which handled all the rape related crimes as well as those involving children. Sergeant Albright promised to keep the information coming as much as she possibly could, reminding everyone that there were going to be times when she wouldn't be able to answer a question or concern if they were deemed invasive in nature or a possible hindrance to the ongoing investigation. She reassured the public every chance she got that the authorities were doing everything in their power to put an end to the serial killer's reign of terror once and for all. Caution, she reiterated, should be exercised by every female member of the population until that task was successfully accomplished.

"And still no suspects have been apprehended thus far in spite of all the manpower the authorities have assigned to these cases, in their massive efforts to stop this criminal from claiming yet another young life." The anchorwoman's voice managed to penetrate through Jill's thoughts, startling her back to the unfortunate news being broadcasted. She touched the blanket spread over the family room couch with icy cold fingers, slowly pulling it over her shaking body. The fourth victim's body had been found by the side of the road alongside the northbound lanes of the Merritt Parkway, between exits 59 and 60 in Hamden. The dark, long hair partially covering the twenty-one-year-old girl's face and exposed breasts was reduced to a mass of tangles that clung to her pale and cold skin. Her denim jeans were down by her left knee, while her right leg was exposed all the way. Next to her right foot laid a pair of ripped pink panties and matching bra. Her wine-colored leather purse, cleaned out of its contents except for a small makeup bag containing a lipstick, lip gloss, and a small hair brush, was located about twenty feet from her body, under a small holy bush. There were ugly bite marks all over her breasts and lower abdomen, while huge bruises could clearly be seen on both of her upper arms and thighs. Blood had trickled down between her legs, testimony to the brutality of the sexual assault she was subjected to before being killed. Around both of her wrists, imprints of her attacker's fingers were outlined in deep shades of purple, as if she had been held down by a pair of large powerful hands. There was an enormous bruise across her lower thoracic spine as well, probably the result of being pinned down against a solid and hard protruding object, which turned out to be the steering wheel. Her lower lip was swollen, and a small amount of blood had dripped down from the corner of her left lip and pooled on the crook of her left clavicle. It was obvious that she had put up a good fight, since her body was far more battered and bruised than any of the previous victims. A third-year student at Southern Connecticut State University, she had last been seen by her mother the night before as she was getting ready to leave for her part-time job as an aerobics instructor at Bally's Fitness Center in Hamden, not very far from where her body had been found. It appeared as if it had been hastily hidden behind some thick brush and covered with several layers of debris and dried-up leaves. One of the traumatized city workers who had come across the disturbing scene while trimming some overgrown bushes near the guardrails earlier that morning, was being treated for shock at Yale New Haven Hospital as reports of this latest attack hit the airwaves.

Nearly two years had passed since the body of the first victim had been found, and the frustrated authorities were perplexed by the total lack of evidence left behind in any of the crime scenes. No witnesses had come forward yet, none they could rely on and confirm anyway–a testimony to the perpetrator's cunning planning and execution of each one of the attacks. Either that or he was the luckiest son of a bitch this side of the equator. The special task force assigned to solve the crimes was kept very busy as they investigated just about any and every bit of information that reached them. They knew they couldn't afford not to, not with four dead girls and a ruthless serial killer on their hands. They knew they were dealing with a clever individual with a callous streak, and a careful killer to boot, undoubtedly the most dangerous and difficult type of criminal to corner and capture.

The only thing that the forensic experts could confirm with certainty was that the semen found inside each one of the victims belonged to the same individual but nothing much else besides that. No hairs were ever collected, pubic or otherwise, except for those belonging to the victims. No skin under their fingernails either other than some cells belonging to each one of the girls, as if the bastard had swiped them clean before disposing of their bodies. No finger prints, no shoe outlines, nothing whatsoever they could use that would lead to his identity. Judging by the bruising marks left around the fourth girl's wrists and by the finger marks noted around the neck of each one of the four victims, they knew that they were dealing with a person who had large hands and was quite strong but little else more concrete besides that. They concluded that he was in great physical condition but only because it was apparent that he had been able to subdue and overpower his victims with relative ease. The only exception was the tall and the very fit aerobics instructor, and she unfortunately had paid dearly for it.

With the frequency of the attacks appearing to have accelerated, the authorities became even more concerned, which only served to fuel their level of frustration with the nearly total lack of clues. The fact that the amount of violence and cruelty inflicted upon the victims had also increased further worried the already overwhelmed detectives assigned to the cases. They were well aware that the mounting fear circulating among the population could easily turn into panic, which would ultimately greatly interfere with the ongoing investigation. Panic had the potential of spreading like wildfire, resulting in a state of pure and compromising chaos. What the authorities feared the most was that citizens would then begin to inundate the special hotline set up specifically for those particular cases with unreliable tips and crank calls. If that happened, the end result would be disastrous, causing the already overworked investigators to be pulled from the calls that were indeed legitimate in order to answer all those that were not.

The authorities were also extremely wary of copycat cases in the aftermath of the enormous amount of publicity the four murders had generated in the past couple of years. Those copycat crimes had the tendency to be committed by people who were looking for their "fifteen minutes of fame," but who ended up not only taking an innocent life but also taking precious time, energy, and concentration away from the pursue of the real serial killer. They were sure that the perpetrator would strike again if not captured, and that knowledge kept many detectives from being able to sleep at night. None of them wanted to have another casualty in their hands, therefore they needed to remain focused on the murderer still at large and on any progress they had managed to make, which was, at best, practically nonexistent and, as a worst scenario, more than still practically nonexistent.

Because there was no set pattern to the attacks and absolutely no connection among any of the victims that they could come up with, the baffling sequence of events that followed the first attack simply led the investigation nowhere fast. The authorities' only certainty up until then was that the attacks had been carried out by the same sick bastard and that the murdered girls had all been young and attractive; that's where the similarities ended. Their backgrounds had nothing in common, neither did their social status, where they lived, went to school, or worked. The authorities literally prayed that sooner rather than later, the son of a bitch made a costly mistake along the way, hopefully before he had the chance to strike again. Thus far, however, they remained more than puzzled and utterly baffled by the total lack of evidence, which was an unusual fact when dealing with multiple murders that were carried out by the same person. It had been their experience in the past in cases similar to the one they now faced that the longer it took for the suspects to be found and interrogated, the higher the possibility that the killers would let their guard down. Buoyed by their ability to cleverly and successfully elude capture, the culprits had the tendency to become so comfortable and ego-inflated that invariably they ended up making a careless mistake. Cocky and buoyed by their feelings of self-superiority and high level of intelligence, they often overlooked a minute detail that lead the cops directly to their front door, and that was what the authorities were counting on. So far, however, the only thing they knew for sure was that they were dealing with an individual that was the by-product of a lethal combination of factors. He was extremely cold, infinitely careful, expertly calculating, dangerously cunning, and very clever. Very, very clever.

*   *   *

Bernie pulled a crisp twenty-dollar bill from the wine-colored leather wallet with gusto. He paid for his third scotch on the rocks with a satisfied smile on his unshaven, rugged face. He had eaten all the salted peanuts on the bowl next to him, but who the hell cared, right? Besides, he had already paid for them by the time he was midway thru his second drink for sure. He scanned the packed bar with a sharp eye, noticing the pretty little thing sitting all by herself at a table for two. He asked the scantily clad waitress to refresh whatever it was that she was drinking as he placed another ten dollar bill on her empty little tray. Looking in the beauty's direction, he lifted his own glass and smiled at her, ready to be promptly turned down as he had so many times before. Not that he was bad looking, with dark blond hair falling over his shoulders, piercing gray eyes, and a tall, muscular, and lean frame. But life hadn't been kind to him, or was it that he hadn't been kind to life? He was never sure which came first. A drifter since the age of seventeen, he moved from place to place, taking any job he could find as long as he did not have to work too hard and paid in cash. A work-phobic, booze-indulgent, good-for-nothing smart ass, a hustler and a slacker, and a moocher to boot, who was born somewhere and fast going nowhere, he was indeed a special type of a guy's guy. With his deep aversion to steady work and a strong penchant for booze and pretty women, he did what he had to in order to live up to his standards, which were always much higher than his means. And whenever he wasn't able to find work, there were always other ways of getting hold of some cash. He was no dummy and had never been one, although there were times when playing one had served him very well indeed. It was amazing how predictable people were; a few well-chosen words and he had them eating out of the palm of his hand! He wasn't afraid to go after what he wanted either, patience probably being his best asset. Who needed a college degree when you had the brains and the balls to get things done? He still had four more twenty dollar bills in the wine leather wallet in his back pocket, along with five tens, a couple of fives, and a few singles. The American Express and MasterCards that were hidden inside would only be used in case of a dire emergency, since he was by no means named Carla Noelle Martin and didn't look like one. He had to be extremely cautious if he ever had to use them, knowing for a fact that only shady owners of small stores in seedy neighborhoods would consider turning a blind eye to the fact that they were "most likely stolen." His well-worn black leather jacket and big Harley Davidson bike were always on hand for whatever the evening might have in store for him.

To his pleasant surprise, the girl smile back, mouthing the words "thank you" as she proceeded to raise her own glass. Bernie wasted no time, slowly rising from his barstool and sauntering over to where she was sitting. "Is this chair taken?" he asked with all the southerner charm he could muster. "Nope," the girl replied, playing with a strand of her long hair in the way women had a habit of doing when flirting with someone. "Can I join you, then?" he politely asked, putting on the performance of his life. "By all means," she answered, her curious light green eyes never leaving his face. Easing his long frame into the empty chair, Bernie offered his large right hand for her to shake, which caused a look of total surprise to cross her pretty heart-shaped face. Darn it if that little trick of his didn't work well every time he used it, and he had done so a lot lately! Who said that gallantry was a thing of the past? Taking hold of her small hand, he leaned forward and placed a tender kiss on the back of it, causing the girl to giggle and flush. "Hi, I'm Kim. What's your name?" she asked, a coy smile appearing on her luscious red lips. "I'm Bernie, little lady," he drawled, keeping his eyes glued to hers, a smile making the dimples on his cheeks appear like two round dots amid his four-day-old beard. "So, Bernie, with an accent like that, where do you hail from?" "What accent," he teased, winking at her. "Just teasing you, pay me no mind. I'm from Tennessee, I'm glad to inform you. Been in the area for about two years now, and I'm getting to like it very much, especially after having the pleasure of meeting you, Kim." "And what's a fine guy like you doing in a place like this?" Kim retorted. She knew that she had just used the most common cliché men used in order to hit on a woman, but she had a feeling that Bernie had a good sense of humor and would get a kick out of it, and she was not disappointed. With a hearty laugh, he brought the tips of his right index and middle fingers to his forehead, in the well-known touché fashion. "Same thing as you, doll, I suppose. Friday night, crowded bar, lonely guy, pretty girl . . . You know how it goes." "And what makes you think that I'm lonely as well?" she retorted, playing with her hair once more. "Just hoping, that's all. Are you? Lonely, I mean," he ventured, a boyish look on his manly face. In the dim lights of the bar, she looked like an angel, he mused with an overwhelming urge to simply ravish her. It wasn't long before he had Kim holding on tight as they sped away from the bar, his Harley Davidson motorcycle headed to the little summer cottage he had rented for a very low rate since it consisted of only one large room with a tiny bathroom attached to it. The mismatched pieces of furniture that came with the place had been more than enough for his meager worldly needs as long as he had what he craved the most–power and freedom.

*   *   *

The shockwave created by the senseless murders was felt throughout the entire country. People from coast to coast followed the cases with a mixture of shock and anger, truly sorry for the victims and their families. Jill felt a great deal of empathy for them as well, knowing firsthand how much it hurt to lose a loved one unexpectedly and how much pain they endured for months and years afterwards. Each time another girl's body was found, she sat down at her desk and wrote a heartfelt note to their next of kin, which she promptly mailed inside a sympathy card. With her words, she tried to console them, sharing her own experience in the process, how she came to lean on her loved ones for comfort during her darkest hours, and how they should try to do the same. "Someday," she wrote in each letter she sent, "the sun will slowly melt the icy grip that has taken hold of your shattered hearts, squeezing them to pieces with ironclad force. But you will eventually recapture the ability to think about the child you have just lost and smile. I know that you are all crying right now and will probably continue to do so for quite some time to come. Crying can certainly be very comforting when your world has just fallen apart, for tears have a way of cleansing a wounded soul. I will not lie to you, for the ache and emptiness that you now feel is overwhelming and will always be there, but it will become duller with the passing of time. But as certainly as that ache in your hearts will continue to be part of your lives, so will all the happy moments that you all shared. Those memories will eventually help you to overcome your sadness and pain, to move on. And the beauty of memories is that they never go away, regardless of how many years go by. They will help your hearts to heal and will sustain you until the day when you will finally be reunited with your child again. Believe me when I tell you that I know what I am talking about; I have been there myself, exactly where you are right now," she candidly admitted, holding nothing back. She didn't expect to receive any replies from the grieving families, and when none came, she was perfectly fine with that. All she hoped for was to somehow be of some comfort to people she had never met but with whom she shared a common bond. Tragedy was tragedy, regardless of the circumstances surrounding it. Grief was a very strong feeling, and the sorrow that followed the unexpected death of a loved one was indeed an emotion that transcended time and place and known to kings and peasants alike. For those left behind to mourn that death, the road to healing was paved with tears, cemented with pain, and preserved with love and hope that someday they will be able to be all together again.

*　　*　　*

The sun had been shining brightly all morning long, causing the temperature to rise to a balmy sixty-seven degrees, which was practically unheard of in New England considering it was late November already. The weekend promised to be a great one according to the weather experts. As the sage-green Jeep Cherokee slowly entered the deserted parking lot, the young couple inside exchanged a sigh of relief. Married for a little over two years, they were more in love than ever, especially since they had just found out that they were finally expecting the child they so longed for. The little known park, located in the rural town of Prospect, had a magnificent hiking trail. Avid hikers, they couldn't wait to get started on their way, admiring the unspoiled scenery as if they were seeing it for the first time instead of at least a dozen times before. Suddenly, a simply beautiful black, red, and yellow bird appeared slightly ahead of them and quickly turned to the left and deeper into the dense vegetation. Because they both shared a passion for wild birds as well as hiking, they decided to momentarily leave the main trail in their eagerness to spot the unknown bird again. They had gone in for about eighty feet or so when they came across the remnants of a massive tree. Although the tree limbs had decayed to nothing more than mulch, the trunk remained amazingly intact except for its bark, which had dried up and fallen off like scales of a fish with the passing of time. As they both continued to look up in their search for the mysterious bird, the wife tripped on something solid under a bunch of old leaves. Kicking at it with her right booted foot, she was startled to see a woman's shoe go flying in the air, landing with a muffled sound on the other side of the large log. Curiosity got the best of her, so she carefully climbed on top of the fallen trunk in order to have a better look. She couldn't stop the terrified scream from escaping her throat even if she tried. The shoe had landed by a small thick bush that had grown right next the log, and she stared in horror at the human leg sticking out from under it. Alarmed by the scream, her husband rushed to her side, trying to figure out what had her so frightened. Hardly believing his own eyes, he quickly jumped off, approaching the gruesome scene with shaken legs. As he moved part of the bush to one side, he blinked a few times as if he was not sure he was really seeing what was right in front of his eyes. A young girl lay there face up and with her green eyes open still. A mass of wavy light chestnut hair fanned out around her head, like the halo of an angel. The astonished hiker hastily removed his hooded sweat jacket and covered the poor girl's naked body, unaware that her clothes were piled in a heap no more than twenty feet from them. His wife's loud sobs caused him to look up at her as she tried to cover her own face with trembling hands. In a robotlike state, he climbed back on the log and helped his wife down to solid ground. They headed back to where they had parked the Jeep in total silence, which was broken off only by the sound of her crying. Once back in the parking lot, the young man wasted no time in dialing 911 then sat with his hands on the steering wheel as if he couldn't wait to get away from the scene. Frightened to the core, his entire body shook so much that even his teeth clattered; he had never seen a dead person so up close except for the very few wakes he had attended. This, however, was altogether different. He wondered where the hell the cops were, for it appeared to take hours before the first patrol car got there even though in reality no more than fifteen minutes had gone by. In the distance, loud sirens could be heard as several emergency vehicles approached the park, their urgency reflected by the shrieking noise they made.

The shocked couple answered all the questions posed to them as best as they could, the police officers intent on getting as many details as possible while the events were still fresh on the witnesses' minds. After being questioned at length, the young couple was let go but not before they provided the sergeant in charge with all their personal information. They cried the whole way home, unable to understand how such a beautiful fall afternoon could turn out so ugly in an instant. In the mean time, the body of the unfortunate girl was being transported to the morgue to determine the cause of death. Her purse, which was found next to her discarded clothes, had been cleared of all of its contents except for her driver's license, a case of Revlon lip gloss, and a pack of mint-flavored Tic Tacs. Kimberly Grace Wilson, twenty years of age, had been a second year student at Gateway Community College in New Haven, the authorities later found out. The oldest of four children, the petite girl had worked part-time as a salesperson at Linens 'n Things located on the Post Road in Milford while going to school full time.

DJ and Jill could not understand how the attacker was able to elude capture for so long, especially in view of the fact that a special police unit had been set up with the sole purpose of apprehending him. The hotline number 1-800-VICTIMS was inundated with calls, but none of them had turned into anything concrete. Jill felt immense sadness for the girls and their families while DJ seemed angry at the fact that the victims, who were all around his age or even younger, had been put through so much suffering before being so brutally killed. "You know that I'm not a violent person, Mom, but I could use five minutes alone with the bastard so that I could give him a little of his own medicine. The coward probably never felt any real pain in his life, and that could very well be why he so 'generously' doles it out every chance he gets. Five minutes is all that it would take to satisfy me!" He paused for a few seconds, his head in turmoil, before he was able to control his frustration long enough to talk again. "Unfortunately, the truth of the matter is that there are a lot of sick people out there, Mom," he added in a sad voice, reflecting on the futility of it all, "and the scariest part is that they, more often than not, look as normal as you and me so that one never knows for sure who they actually are." Mulling over the truthfulness of his words, she remained silent for a few seconds, trying to come up with something to say. When she couldn't, she simply nodded her head.

Who could argue with the wisdom of his statement, as horrifying as it was? "I know, honey, I know," Jill answered with a heavy heart, hugging her beloved son with so much intensity that she started to tremble. She was really proud of her kind-hearted, sensitive, and respectful child, especially in a world where so many temptations or hardships could entice a relatively good person to stray from the right path, the path that would lead them to a productive, honest, and fulfilled life. Sometimes all it took was one wrong choice to cause an otherwise decent life to unravel out of control, regardless of how decent a person they were or how well they had behaved until then. Having worked for many years as a school guidance counselor, she was very aware of the perils that some children faced. And unfortunately, some of these perils were created by their own misguided parents, whom, for a variety of reasons, often times held their kids to a very high standard, pushing them to the max. What most of them didn't seem to realize was that they were actually doing nothing more than projecting their own failed dreams onto their child without realizing they were doing so. With high expectations they, more often than not, accomplished little more than setting themselves and their children up for a huge letdown. If nothing else, her experience had thought her to never push her son to do more than she knew him to be capable of. That wasn't to say that she did not expect and often times even guided him to always do the best that he possibly could, reminding him not to shortchange his own potential by choosing to simply coast by instead of applying himself in order to reach for and ultimately achieve his greatest potential. The only thing she truly aspired for DJ was for him to always treat others with politeness and respect and for him to be an all around good person with a good mind and heart, and that he had proven to be, she thought with gratitude. "I know that some people are capable of just about any cruelty imaginable against their fellow humans. I just wish it weren't so," she added with a sigh, unable to get the images of the murdered girls out of her mind. No matter how hard she tried to move on, the smiling and innocent faces of the young women keep on haunting her, both day and night, for quite some time after they were gone. It was as if they were trying to remind Jill not to forget about them for some reason, as if she ever could even if she tried, which she knew in her heart she wouldn't either. Not then, not ever.

*   *   *

Bernie entered the bar, one he had never patronized before, with the sixty-seven bucks inside his pocket begging to be put to good use. The wallet he had taken from Kim came in the nick of time, since he only had eighteen bucks to his name by then. Call it payment for services well-rendered, he chuckled, completely happy with his overall performance the previous night. After taking the cash, he was pleased to find another couple of bucks in quarters, dimes, and nickels in the tiny coin compartment. No pennies, praise the Lord! He hated pennies, which he considered to be totally useless to someone with his refined taste for the good things that life had to offer. He would use the coins to buy the morning paper. He liked to be well-informed about what was going on in the States and abroad. It paid to make sure you knew what was going on around you at all times, he laughed with undisguised sarcasm. He toyed with the idea of keeping the three credit cards he found inside but thought better of it. He had gotten away with his quirky lifestyle so far, so why rock the boat now? Giving up the ones for Express and Eddie Bauer had been hard enough, especially for someone with a penchant for refined clothes to begin with, but the Chase MasterCard almost drove him over the edge. In the end, though, his common sense prevailed, beating his greedy hands down. Who knew, perhaps one of these days he would get really, really lucky and come across some chick that had a fat wallet to match her equally fat head. Wouldn't that be great?

*   *   *

With five killings under his belt, the audacious criminal became the most wanted person in the State of Connecticut, and yet the police knew as much about him by then as they had after his first attack. The crimes were first-page news for days on end every time another body was found. DJ seemed to be even more disturbed by the senseless deaths than ever. "It scares me to know that this lunatic is out there and could be virtually anywhere at any given time. I wish that I could be with you whenever you go out, but I realize that I simply can't, so promise me that you'll always be on the lookout, all right? Like they advised, Mom, carry a can of mace everywhere you go. And that trick with the key is a real good one. And if all else fails, a swift kick in the groin could give you the precious time you'll need to try and get away," he added, his forehead creased with the weight of his concern for her safety. "And here, Mom, please wear this whistle around your neck when you are out and about, regardless of where that happens to be. I had it especially made for you in gold, chain and all. Don't let the whistle's small size fool you because although it is quite small, it packs a lot of punch and is as loud as those used by sports coaches during practice." Jill was really touched by her son's open show of concern for her. It was very rewarding as a parent to have raised such a fine child, especially given the fact that she had done so practically on her own. The heartaches and sacrifices that she had gone through over the years were all well worth it, and she would do it all over again without a moment's hesitation if she had the chance.

"I don't consider myself a naïve person," Jill told her son one day, "and I'm well aware that there are many people who are capable of unspeakable acts of cruelty against others. But it shouldn't be that way. Even the most wild of animal only kills for survival, to protect their young or their territory, for self-defense, or as a last result when they are cornered or provoked. We could all learn a lot from them, I tell you. I often wonder which species is really the civilized one." All DJ could do was nod in agreement, especially after the events of the last couple of years. We could all indeed learn a lot from the species known as the wild ones, for humans certainly left a lot to be desired, all in spite of our supposed ability to think and rationalize, not to mention our knowledge of the difference between what was right and what was not. With a sigh, Jill continued to hug her son, reticent to let go. The smiling faces of all the murdered young women inundated her thoughts and would continue to do so for quite some time to come. She knew that she would never be able to forget any of them, not then, not ever.

*   *   *

The body of the sixth victim came as a huge shock to everyone. It had been over seven months since the last girl had been killed, so the authorities, who were still investing a lot of manpower trying to solve the previous cases, were hopeful that the serial killer had gotten his fill, putting an end to the spree of terror, brutality, and violence he was so well-known for. Needless to say, they were deadly wrong.

As the middle-aged couple sat in the office of Police Lieutenant Michael Williams, they held each other for support as tears ran down their pallid faces. The North Haven residents had arrived at their local police precinct a few minutes earlier in a total state of panic. Mr. and Mrs. Gordon were there to report that their seventeen-year-old daughter, Emma, had failed to return home from the birthday party of her best friend, Madison, the night before. Speaking in pieces and bits, the agitated couple often cut each other off, trying to relay their story to the policewoman at the front desk. Without hesitation, the officer quickly ushered the frantic parents to Lieutenant Williams's office. As soon as the lieutenant walked in, they both got to their feet, speaking over one another in their need to tell him why they had come to the police station, which was two blocks from their home. "It is our daughter, Emma. We haven't seen or heard from her since yesterday afternoon. Please, help us find our baby." With Mrs. Gordon sobbing by then, her husband continued to tell what had happened to cause them to be so upset. Emma, he said, had left the house at around 6:00 p.m., on her way to the birthday party. Since the celebration was on a Saturday night and assuming that Emma had gotten home later than usual that evening, Mrs. Gordon decided to let her daughter sleep a while longer. When she still hadn't gotten up by twelve noon, her mother knocked on her closed bedroom door to wake her. Hearing no response from within, she opened the door and was startled to find Emma's bed empty and with no sign at all that she had slept in it. Extremely worried, for her daughter had never slept away from home without asking for her parent's permission first, Mrs. Gordon immediately called Madison's house in hopes that Emma had stayed there for the night instead of driving all the way back home. Madison, surprised by the question, quickly told the worried mother that she hadn't. Yes, she had come to the party, but she only stayed for a little while, telling her best friend that she was meeting someone at around 9:00 p.m. and asking her not to say a word to anyone. And that was the last time Madison had seen Emma. Devastated by the news, Claire Gordon called her husband at work, and they had both come directly to the police station. Lieutenant Williams, having received word that the body of a young girl had just been found earlier that morning asked the parents to describe their daughter to him. The overwhelmed couple were so intent on complying with his request that they failed to see the look of dread that suddenly appeared on the cop's face. Yes, the victim had long straight dark blonde hair. Yes, she was petite and around five feet two inches tall.

Yes, she weighed no more than 105 pounds. And yes, her eyes were hazel-colored, and she had been wearing a pair of black jeans and a powder blue cashmere sweater.

A dedicated police officer in the truest sense of his chosen profession, the seasoned cop remained calm and composed on the exterior, but inside he had turned to mush. He would make sure to hug and kiss his own seventeen-year-old daughter the minute he got home, regardless of what time of day or night that happened to be. Keeping his voice steady, he chose his words carefully when he resumed talking again, which would take a very heavy toll until later on when he could let his guard down and cry like a baby for the dead girl, for her poor parents, and for himself for what he was about to put the Gordons through. Lieutenant Williams gently informed the couple that he had just found out that a young woman had been found but that her identity had not been established. "Would you mind coming with me so that we can make sure that she isn't your daughter?" He would be damned if he was going to let on that he was pretty sure that it was indeed Emma's body that had been found. Let the poor parents hold on to the hope that it wasn't for as long as they could. They would soon enough find out.

The Gordons didn't say much as they got up to follow the officer, but they held on to each other for dear life, afraid that if they let go, they wouldn't be able to take a single step. At the city morgue, the coldness of the place was like a sharp icicle penetrating their heart through and through. Inside the massive room, the stainless steel gurneys and tables were shocking enough, but what caused the already shaken couple to almost faint were the rows of stainless steel doors that lined two of the four walls. Mrs. Gordon started to weep as the medical coroner walked over to the one with the number nineteen on it and proceeded to open it. He pulled out a sliding shelf with ease, revealing the still form of a person covered with a crisp clean white sheet. As he motioned for the Gordons to approach the drawer, Mrs. Gordon began to sob and shake her head from side to side, clearly too distraught at the thought that it could be Emma's lifeless body lying under the sheet to take a step forward. Even though Mr. Gordon was just as scared and all he wanted to do was to turn around and leave the awful place behind, he forced himself to come closer. Lieutenant Williams stayed behind with Claire Gordon, his right arm around the poor woman's trembling shoulders. As the coroner lifted the sheet, exposing the deceased's face, he let out an agonizing scream. With tears falling rapidly down his ashen cheeks, he whispered the words that Lieutenant Williams had dreaded from the moment they had described their daughter to him. The young girl lying lifeless on the cold slab of stainless steel was indeed their Emma, but she was no longer the daughter he cherished with all his heart. That Emma had been "their menopause surprise," Claire Gordon used to say, since she had absolutely no idea that she was pregnant until the middle of her fourth month. She didn't have to be told by any doctor then; having given birth to three other children, she recognized the symptoms right away the moment she felt the baby moving around in her womb. His little girl looked now like someone had applied opera makeup all over her delicate face, and her lips had a sickening blue tint to them. Her beautiful eyes, once so full of life and happiness, were closed, and dark circles underlined both. Her hair, always so shiny and soft, looked as if it hadn't been washed in months. Sobbing loudly by then, he could no long look at the still face before him. Gone was the smile that illuminated her entire face, the light that shone brightly in her beautiful hazel eyes, and the pink color that dotted her cheeks when she was excited. Gone was the sound of her voice as she said "I love you this much, Daddy"–her arms over-extended to her sides to further emphasize her words. And gone was the bubbling energy that poured out of her petite frame like lava from an erupting volcano, fueled by the pure joy of being young and full of life. Like a wounded animal, he recoiled from the sight of her body and retreated to a corner, his fists pounding on both sides of the walls in front of him. As the coroner closed the door, he unknowingly opened a wound in the poor parents' hearts that would never completely heal. Walking like a robot to where his wife stood, he placed his arm protectively around her slumped shoulders, both turning around as if in slow motion and leaving the room as mere shells of the people they had been when they first came in. The humbled officer thanked the coroner and took one last look at the rows of stainless steel doors. How many bodies laid behind them besides that of Emma's, he wondered, wishing with all his soul that the answer was no other, but he knew that the chances of that being the case were probably zero to none.

Lieutenant Williams accompanied the Gordons to their car and told them how sorry he was for their loss. Too heartbroken to talk, the grieving parents simply nodded their heads, tears no long bringing them the solace they were in such dire need of. As he drove back to the police precinct, he continued to think about the poor couple, the image of their little girl's lifeless face taking over his mind. Thankfully, the Gordons would be spared the details surrounding their youngest child's death, other than the fact that her body had been discovered by a teenaged boy.

Ironically born on the exact same month and year as the dead girl, he came across the body while riding his dirt bike in the woods surrounding the Sleeping Giant Mountain in Hamden. The teen, named Jeremy, knew the woods well, having been born and raised in the area, and loved to ride there, his daredevil stunts not interfered with like they usually were when in the presence of others. As he jumped up in the air, as he had done literally thousands of times before, he lost his balance and ended up flat on his belly over a pile of brush. As he placed his hands over the thick ground-covering vegetation, his left hand landed on something unusually soft for the surroundings he was in. Moving some of the brittle brunches around, he jumped back as if bitten by a rattle snake. The arm he had uncovered was slender, as was the body it belonged to. The girl was lying on her left side, her long hair trailing behind her small head. Her black jeans had been completely pulled off her slim frame, as had her black lacy panties. Naked from the waist down, her blue sweater was embedded with shreds of old leaves and fragments of wood, as well as thin pieces of twigs. Her black sandals were tossed next to her body, the back strap on the right one missing. As hard as he tried not to, Jeremy couldn't help but stare at the poor girl. Her buttocks and thighs were covered with ugly bruises. Looking for his bike, he found it about ten feet away, almost hidden by the thick ground coverings and tall weeds. He retrieved his cell phone from his back pocket, grateful that he had landed on his stomach instead of on his butt. He paid no attention to the blood oozing from a deep cut on his right knee, caring only if the phone worked or not and whether he would be able to get enough reception to call 911. Before long, several emergency and police vehicles had a large area around the girl's body surrounded by yellow plastic tape. The teenager was questioned repeatedly by a series of men and women, telling them exactly how he came across the girl's body. It wouldn't be cool to cry in front of all those people; he would do that later on while taking a long, well-deserved hot shower.

Two days later, a homeless man was ecstatic when he found a small navy blue purse while going through the trash at the Dunkin Donuts on Dixwell Avenue in Hamden. Looking around to make sure nobody saw what he had found, he quickly hid the purse inside the shopping cart he dragged wherever he went, and which held all his worldly possessions, right between his precious heavy blanket and his make-believe pillow. He would look inside the bag the minute he got to his spot, a small niche carved out of a junction between two sections of the concrete wall supporting a low bridge located near one of the many buildings that were part of the famous Yale University Campus. With equally eager and dirty fingers, he retrieved the bag from where he had hidden it, turning it upside-down and spilling its contents over the cracked walkway. Anything inside would be a major bonus for someone who had so little, but money would come in very handy anytime! The pink lipstick, he could do without, but he knew a homeless lady who would love to get her filthy little hands on it–but for a price, of course. In the streets, everything came with a price, in exchange for the "privilege" of being free of the conventional trappings that usually plagued all those who lived a "normal life." Perhaps he would even get some well-needed sex in the bargain, he figured, growing excited just thinking about it. The lip gloss he would keep; his lips could really use a little TLC just about now. The face powder, well, that was a different story altogether. He would certainly get sex for that one! The hairbrush was totally useless to him since he was as bald as a billiard ball, but he could always use it to get something from somebody else. The pack of chewing gum was a real treat though. He couldn't remember the last time he had been treated to gum that hadn't been chewed by someone else before he got it. He left the matching wallet for last, already salivating at the thought of how much money could be in there. Unfortunately though, there were only two ten-dollar bills inside the darn thing. He would use one of them to buy enough booze to get him drunk enough not to feel the hardness of the solid concrete under his tired old bones. The driver's license he held in his hand showed the face of a real pretty girl with a beautiful smile and dark blonde hair. Even her name sounded pretty–Emma Nicole Gordon. Since he had no use for it, he would drop it in the first mailbox he came across during his long daily search for food. The purse and the wallet though, he would keep. Maybe he could sell them to someone for some cash, but who would want a bag that had the name Coach stamped right on the side? Too bad it didn't look that expensive at all.

CHAPTER 13

Jill loved reruns of *Little House on the Prairie* and was watching one of her favorite episodes, a particular one that was so hysterical that it made her laugh out loud every time she happened to see it. In this segment, Nellie Olsen, who had never worked a day in her privileged life, had to learn how to cook in a hurry, all thanks to her mother. Good old Harriett Olsen, during one of her many brainstorming frenzies, had bought a restaurant for her only daughter, thinking that it would serve to improve Nellie's chances at finding *a beau*. Once more having bitten more than she could chew, Mrs. Olsen was having one hell of a time showing the thoroughly spoiled girl how to prepare even the simplest of meals. Everything that Nellie touched she ended up burning, including, soon enough, her mother's practically nonexistent patience. Jill was still laughing when she heard the phone ring but stopped the second she answered the call. By the sound of her oldest brother's voice, she instinctively knew that something terrible had just occurred. "Jill," Daniel said in a tone barely above a whisper. "Dad collapsed while he was trimming the hedges out front a few minutes ago. Can you meet us at Saint Vincent's Medical Center? The ambulance is on the way to the emergency room as we speak," he concluded, his words lacking any quality whatsoever and so low that she wasn't quite sure if she heard every word he had said. Hanging up the phone, Jill dropped her head in her hands and wept. After crying for a couple of minutes, she composed herself just long enough to grab the bag and car keys and run to the garage.

Her calm, soft-spoken father, William, had been an educator all his adult life. He started teaching seventh grade math and science in the late summer of 1945 at Woodland Middle School in Stratford. He had remained at the same school during the duration of his brilliant and very successful career. He had been promoted to assistant principal in 1959, after fourteen years of dedicated teaching, and became the school principal seven years thereafter. He had maintained that prestigious position until he retired at the end of the school year, in the summer of 1987. A gifted teacher through and through, he

124

had loved nothing more than to be among his students and it showed, for they clearly loved Mr. Chandler in return.

Though he had been offered much higher positions throughout the years by the Department of Education, his answer had routinely been the same save when he accepted the assistant principal and then the principal's positions. Politely but firmly, he always declined the honor, since he knew that by accepting any of those offers meant he would have to also accept the changes that invariably came with any new position. Because he was only professionally happy when he was able to be among his students, the prospect of sitting behind a desk, giving orders he didn't want to give, and in a building far removed from an actual school setting had never appealed to him. Even the prestigious and very lucrative position as superintendent of schools, an offer that was presented to him on more than one occasion over the years, never swayed him in the least. Many of his colleagues had often asked him why he wouldn't accept a promotion that most would kill for, but he had simply shrugged his shoulders in lieu of an answer. He knew that he had more than enough credentials to continue to climb the ladder to success and financial stability, but it was something that he hadn't wasted any valuable time dwelling on. For her part, Sophia always supported his decisions, having realized a long time before that money was hardly in the equation as far as job satisfaction was concerned. And besides, they had been lucky enough that it had never been an issue in their long-lasting marriage, since they both had been privileged enough to have come from financially stable backgrounds.

After retiring in 1987, William began to take enormous pleasure in traveling to different parts of the globe, always eager to learn about other countries and cultures, with Sophia always by his side. Both of them still lived in the same comfortable colonial-style house where their four children were raised. The house, located in the "Berries" section of Huntington, was definitely too big for them now that their kids were all married and had homes of their own, but they vehemently refused to downsize whenever any of them brought up the subject. Daniel, who was well-known by his siblings to possess the gift of always thinking things through, thus being the family's official advisor, never had any luck either. On several occasions, he had tried to reason with his parents how a smaller place, a waterfront condo perhaps, would fit their needs much better, since there were only the two of them living in the six-bedroom house by then. It would be much more practical for them, he had argued, voicing the concerns he had heard from each one of his siblings whenever they got together, but always when their parents weren't present. In the long run, he had emphasized, less would be a much better fit in this new and exciting stage in their lives–less work, less worry, less upkeep, and so on. William, however, had other ideas in his mind and was never shy about sharing them. He loved to say that they needed every single one of those bedrooms to comfortably accommodate the ever-growing Chandler brood whenever any of them, or all of them for that matter, wished to sleep over, which they indeed did on a regular basis.

William was very fond of boasting that, besides their own four children, their beloved grandchildren were their pride and joy, all ten of them and still counting. "The more, the merrier," he would proudly say, and any holiday with the elder Chandlers was always a memorable event, with people and kids everywhere much to William's delight. He certainly cherished all of his grandchildren equally, but DJ had somehow stolen a huge chunk of his grandfather's generous heart ever since he was born but even more so after his own father's death when he was just a little toddler. He always looked up at his grandpa with adoration in his big blue eyes, and that had struck a protective chord in the older man's soul. DJ had been given the middle name of William in his grandfather's honor and was very proud of it, a fact he often told him, thus further cementing the already strong bond they shared. Often they would go on long walks together, just the two of them, for they liked nothing better than spending time on a one-to-one-basis without interruptions from anyone. They managed to laugh at everything or at nothing at all, often seeing the true beauty and mystery of the amazing world around them through each other's eyes. Always the educator, William delighted in teaching his attentive grandson to examine Planet Earth as the truly vast and wondrous miracle that it really was, a place to explore and discover time and time again. They looked under every rock they could move, marveling at the amount of activity carried out by hordes of insects and worms that lived beneath each one of them. They sat under every majestic tree they came across, wondering how many years it had taken each to grow from seedling to their fully grown size. DJ, for his part, was able to teach his grandfather a thing or two as well. From his grandson, William rediscovered the ability to see their surroundings through the eyes of an innocent child, his infinite curiosity and imagination a gift in itself, and for that he was eternally grateful. He regarded those times with DJ as brief but treasured glimpses at his own childhood, now long gone but never totally forgotten, and as a return to the carefree ways that only a child was fully able to enjoy. With a touch of nostalgia, he would affectionately kiss the top of his grandson's blond head with a mixture of pride and joy for the child's existence. He had been very fond of Drew from the first time he met him, and now his little boy kept on showing the same kindness of heart and capacity to give that his father had so generously shared with those around him. "I still have you, Drew, through your child, my dear friend. You are never too far from me," William thought often, the immense emptiness that his son-in-law's death left within his soul slowly being filled by the love he shared with their DJ.

*   *   *

Upon reaching the hospital, Jill didn't have to ask anyone about her dad's condition. Her mother, always the picture of poise and grace sat alone, both knees pressed together, hands so fiercely clasped on her lap that her knuckles had become practically blood-drained. Tension was written all over her usually relaxed body, now motionless, dormant. Her face, which always radiated from the unspoiled joy of just being alive and happy, was drawn and devoid of any hint of color, a human mask of pain and fear. Her shoulders, always held upright with elegance and pride, now stooped by the unbearable weight of her sorrow and shock, starkly contrasting with her rigidly erect spine. Her eyes, those happy green eyes that conveyed everything that she was even before she had a chance to utter a single word, simply stared vacantly at nothing in particular, the warm spark of life extinguished by the enormity of her loss. They showed in detail the depth of the damage caused by the mortal wound she had just received. There was no need for words at a time like that, for those haunting eyes said it all, things that Jill was not ready to hear, understand, or accept. By the time she reached her mother's side, Sophia had dissolved in a deluge of tears as she opened her arms to accommodate her youngest child's slim frame, her need for the comfort of her daughter's embrace as fierce as her love for her.

Jill saw Nicholas and Tara right away as she protectively and instinctively scanned the large emergency room for her sibling's whereabouts. They were sobbing in each other's arms, totally oblivious to what was going on around them, giving in to the pain that was unmercifully tearing their hearts to pieces. Looking for Daniel, she was finally able to spot him off in a secluded corner. He stood by himself, both hands deep in his pants' pockets, seemingly unaware of his surroundings. It was not until she gently called out his name that he showed any signs of actually being there. When he turned around to face her, she nearly gasped, struck to the core by the hollow, blank stare on his otherwise handsome face. He remained completely motionless, the deep and dark circles under his eyes testimony to his sheer agony, which threatened to reduce her quiet and strong brother to a quivering mass of anguish and despair at any given moment. She never loved him more than she did then and there, at that precise moment. Daniel was so much like their father, Jill suddenly realized in awe, her feelings for him crushing her heart with equal amounts of enormous pride and overwhelming pain. He was always a pillar of strength, even when everyone around him was literally falling apart. And now, she acknowledged with profound sadness, this pillar of strength had received a major blow that could very quickly reduce him to nothing more than a pile of rubble and dust.

Her father never had any type of cardiac problem that she was aware of, and her mother saw to it that he ate well-balanced meals and went for his yearly physical exam every May. Although he had gained a few pounds over the years, he wasn't by any means considered to be overweight, making any type of physical exercise part of his daily routine. At six feet three inches tall and 210 pounds, he was the picture of health. He was proud of the fact that he had never smoked in his life and only had a drink or two during special occasions such as weddings and the holidays. In spite of it all though, William Richard Chandler, seemingly healthy and fit, died as a result of a massive heart attack on July, 11, 1995, at the age of seventy-three. In spite of the continuous attempts to resuscitate him, both at the scene and during the short trip to the hospital, he didn't survive the severity of his cardiac damage. He had already passed away as the paramedics doubled their efforts to revive him while the ambulance rushed him to Saint Vincent's. By the time they arrived there, it was already too late to try any other intervention to bring him back, for he was long gone. No "golden hour" to speak of, for he had died instantly as he keeled over on his front yard, hedge trimmer in hand, on a sunny and balmy summer afternoon that instantly turned cold and dark for the family left behind to grieve him. Unfortunately, he didn't even have the chance to say good-bye to those he cherished most in the entire world. Memories, once more, were all that remained of such a wonderful and caring man, those ever so precious and irreplaceable memories. They had no monetary value whatsoever, yet they were truly priceless for those who had the privilege to create and share some. They were the only thing that a person took with them upon their death while at the same time leaving them all with their loved ones, to console them as they mourned their passing. All of their material possessions stayed right where they were, all the money, the cars, the successful careers, the power and prestige, and so forth. When everything was said and done, life ultimately came down to only one thing in the end, and that was the love that was given and received, along with all the happiness and laughter that was enjoyed and passed along for others to remember them by. Everything else paled by comparison, for it was all lost the second a person's time in this world finally came to an end.

Upon arriving home from the hospital, the first thing that Jill did was to call Jack, wanting to hear his voice and be reassured by him that everything was going to be all right. Jack quickly offered to come over, if only for a little while, but as tempting it was for her to crawl into his arms in order to feel protected and secure, she told him that it would be best if she processed her loss on her own. All she needed, she told him, as an unexpected sob escaped her throat, was to hear his voice, and that would suffice to comfort her until the following day. It was close to midnight by then, and she knew that he needed to get up very early the next morning in order to get to work on time. Before hanging up though, Jack promised to come straight to her house after school was out and spend the rest of the afternoon and evening with her. True to his word, he showed up at around 4:00 p.m., a huge bouquet of peach-colored roses in his arms. He knew that Jill's favorite flowers were yellow roses, but that was something very intimate and personal she had shared with Drew. Since he would never try to come between Jill and Drew's special bond, he decided that peach was the closest he could come to yellow without risking hurting the woman he loved with his heart and soul. That was the reason why peach-colored roses became their own way of sharing what they had been blessed to find together, without negating the importance that Drew would always occupy in Jill's life. Touched by his thoughtful gesture, she hugged him tightly to her heart, enjoying the feel of his long and strong arms around her petite frame. Laying her head on his chest, she allowed the tears to come, crying her eyes out until they seemed to run dry. Jack ordered some Chinese food, but Jill hardly looked at any of it, and Jack could understand why. She had always been daddy's little girl, and now he was gone forever. He suspected that she would cry herself to sleep after he left, and it would do her a world of good. Grieving properly was detrimental to a person's emotional healing and future well-being. The thought of asking her if he should stay the night never crossed his mind, for he was almost sure that she would probably ask him not to. This should be a private time, giving her the chance to mourn alone for the dad that had meant the world to his child. He had never spent the night at her place, out of respect for Drew, for DJ, and for Jill, and he knew that it should remain that way; for how long, he simply couldn't begin to guess. He left slightly before 10:00 p.m., hoping that she would be able to get some well-deserved sleep, which, unfortunately, he was sure that she would not.

During her father's wake and funeral, Jill tried hard to remain strong for her mother and for her siblings. Daniel especially worried her more than anyone else, for he seemed to be hanging on by a single thread. She had written a long farewell letter to her dad, which she quietly slipped inside the breast pocket of his dark gray jacket when she had kneeled by his solid oak casket for their final good-bye. During the funeral mass at Saint Lawrence Church, she shared some of the passages of the letter with the mourners, an intimate collage of memories, thoughts, feelings, and experiences they had gone through over the years. Looking for Jack before she started to speak, she was relieved to find him right away, sitting three pews behind her immediate family. She tried to lock eyes with him in an attempt not to breakdown, finding great strength in his calm expression, which spoke volumes to her. By the time she finished paying tribute to the father she loved with such intensity, there were hardly any dry eyes inside the quiet church. The mourners, so touched by her words, were literally brought to tears, many of them immersed in their own recollection of the man they had all called a loyal friend. Thankfully, DJ remained next to his mother throughout the agonizingly difficult day, often squeezing her hand or gently rubbing her upper arms, thus letting her know that he was right there for her. His grandfather's sudden death hit him hard, but his main concern was for his mother's well-being first and foremost. He would probably fall apart later, in the privacy of his room, where his mother could not see the depth of his grief. She had enough of it on her own to have to handle his as well. Having known Jack practically since he was born, he was grateful that his ex-elementary school principal had become such an important and comforting person in his mother's life. She certainly had gone through more than her share of heartache, and it was about time she thought about herself for a change instead of always worrying about everyone else. She had been a widow for nineteen years already, and aside from Brian, the Shelton High School coach she had tried to date several years back, she had remained true to his father's memory for far too long. It was about time she allowed her heart to freely care for someone again, and he could not be happier with the choice she finally made. Besides that, he was truly fond of Jack, who had always been a tough but very fair disciplinarian during the nine years he studied under his care, and very easy to talk to when the need to do so presented itself. Grabbing hold of his mother's right hand, he squeezed it three times, their secret code of saying "I love you." It felt amazingly reassuring to Jill to have such a devoted son by her side, and she vowed to never take his love for granted, just as she had and would never take her father's love for granted either, whether or not he was still among them.

Jill fondly recalled often telling William how much she adored him while he was alive. Now, as he was being prepared to be lowered into his final resting place, she again told him how much she adored him still, and what a wonderful dad he had been to her and her siblings. She felt herself transported back in time, no longer a grown woman who was burying her father but a little girl who had just lost her daddy. She tenderly kisses the beautiful yellow rose before she placed it on top of his casket, and that single rose carried with it all the emotions and feelings that a small child-woman felt as she said good-bye to her dad for the very last time, sad and totally heartbroken. As the early afternoon sun streamed through the thick trees, it lent a special glow to only that single rose among all the others, as if her father was telling her "I know, darling, and I love you too." It was the same glow her dad had left behind in everyone he had ever loved, met, touched, or knew, most of who were openly weeping as they said good-bye to this tender giant of a man with a huge heart to match. Again, it was up to Father Mancini, now well into his eighties and no longer working as a priest, to bless the casket containing the remains of his friend one final time. He sincerely hoped that this would be the last funeral of a dear one he had to suffer through, for the pain of losing someone as close and as important as William had been to him was getting harder and harder to recover from. He also hoped that the next funeral would be his own, for he felt that his work here on earth had come full circle and that it was more than about time he joined all of those who had gone before him, both in the U.S. and in his beloved Village of San Clemente, in the Abruzzi hills of Italy. All he prayed for was that he did not become ill for too long before moving on, for he didn't want to become a burden to anyone he loved.

CHAPTER 14

A few days had passed since her father's funeral, and a sad and sullen Jill found herself somewhat restless, not at all sure as to the reason why. She needed something to do, something to immerse herself into, in order to keep herself too busy to allow her thoughts to wander aimlessly and invariably back to the fact that her dad was now forever gone as well. Since she had never gotten around to performing the annual spring cleaning that was usually all done by late May or early June, she decided that it was definitely something she could really get into then. Feeling suddenly reenergized by the warming weather and the promise of the long and lazy summer days ahead, she changed into old clothes in order to better accomplish what she set out to do. Her father's sudden death had literally sent her into a tailspin, her cleaning ritual the last thing on her mind in the days that followed. But now, she realized good old-fashioned physical hard work would the best antidote for her morose and melancholic mood. She knew that she had to remain as physically active as she could in order not to totally fall apart emotionally. So many people needed her at the moment, and she was determined to do everything necessary to make sure that she didn't let anyone down. They had been there for her when Drew died so many years before, and now it was her turn to do so.

Growing even more restless as the morning progressed, she decided to start her cleaning marathon in the family room–by far the most utilized room in the entire house. Once she was satisfied that everything was in perfect order there, she moved on to the kitchen and bathrooms, rolling up her sleeves as she got ready to attack and conquer the dirt and grime she knew tried to hide everywhere. When everything seemed to be sparkling, she moved on to her bedroom, deciding to exchange the dark, heavy comforter set for a more summery one, which was her favorite–the one with many dainty pastel-colored flowers set in a creamy yellow background. Down came all the insulated draperies, replaced by lacy beige curtains that gently swayed in the warm summer breeze. The fact that the windows were wide open felt wonderful both physically and psychologically especially after the endless months of harsh cold weather, wind, and rain that were so typical of the New England's winter season. When she was done with all the last touches, such as the contrasting throw pillow she piled on top of her bed, her room looked cozy and sumptuous, reminding her of those she had often seen in all the decorating magazines she loved to read. "A true bed and breakfast *boudoir,* if I ever saw one," she proclaimed, managing to chuckle a little as she realized that she had just praised herself.

Once she was done with her room, she crossed the hallway and entered her son's, which he often referred to as his very own "chaotically organized kingdom." Indeed, everything in there appeared to be in order, at least until you opened a dresser drawer or a closet door. Then you would be confronted with carelessly overstuffed drawers, their contents usually rolled into a ball or turned inside out and scattered all over the place. Half of the clothes inside his wall-to-wall closet laid in piles on the floor, dirty ones mixed in with freshly laundered ones, in heaps the size of Mount Rushmore, hence the term "chaotically organized." The other half barely hung on their hangers but not for very long. Having waged a losing battle with DJ about his messy ways, Jill had long since reached a truce with him but not after years of endless strife. God only knew how she tirelessly tried to get her son to put away his clean and neatly folded clothes in an organized and fashionable manner, only to find them in piles once more before long, stuffed anywhere he found any space still available. Their pact was a simple one; she would place his newly washed and folded clothes on top of his bed, vowing to never open any of his drawers or closet doors again. It was then up to him to put his clothes away. But she would only wash the clothes that he placed in the hamper inside his bathroom because she simply refused to go searching for them. And if DJ wanted to wear a particular item of clothing that was all wrinkled due to his carelessness, he'd better learn how use the iron fast, for she wouldn't do it for him. Because she had already ironed all the shirts and pants that needed to be ironed before placing them on his bed, she refused to do the same job twice. In order for her not to nag him any longer about the messy state of his closet and drawers, DJ quickly agreed to the rules, knowing a fair deal when he saw one.

With great care, she dusted all the pieces of his dark mahogany furniture, an absolutely beautiful set he had inherited from Drew's parents when they moved to California, tidying up here and there as she went along. Next she started to vacuum the thick caramel-colored rug she had replaced the year before. She has just started to clean underneath his large queen-sized bed, when the vacuum cleaner hit something solid with a muffled, thumping sound. Getting on her knees, she lifted the bed skirt to see where the strange noise was coming from, and that is when Jill spotted a silver-colored metal box that she had never seen before, stashed under the headboard. Laying flat on her belly, she inched her way until she could grab a hold of its handle, slowly pulling it out. With difficulty, she was finally able to place it safely on top of the bed so that she could finish vacuuming under it. She had always been extraconscientious about respecting everyone's privacy, and her son was no exception. After the vacuuming was completed, she carefully picked up the box in order to return it to where she had found it but, being quite heavy, it simply slipped from her grasp, landing with a solid thud on the floor. The lid, which was not locked, opened up all the way, spilling some of the contents of the box all over the carpeting. Scattered birds' feathers caught her attention right away, their sheer number an overwhelming sight. Of a variety of colors, ranging from black ones to bright yellow and to every other color in between, their shapes were as uniquely varied. Their sizes, just about every single one she had ever seen in her forty-six years of life, were impressive as well. With a puzzled look on her face, she started to pick them up, one by one, careful not to damage their delicate beauty. Her eyes then turned back to the mysterious box, and against everything she believed in, she felt a compulsion to look through the contents still remaining inside. Along with literally hundreds of bird feathers, there were several dozens of butterfly wings, from little ones to the huge wings of monarch butterflies, their bright orange and black coloring hard to miss among all the others. They were a myriad of sizes, shapes, and shades, from bright blues, to creamy whites, to yellows, to grays, to lavenders, to black, all neatly piled one on top of the other in several rows. Pepper's bright pink collar, the tags still attached to it, was also inside the box, along with her favorite chewing toy, a black and yellow rubber squeezer in the shape of a rolled up newspaper. "What the heck is going on here? I don't understand any of this! It makes absolutely no sense to me, no sense whatsoever. Why would DJ want to save all of these things? What for? "she asked herself, getting increasingly more confused by the second. "And Peppy's things . . . I know for a fact that I buried them with her because I placed them next to her myself just before I closed the plastic container. How can they possibly be right here in my hands now? And more to the point, why? *Why*? I really don't understand any of this. Can someone please tell me what the hell is going on here before I lose my mind altogether?" Jill pondered out loud, her voice elevated to a shriek by then, her pleas directed at no one in particular. With her thoughts in total disarray, she continued to stare at the items in the metal box, not really believing what her eyes were actually seeing. With trembling hands, she tentatively began to move the chewing toy aside, overwhelmed by the sheer number of items inside the large container. And that was when she spotted what appeared to be a few locks of hair, individually wrapped in plastic wrap, and tied with a thin purple elastic band. With her hands violently shaking by the odd findings, she slowly picked them up, mesmerized, and carefully examined each one through misty eyes. One lock was pale blonde, almost the color of ginger ale; another was of a darker shade of blonde with reddish highlighted strands mixed in. The third was brownish red, very much like the color of freshly ground cinnamon, and another was a dark shade of chestnut that, at first glance, appeared to be almost black. The fifth was of a very light shade of brown, almost the color of cream-flavored soda pop. The last one was dark blonde, like the pieces of chewy caramel candy she was so fond of. Six locks of hair in total, each one of a specific color and texture, and clearly belonging to six different individuals, carefully wrapped and preserved at the very bottom of the silver-colored metal box. "What is going on here?" Jill asked loudly once more, her voice having taken on a tone of frustration and desperation, what was left of her mind running wild back and forth without any sense of purpose or direction. She was more confused than she had ever been in her life and continued to get even more confused with each second that ticked away. Rubbing her temples in a feeble attempt to reign in her erratic thoughts, she felt an urgent need to let go and just scream at something or someone, not quite understanding where it was coming from. All she knew was that she felt truly scared to death, but she didn't know the reason why. "Can anyone please tell me what is going on? Please . . ." Jill asked again, even though she was aware that she was home alone at the time. Suddenly, as if she had fallen in a trance, the smiling and innocent faces of six young women paraded vividly in front of her eyes as if they had been preserved in the recesses of her mind for a very specific reason, one she had absolutely no idea as to what but was simply terrified to find out why. The faces, which had been burned in her memory for quite some time belonged to the six girls that were brutally raped and murdered during the last few years. And then, as if a light switch was abruptly turned on, the pieces of the puzzle began to fall neatly into place. "Nooooooo!" she screamed, pulling away from the box as if she had received a powerful electrical discharge. "*Not my son! Not my DJ! It can't be. Please, don't let it be!*" her mind shouted, and Jill was terrified that if she dared to speak her thoughts out loud, they would become a hellish reality. "It just can't be . . . It must not be . . . It must not," she began to whisper, her whole body a mass of convulsing chills as she started to fear the worst. She felt her blood instantly turn to ice, from her exploding head to her now completely numb toes. With a deadly combination of dread and horror, the names of several girls bullied their way into her fragmented thoughts. Somehow they managed to penetrate through the barrier she quickly tried to erect around her mind for self-preservation. But the faces and the names weren't going to be stopped, and they continued to forge ahead, slipping through the cracks of her crumbling self-control, destroying her soul in their justifiable need for justice. *Nicky this, Beth that, Meghan, Carly, Kim, Emma . . . Those names . . . Those faces . . . Stop this, please, just stop it . . .* , her heart shouted, but she remained silent, unable to accept that her son had anything to do with any of their deaths. She squeezed her eyes shut in an effort to block out the images that continued to assail her mind, but it was useless. Fighting an internal battle she had already lost, the significance of the names became increasingly clear to her, their possible connection with her son something she struggled hard to suppress. With denial playing a major role in her thinking process and added to the self-conflict and doubt that it generated, Jill tried with all the power she possessed to delay the unstoppable remembrance from gaining ground, but she soon realized that she had lost that battle as well. Methodically, the many heart-to-heart talks she had with DJ came rushing back, causing her to remember what she wished she could not. How often had her son mentioned those names during their conversations, leading her to believe that they were girls he had been romantically interested in at one time or another?

As if struck by a lead fist that slammed into her like a tidal wave, she stumbled sideways. Leaning on the bed frame for added support, she simply allowed the truth to finally come crashing down over and around her, knocking the wind right out of her lungs and robbing her of any defense mechanism she could tap into. *Nicky–Nicole Elysse Keane*, blonde and only eighteen, her smile so happy and innocent that it had caused Jill to cry like a baby when her lifeless body had been found over three years before, brutally raped and murdered before she even had a chance to start living as an adult. *Beth–Elizabeth Marie Russo*, a twenty-year-old strawberry blonde, the second victim that was found a few months after the first one, masses of curly hair framing a simply enchanting young and carefree face, the sprinkling of freckles across the bridge of her nose making her appear even younger than she already was. *Meg–Meghan Lynne Morris*, nineteen, a beautiful red-haired young woman killed just like the previous two, her sparkling green eyes reflecting the joy of simply being young and alive. And then there was *Carly–Carla Noelle Martin*, the pretty twenty-one-year-old girl who was found six months later, her body much more battered than those of the previous three. *Kim–Kimberly Grace Williams*, twenty, her long light brown hair reaching her waist, light green eyes like two shiny glass beads, and found just that past spring. And then there was Emma–*Emma Camille Gordon*, the youngest of them all. Only seventeen at the time of her murder earlier that very month, she had a contagious grin and beautiful hazel eyes, both still clearly imprinted on Jill's mind, and her death had come just a week before her own father's. *Could this all be nothing but a cruel coincidence*, her bewildered mind questioned, *or was DJ actually mentioning the poor girls' names to me right after attacking and killing them*? *Could he really be that cold, that callous*? "*It can't be. It just can't be. Not my son, please. Not my DJ . . .*" Jill wailed over and over again as her numb fingers let go of the locks, and they fell back into the box as if in slow motion, one right after the other. "Oh, Drew, what have you done, son?" she screamed like a wounded animal, cradling her exploding head in her trembling hands, and rocking back and forth with the intensity of her anguish.

Her mind drifted back to the hundreds of small creatures she had helped DJ bury in their backyard over the years, the graves, the crosses, the tears. She began to remember pieces and bits of conversations between herself and DJ, starting when he was just a little boy. "Mom, I found this baby bird in our front yard when I got off the bus. I think that he is really hurt. Can you please make him all better just like you always do when I am sick? Please, Mom." "Poor thing, I think his tiny wings are broken! No, I don't know how it happened, I swear. I just found him like this, just lying on the sidewalk, not able to fly . . ." "Mom, why can't this pretty butterfly fly like all the others? I feel really sad that her little wing is all ripped up like this. Do you think that another animal did this to her? No, Mommy, I have no idea how it happened. I found her just like that, sitting on the grass in the backyard, the poor little thing. She is so pretty, isn't she, Mom? Even with half of her wing gone, she is still so pretty!" "I don't know why Pepper is acting so weird all of a sudden. Why are you asking me that, how should I know?" "No, I have no idea why she cries so much. Why do you keep on asking me that? How would I know what is wrong with her?" "No, I didn't bother her, I swear, Mom. She just turned around and bit me in the hand. For no reason at all, honest!" "Please, Mom, don't kill my little dog!" "The truth is that we live in a very violent world, Mom. I shudder to think how much that poor girl must have suffered before she died at the hands of that bastard . . ." "Unfortunately there are a lot of sick people out there, Mom, and the scariest truth is that most of them look as normal as you and me. You never know, that's for sure, do you?" *Nicky . . . Beth . . . Meghan . . . Carly . . . Kim . . . Emma . . .* And in a split second, as if stricken by a second powerful bolt of lightning, things began to finally make sense to her, methodically at first but quickly escalating into a dizzying succession of lies, cowardice, brutality, and destruction. The jigsaw puzzle, which had started out small but became gigantic in size, finally uncovered some of the most vital details of the total picture, one of unbelievable horror and pain. Whether Jill had the strength to handle it or not, there it was, staring her in the face, inside a silver-colored box she wished with all her heart she had never seen. A lifetime of sacrificing as you raised a child you loved beyond life itself and whom you thought you knew better than you knew yourself, wiped out in a second with the discovery of that damned silver box!

As the last of the strategic pieces fell into place, the final story that emerged was far more horrifying than any human mind could assimilate, especially the mind of a loving mother that had made her child the center of her existence. And now, that same child was the culprit of a brutal and macabre nightmare. She recalled all of her little boy's tears, the graves he so diligently dug as a dignified final resting place for all of his small innocent "friends." The crosses he so patiently made from the twigs he searched around for hours until he finally found the ones that were just about the right size so that he could make his last gift for the poor little creatures. As Jill painfully recalled those sad events of long ago, the sequence and manner in which they occurred were quite different than she had recalled. As DJ placed a tiny cross on top of each small grave, a wide grin threatened to come out of its hiding place and spread across his seemingly distraught ashen face, but he managed to keep it under control at the very last second. And Pepper, sweet and loving Pepper, whimpering for apparently no reason then limping a for weeks on end, her left hind leg clearly hurting her then growling at "nothing in particular" based on what Jill could tell and what DJ swore up and down to. His innocent misty eyes never betrayed him, his cleverness at a very high level even for one so young. A pathological liar already, the budding psychopath continued to evolve as he grew older, earning a well-deserved spot among the best by the time he entered his junior year of high school. His mastery in the art of manipulation was his best tool. He knew exactly how he should behave in order to gain the trust of anyone who could be of any use to him, either then or at a later date. His only reprieve had been the time during which he was so ill, but he quickly returned to his old ways. He also mastered the gift of expressing himself in perfectly phrased words that had everyone eating from the palm of his hand and to conduct himself in a way that left no reason for someone to doubt his sincerity and good heart. Having the looks to complement his extreme politeness, kindness, and impeccable manners was an added bonus, and he used it to get precisely what he was after regardless of what it ended up costing the others. Remorse was a feeling that was foreign to him, and guilt a word that was hardly part of his extensive vocabulary to begin with. And nobody had any inkling as to the callous and heartless person he was growing into or of what heinous "discipline" he was capable of doling out, least of all his devoted mother. She truly considered herself to be the luckiest mom on earth for having such a sweetheart of a boy for a son.

The acts of cruelty he had inflicted on all the defenseless little animals he happened to come by were only the tip of the iceberg. Poor Pepper who had done nothing but love him unconditionally, as most dogs did, had been the recipient of repeated abuse from her supposedly best friend. And she had continued to love him in spite of it all until her tormentor became increasingly meaner to the innocent creature. Then and only then did her love and devotion begin to wane, culminating on that fateful afternoon when the little dog, out of pure fear, retaliated the only way she knew how. The ironic tragedy though, was that she had been put to sleep as a result of that one incident, when she had endured so much pain at the hands of the cunning child already. Images of her incredibly sad eyes took over Jill's mind, haunting her so that she literally recoiled from the pain of it all, hiding her face with numb hands and an even number heart. "Oh, Peppy. If I had any idea of what was really going on, my sweet girl, I would have put an end to it immediately, little one. My only consolation is that I can honestly say that the thought of DJ hurting you never crossed my mind. He appeared to love you so, but I now know that it wasn't always like that, was it? I can only reassure you that I would have protected you any way that I could, even from my own son, and this I can tell you from the bottom of my soul, my darling girl. And to think that I had you put to sleep after all that you had gone through already at my DJ's hands, I can't even begin to tell you how sorry I feel. That was unconscionable, if not downright criminal, and I'll have to live with that knowledge for the rest of my life." Jill sobbed. The injustice of it all was more than she could handle as thick tears kept on soaking her pale face, her agony so overwhelming that she found it difficult to even breathe. "Oh, Pepper. My sweet, loving Pepper. Please forgive me, little one. If I only knew then what DJ was doing to you, I swear that I would never have allowed him to do that to you again. This is not, by any means, an excuse, for there is no excuse for what he did to you, but I didn't I find any of this out while there was still time to correct the situation, my love," Jill lamented, tormented by the cruelty inflicted upon the innocent little dog, and the worst part was that it was all done by her child. Painful thoughts flooded her mind, one horrific image after another, images she fervently wished she could block out but which she forced herself to face in spite of how deeply it hurt her or perhaps because of it. Nowhere to hide now, she finally acknowledged the truth, crushed to the core by the severity of the events that continued to slowly unfold before her swollen eyes. DJ, begging his mother to "please don't kill my dog, Mom. Please . . ." There was an unmistakably victorious glee on his tear-soaked eyes, had one known what to look for back then. The twig cross, carefully fashioned and somberly placed on Peppy's grave by a sobbing, pale-faced ten-year-old child who, for once, wasn't able to contain the grin that suddenly spread across his mouth. He had cleverly turned his face downward at the precise moment so that his mother couldn't catch the smile that contradicted all the tears he elaborately shed that grim afternoon.

DJ's job at the mall couldn't have served him better if he tried, for it gave him easy access to an endless supply of young and pretty girls, who equally attracted and repulsed him, both in the same breath. And as if his extraordinarily handsome features and trim physique weren't enough, his easygoing personality compounded by his extreme politeness and good manners sealed the deal, presenting what could be called the perfect package, if ever there was one. He never had any difficulty gaining the attention of members of the opposite sex. Young or older, they were drawn to him like moths to a bright light bulb. He had the looks, the opportunity, and the time to approach any female who caught his eye. Extremely intelligent and far more cunning than anyone ever gave him credit for, he had planned the attacks down to the every minimal detail except for the first one; that had been pure luck. He had been extra careful not to "date" any girl that could, in any possible way, be traced back to him. He made it a point to never become involved with any of his fellow students at Quinnipiac University, with girls that he was even remotely acquainted with, or anyone from his immediate neighborhood. Detail-oriented, all his methodical planning had paid off big time, for he had gotten away relatively easy with his actions, and had absolutely no intention of ever getting caught, thus the need to always follow his well-devised and executed course of action every single time. *See how clever I am?* He wanted to shout for the world to hear! But he wasn't a fool and was fully aware that it would never happen. That fact literally killed him and more than pissed him off because he would never be able to gloat, not even once. Unfortunately he would have to make do with the personal satisfaction of knowing that he was smarter than anyone he knew and certainly more clever and capable than most. In his sick and twisted way of thinking, his accomplishments were an eternal source of immense pride and intense pleasure, a lethal boost to his egotistical sense of superiority and self-worth. He simply basked in the glory of knowing that he could go on for as long as he wished to, provided that it continued to bring him the fulfillment that it had until then. That knowledge gave him the extra push to move forward, the boost that he hardly needed to indulge in his sadistic pursue of power. His already overinflated sense of invincibility was more than enough to last him a lifetime twice-over. "Life is good," he often said to himself, a self-indulgent grin on his handsome face, and his bright blue eyes shining from what he considered the sweet taste of success. "Life is really good."

*   *   *

The full scope of her discovery, along with its meaning and subsequent ramifications, sent Jill to her knees, her legs giving out under the full weight of her conscience and despair. As she dropped her throbbing head on DJ's bed, she gave free reign to her anguish and desperation, allowing her emotions to drain every ounce of fight she still held onto. Life could be so cruel, but that fact had never hit her as strongly as it was doing now and was much more than enough to literally destroy a person's entire world in a matter of mere minutes. No one seemed to be spared from their fate or to be able to escape from its iron clutch. It struck with indiscriminating speed and lacked any rhyme or reason, no matter how hard one tried to dodge it. What was meant to be was ultimately going to be, she forced herself to acknowledge, especially when it went totally against all that she ever believed in. The deep sadness that assailed her came with a large dose of resignation, which was a far cry from saying that she was able to understand it or ready to accept it. The horrendous truth she had just uncovered refused to be denied, no matter how fervently she wished it could be done, and it felt like literally thousands of sharp daggers jabbing at her heart, trying to wipe out what was left of her soul. Unlocking a horrible memory she swore never to release again, she drifted back to the time when she had to make the crucial decision to sacrifice the precious life of an innocent child in order to save her own son's. What mother wouldn't have done the exact same thing had they been in her place? Her overloaded mind refused to stop, in a feeble attempt to justify a choice that defied justification. She was still trying to appease her guilty conscience even after the many years that had already gone by. Back then she had been given the chance to prevent her beloved child from dying but was the price ultimately paid by so many people worth it? she questioned. Had she known then what she had just found out, would she still have chosen the same course of action? As it was, due to a decision she had been literally forced to make so long ago, the lives of that little girl and that of an additional six bright, beautiful, and innocent young women had been taken. And what about the lives of all those little creatures that had the misfortune to come across her son's troubled and destructive path while he was growing up? And Pepper. Poor, sweet Pepper. *So much pain and sorrow,* she agonized, *for those unfortunate girls, for their parents, their siblings, their loved ones . . . Why, DJ, why did you do it, son? What was it that caused you to do all of this? What could possibly have happened to cause you to lash out and hurt so many people? And all those poor, defenseless creatures, what did they ever do to you, son?* She continued to cry, unable to stop all the violent and disturbing images from literally destroying her as they continued to decimate whatever was left of her mangled heart. *Was it something that I did or neglected to do? Was it my fault as much as it was yours? Could it have been more my fault than it was yours?* Unable to stop, she simply went on, in a self-destructive yet cathartic purging of past sins, beating herself beyond the realm of plain torture. *And all of it because I simply and honestly could not bear the thought of losing you, son, not then, not now, not ever!* The utterly sick feeling at the pit of her stomach was minimal when compared to the one that powerfully buried her soul under a sky-high pile of loathing and self-abhorrence. *What do I do now? Where do I go from here, DJ? How do I rectify all the wrong that I unknowingly caused to so many innocent people? How do I make up for the tremendous amount of suffering and misery that resulted from a decision I made so long ago, out of nothing short of animalistic desperation and a need to protect you, my love? How do I go about restituting some of what I so selfishly took from another mother just like me? I had absolutely no idea that in my eagerness to save your life, I would end up feeling responsible for the loss of so many others. I haven't the slightest idea as to where to start from,* she agonized. *I know that if I don't stop you, chances are that you will continue to harm and kill more innocent people, and as much as I adore you, son, I simply cannot live with that. I have sinned so much already and made so many mistakes along the way. I simply cannot justify my past mistakes by making an even bigger one now. I simply can't . . .* , she reasoned, still unable to face the decision she knew she must make. And once that decision was made, she feared that she wouldn't have the strength she knew she would need in order to carry it out.

The icy numb fingers that dialed 911 felt foreign to her, as if they belonged to someone else. Still not sure whether she possessed the courage necessary to do what she had to, once the phone was answered, she felt extremely tempted to simply hang up and just live with crushing guilt for the rest of her miserable life. Anything was better than what she was about to do, she wailed, even if no sound ever came out of her clenched mouth. Her voice was barely audible when she asked to speak to the person in charge, her heart doing somersaults inside her suddenly compressed chest, bouncing off her rib cage like a ping-pong ball during a do-or-die match. She continually fought the overwhelming urge to quickly hang up, the fear of what was to come as great as the fear of what had already happened. Knowing that she was doing the only thing she could live with didn't compare to the knowledge of what she knew she was about to do live without. It seemed to take forever for the police sergeant to come to the phone and yet, when he finally did, she silently cursed him for answering the damned phone so damned quickly. By the time she was done relating all the facts to the stunned officer on the other end of the line, she felt numb and empty inside. She hung up the phone with a robotic hand, functioning totally on automatic pilot by then. Slowly she lowered herself to the floor, where she proceeded to sit with her legs bent at the knees and under her body, loud sobs shaking her frail body from head to toe, her bony back banging against the kitchen wall with painful force. Life as she had known was completely and irrevocably over, never to be had again. Guilt was such a useless feeling, especially when there is absolutely no way of rectifying the harm that caused the guilt to begin with. As it was though, it became the dominating factor in her shattered world, quickly followed by that of remorse, another completely doomed and useless feeling at a time like that. What she needed more than anything else was forgiveness, but that wouldn't be in the cards for her any time soon, for in order to be forgiven by someone else, one had first be able to forgive oneself. Not only wasn't Jill anywhere near that point yet, she probably would never be.

She knew that her son would be back at around 4:00 p.m., and she politely requested that the patrol cars responding to her call not use their sirens or flashing lights as they approached the house so as not to call attention to the situation at hand. It was without any fanfare that two squad cars stopped in front of the spacious ranch-style dwelling on Rydell Drive. The blue Grand Am was parked in the driveway, the engine still warm. DJ was in the family room, lying on the couch and sipping a coke, watching a movie on the VCR, as Jill silently opened the front door, giving the police officers full access to her home and, more devastatingly, full access to her son. Caught by surprise, a highly confused DJ offered no resistance whatsoever as one police officer read his Miranda rights while a much younger one produced a pair of handcuffs and placed them snuggly around DJ's wrists. With one last bewildered look in his mother's direction, he was led out the door without saying a single word. Jill, her heart racing totally out of control, simply allowed herself to slide down the front door, landing on the cold ceramic floor without making a single sound. She remained there for a very long time, unable to think, to feel, to cry, or to move. Where were those merciful tears when you needed them the most, she despaired, looking for relief from the darkness that had enveloped her heart, mind, and soul? She sought solace from the events that were just starting to unravel without success in her past, but what she needed more than anything else though, was to find refuge from the cruelty and devastation of the present. Unfortunately, none came her way regardless of how much she begged for it, and the only thing she could be sure of was that no respite would be coming her way anytime in the near future. Completely losing track of time, she had absolutely no idea how long she just sat there, on the cold foyer floor, moving only when she noticed the first rays of daylight coming in through the etched glass panes on the front door. Still operating solely on automatic pilot, she slowly got back on her feet, her muscles stiff and her bones aching all over. Heading to the kitchen, she brewed some fresh coffee, which she absentmindedly began to sip, her mind nothing but a blank space inside her head, and her heart simply a huge hole which has been painfully carved on the left side of her chest with a very dull knife, inch by painful inch. Only the depth of her immense sadness managed to penetrate through the shell of the pathetic creature she had become, one who only twenty-four hours before had been a strong and vibrant woman with a lot to live for. When the phone rang, she simply ignored it, even when Jack's loving voice came through the answering machine.

CHAPTER 15

The evidence was piled high against DJ. Just like Jill had feared all along, the locks of hair found in the metal box under his bed turned out to be a perfect match to the hair of each of the murdered girls. DNA obtained from DJ's semen matched the samples found inside the raped victims as well, without the slightest margin of doubt. With such concrete and incriminating proof already in the prosecutor's hands, Jill was mercifully spared the ordeal of having to take the stand, and for that she was deeply grateful and relieved. She doubted that she would have been able to do so anyway, she sadly acknowledged, if not to anyone else, at least to herself. That was one of the many casualties in a situation as devastating as the one she found herself in; you could always deny the truth to just about anyone else, but how do you deny the truth to yourself? Jill was far too intelligent to play that game even though admitting something was very different than accepting it. The backlash of what DJ had done had just started to emerge, and the fallout from his crimes would catch up with all those affected one way or another. Having had to turn her own son into the police was the hardest thing she had ever faced, even harder than losing her darling husband after only four years of marriage. She would have done absolutely anything if only she could only go back to that rainy April morning in 1976, anything to prevent Drew from getting behind the wheel, but she was well aware that she simply could not. Neither could she have prevented what happened to them since that fateful 911 call, for she saw no other way out whatsoever, or at least none that she could have lived with anyway. And the worst was yet to come, she was sure of, a truth that gave her a feeling of helplessness that was completely foreign to her. Damned be destiny, fate, guilt, powerlessness, and all the other feelings and emotions that had the ability to literally destroy a person's life, regardless of whether they brought them on themselves or were merely a casualty of someone else's behavior.

Thank God she didn't have to testify against her own flesh and blood, for it would have been the end of her, she was sure of it, since he was the most precious person in her life and her entire world, a world that, unfortunately, had been reduced to a mere speck of dust in the vast universe of actions, consequences, and accountability. Sitting very still in the courtroom everyday of the trial, it tore her apart to see the pain and grief reflected on the ravaged faces of the murdered girls' parents, siblings, and relatives–a look she was more than familiar with herself on a few occasions. One by one, they all directed their anger and disdain toward the person who had caused them so much grief and sorrow, and that person was none other than her own child, her beloved DJ. Sitting a mere few feet away from where she sat, he seemed far removed and much more distant to her than ever before. The raw emotion that was palpable inside the packed courtroom was nearly too much to bear for many of those in attendance; for Jill, it felt like being buried alive. Every single morning during the proceedings, DJ was brought into the courtroom handcuffed and in shackles, the bright orange hue of his prison-issued jumpsuit in stark contrast with his dark blonde hair and captivating blue eyes. Much to Jill's distress, DJ never gave her a second look, acting as if she wasn't even there. Her hungry motherly eyes though, remained glued to his face, a face she knew and loved so much, the face of her precious child. Even though her brothers and sister were still mourning the loss of their father, they took turns coming to sit by Jill's side. Thankfully their spouses took over the care of their respective families so that each could lend some needed support to their baby sister. They knew how much she had gone through already, but nothing was quite as difficult as what she now had to endure. Daniel, Nicholas, and Tara had all lost quite a bit of weight after finding out what unconceivable crimes their beloved nephew had been accused of and was now on trial for. Although this latest tragedy further added to their already heavy burden, they continued to come to the trial as often as they could. Their mother, however, was a different story. She simply couldn't get over William's death, her fragile physical and emotional state a cause of great concern to her children. They had all gathered at her house one day, all four of them, and begged her not to come to the proceedings. They realized that she was in no shape to hear the horrendous things that would be said against her darling grandson, day in and day out. They also didn't want Sophia to see DJ under such horrible circumstances. Jack, kind and loving Jack, made the trip on a few occasions, using some personal time in order to get the day off, protectively placing his arm around Jill's thin shoulders in an effort to shield her from the horror she was being exposed to on a daily basis. He always left the courtroom devastated by what he heard and by all the suffering that Jill was being put through, feeling helpless as to how he could be of any further support to her during her hour of need. After all, this was the woman he loved, and DJ was not only her only child but that of his late friend Drew as well, so he kept coming every chance he got. Even Marissa, fearing for Jill's emotional and psychological health, showed up several times, simply holding her cold and clammy hands between her own, often squeezing them when they began to shake after hearing of some particularly grisly detail in one of the cases. She felt helpless as well, wanting to do so much for her best friend yet not knowing what. Little did she know how much she was helping Jill already just by being there.

DJ seemed totally out of place dressed in prison-issued clothes. He was indeed a very handsome and well-mannered young man and didn't fit the typical profile or the stereotype that was often associated with a serial killer. He didn't look or behave like one, and his background certainly didn't match that of most hardcore criminals' or the circumstances under which they were often brought up. Instead, he could very well pass as the poster child for the all-American boy next door. This good-looking, well-educated, well-spoken, polite young man had been raised in a financially stable home, surrounded by a large and close-knit family and had been loved by people who simply adored him, like his grandfather William for example. He had never been physically, sexually, verbally, or emotionally abused, which was often the case in most violent criminals' histories. He had indeed lived a very privileged life many only get to dream about, always getting all he ever wanted, which was far more than he ever needed. What was it that caused him to turn out to be so cold, callous, and calculating, an enigmatic and pragmatic being that many did not even consider of the human race? What could have gone so wrong, and when did this dramatic change manifest itself? What caused such drastic deviation from the right path to follow, especially given his supportive background? What prompted him to literally destroy dozens of lives along the way, including his very own? Was it a touch of self-indulgence, or was it just a large dose of self-entitlement? Could it have been, unfortunately for all his victims, simply a case of total disregard for life in general? For his devastated mother, no possible explanation would ever suffice; peace and acceptance something she would strive for but perhaps never attain. Her hell on earth had officially started.

The nauseating truth about the sinister nature of DJ's attacks was never alluded to during the course of his trial, not because they were irrelevant, but because they were never discovered. In a way, it was better that they remained unknown, for that fact was a blessing in disguise for the murdered girls' relatives and friends. They had gone through so much pain already; discovering the whole truth would only serve to add salt to the already bleeding wounds. Besides, DJ wasn't about to volunteer all the sinister information to anyone, reserving that knowledge for his own personal satisfaction. It was proof of how truly gifted and brilliant he was and a source of tremendous personal pride, not only then but for many years to come. Besides, it wasn't really anybody's business if he had already killed each girl before having the pleasure of "making love to them." It was and would forever remain their little secret, shared only between him and his "lovers." He considered the way in which he had outsmarted every so-called "expert" that the prosecution hired to evaluate him to be a major victory. He had easily fooled them all, he silently laughed, proud of all of his performances. But what a waste of taxpayer dollars, he smirked! And the authorities still had no inkling as to his true talent, which was a shame, really. The macabre details of each killing were undoubtedly unparalleled to any they could have suspected unless they were to be told about them, and he had absolutely no intention of ever doing so. He would remain the only living person privy to every juicy detail, and for that he felt beyond honored. Let them all think what they wanted to about him, for he couldn't care less. Let them believe that perhaps he was nothing more than your run-of-the-mill serial killer; he wasn't about to waste a single brain cell thinking about any of that crap! What really mattered to him was that he knew the truth, and that in itself was a coup as well as a valuable triumph to be savored and relived time and time again. He simply didn't give a damn about what the hell anyone thought about him anyway, never had and never would. His politeness and easygoing personality were his best tools and his good looks his best asset, for they had opened many doors along the way. The only reason he comported himself in a respectful, well-mannered, and caring way was because he benefited immensely from the freedom to do whatever pleased him that it provided. By behaving so, which was a truly typical psychopathic trait, he had avoided raising any suspicions from those he came in contact with, which had suited his needs fine. His family had no inkling as to who he was or what he did over the years, not until the woman he had called mother for over twenty-one years decided to stick her nose where it certainly didn't belong. *Damn you, Jill, for turning against me, your own son,* he silently cursed, lashing out in frustration, especially when in the privacy of his cell, where no one could witness his true dark side. *Someday I'll be able to return the favor, Mother, and I'm truly looking forward to the chance to repay you in full, of that much I can assure you,* he vowed, jaw clenched and both fists pounding on his mattress until he was able to regain the cool and collected role he had mastered over the years.

As disgustingly gruesome as it was, the secret he carried was a source of great personal fulfillment in his ego-crowded mind. With his ability to turn on the charm at will, he became a formidable hunter. With the face of an angel and the heart of a monster, he had packed more cruelty in his short life than anyone could ever guess. With his mind so distant from what was deemed right and wrong, the fact that he had violated a dead body, not once but a total of six times, was viewed by him as nothing to lose sleep over. In fact, that knowledge gave him an extra boost of pride and self-worth, a feeling that spoke volumes about his deviant character. With the exception of those who acted in the same manner, desecrating a body was considered to be an evil act even by the most depraved of criminals, who would probably be repulsed by the simple idea of it. Someday DJ would have to answer to a higher court than that of his peers, and his punishment would certainly be much harsher than any that society's laws could ever hand out. In DJ's sick world, however, there was absolutely no room for anyone or anything else other than himself and his needs, so he actually didn't give a horse's ass to anyone's opinion except for the twelve people sitting in the jury box. He wasn't all that concerned though because he believed that he had more than enough time to work on them. In a world that placed such emphasis on someone's looks, his attributes were not going to be overlooked by all twelve of them. There had to be at least one juror that he could still charm. After all, he hadn't lost his touch!

Not one to miss any detail, no matter how insignificant it might appear to others, he had noticed how some of the women in the jury looked at him whenever he entered the courtroom. One of them in particular, a young little bitty thing with long dark hair, seemed to keep her attention on his face a fraction of a second longer than the others. It wasn't something that anyone in attendance could have picked up on, but for DJ's acutely perceptive eyes, it was as if she was holding a sign that said: "you got me, handsome one!" A second lady, perhaps the oldest one in the group, often had what he could swear were signs of pity on her pleasant features on few occasions when they had briefly locked eyes. Pity was definitely something he simply abhorred, and had all his life, but not in this instance, when it came from a silver-haired juror that could very well have been his grandmother. At least two female jurors, one in her twenties and the other probably in her late sixties, could be of great help to him when decision time came around.

DJ was right on target as far as jury deliberation was concerned. Although the majority of the jurors were firm in their belief that he deserved the death penalty, the two female ones were just as adamant as to why they didn't agree with the harsh sentence. Their argument, which was nothing but a veiled attempt to spare his life, was that putting him to death would serve no purpose whatsoever, except to shorten his time of suffering. True justice would be better served by a sentence of life in prison for each of the six crimes he was guilty of. The jury deliberated for a full nine days, completely deadlocked between the death sentence and the life in prison. As totally convinced as the ten jurors were of their decision, so were the other two of their position, with both sides holding firmly to their beliefs. As DJ had counted on, his good looks and impeccable behavior served him well once more as they had so many other times in the past. He had managed, with carefully orchestrated subtleness, to even accidently lock eyes with the young juror, thus starting a mutual flirting game that went unnoticed by everyone except for the only two players involved. He even saw the hint of a well-concealed smile on the pretty brunette's luscious lips. If the outcome came in his favor, as he predicted it ultimately would, he would find a way to send her some flowers. Pink roses would be a good choice, he figured. Yes, two dozen of long-stemmed pink roses with plenty of white baby's breath to enhance their beauty.

With the possibility of a mistrial hanging right above their heads if they couldn't unanimously agree on a verdict and completely wiped out from the deliberations and the heated arguments they provoked, the ten jurors decided to simply give in and join the remaining two in their decision. Truth be said, at that point all that they could think of was the prospect of finally going home and forgetting all about the stress that the trial inflicted on them. They couldn't help but feel deep disappointment as the folded piece of white paper on which the final sentence was written was passed from the foreperson, who happened to be the silver-haired lady, to the presiding judge. With an unreadable expression on his seasoned face, Judge Trevor Wilcox paused for a full minute before handing the paper back to the foreperson, Mrs. Joyce Cassidy. His withheld breath and lack of emotion spoke volumes in the packed yet eerily silent room. Mrs. Cassidy's voice never betrayed what she was feeling inside either, except for the almost undetectable tremor in the tone of her voice, which was recognized only by her husband, who sat quite still on a bench to her right. Life in prison without the possibility of parole, she repeated as each of the victims' names was pronounced. After each sentence was read, a loud murmur could be heard from the area where the families of the victims were seated during the trial. After the last verdict was declared, Judge Wilcox thanked the jury members for their hard work and dismissed them. As they left the courtroom, none of them looked directly in DJ's direction, not even the pretty young brunette, for she didn't want to raise any suspicions against herself. She did, however, manage to discreetly look at him sideways, her head bent to shield the faint smile that almost escaped her lips. And as usual, DJ missed none of it, his heart beating much faster at the knowledge that she had been true to him in her determination not to let him be put to death. *Way to go, little one! I knew that I could count on you. Perhaps I can pay you back sometime,* he thought, the sweet fragrance of roses suddenly surrounding him, and an equally faint smile almost escaping his sensual lips. *If only we had met under different circumstances, my little jewel. We could have shared such a memorable time together. Of that I'm sure.*

It was on a dismal rainy day on September 11, 1995, that Drew William Millner Jr., affectionally known as DJ to all who loved him, was officially sentenced to life in prison without any possibility of parole. Jill's heart dropped to her feet as the devastating words were repeated over and over, painfully reinforcing the truth that her son would never be coming home again. In a second, a tremendous wave of nausea suddenly reared its ugly head and overpowered all of her other senses. With her eyes riveted on her son's face, she didn't blink once and remained as silent and still as a stone. It felt to her that she had just died right there, sitting on that courtroom bench. DJ remained totally impassive, giving the impression that he hadn't even heard the sentence. He acted as if he wasn't the one being condemned but simply a curious spectator at his own trial, thus completely detached from the final decision. The only outward sign that he had heard the verdict was the subtle twitching of a few muscles on both sides of his temples and the almost imperceptible clenching of his jaws. As the last of the sentences were read, loud cries of injustice and disapproval erupted inside the packed courtroom and clenched fists were raised in a clear expression of exploding tempers and unquenched need for revenge. Most of those in attendance felt totally cheated out of the death penalty that they unanimously felt DJ deserved; anything less than that was like a slap in the face of all his victims. With outraged cries that a miscarriage of justice had been just handed out echoing throughout the still-packed room like clashes of thunder, DJ was expediently escorted through a small side door. The loud shouts and sobs continued to grow, reaching an all-time high as the door closed behind his odious figure. Just before he left the courtroom though, DJ suddenly stopped dead in his tracks and turned his full attention to his mother, fixing her with such an intensely frigid stare that instantly froze all the blood in her veins, icicles piercing the length of her body from the inside out. With chills running rampant up and down her spine, it wasn't long before both of her arms and legs went simultaneously numb and cold. Buckling under the weight of her frail body but heavy conscience, her legs wobbled, rendering Jill unable of keeping herself in an upright position. Holding his destructive and incapacitating stare as long as he possibly could, and with daggers shooting from his eyes, he continued his verbal assault on her even though not once did he ever utter a sound. Before long, the correctional officers were leading DJ out to a waiting van that was inconspicuously parked behind the courthouse. The unmarked vehicle wasted no time in transporting him to the Raymond Corrigan Correctional Facility, a well-known maximum-security prison located on New London Turnpike in Uncasville, Connecticut. There, a dark and dingy nine-by-five foot cell patiently waited for the return of its infamous occupant. And as soon as DJ got there, the heavy iron gates would slam shut behind him with a loud bang, forever keeping him away from the world he once knew but chose to discard, a world that held nothing but contempt for the inhuman creature he had become. And that world would certainly be much safer because he was no longer a free man

*　　*　　*

Leaving the courthouse by the rear door, DJ was briefly greeted by the heavy rain on his face, forcing him to immediately lower his head against the wind-driven downpour. Once inside the back of the van, he fidgeted for a while, trying to find a more comfortable position as he sat on the hardwood bench, both hands securely handcuffed behind his waist and both ankles in shackles as per police protocol. He was still seething from his encounter with his mother. What a real disappointment she turned out to be, he swore under his breath, consumed with hate and contempt. He was still unable to understand how the bitch could have turned on him, her only child, like that. "How dare she?" he almost screamed. A litany of cursing words escaped his clenched jaw, his head ready to explode from his mounting fury. The thought of being caught had been the furthest thing from his mind; so certain was he that he was the most astute person he knew by a mile, thus more than capable of eluding capture forever. He was sure that he would still be out there, doing his thing and not bothering anyone had his darling mother not stuck her stupid nose where she shouldn't. She had no right to do that, he fumed, both nostrils flaring in his rage at the injustice of it all. She could try to apologize all she wanted, he sneered, but he would never forgive her for her audacity to interfere in what he considered to be his business and his business only. The ultimate betrayal she committed against him, her very own flesh and blood, would never ebb away no matter how hard she attempted to make amends from that point on or how much time ultimately passed. With his disgust threatening to unravel his always-in-control demeanor and not wanting to waste any more of his precious time on someone who was not worthy of a second thought, DJ decided to think of far more pleasant things than his miserable excuse for a mother. Shifting gears as quickly and as easily as he had already dismissed all of the lives he had taken, human and otherwise, he began to reminisce. Soon a cocky grin had replaced the fierce and menacing frown he had sported on his forehead a mere few minutes before.

Ah, my sweet, Alyssa! He recalled with a smile his pretty date for the high school prom. *You were a real beauty, that's for sure. I did make you purr, didn't I, kitten? I know that you wanted and expected much more from me, but I simply couldn't deliver, and that's the truth! We just didn't click, that's all. Sorry, sweet pea!* He had behaved like a perfect gentleman that evening, very attentive and well-mannered. Even the chaste and tender kiss they exchanged as they stood at her front door when he dropped her off had been beyond reproach. He quickly realized, after spending some time with her, that she was simply not his type after all, so why waste both of their time with something that wasn't going anywhere? At the dance, however, a petite blonde girl caught his attention from the second he saw her, and she appeared to have noticed him as well. Nicole was her name, he overheard someone say. She danced with her date most of the evening, a fellow student by the name of Roger that he knew only in passing. As Nicole and DJ both approached the refreshment table, she quickly slipped him a folded piece of paper, which had her phone number neatly written on it along with her name. Extremely pleased with this sudden turn of events, he returned to Alyssa with two glasses of soda in his hands and a satisfied smile on his devastatingly handsome face. Throughout the night though, he caught Nicole looking in his direction every time he sneaked a peek at her. The coy smile she gave him only served to pique his interest in her even further, images of good times to be had flooding his mind with a mixture of promise and pleasure. *Yes, Nicole, you certainly managed to catch my attention all right, you pretty little thing! I think that we are in for a real good time together, you and me, darling girl!"*

He decided not to call Nicole right away. *Let her sweat it a little bit longer*, he reasoned. He wanted to play it cool after all and not look like an overly eager, inexperienced, and horny teenager. He was, after all, a full-grown man and not a little boy. Waiting for about a week after they first met, he dialed the number she had given to him at the dance. For some unknown reason at the time, he decided to use a public telephone from a gas station along the Merritt Parkway to make the call instead of calling her from his phone at home. He was extremely pleased indeed to hear the excitement in her voice when she finally answered on the fifth ring. She was pretty enough, he conceded, a smug expression on his handsome face. Her long pale blonde hair was shiny and smooth and reached just above her tiny waist, just the way he liked it. Her beautiful large eyes, however, were her most attractive feature, he recalled with a wide smile. Their light honey color was of a shade he had never seen before, almost matching the color of her silky hair, very captivating indeed. They made plans to meet at a movie theater in Fairfield but decided to skip the movie at the last minute, opting instead to go for a ride in his old Chevette. If she noticed that the car had seen better days, she didn't mention anything at all about it, earning her a gold star in his book. She was quite friendly and outgoing, perhaps a bit too forward for his taste, but who cared, right? He behaved like a total gentleman once again that night, and their first kiss was pleasantly tender and sweet. Another gold star, this one given to himself. He could tell that she really liked him from the get go, and that was an added bonus in his favor. They went out a couple more times after that initial date but never to a restaurant or other public place, a fact that seemed to go unnoticed by the clearly smitten young girl. On their fourth outing together, he decided to take her to Belle Island, a quiet park in Rowayton, a quaint and affluent seaside section of Norwalk. He tenderly held her hand all the way there and parked the car in a secluded dark spot. They started to make out the minute the engine stopped running. She was a willing participant and quite passionate to boot, not the innocent girl he had imagined her to be when they first met at the dance, coy smile and all. He wasn't sure whether he liked that fact or not, but it didn't really matter anyway, for he was by then fully aroused by the little minx. Tentatively, he started to run his right hand gently up and down her left inner thigh, an easy enough move since she was wearing a short pleated skirt. To his pleasant surprise, she made no effort to stop him; quite the contrary as a matter of fact! With uncontrollable urgency, she took hold of his hand and guided it to the spot where her thighs met, the small triangle there cushioned with amazingly soft pubic hair, deepening the kiss as she did so. Her panties were made of some sort of silky material that felt wonderful to the touch as it met his gentle yet eager fingers. Before he realized what he was doing, he began to stroke her in a very slow, erotic, and clearly pleasurable up and down motion, faint sounds escaping her lips in between lust-filled kisses. In one fluid and smooth move, she lifted her skirt and quickly removed her red panties, tossing them into the backseat with that coy and seductive smile of hers that had caught his attention to begin with. Just as quickly, he unzipped his pants and pulled them down around his ankles, his Corona beer boxer shorts soon following, leaving his engorged penis fully exposed for her hungry eyes and hands to feast on. With an expertise he had no idea she was capable of, she wrapped her slender and delicate fingers fully around his magnificently rigid erection. As she started to slowly move her hand up and down, the feel of his hardness and considerable girth made her hot and moist with anticipation and desire. He quickly pushed the driver's seat as far back as it would go in order to better accommodate the two of them within the cramped space. He was just about to lower her hungry hot little bottom down onto his hard erection when, to his horror, his penis started to go flaccid all of a sudden. He tried to concentrate on what they were doing in order to regain the splendid erection that he had just a couple of minutes before but failed miserably in his efforts. Unfortunately, the harder he tried, the more he failed in his attempts. Nicole's expression went from passionate to urgent to confused, all in the span of mere seconds, but she wasn't about to let this happen to her. She wanted him so much that she wasn't about to give up, craving the wonderful sex she was sure they were capable of having more than anything else at the moment. She was absolutely certain that her date, which she happened to like much more than any other guy she had ever gone out with before, deserved better from her as well. Guided by pure instinct and animalistic need, she found herself doubling her efforts in order to get help him recapture his response to all the sexiness and allure she knew she possessed. "What's the matter, stud?" she cajoled, in a sincere attempt to lighten the mood, trying hard to take some pressure off of him. "Am I too much of a woman for you to handle, big boy?" she teased, licking her red hot lips in a seductive manner, her small tongue suggestively moving slowly over her pouty, sexy mouth. She was so intent in reigniting the fire of the passion she knew they were both capable of, that she failed to notice how his expression had suddenly changed upon hearing her words. Unfortunately, he totally misinterpreted their meaning, mistakenly viewing her innocent remarks as being an affront to his prowess and masculinity. Little did he know that all she had meant to do was to give him the go ahead, the gentle nudge he might be looking for, and not be deterred by what she considered to be simply a direct result of them being first-time lovers. The thought that he was a lesser man or an inadequate sexual partner was the furthest thing from her mind. *What is wrong with you?* her eyes seemed to shout at him. *Are you gay or something?* They continued to scream, those accusing eyes of hers, no longer as beautiful as he had first thought them to be. He wasn't sure as to how he wanted to proceed, but he was really beginning to dislike this girl with the face of an angel and the manners of a common whore. Nicole was completely unaware of the turmoil her words had caused in his mind or the ire they had unleashed, words she had spoken in a sincere attempt to let him know that it was all right with her, trying only to put him more at ease. Tentatively, she kissed his sensual lips, urging with her tongue some response from him, using all her charms to attempt to calm the clearly upset young man she happened to like so much. His hands were now at the back of her slender neck, his fingers slowly pressing against the vertebrae he could easily feel through the fabric of her thin blouse. She was looking at him with what he could swear was a mixture of disappointment, disgust, and pity. *How dare you look at me like that, you filthy, cunning bitch?* He went on, silently accusing the naïve and totally oblivious girl who continued to minister to his needs, trying hard to get him to respond to her again. He could feel his anger escalating as he started to move his hands slowly, bringing his thumbs together over the hollow spot at the base of her throat, ever so gently rubbing them against her warm and soft skin. He felt himself getting aroused again at what he perceived to be total submissiveness on Nicole's part. As the hands around her slender neck continued to increase their pressure, his arousal responded by increasing as well. What had started as a pleasurable massage to her neck became something else altogether in no time at all. Soon Nicole realized that the pressure he was exerting was way too heavy for comfort, a sick and uneasy feeling sneaking deep into her head. Frantically, she tugged at his hands, trying to lessen their grip on her, thus easing her mounting discomfort. His hands, however, simply refused to budge as they continued to squeeze tighter and tighter still. She found herself using all the strength she had trying to loosen his tight grasp. By then, the pressure his hands were exerting bordered on torture, her eyes wide with fear and her legs jerking around in a frantic dance of life and death, quickly exhausting her in her efforts to break free. As her fear and combativeness grew, so did his erection. He continued to escalate the intensity of the pressure on her neck for a couple of minutes longer, and the more she fought, the tighter he squeezed, and the more aroused he became. The vicious cycle became a sick repetition of torture and pleasure, of domination and abandon. All of a sudden, the mortal game came to a halt, and she went totally still, arms limp by her sides, and her legs sprawled at an odd angle. He was so aroused by then that he tried to raise her small bottom up from him in order to immediately penetrate her so that he could satisfy his immense sexual need. Her lifeless body, however, seemed to have doubled in weight, becoming too heavy for him to lift, rendering him unable to accomplish what he wanted to inside such limited and cramped space. He grew more than frustrated then, sandwiched as he was between the back of the driver seat and the steering wheel. With an exasperated sigh and a few choice words, he barely managed to shove the girl's body over the gear box between the two front seats. With his anger quickly escalating, he got out of the car and tersely walked to the passenger side. He roughly pulled both of her legs out of the car, letting her body clumsily fall across both seats, her head making a muffled sound as it hit the leather upholstery. He wasted no time in penetrating her, and it took him only one thrust to cause waves of pleasure to take over every inch of his body, making him shake from the intensity of the exquisite sensations. His final orgasm was so intense that he thought his eyes were literally going to fall out of their sockets. He had never experienced anything as amazing as that before, in any of the hundreds of times he had masturbated while watching pornographic flicks in the sanctuary of his bedroom. No one would ever guess that this was his first sexual encounter with a member of the opposite sex, he thought with a truly satisfied grin, but what a first encounter it had been! The fact that the girl was dead didn't disturb him in the least; as a matter of fact, it had quite the opposite effect on him, multiplying his orgasm tenfold. Nicole was no longer mocking him or pitying him because he had quickly put a stop to it, he thought triumphantly. He was still unable to believe the feelings of power and well-being that pulsated through his veins, flooding his mind with unending pleasure still. Long forgotten was the untamed anger of only a few minutes before, and he was once again in control of his emotions, as cool and collected as a satisfied cat napping on a sunny windowsill. Returning the girl to a sitting position, he carefully secured the seatbelt around her lifeless body; he didn't want to get a ticket just because his passenger was not wearing her seatbelt. It was, after all, the law, and he always made sure not to break the law! He laughed hard, amused by the irony of his own perverse joke. Getting behind the wheel, he started to drive slowly out of the park. He didn't want to risk getting a speeding ticket either. He laughed again, amazed at his wit and sense of humor. "I'm on a roll tonight, man," he said, still laughing as he reached into the backseat and retrieved her silky red panties, the same ones she had so willingly tossed away a little while before in great anticipation of what was yet to come. In one fluid movement, he reached into his pants' right pocket and retrieved a multipurpose Swiss Army knife that his grandfather William had given to him on his tenth birthday, and which he carried with him everywhere he went. Swiftly, he cut a small lock of Nicole's pale blond hair and carefully wrapped it in some tissue paper, which he immediately placed in the glove compartment. This ritual of keeping some sort of memento from each of his special "adventures" had been repeated many times before, granted not to this unbelievably degree of enjoyment. It had started when he collected his first bird feather and butterfly wing from all those pesky weaklings that he had come across as a child. It continued with Pepper as well, who had pissed him off to no end when she began following his every step, so needy that she literally became suffocating. All of a sudden she appeared to never leave him alone, not even when he had to go to the bathroom, the pain in his ass nuisance. He treasured those items he so carefully collected like a trophy to remember them by, which he kept in a silver metal box stashed away under his bed for safekeeping. Just before he reached the southbound entrance leading to the Merritt Parkway, he stuffed Nicole's panties in her mouth with a lazy grin on his smug face. Unbuckling her seatbelt, he opened the passenger door and callously shoved her slumped body out of the barely moving vehicle in one swift movement. He watched in total fascination as she slowly rolled down the slightly descending slope, landing face down on a deep ditch parallel to the seldom-traveled road. He was still under the spell of the absolutely incredible high he had experienced not that long before and far too cocky to entertain the thought of ever getting caught. "It will never, ever happen," he proclaimed, his voice brimming with confidence and self-importance. Totally hooked now, he made a solemn vow that he would indeed seek and find that intoxicatingly pleasurable feeling he had so enjoyed with his now late partner as often as he could in the months and years to come. Without even a glance back, he wasted no time in driving away from the girl lying lifeless, the cause of his unbelievable ecstasy and newfound sense of power and satisfaction. The fact that he had killed the beautiful girl in such cold fashion never caused him the slightest remorse or worry. The only thing he remembered and did for quite a long time afterwards was the incredible, mind-blowing orgasm she had gifted him with. He hoped that she had enjoyed herself at least half as much as he did. It would be a real shame if she had not. A total waste of a damn good time.

Since he had every intention of continuing what he had started with Nicole, he came up with what he devised as a foolproof plan of action, concentrating mostly on where to safely take his next "date" when he was ready to act again. He decided that he would stake out secluded spots in different towns for at least six consecutive weeks in order to see which days of the week had the least number of visitors to the particular spot he had in mind. He would then take his unsuspecting companion there on the day of the week he saw no other people around, which was usually on a Monday or on a Wednesday night, depending on the place and the season. He felt very confident with this arrangement, since he could always change it at a second's notice if he spotted anyone around or if he felt uneasy about any part of his plan of action. After all, time was on his side, so there was no need to take any risks regardless of how low they might appear to be. For a very short while he even entertained the thought of looking for another job, one that perhaps paid a little better, but now he was more than glad he had not. Besides the fact that he somehow managed to hardly do much more than walk around the mall during his shift, an easy enough task that suited his lazy attitude and his total lack of work ethics to perfection, his job at the mall was the perfect venue for meeting women of all ages, ethnicity, cultural background, and social upbringing. Not that he gave a dam about any of it though, but he was extremely attuned to the fact that he needed to avoid setting a pattern that could lead the authorities to his front door. He never had to go out of his way to meet any of them, for they seemed to simply gravitate to him wherever he went. The fact that he was six feet two inches and 190 pounds of lean muscle, compounded by his exceptional good looks and truly amazing blue eyes, helped a lot, not to mention his on-the-spot polite demeanor and good manners. That combination of attributes made him a prime target for the undivided attention and interest of members of the opposite sex. Attracting women was never a problem, as effortless to him as the natural act of eating or breathing he soon realized, wasting no time in putting his charms to work for his benefit whenever it was convenient to him. Because he didn't want to act impulsively, he decided to wait for a while before setting up another "date." *Let things cool off a bit,* he wisely thought, and then it would be safe to go on the prowl again. *Prowl.* He loved the term and the meaning it instantly brought to mind, that of a stealthy, fluid predator patiently stalking his next meal, one that would truly satisfy his voracious appetite if only for a while before it needed to hunt again.

In a matter of four months, he was able to easily recruit his second victim, a petite strawberry-blonde beauty he spotted as she was window shopping at Macy's. *My type of girl,* he thought immediately, *very young, big on looks, and small in stature!* Feigning interest in an item of clothing on display at the same store window front she had stopped at, he approached the unsuspecting girl and soon they were enjoying a cup of coffee, conveniently seated at a very secluded table in the food courtyard. Her name, she gladly told her attentive companion, was Elizabeth, but all her friends called her Beth, she stated with a smile. Her twentieth birthday was just around the corner, she added in a demure and shy way that DJ found quite attractive this day and age. They sat and continued to chat for a little while longer, the conversation flowing easily back and forth between sips of hot coffee and a shared chocolate-filled croissant. Before they parted ways, she gave him her phone number, hoping that the handsome young man would call her sooner rather than later. She really liked him, she realized with a tug of her heart, this gorgeous, charming, and polite stranger. And she loved his name, Drew, and had ever since she was in the first grade and had developed a major crush on a classmate with the very same name. *Please call me, Drew, please, please, please . . . I would really love to see you again,* she thought as she continued her perusal through the rest of the shops at the mall, hoping to "casually" come across him once more before she had to go back home.

Again DJ waited a few days before calling Beth because he was determined not to be perceived as being too eager or too smitten by the pretty girl no matter what. As he had done the previous time, he called her from a different public phone and again felt a boost to his already swollen ego when she sounded so relieved and pleased upon hearing his voice. By the time he took her out on their first date, his old Chevette was history, replaced by the shiny brand new Grand Am. Beth seemed to be quite impressed by his taste in cars and congratulated him on it as soon as he took his place behind the wheel. The bright shade of blue was absolutely beautiful and "a very close match to the color of your simply amazing eyes," she added with sincerity. She blushed profusely when she realized how forward she must have sounded to him, which wasn't her intention at all. The bright smile he directed at her lessened some of her worries about giving him the wrong impression, reassuring her that he was actually pleased by her honest and naïve nature. "Fasten your seat belt, little lady. We don't want anything to happen to you, do we"? Appearing all of a sudden to have become a bit shy himself, DJ tentatively reached for her small left hand with his large right one, and she was caught completely off guard by the jolt of electricity that seemed to instantly pass between the two of them. Even more surprising though, were the butterflies she felt in the pit of her stomach, not to mention the sudden yearning she felt all the way down to her groin, something that was totally out of character for her to say the least. *Oh, boy! I might be in real trouble here!* she fretted, trying not to let DJ suspect her true feelings. *Perhaps I like Drew a lot more than I should, and that can be a dangerous game for me to get involved in or hooked on!* She continued to worry, knowing that she was traveling through totally uncharted waters. *I better watch myself. I really don't want Drew to have the impression that I am easy because I certainly am not and have never been,* she chastised herself. The truth, however, was that she had never felt so strongly about a man so quickly and was not at all sure as to how she should comport herself with her dangerously handsome date. His looks were so devastatingly gorgeous that they made her weak at the knees, and she was not only innocent in the ways of men but quite inexperienced in the dating department to boot. As a matter of fact, until meeting him, she was very proud of the fact that she was still a virgin, never before having felt the need to enter into a sexual relationship with any of her previous boyfriends. She honestly hadn't felt ready to do so anyway, not that she had even dated that many men to begin with, this being her third boyfriend in four years. To her amazement though, DJ behaved impeccably, seeming unwilling to push the envelope by making her do anything she might not be ready for or come to regret later. Little did the poor girl know that his behavior was nothing but a ruse, a carefully plotted and very well-thought-out plan of action, a predator patiently yet stealthily stalking his prey before the final attack and kill. By their fourth date, he had her to the point where she was the one making most of the moves, and that was exactly how he wanted it to be. She was becoming increasingly more and more into the mysteriously well-mannered young man, a fascination that only increased with each subsequent encounter. And his unbelievably handsome features, added to his strong yet trim physique, made him someone no sane woman could or would want to resist. It really impressed her that he seemed to like and respect her so much that he never tried to take advantage of her deep infatuation with him, an endearing quality that made her want him even more. She hardly recognized herself when she was with Drew, the depth of her passion for him scaring her beyond believe. On their fifth outing, Drew drove to Indian Ledge Park in Trumbull, a place she didn't even know existed until they were already there. The small yet cozy area had a small brook-fed lake in the center and was surrounded by thick, lush foliage and numerous tall trees. There was a children's playground to one side and a few picnic tables and benches across from the lake. A charming bridge crossed over the narrow brook where the stream fell into the lake, a drop of approximately twelve feet. The sound of the falling water made for a truly romantic background for all lovers, young and old alike, making the natural setting more than ideal for romance. Just as it had happened the first time around with Nicole, they started to make out as soon as he shut the car engine. Beth, who felt an instantaneous and irresistible attraction toward her companion from day one, was by then more than ready to go all the way. She was as sure of that as she was of her feelings for DJ, she realized with a mixture of fear and anticipation, for she had never been even close to being sexually involved with a man before. The furthest she had ever gone was the deep kissing stage and some light touching, always stopping before things got out of hand. But that was then and this was now, she admitted, the bit of hesitation she still had dissolving as quickly as it had appeared. Before she realized what had taken over her and as if she had plenty of experience with the act of being sexually intimate with a man, she found herself straddling him, her face only inches from his. She started to run her fingers up and down his muscular chest, playing with the curly hairs there, thick and slightly coarse just like she had imagined them to be. Eager to move things along, a daring response from a nearly inexperienced girl, she found herself resting her small hands on the pulsating bulge that filled his jeans' front, threatening to split the zipper apart at any given moment. As he reached for her, the soft feel of her lacy underwear further inflamed his desire. Gently, he urged her to lift her nicely round and firm bottom up in order to remove her panties, which he quickly did. With amazing dexterity, he managed to unzip his pants and simultaneously pull them and his boxer shorts down his muscular thighs and knees, just far enough to free his engorged penis. And then, just as it had happened before, the minute he was ready to enter the warm moisture of her young, ripe, and ready hot body, he felt his erection soften a little. With a hollow feeling suddenly lodged in his throat, and his stomach literally in knots at the mere thought of not being able to maintain his arousal, he tried to concentrate harder on the beauty on top of him. Fearful that he was going to go flaccid again, he deepened the kiss they were exchanging, all the while holding her small head firmly cupped in both of his large hands. Without even thinking about what he was doing, his thumbs rested on the hollow space at the base of her throat, caressing the tender skin there with hardly any pressure at all. As his penis continued to soften, he started to augment the force his thumbs were exerting on the girl's neck ever so slightly. At first, mistaking the increase in pressure as some sort of sexual urgency on his part, she responded by rubbing herself against his lap, matching the passion of his kiss with an equal dose of her own. As the pressure of his hands increased, however, her eyes began to reflect a hint of the uneasiness that was slowly creeping into her mind, warning her that things could very well get out of hand at any minute. Before long, she found herself tugging at his hands with increasing effort, panic rapidly taking over as she frantically tried to lessen his unrelenting grip on her throat, her breathing raspy and harsh. Her eyes showed the unmistakable recognition of approaching danger as her lungs were being deprived of the air they were starving for, and waves of nausea assaulted her dazed senses. She attempted to slide off of him but he had her pinned against the steering wheel, which was now digging painfully into her mid and lower back. Eyes bulging out of their sockets in her struggle to breathe, she found it hard to continue her fight to free herself from his iron grip, his hands, once so gentle and tender, were now squeezing the very life out of her. The more she tried to fight him, the more aroused he became, the vicious and violent cycle repeating its deadly dance, time and time again. The last thing that Beth saw was the dark, almost demonic look in Drew's once beautiful eyes, death imminent upon her by then. With her life forever extinguished, she sagged against him, the sudden heaviness of her lifeless body causing his erect penis to painfully twist to one side. With a series of irritated "fucks" directed at situation at hand and the arrogant and self-assured smirk instantly erased from his otherwise very sensual lips, he unceremoniously pushed the girl's limp body to the right. The rough move caused him to cry out in pain as his penis momentarily bent even further, upsetting him to no end. A litany of curses soon followed as a wave of excruciating pain assailed him. Once more, he walked over to the passenger side of the car and literally yanked the heavy door wide open. Unceremoniously pulling her slender legs out of the vehicle, he crudely spread them apart and, without preamble, tried to enter her. Even though she was very moist from having desired him so much not long before, he wasn't able to penetrate her during his first attempt. Swearing like a drunken sailor, he had to try quite a few more times before he could feel himself fully inside the unusually tight space. Another barrage of curses was issued as he felt her flesh rip around his enormous penis. This time, however, it took him a few deep thrusts, but the explosion of sensations and the waves of pleasure that soon flooded his brain made all the extra effort well worth the wait. For a few seconds, he debated whether or not he should go for a second climax, since his penis seemed to refuse to go down but, in the end, he ultimately decided against it. Better safe than sorry, he was fond of saying, and he didn't want to risk getting caught, not now, not ever. After all, the extraordinary orgasm he had just experienced was probably worth ten regular ones. The fact that his penis was covered in blood, an indication that the poor girl was probably still a virgin, didn't affect him at all, one way or the other. He sat Beth upright once more, straightening her clothes before he fastened her seatbelt snuggly around her chest and lap, just like he had done with Nicole. He drove to Cheshire, a town about forty minutes away from where they had "made love," being sure to stay well within the posted speed limit. He wanted plenty off distance between where he had killed her and where he would ultimately get rid of her body, mentally going over every detail with a fine tooth comb. *No margin for errors here! None whatsoever, not now or in the future!* Extremely thorough in his way of thinking, he wanted to make sure that he left no traces behind that could somehow, someday, link the girl's disappearance and death back to him. Upon reaching Cheshire, he drove directly to a park adjacent to the town's high school. He dumped her body behind some rhododendron bushes, tossing her black lacy panties next to her head, her denim jeans pulled to her narrow hips, leaving her pubic hair partially exposed above her unzipped pants. Her jeans were caked with blood between her legs and on the seat of her pants, a fact that did not register with him at all. He didn't even have the slightest hint of remorse on his conscience whatsoever over having robbed the poor girl of her virginity as well as of her life. He drove all the way back to Shelton at a steady fifty-five miles per hour. Fortunately, his mother had already gone to bed by the time he got home. Going directly to his room, he reached under the bed and retrieved his precious metal box, where he deposited his latest memento with great pomposity and satisfaction. It had become a well rehearsed and revered ritual for him as he continued to add to his continually expanding eclectic collection of memorable mementos. He often went through the contents in his "treasure box," deriving enormous pleasure and satisfaction at the memory that each item revived, and he counted on the box to brighten his day whenever he was feeling down or bored. Pulling off his clothes, he put on a clean pair of boxer shorts and a cotton T-shirt. He would make sure to carefully wash the blood out of his dirty ones first thing in the morning with some peroxide, an easy enough way to remove blood stains, before tossing them into the hamper. He would also add a pile of dirty clothes to the wet ones for added precaution, which could always be found in a heap on his closet floor. He was fast asleep even before his head had the chance to hit his pillow. He woke up late the following day with a tremendous erection still. His thoughts automatically drifted back to the previous night, and his unbelievable encounter with the sweet yet sexy Beth and her little tight jewel. He experienced an exhilarating high as he once again realized that his hands had the power of life and death over another human being. That high turned into raw, unleashed sexual energy, and he ejaculated even before he had a chance to touch himself. He was beyond totally hooked by the time he went out with his third victim; no turning back now. His hunger for the ecstasy that followed each encounter continued to grow like a powerful drug, one that his body never seemed to have enough of.

The third girl, Meghan was her name if he remembered it correctly, he had again met at the mall, her long red hair and bright green eyes catching his fancy immediately. He first noticed her when she came into the mall via the JC Penney entrance, carrying at least three large bags from that same store. He followed her at a safe distance, stopping here and there in order to make believe that he was looking at something so that it wouldn't become noticeable to anyone around that he was actually following the beautiful girl. He kept his eyes on her whereabouts, never letting her off his sight. He was definitely on the prowl, and it had become sort of a game, making him feel like a dangerous, famished, lean and mean black panther. He managed to "accidently" bump into the stunning girl as they both approached the escalator going down to the ground level. With a smile oozing nothing but pure charm on his handsome face, he tried to sound very sincere as he apologized for the incident. He teasingly told her that her beauty was to blame for his lack of attention, clearly flirting with the pretty teen. The poor girl was instantly hooked from that point on. The sequence of events that followed that first "casual" encounter was basically the same as with the previous two girls. DJ, however, was slightly disappointed that she didn't fight quite as hard as he would have liked her to, when the actual final encounter occurred after at least a half dozen perfectly harmonized dates. Perhaps the completely smitten girl was simply too scared to fight back since, until then, she hadn't had any reason whatsoever to fear her impeccably well-behaved companion, he reasoned. Or it could have been that he simply caught her totally by surprise, thus giving her no time to react at all. The ultimate fact, though, was that she didn't start to react until his strong hands had already started to exert the powerful pressure they were so capable of, thus far beyond any possible defense on her part. After he was done with her, he drove directly to a filthy, dark, and narrow alley in a questionable neighborhood in Orange, where he quickly disposed of her body next to a dumpster. Covering her with a few cardboard boxes before taking off, he again left without a single look back, for that was no longer anything in the alleyway that interested him in the least. That third conquest lead to a fourth, and each encounter was even better than the one before, always blowing his mind and boosting his sense of power and engorged ego. Each girl surprised him in her own unique way, far surpassing even his wildest expectations, blessed their little hearts, and each orgasm was far more intense than the previous ones, if that was even possible. As his power over his "lovers" grew, so did his ultimate reward . . .

Unfortunately, as his level of pleasure increased, so did his cruelty and violence toward his victims. The fourth one, Carly, who worked part-time as an aerobics instructor, was in excellent physical shape, and fought DJ off much harder than any of the previous ones were ever able to. She defended herself so fiercely that, for once, he did not feel as confident about his own power over every woman this time around, something that had been unquestionable until then. Not only was Carly stronger, she wasn't as petite in stature as he usually liked, being quite taller and muscular than any of the others. Frustrated by his difficulty in subduing his feisty victim as swiftly as he wished to, he unleashed his full wrath against the twenty-one-year-old like he had never done before. Death must have come as a release from her suffering once she was overpowered by the unscrupulous killer. It was evident by the huge bruises, welts, and scrapes covering her arms and upper legs as well as her entire genital area. Both of her wrists had turned deep purple and blue in color all around after DJ had pinned them behind her back with every ounce of strength he could muster. Completely mindless of her pitiful cries for mercy, he continued to inflict great pain upon his terrified captive. Her emotional agony must've been of unimaginable and unbearable cruelty, probably much more so than any physical pain he could further deliver to her already battered and broken body. Many ugly bite marks covered her breasts and abdomen, blood having oozed from some of them. Even her ears had been bitten, teeth imprints clearly detected among the dark purplish hue of her earlobes. Several vaginal tears and vulva lacerations completed a picture of a brutality extremely hard to fathom and not seen on any of the previous ones. It wasn't until the poor girl was no longer breathing that DJ was able to finally regain his full sense of power, his most addictive vice by far. With his perceived manhood restored by ultimately regaining control of the situation, his attention immediately switched to the still unfinished task at hand. With his feeling of unmatched power quickly escalating into a sexual frenzy, his effort culminated into multiple orgasmic spasms, leaving him feeling as exhausted as he felt exhilarated and fulfilled. With all those emotions all rolled up into one, he felt on top of the world–cleverly capable, masterfully unstoppable, and fearful of absolutely no one. At least that is how he chose to view himself even though the real truth was nothing like that, mastering nothing more than a large dose of unadulterated cowardice under all that false bravado. He seemed to have absorbed more energy and become even less concerned with the damage he inflicted upon his victims with each consecutive attack. It was a lethal combination that had the potential of doling out much more torture, tragedy, and terror than what had been witnessed until then, should he continue to successfully elude capture. Considering himself the best at his craft, he was already looking forward to the next time, his ferocious appetite multiplying at an alarming rate of speed. Taking on a disturbingly unnecessary brutal undertone, the level of his incredible violence became a source of great concern to the authorities involved in trying to solve the baffling cases. Unfortunately for his victims, they were quite far from finding out who the serial killer was. They had nothing on him even though he became their primary "most wanted" criminal by far.

Having learned his lesson with Carly, DJ became much more careful with the girls he chose to "interact" with from that point on. Both his fifth and sixth victims were very slim and quite shorter than him, just the way he liked it. Kim, whom he met at a carnival in New Haven, was very friendly and outgoing. He liked the way her curly light brown hair framed her angel-like face. Her engaging smile managed to illuminate her features with the magnetic power it projected from within, while her well proportioned figure had him hooked the moment he spotted her walking around all alone. In less than five minutes, he had her fully engaged in trivial conversation, her light green eyes never leaving her smiling face. The fact that she immediately agreed to leave the noisy chaos of the carnival grounds for a quieter, more private setting, had him literally walking on air. That casual encounter was innocent enough to secure an official first date, during which he found out a little more about the charming twenty-year-old. She told her handsome and very attentive companion that she worked part-time at the Linens 'n Things store in Milford and was a full-time student at Gateway Community College in New Haven. That date led to a few more, and by the time Kim realized what was happening, it was already too late, for the world had ceased to exist for the pretty young girl. Emma, on the other hand, had captivated him from the get go. Her shiny and dark blonde hair reached below her tiny waist, and her vibrant hazel eyes were a perfect complement to her light olive complexion. Only seventeen, she was the perfect age to be swiped off her feet by a masterful older guy. A beauty on the making, her petite frame was exactly the way he liked, and her inexperience a quality that worked totally in his favor. The top of her head only reached to his chest, and yet she fit inside his arms as if she had been tailor-made to be embraced by him. When he told her that, she went mellow with desire, just as he knew that she would. Of all the girls he had the privilege of "dating," Emma was by far the prettiest. What a shame that they would have to end their blossoming "love" story much before she could ever have anticipated.

He never lost a single night's sleep over any of his victims, continuing to live his charmed and carefree lifestyle to its fullness. Sure his grandfather's death had affected him, he couldn't deny that, but he had needs that had to be met, his hunger for power the strongest driving force behind every action he took. He was already working on his newest conquest, an oriental little thing called Jasmine, when his surprising arrest had taken place. And to think that he had been more cautious than ever before this time around made him laugh at the irony of it all. He had been the model of patience and had waited until the timing and conditions surrounding the final strike were all above and beyond perfection in order to proceed with his well-thought-out plan of action. He was all set to meet with Jasmine on the same evening he was arrested. That would certainly never happen if his "devoted" mother hadn't gone meddling in his affairs. "Judas," he hissed, contempt for her momentarily overpowering his usually well-reigned-in emotions and behavior. With a little effort on his part, he quickly regained control of them once more. Being able to remain cool and collected at all times had served him well throughout the years, enabling him to get away with every endeavor he had tried to accomplish with relative ease. He was not about to relinquish this gift to anyone, not then or ever.

The perky brunette would've been the perfect "date," he was certain of, for she was petite, was very young, and seemed to be on the innocent side–a triple grand prize if he ever saw one. There was so much he was more than willing to teach Jasmine. Even the sound of her name pleased him. They could have had a fabulous time together had he not been so rudely interrupted by his own mother and those sons of bitches police officers. "There was so much that I wanted to share with you, my little oriental jewel. It is a shame that I didn't get a chance to! Unfortunately for both of us, we were deprived of our right to go on our special adventure together and by events that we simply had no power over. I was really looking forward to getting to know you better, I swear. Scout's honor and all that," he whispered, filled with false and misplaced regret. Brooding about what could've been would serve no purpose for him whatsoever, so why waste precious energy on something he could never change or achieve anyway? he prudently realized. He was way better off thinking of more pleasant things, and there were plenty of those to occupy his mind for the rest of his natural life, little tidbits that only he was privileged enough to know.

He was so involved in reminiscing about such pleasurable events and times, that he failed to notice they had arrived at their final destination until they were already there. Neither did he realize that he had become fully aroused while lost in his forage into the past. The guards, however, who were responsible for his safe escort from the prison to the courthouse and then back again, missed absolutely nothing; after all, they were trained to do exactly that. Once inside the compound and with the heavy iron gates securely locked behind them, they wasted no time in ushering DJ out of the back of the van, noticing his state of full sexual arousal the second he set foot on the ground. There was also what appeared to be a large amount of ejaculated fluid on the front of his jumpsuit as well. Between a barrage of curt commands and crude remarks, they urged their charge to move faster–*if his present condition allowed*, they added sarcastically*, taking great pleasure at the chance to mock him. They were quick to remind him not to try doing anything stupid or he would have to pay the consequences later, their voices barely disguising their amusement at his obvious state of discomposure. They smirked behind his back, wondering what the hell had happened during their relatively short one-hour trip from the courthouse to the prison to cause their illustrious guest to become so visibly aroused. They understood that he had plenty of time to masturbate, but they also knew that it was an almost impossible thing to do with both of his hands handcuffed behind his back unless he was Houdini or someone like that. *You ingenious little bastard. How in hell did you manage to pull this one off? We would indeed love to find out how* *you did it, old champ. You either have a very long dick or an incredible set of flexible hands and fingers. Which one is it, pretty boy?* they wondered, literally scratching their heads over the mysterious feat. They crudely grabbed at their own crotches, running their hands up and down the length of their penises in a flagrant attempt to imitate the act of masturbation. Laughing among themselves, they took immense pleasure mocking the young man they hardly knew and didn't really care to. In their position as guards in a maximum security facility, they had been exposed to all types of criminals. Some of the acts that many were ultimately convicted of having committed were so heinous in nature that, over a period of time, most of the guards became desensitized to practically every act imaginable. Those crimes carried out by real hardcore inmates against their poor and defenseless victims were a common fact among the prison population. When all was said and done, however, those same guards were still part of the human race, even though they often wondered if some of the incarcerated men they had to look after were also human as well, for they acted as if they were not most of the time. All of the guards had completely different lives outside the prison and certainly had mothers, wives or girlfriends, daughters, sisters, or a varied combination of all four. If any of these same correctional officers had the slightest inkling as to the reason behind Drew's obvious state of sexual excitement, they would be hard-pressed to find any reason to laugh so loud, if at all. Some acts were just too disconcerting, too cruel and macabre, for even these tough-as-nails guards to digest. Yes, if they had any idea of the particulars of DJ's crimes and of the sick fact that every single girl he had attacked was already dead by the time he brutally violated them, they would be hard-pressed to find any reason to laugh at all.

*   *   *

With the weight of the world seeming to have settled upon her hunched shoulders and her numb legs simply refusing to sustain her beaten body, Jill remained seated until almost everyone had the chance to leave the courtroom. She hoped that by waiting so long she would be able to safely exit without being noticed. After about what felt like a lifetime to her, she managed to stand up, trying to leave as quietly as possible, but it turned out to be something far more difficult to accomplish than she had anticipated. A pack of perpetually news-hungry reporters who had obviously stayed behind waiting for her to emerge from the building, descended upon the unsuspecting mother the minute they spotted her. Like a school of starving sharks during the ferocious act of a feeding frenzy, and without the slightest sense of respect, decency, or pity for her deeply hurting soul, they proceeded to shove several microphones directly in Jill's ashen face. They immediately began to shout a barrage of questions she was in no condition to answer and had absolutely no intention of doing so anyway. In the meantime, several photographers clicked away with their high-powered cameras, in their eagerness to capture that one particular shot that was sure to pay them big bucks when sold to the highest bidder. With tears threatening to spill from her sad eyes and down her sunken cheeks, and a "no comment" automatically on her trembling lips, she raised both of her arms in front of her face. In a feeble attempt of self-protection, Jill bent her head, literally fighting her way through the dense crowd who demanded even more from the already destroyed mother. It was a tough struggle to reach the safety of her car as quickly as she could, a task she found to be much easier said than done. Finally able to get to where she had parked, she opened the driver's door with fingers that shook so much that it ended up taking her far too long to unlock it. In her haste, she managed to drop her keys a couple of times before she was ultimately able to successfully get the darn door open. Once inside the car, she didn't even stop long enough to fasten her seatbelt; so desperate was she to get away from them as fast as humanly possible. She desperately needed to get far away from all those unfeeling people who simply didn't give a damn about what she was going through and who didn't appear to care, one way or the other. They would not think twice about whether or not they were further wounding her as long as they got the scoop. They wouldn't think twice about drawing blood if it served them well in the process. There was no compassion, no empathy, no morals to speak of, she reflected, greatly repulsed at the level they were obviously willing to stoop in order to get the story, which was a sorry reflection on some members of our society. They seemed totally unfazed about the price that the object of their interest had to ultimately pay, their eagerness to get the story out ahead of any of their competitors the only thing that really mattered to them in the interim. She drove off without looking back, in total disgust. If she had, she would have noticed the dark shadow following her so close behind, the shadow of a totally beaten mother's failed hopes and dreams. The hopes and dreams she once had for her family, for herself, but above all, for her son, the person she loved most in her entire world and now the source of such deep consternation and pain. The preciousness of life and living were slowly ebbing away, starting with DJ's, she sadly admitted, realizing that hers was not that far behind. "Why, son? Why did you do that to those poor, innocent girls? I just don't understand how you could have done what you did. How could you DJ? Why and how, son? Why? How?"

CHAPTER 16

At home, Jill felt like she was as much a prisoner as her son, who was behind bars for the rest of his natural life. Every time she turned on the television, flashes of DJ's handsome face filled the screen, usually alternating with the pictures of his young victims, a constant reminder of the horrific crimes he committed in the span of three long years. For the distraught mother, it was an unendingly and excruciatingly painful nightmare that had just begun, and her anguish only in its early stage, an unbelievable amount of suffering still yet to come. Try as she might, there was no way of escaping the brutal reality that her own son was the sole person responsible for acts of unfathomed cruelty and unprecedented torture against so many innocent young women. It tore Jill apart to imagine the level of raw pain and fear that the poor girls were subjected to before being killed; that knowledge alone soon began to chisel away at whatever was left of her wounded soul. The fact that the infamous serial killer who singlehandedly managed to elude the authorities for nearly three years had finally been apprehended and convicted, dominated every major newscast and newspaper from coast to coast, driving the truth home to his poor mother with undeniable vengeance. The fact that he was a charismatic, polite, and very handsome young man only served to add fuel to the fire his crimes had created, causing many to question the validity of his final sentence. Had he been of average looks, he would have gotten the death penalty most of the population knew he deserved six times over. However, it was the way in which he was caught, being turned in by his own mother which had mitigated the outcome of the totally unbelievable case. It was common knowledge that the vast majority of the country was extremely grateful to Mrs. Millner for unselfishly having found the strength and courage to ultimately do the right thing, even if it had meant turning her own child in to the authorities. Her actions were something that the majority of parents like her would probably not have been able to do in spite of their best intentions, no matter how fair they might have tried to be.

As it was, cries of injustice were heard everywhere, intermingled with widespread outrage, especially over the fact that DJ didn't receive the death penalty, which most felt he more than deserved. The barbarity of the crimes he was convicted of having committed were such that everyone questioned felt that he certainly merited a double dose of the lethal injection, to say the very least. Stories of how well this person or that one knew the young serial killer quickly sprouted from the lips of people who had never even met him. It became the only topic of conversation in many diners and fast food establishments in the Shelton area and all the surrounding towns. Each storyteller tried to outdo the previous one, their tales being paraded around as if they were something to be proud of or worthy of being paid attention to. The details naturally got more and more exaggerated with each recounting of a particular encounter or incident, with the majority way off the mark as far as the real truth went. The circuslike atmosphere created by the cases ended up affecting those closest to DJ in a personally destructive and heart-wrenching manner. Jill's doorbell was now disconnected after days of nonstop ringing by curious people she had never seen before and never wanted to see again. She stopped picking up the telephone as well, letting the answering machine do the job for her. She lifted the receiver only if she recognized who the caller was, and even then she was extremely selective as to whom she would actually speak with. Eventually the answering machine reached its capacity, becoming so full that it stopped recording any of the consecutive messages after that. Before long, she ended up taking the phone off the hook altogether, letting it run out of charge once and for all.

Her family tried hard to reach out and support her, all the while simultaneously still grieving for William. Totally overwhelmed by DJ's actions, they were often assailed by such conflicting feelings that they didn't know how to react any longer. On one hand, there was the deep love they still felt for the fatherless boy who grew up to be such a charming and polite young man. On the other, they felt totally betrayed by him, all the while feeling utterly disgusted by the magnitude and the callousness of the crimes he was now behind bars for. Shame, more than anything else, made an already difficult situation seem insurmountable and impossible to comprehend. The sympathy they felt for the innocent young victims and their suffering families far outweighed their mortally wounded love for DJ. Jill tried to see her son on several occasions, always making the trip filled with great hope that he would finally agree to see her, but she always left the prison with her heart shattered. The second he was told who his visitor was, he flatly refused to even leave his cell, suddenly becoming agitated and downright vicious, shouting for all to hear that he no longer had a mother. No matter how often she made the trip to the jail, he made it very clear that he would never give her the satisfaction of thinking that he wanted to see her again. "She can rot in hell, for all I care! She certainly deserves no less, if I have any saying on the matter. Tell her to stop wasting her time and mine once and for all. As far as I am concerned, she is dead!" he curtly instructed the guard who usually came for him. After several more unsuccessful attempts, Jill eventually realized that he meant every single word he said and stopped trying to see her beloved child ever again, hoping that he would someday forgive her just long enough to give her a second chance. It ripped her apart, but she knew that she had no other choice but to abide by his wishes, when all she wanted more than anything else was to cradle her son in her loving arms again, just like she used to when he was just a child. She missed the days when he had been simply her little boy.

*   *   *

Jill refused all attempts made by her concerned mother and siblings to reach out to her. Her best friend, Marissa, worried out of her mind about her as well, made it a point to stop by the house almost daily since DJ was convicted, only to be met by a front door that remained shut. Knowing how deeply Jill must be hurting, she persisted in her efforts to help her, but eventually even Marissa had no choice but to accept Jill's decision to work through her grief alone, at least for the time being anyway. Unfortunately, she came to the painful realization that there was absolutely nothing else she could do but to respect her best friend's wishes. She prayed that God would continue to remain by the hurting mother every step of the way, guiding her back to some semblance of emotional stability, for He was probably the only one who could offer any kind of help to Jill during her hour of need. A mother of three by then, Marissa more than empathized with her distraught friend. DJ was not only her godson but someone she loved as if he was her own son, suffering right along with his mother and family ever since the news of his involvement in all those horrific crimes was first revealed. She sincerely hoped that Jill would be able to hold on long enough to allow the healing process to take root and to begin to evolve from the inside out.

Even Jack, who probably spoke with Jill more often than anyone else on the days following DJ's arrest and subsequent trial, had hardly been able to get in touch with her following his conviction. For the last two weeks, to his great disconcertment, all his calls to her weren't answered, and she never came to the door whenever he stopped by. Just like Marissa had to, he also came to the sad realization that he had no choice but to abide by Jill's wish to be left alone. Knowing her as well as he did, he was aware that absolutely no one could make Jill do anything she didn't want to. As much as he loved her, and he certainly did, he knew better than to push too hard or too soon. Her message to all of them had been loud and clear, whether or not they agreed with it. She needed time away from everyone and everything in order to get a handle on the overwhelming pain that had become her only companion since that fateful day when she had turned against her own son. Yes, she had done the right thing, but that was of little comfort to her now that she knew he would never be coming home again. His bedroom remained as empty as her godforsaken soul.

As the days slowly turned into weeks, Jill began to spend more and more time in bed, with the window blinds closed in order to shut out the world that had been so cruel to her. In total darkness, she held a picture of her formerly happy family clutched tightly against her chest. In the picture, taken during the very first Christmas after DJ was born, Jill and Drew were simply beaming for the camera as they tenderly embraced their happy seven-month-old son, who contentedly sat between his proud parents. "If I could only turn back the clock and return to this time," she often cried. "We were so full of joy then and on top of the world. I had my Drew and our DJ. And now, Drew is gone and so is DJ. Why did it have to be so? What did I ever do to deserve such punishment?" Her Drew, her better half, the only man she had ever truly loved with her whole heart, had been taken from her in such a tragic way that she had never quite recovered from. Even now, twenty long years later, his death remained one of the two saddest days of her entire life. Yes, she did care about Jack, and how could she not? He was, after all, a very caring and loving man and had woven his way into her heart, through friendship at first and then through his kindness and caring ways. Yes, she did grow to love him in time, but she would never love again like she had loved Drew. That kind of love came around once in a lifetime to a lucky few, and she had been one of them. And then DJ, the person whom she cherished above and beyond all else in her entire world and who had been taken away from her as well but not before he had a chance to inflict unimaginable anguish, horror, and suffering to so many others. "Why, DJ? Why, my darling son? Why, why, why . . ."

Soon Jill forgot to eat on a regular basis, and bathing became less and less important to her, nothing more than a chore she'd rather skip. She began to lose weight at an alarming rate even though she could hardly afford to. Grooming being the last thing on her mind, her blonde hair, once luxuriously thick and shiny, became a dull and lifeless mass of tangles and knots in no time at all. In her bed, still holding onto the picture she stared at but no longer saw, Jill slowly allowed her tormented mind and soul to completely obliterate any and all reasonable thinking. Jillian Elizabeth Millner, the youngest daughter of the late William Richard and Sophia Marie Chandler, loving sister of Daniel, Nicholas, and Tara, loving wife of the late Drew James Millner, adoring mother of Drew William Millner Jr., devoted daughter-in-law of Raymond Joseph and Deborah Christine Millner, caring sister-in-law of Phillip and Hannah, and caring aunt to several nieces and nephews, loved by more people than she could ever imagine, suddenly wasn't alive any longer, even though she continued to breathe and her heart went on beating still. In her place, a shadow of her former self lay wasting away in self-imposed exile. And life, as she had once known, ceased to exist altogether.

Sophia, extremely worried about her youngest daughter, tried repeatedly to get in touch with her, leaving message after message on her answering machine, none of which were ever returned. Jill's siblings and close friends continued to stop by the house on numerous occasions, ringing the doorbell repeatedly, but the front door remained closed. No one realized that Jill had disconnected the doorbell soon after DJ's conviction because she could not handle the number of times that it was rung every single day. She grew so angry with the constant intrusion that she simply decided to get rid of the offensive thing altogether, just as she did with the telephone, which she simply decided to keep off the hook. Sophia was aware that her poor daughter was hurting deeply but could never have imagined the full extent of her suffering. At Jill's doorstep one morning, she again rang the bell repeatedly, her apprehension multiplying tenfold with each second that went by. When she got no answer as usual, she started to pound on the solid wood and glass door with her small fist, trying to get through to her daughter who she was determined to see this time, came hell or high water. Her apprehension soon turned to a mixture of sheer frustration and raw panic when the door remained shut still. Her inability to get to Jill had taken a heavy toll on the worried mother. Not about to turn around and leave as she had done almost every day for a few weeks already, Sophia finally reached her breaking point, realizing that the current situation couldn't go on like that any longer. No matter what she had to do, she was more determined than ever to get to her daughter, but how? Not knowing what else to do, she got back in her car and drove to the nearest police station she knew. Shaking with fear, she begged the officer at the front desk to please allow her to speak to the person in charge. The young cop must've seen something in the older woman's eyes that convinced him, for he placed a quick phone call before escorting her to Sergeant Warner's office. After listening to her tale for a few minutes, the seasoned officer tried to explain to Sophia that, unfortunately, there wasn't much the police could do since no law had been broken and that choosing not to answer a door was not a crime. But she wasn't about to be swayed by his words and wouldn't be deterred by anyone or anything no matter how hard she had to argue on her daughter's behalf. *Not this time!* She silently vowed, both of her small hands balled into tight fists and shaking with the sheer strength of her conviction. Her motherly intuition told her that something was drastically wrong with her child, and she was going to find out exactly what it was, regardless of what she had to ultimately do to accomplish that. She was so firm in her belief that Sergeant Warner finally caved in just to appease the distraught lady. Sophia was so thankful and relieved that she impulsively hugged the veteran cop without even thinking about it, causing both of them to blush but for totally different reasons.

Within a few minutes, a Shelton police cruiser was following Sophia's car back to her daughter's house. As the seasoned officer got out of the car, he automatically began to scan around the property, his trained eyes trying to find some indication that anything was out of the ordinary outside the sprawling residence. The overgrown flower gardens were the first thing that caught his eye, followed by the sight of overripe and spoiled tomatoes pooled around the bases of their vines, all of which had turned yellow and brown by the lack of watering. Peeking through the two large windows facing the front yard, he saw nothing out of the ordinary inside the quiet and undisturbed living and dining rooms. Walking toward the back, he headed straight to the rear door. Unable to hear any kind of noise coming from inside the house, he decided to break the large glass panel insert that took over a good portion of the solid oak door in order to gain access inside the eerily silent place. Finding himself in the laundry and mudrooms, he stopped for a second to check a bedroom that had been turned into an office at the very rear of the house. Finding it empty, he then checked the half bath adjacent to the mudroom. Suddenly, he was overwhelmed by the pungent odor of decaying and rotten food, which was the first indication that something was indeed not right there. Moldy remnants of uneaten meals overflowed from the top of the kitchen trash can, a mixture of spoiled food and garbage spreading in great heaps all around the overpacked container. The numerous houseplants on the expansive window sill, according to Sophia her daughter's pride and joy, had all dried up and stood in odd contrast against the brightly colored ceramic pots they had been placed in. Brown and lifeless from total lack of watering and care, they had lost most of their leaves, which had fallen from the plants and lay scattered all over the oak sill and on the floor in front of the large bow window. It was, however, the putrid stench emanating from the master bedroom located at the end of the long hallway that caused both Sophia and the seasoned police officer to actually gag. Fearful of what he might find once he turned on the lights in the pitch-dark room, Sergeant Warner carefully entered it ahead of Sophia. Judging from the odor alone, he could almost visualize a body laying dead somewhere inside the room. He felt much more afraid for the mother, who walked with uncertain steps just inches behind him, than for himself. He had been a cop for forty of his sixty-one years, therefore he had encountered all kinds of sad and scary situations, but this one had him really spooked and shaking on the inside. Once he turned on the lights, though, he felt an overwhelming need to shut them off again as quickly as he could, thus sparing Sophia from what he had just seen. The heart-wrenching scene right in front of him was so devastating that he would never be able to erase it from his memory, and far worse than he had ever anticipated or prepared for. It tore right through his armor, and he had to fight hard to maintain his composure and professional demeanor, images of his grown children instantly crowding his mind and shattering his fatherly heart. Being a police officer was set aside for the time being, for the horrible drama contained inside the dismal room caused his eyes to instantly fill with tears. He was horrified by the sight he wished he didn't have to see but had to face head on. However, it was a sight of such devastating proportions that he knew he would never forget it.

In the middle of the filthy, rumbled bed, a fragile, emaciated, and cachectic Jill laid in a large pool of her own excrements, her eyes open but clearly unseeing and not moving at all. The overpowering smell of urine, feces, and unwashed human flesh permeated throughout the confined space, making it nearly impossible to breathe. Jill still held onto the picture she had grown to love so much, the smiling faces of the three happy people captured there in heartbreaking contrast with the human suffering that lay motionless in the middle of the huge bed. Those young radiant faces were the only hint of the kind of happiness that this poor woman had once possessed but had lost quite a while before. With eyes that had long stopped really seeing, her vacant stare was fixed on the ceiling right above her head. Those eyes which appeared to be even bluer than before, seemed to be totally out of place against the ashen background of their surroundings. Directly below her unblinking eyes, dark circles literally took up half of her small face while sunken cheeks further accentuated the skylike hue of their shade. They were the only hint of color to be found in the pale–and gray-toned skin of her face and neck. Even her dry and cracked lips were devoid of any hint of color, seeming to just blend in with the rest of her features. The hands holding the beloved picture were so small and thin that their skin had become translucent, faint blue veins easily visible even from afar. Her nails, having grown very long, curved over the tip of her slender fingers, their base a sickly shade of gray. Fecal material was seen underneath every single one of those nails, deeply imbedded and beyond dried up; God only knew how long she had been in such deplorable condition. *The hands of a very old person*, Sophia thought with a painful knot at the pit of her stomach, afraid that she wouldn't be able stop herself from the urge to recoil from such a pitiful sight. It was the sight of her youngest child's imminent demise, she realized with tremendous sadness, her heart being decimated as quickly as her soul. "Oh, Jill," her mother cried out in horror, no longer able to control the tears that began to fall down her cheeks, loud sobs taking over her trembling body as she cradled her child in her aching arms. "Oh, Jill," she repeated over and over again, unable to handle the haunting scene that her eyes refused not to see, in spite of how many times she begged them not to. Her mind continued take in excruciatingly detail the full scope of her daughter's misery, every nuance, every nook and cranny, every declining step. And even though she found it absolutely unbearable to witness and ultimately acknowledge what had really taken place, Sophia forced herself accept her part in it. The depth of Jill's agony and the utter devastation that it evoked was a much-needed wake-up call to her numb but guilt-ridden soul. How could she have allowed this horrible situation to go on as long as it did? she now berated herself.

"What has happened to you, Jill? How could things have gotten to this point? You never let go before, not even after you lost your husband and your dad. But DJ, that was another story, wasn't it, darling? I know, my love, I am a mother too! I could have helped you, you know? And I should have helped you, sweetheart, even if you refused my offer to do so. The fact that you simply wouldn't let me in should've been a red flag, and now I hate myself for not having been more persistent, sweetheart. You shut me out like you did everyone and everything else around you, but I'm your mother. I should have tried harder and didn't, and that is something that is going to haunt me for the rest of my life. Why didn't I, my little girl? Why . . ." Sophia agonized, her voice drowned by the sound of her wrenching sobs. Unbearable pain was literally splitting her heart into a million pieces, each one clawing at her like the paws of a beast called a mother's sense of helplessness and guilt. Chastising herself for not having intervened much sooner, she fervently prayed that she wasn't too late already. "Bill," she whispered, talking to her late husband as if he was sitting right there next to her, "please, just stay by our daughter's side. Don't let go of her hand, not even for a second, or we will lose her forever. Hold on to daddy's little girl, please darling, and help her now, since I failed so miserably at doing so," she went on, her head bowed in total defeat. "And Lord," she continued, her voice cracking with each word she spoke, "have mercy on my child, I beg of you. Don't let my daughter suffer any longer. She has suffered so much already in her short life. She needs you far more than she needs me. Please, dear Lord, carry my child in your loving arms now that she can no longer walk by herself. I beg you, Lord, please carry her until she can stand on her own again," she concluded, her thin voice slightly above a murmur by then.

Sergeant Warner made no effort to hide the tears streaming down his face, for the scene was just too traumatic even for the veteran cop to handle. Jill Millner's act of courage and sacrifice as she turned her only child into the authorities a few months before was a well-known fact in every police precinct in the State of Connecticut. Every law enforcement officer he knew was extremely fond of the young mother, holding her with the highest level of awe and respect. They also owed her their genuine gratitude for having helped them to finally break the baffling case, which had until then failed to yield any clues as to the identity of the perpetrator. And to see the price that this courageous woman ended up paying in order to make sure that her son never had the chance to harm or kill another person again simply broke his heart to pieces. He had felt such admiration for the young mother at the time, the same woman who was now less than a shadow of her old self, laying in a cesspool of oblivion and neglect. He walked back into the kitchen in order to summon an emergency vehicle to 175 Rydell Drive, trying hard to regain control of his emotions. He instructed the dispatcher to tell the driver not to use any sirens as they approached the address that was given, for he intended to honor Jill's need for privacy even if it turned out to be for the last time. After shutting off his police radio, he slowly walked over to where Sophia sat tenderly stroking her daughter's fragile hand. Sitting besides the heartbroken mother, he gently placed his left arm around her frail shoulders. The police academy certainly never prepared any cadet to handle a heartbreaking case such as this one, by far the saddest he had ever seen. He was lost among all the feelings trampling through his mind at the time, with sympathy, empathy, and helplessness just a fraction of what he felt as he looked at both mother and daughter. What he failed to realize though, was that he had already done much more than he would ever know, for he had taken the time to listen to a desperate mother's worries about her child at a time when Sophia had needed to be heard the most. What a wonderful gift the art of truly listening was, when one person gave another their full attention, thus really paying attention to what they were saying; it was a gift that most went without giving or receiving. Thank God Sergeant Warner and Sophia were not among them.

Even though he still wasn't sure if Jill was going to make it or not, Sergeant Warner shuddered at the thought that this beautiful woman's life could have easily come to a horrible end had her mother not insisted that he listen to her concerns. Thank God her persistence had ultimately paid off, for she got the help she was sure her daughter desperately needed and hopefully just in the nick of time. And to think that he almost sent her away, dismissing her worries as being just like all the others he had heard before from so many overprotective parents. Her pleas, however, had been so genuine that they were able to tear down the wall of doubt her incredible tale had forced him to erect, for the sake of objectivity and self-preservation. With only her premonition to go by, most officers would've simply tried to calm her down before dismissing her, giving no credence to her fears unless they had more concrete reason to; a mother's intuition alone was hardly enough to get anything done. It was, after all, this same wall of doubt honed in by many decades in the police force that allowed officers to remain objective and to view each case and analyze each situation based on something quite more viable than mere hunches. In this instance though, Sergeant Warner was beyond grateful for Sophia's persistence as well as his increasing gut feeling that the peril she described was indeed real. And Mrs. Chandler, bless her heart, had not given up, begging him not to dismiss her concerns as unimportant, as nothing more than the product of an overactive imagination or the ravings of an overzealous mother. God only knew how officers everywhere were daily confronted with cases similar to this one only to find out that they were fortunately not always warranted. That was why there was such a high level of skepticism among the police force at large and with plenty of reason. Sergeant Warner was glad that for once he had allowed his heart to override his rules. He would never have forgiven himself had he sent Mrs. Chandler away only to find out later that Jill Millner had starved herself to death.

Once the paramedics got there, Sergeant Warner politely pulled one of them aside and asked him to be kind enough and allow Mrs. Chandler to ride in the back of the ambulance with them. The overwrought mother simply refused to allow her daughter out of her sight, and he sincerely believed that Jill would fare much better if her mother remained by her side, talking to her as she was being rushed to the nearest hospital. God only knew whether she was going to survive or not, so why not prolong whatever time she had left with her mother. This could turn out to be a situation where every second really mattered to both. Reticent at first, the paramedic finally relented when Sophia's determination to be by her daughter's side didn't abate no matter how hard he tried to talk her out of it. When Sergeant Warner was finally able to get back to his patrol car, he just sat quietly for quite a while, still trying to deal with the trauma and shock the entire incident evoked in his heart and mind. His emotional status had taken a beating, and he was sure that he would never be the same man he was after witnessing how much suffering a person could be exposed to through no fault of her own. The scene he had encountered once he flicked on the lights replayed over and over in his head, impacting him like nothing else ever had until then. He already knew that he would be a better man and a better cop as a result all of this, for no person could walk away from truly devastating tragedies such as this one without learning something about himself, about his life, and about the world we all lived in. Some of life's most significant and memorable lessons many times came from the least expected source. The trick, however, was being able to learn something from them; it was a gift well worth the effort.

*   *   *

The ambulance driver kept the sirens off as he backed out of the driveway, not wanting to call any more attention to the situation than absolutely necessary. Once they turned from Rydell Drive onto Mohegan Road, he turned them on as they sped toward Saint Vincent's Medical Center in nearby Bridgeport. In less than ten minutes, Jill was being wheeled into the packed emergency room where she was quickly whisked away before anyone else as soon as the triage nurse took one look at her. November 6, 1995 would either mark the beginning of Jill's journey back from the brink of death or the beginning of her journey to join her beloved husband. DJ had been sentenced nearly two months before, but Jill had no notion of person, time, or place, her mind having shut down completely almost as long as DJ had being incarcerated for life.

After a thorough evaluation, Jill was taken directly to the ICU Unit. Unfortunately, she was comatose by then, and the odds were stacked high against her survival. She was so critically dehydrated and malnourished that her kidneys were in the process of shutting down due to the dangerously low amount of fluids in her system. The team of doctors who took over her care worked feverishly in order to try to reverse the damage caused by the renal failure, rehydrating her emaciated body as they continued to address the multitude of other problems that went along with such prolonged time without any food or water. It was a labor-intensive undertaking by all who were involved in caring for the gravely ill woman, but they gave it their best shot. The exceptionally knowledgeable and well-trained ICU nurses, many of whom were around Jill's age, were totally committed to doing everything possible to prevent her from dying as they did with every patient under their care. Without delay, Jill was promptly hooked up to a heart monitor because her electrolytes were all out of whack, resulting in a multitude of health problems and issues. The most troublesome by far was the life-threatening cardiac arrhythmia she was suffering, an oftentimes fatal alteration in how effectively her heart was performing. She was having a hard time breathing, so she was immediately placed on a respirator, thus making sure that all of her major body organs received the oxygen they needed in order to continue functioning, thus buying her more time. This would hopefully prevent them from shutting down completely, most especially her brain. Her red blood cell count was so low that it was a miracle she was still alive. Her anemia was so severe by then that she required several blood transfusions just to raise her hemoglobin level enough to prevent further injury to her vital organs and tissues. Because her veins had all collapsed, again due to the extremely low volume of fluids traveling throughout her body, a special device called a triple lumen catheter, or TLC as it was commonly referred to, was quickly inserted on the right side of her neck, just above the right clavicle. The device had three independent tubes projecting from their point of entry, which were all connected at the base. These individual tubes were contained inside a wider single one, which then sat inside a major vein by the right atrium of the heart, where the volume of blood was quite high and flowed at a very fast pace. This was the safest way to give medications directly into the patient's blood stream, where they would be quickly diluted by the high volume of blood passing through the major blood vessel. Thanks to the device, the nurses caring for Jill were able to hook up several bags of intravenous fluid at once, making the delivery of the necessary medications possible while avoiding any problems that could occur if any of them were incompatible with one another. Even blood transfusions, which Jill so desperately needed, were given through the triple lumen catheter. The device also provided easy access to all the blood samples that were taken so often day and night, especially during the most critical period of a patient's care, when someone's condition could take a turn for the worse without warning and literally from one minute to the next.

After two full weeks of intense monitoring and care, Jill was finally stable enough to be safely transferred to a regular medical unit, where her treatment continued for another ten days. After more than three weeks at Saint Vincent's, she was deemed physically stable enough to be transferred once more, this time to a psychiatric facility that would provide the rest of the care she was still in such need of. Her mental status showed no changes at all as her physical condition continued to improve. If anything, she appeared to have fallen even deeper into a black hole of mental oblivion, appearing as if she no longer occupied her frail and motionless body. She couldn't even manage to maintain eye contact with anyone, not even with her mother. The ever-present vacant stare was the hardest thing to see and the most profound sign of her deeply wounded and disturbed her mind was.

Once more, Jill was transported by ambulance to Silver Hills Psychiatric Hospital, located in New Canaan, on November 30, 1995. Sophia, who sat right next to her stretcher, held her totally unresponsive hand with mixed feelings of concern, hope, and resignation. She was admitted under the care of Dr. Joseph Brauer, chief psychiatrist at the renowned facility. Not wasting any precious time, he expediently put together a team of nurses, counselors, and therapists, all handpicked to assist him in the care of the severely afflicted woman. Her case was so complex that Dr. Brauer wasn't sure that a full recovery could be achieved, but he refused to give up on the chance that they would somehow succeed, not until they had at least tried. He held on to his belief that in time, and with continuous and consistent care, they might eventually be able to penetrate the thick walls that seemed to have engulfed Jill, enclosing the poor woman in an extremely hard-to-reach place within her own body. The lonely, dark, and isolated space where many patients found themselves locked in after they have suffered a nervous breakdown of this magnitude was a complex labyrinth that few were able to find their way out of. He made it a point to meet with each member of his team on a one-on-one basis first and then with them all as a group. Unanimously, they came to the same conclusion about their patient, hoping to eventually be able to reach Jill wherever her mind had taken her. Praying for the best possible outcome, they worked out a carefully mapped-out plan of action, thoroughly encompassing all aspects of her immediate care as well as any of her possible future needs. The nurses would administer a precisely selected combination of medications to Jill while the counselors and therapists would be in charge of handling the psychological support her condition required. It was their belief that by being extra careful and consistent in their handling of her daily care, they would finally find a way to start pulling her out of the deep crater she had fallen in. The road ahead would be nothing but persistent hard work, but they knew that they had nothing to lose. Jill, on the other hand, had everything to gain.

With Dr. Brauer at the helm, personally coordinating and overseeing her overall care, the staff felt a little more confident about the difficult task they were faced with. Their combined efforts, if everything went accordingly, would give Jill the best possible chance to eventually get well again. Such a fully orchestrated and well-planned course of action was the way to go if they were to ever achieve their ultimate goal, and that was to get Jill started on the long and arduous road to recovery. The all-encompassing undertaking would require the full commitment of every member of the knowledgeable team, and they all vowed to do their best to aid the clearly concerned Dr. Brauer. No one involved in her care wanted to even think of the alternative, should she fail to respond to the rigorous yet necessary treatment plan, and shock therapy could not be excluded; they all fervently hoped it didn't come to that although they wouldn't vacillate in carrying it out should she need it. "I don't want to mislead anyone, least of all myself, that's why I'm being so upfront with all of you. This is just about the saddest and most complicated case I have come across during my twenty-seven years of practice. This poor woman simply gave up on life and would have died if she wasn't found when she was. There are absolutely no sure bets in our line of work as you well know. The only guarantee I can give you right now is that this is not going to be easy," Dr. Brauer iterated. "In fact, I expect it to be quite the opposite. But with God's help and a large dose of perseverance from all of you, we shall succeed," he added with far more hope than confidence. "I don't expect any overnight miracles and neither should any of you, or you might find yourselves very disappointed, if not downright disillusioned. I don't want to see it come to that. We will need to make sure that we are always completely open and honest with each other if we are to see any progress being made at all. Each small step in the right direction will translate into a huge milestone in the long run. And never, ever give up. The life of this desperately ill woman is literally in God's hands, with a huge assistance from each and every single one of you. We all, together as well as individually, have an extremely important role to play in the final outcome of this case. And whatever happens, please remember the oath you took when you started your careers in this field and never give up. Time, more than anything else we can offer or do for her, will ultimately turn out to be the best medicine of all, especially in cases as extreme as this one. Fortunately, we have plenty of time to give her, don't we? She deserves no less than our total commitment on her behalf; remember, she is not capable of thinking, speaking, or doing for herself at the moment. Each one of you will be her eyes, ears, voice, and guardian angel for quite some time to come. If anyone at anytime has any question whatsoever, please, for Jill's sake, speak up. It could very well mean the difference between success and failure, and I'm sure none of us want for this young woman to fail. All we can do is to try and try, I assure you, we certainly will! And then some . . ."

It did indeed take quite some time to see even the smallest hint of the progress Dr. Bauer had spoken about. During Jill's entire first month at Silver Hills, there seemed to be no improvement at all in her mental status. Her actions were simply those of a robot that had been programmed to do exactly as she was guided to and nothing else. Because she didn't respond to any commands or gestures, touch became the only means to get her to do what she had to. She was bathed, fed, her diapers were changed when she soiled herself, and she only went where she was taken to. All her movements were performed in a methodical fashion and totally devoid of any emotion. She went to bed when taken to it and got up when helped to. Most nights, she just lay in bed, not even moving or tossing from side to side. The position she was placed in at bedtime was exactly the same position in which the staff found her at daybreak. She never uttered a single sound, be it of approval or disapproval. When not asleep, she usually spent hours simply staring at the ceiling, never doing anything to show she was still there, somewhere inside herself. She never disrupted any of the other patients or members of the staff either. The second month came and went as well and still no response from Jill. She was brought to the common room right after breakfast each morning in the hopes that she would eventually be able to respond to even the simplest form of interaction with one of the fifty or so patients that were there at any given time of day. And she was taken to bed every night at around 8:00 p.m. without giving any sign of life, much to her caregivers' concern. Would they ever get a glimpse of the person she used to be? many wondered.

Jill was taken to the same high-backed chair by a tall window, in one of the corners of the massive room. Always the same chair and window, since daily routine and repetition were extremely important at this stage of her care. The essential aspect of consistency had proven to be crucial and beneficial for the patients' sense of security, regardless of the condition they were admitted for or the severity of their affliction. Any change in their usual routine could send mentally disturbed patients into a virtual tailspin, spiraling out of control until their routine was reestablished, and this was basically due to the high level of anxiety and stress that stemmed from anything that wasn't familiar to them. Once in the main room, Jill remained seated, unmoving until she was taken to wherever she needed to go. Wearing an adult diaper, she soiled herself constantly without giving any indication that she was aware of what she had just done.

Slowly though, the staff caring for her started to notice almost imperceptible signs that she was finally beginning to pay a little bit of attention to her surroundings. At first, they believed those signs to be more a case of wishful thinking than real progress, but they continued to observe her very closely. The responses were so subtle that they were almost nonexistent, such as slightly, almost minimally moving her eyes when another patient crossed her line of vision. Her head, however, never moved an inch, remaining completely still. These episodes, lasting no longer than a split second, happened only occasionally and too far in between. To untrained eyes they would simply pass as nothing more than mere coincidence. After a couple of weeks though, Jill appeared to slowly lower her gaze just a bit when spoken to. Again, these episodes were so rare and far apart that they went almost unnoticed, except for a few members of the staff. In the large common area, she continued to sit very still in the same chair she had been brought to on the first morning after her admission.

It wasn't until one afternoon, a few days later, that one of the nurses observed that Jill appeared to become aware of the sunlight streaming in through the panes of thick glass on both sides of the tall window. The sun, spreading its warmth over her head and body, caused her to slightly turn her face toward the fading rays as the afternoon progressed and the sun began to set. A few days after, the staff noticed that there were times when they could swear she was following some of the other patients with her seemingly vacant eyes as they paced across the vast room. From one side to the other they walked, over and over again, in a steadily paced journey that lead them nowhere. While her head remained still, she indeed moved her eyes off and on, albeit in a very minimal way. Some of the patients spoke and quite often shouted at themselves as they continued their endless pilgrimage, but their chatter failed to elicit any response from Jill.

Eventually, she seemed to notice other minor things as well, such as how some patients sat on straight-backed brown vinyl chairs all by themselves. With their stiff upper bodies leaning forward, their legs maintained a constant cadence as they rhythmically tapped on the floor with one or both feet, following a tune that only they were able to hear. The changes observed by the staff were indeed subtle, but they were undeniably there nevertheless, almost imperceptible at first but becoming more pronounced as the weeks went by, a fact they reported to an exuberant Dr. Brauer during their daily meetings. It appeared that each individual team member had witnessed a minor change at one time or another, a very encouraging sign indeed, which infused a wave of new hope into their tireless efforts. Those baby steps reinforced their commitment to work even harder to see Jill well again, and the sooner the better for the quiet woman they had come to care so deeply about. Her plight had touched everyone on a different level and for different reasons, but they were all united in their wish to see Jill emerge from wherever it was that her desperation had caused her to hide.

On the opposite corner of where she sat, she eventually began to notice a few of the other patients rocking back and forth, back and forth. They seemed to be guided by an invisible power that caused them to never cease their constant motion even if they wanted to. Here and there, groups of patients were engrossed in really animated conversations, which upon closer attention were directed at themselves and not at each other, their topics as varied and odd as the speakers themselves. The nurses, she finally realized one day, mainly stayed behind enclosed counters, observing their charges with experienced eyes, never missing a thing. They couldn't afford to, when caring for so many mentally disturbed adults congregated together in a single space. They expertly and consistently handled each and every situation as it occurred, proof of their excellent training and professionalism, even though some patients seemed to enjoy testing the limits of their patience on a regular basis. The nurses hardly lost their composure, no matter how challenging the situation at hand happened to be, maintaining a cool exterior that clearly reflected their competence. They often worked in pairs, in order to better accomplish any task with as little upheaval as possible. Male aides were always around to handle the more serious episodes but only if there was any need for an added dose of strength in order to subdue a particular patient. Otherwise, they just went about doing their job, often interacting with many of their charges in the course of the day.

The nurses took turns handing out medication to their patients, a task that was safely accomplished through a ten-inch opening along the front of the nurses' station, between the one-inch-thick plexiglas panels and the Formica countertop. Most of them, Jill realized, were nice enough, especially given the level of difficulty their jobs entailed. Having to deal with argumentative and, often times, violent and extremely unruly patients on a daily basis was certainly not an easy job. One nurse in particular though, appeared to have taken a special interest in her, Jill thought. Her ID tag indicated that her name was Rose and that she was an RN. Rose often sought her out, usually spending far more time with her than with any other patient in there, talking mostly about all kinds of light topics in general and trying to engage Jill in simple conversation. At first, she just listened, never saying a single word, positive or negative, but Rose didn't seem to mind the one-way conversation at all. After a couple of weeks though, Jill found herself actually answering when Rose called out her name in greeting, turning her head in the nurse's direction upon hearing her voice. Very slowly, she began to exchange a few words with the soft-spoken nurse, mostly yes, no, or okay, her own voice sounding oddly strange to her for she had not heard it for so long. Rose's kind words had finally penetrated through the thick fog that had surrounded her for some time; how much time, she simply had no idea. The only thing she knew was that Rose was the first person to really get her undivided attention, however minimal that had been to begin with.

Before long, Jill found herself actually looking forward to seeing Rose, even enjoying their one-on-one time together more than anything else in her daily routine. She had no way of knowing that strict institution policy prevented mental health providers from forming personal relationships with their patients, and Rose was always very careful not to cross that very thin line. Still though, she found subtle ways of letting Jill know exactly just how much she cared and how special Jill had become to her. That proved to be precisely the push that Jill needed to want to get better, the best incentive she could have received to propel her to continue to move forward, toward a more stable, therefore much healthier state of mind. In time, with her doctor and her therapists' help but more importantly, with Rose's support and encouragement, Jill slowly began to emerge from the darkness that had settled over and around her. The painful day when she had no choice but to turn her only child in to the police was only surpassed by the day of his conviction, the hate she saw in his eyes something she couldn't come to terms with. It was by far the worst day of her entire life, a day she would never be able to forget but would try very hard to overcome. Once she started to openly show signs of progress, her recovery took on a speed of its own, encouraging her amazed caregivers to fight even harder on her behalf. Dr. Brauer seemed to be the most enthusiastic of all, right behind a triumphant Rose, who couldn't contain her happiness and gratitude at the sheer miracle that was happening right in front of everyone's eyes. There had been a time, not that long before, when they all sadly doubted their ability to help Jill, fearing that her mind was too far gone for anyone to expect any meaningful recovery. Now here they were, sharing in her victory and her return to the real world. Dr. Brauer felt incredibly honored and privileged to have witnessed such admirable progress, which was nothing short of absolutely unbelievable! In a relatively short amount of time, given her original state of mind and physical decay, Jill had morphed from an average-looking caterpillar into the most delicate and beautiful butterfly.

It was with a mixture of pride and joy that the day came when Jill was deemed well enough to be discharged, a word that took on a special meaning to those who had grown to love the quiet woman with haunted eyes. She became their symbol of hope, this patient that had come to them after having lost her will to live. Her impending departure came with a mixture of one-tenth of sadness and nine-tenths of sheer joy, along with their best wishes for a full and enjoyable life in a world that had faded away from her memory for quite some time before reappearing again. If anyone deserved to be happy, they unanimously agreed, it had to be Jill. Chances were that they would not see her anymore once she was gone, and they were just fine with that; none of them wanted to ever see her under the simply dreadful circumstances that had brought her there in the first place. Not wanting to cry anymore than she already had, Jill opted to say her good-byes silently to every dedicated man and woman who had worked so diligently in order to give her a second chance at a meaningful life. Knowing that words still came hard to her, she wisely decided to express her gratitude with written ones. The night before her discharge, she wrote a heartfelt letter, thanking all who were so crucial in getting her from the deep crevices of total darkness that had engulfed her body, mind, and soul back into the world of light and living again. In the candid letter, she named every one of them, careful not to overlook anyone, again thanking each one individually for their support, kindness, persistence, and caring attitude during a time when she had needed their help the most. "What a truly wonderful job you all do, day in and day out. Even though you might be going through a tough time yourselves as I'm sure some of you often must, you never fail to be there for those who need you. I would not be sitting here, writing this letter, had it not been for you dedication and perseverance. When the world around me became nothing more than darkness and oblivion, your dedication became the light that guided me, inch by inch, back to where I belong. There is nothing worse than being dead inside while your body is still alive. You gave me the chance to live again. I can't honestly say that I envy your jobs, but I'm eternally grateful that you were there when I needed you the most. How do you thank the people who returned to you the will to live you so completely had lost and given up on?"

The letter, which was found on top of her carefully made bed after she had left the facility, was read by several pairs of misty eyes. Her words were so kind and sincere that they managed to touch every single staff member she ever came in contact with. She went on to say that she was humbled by their patience, never showing any signs of getting tired or discouraged when a patient relapsed or took too long to get better, using her own case as an example of the later. She also thanked them for making her plight a crusade they had no intention of not seeing through, even when the odds seemed to be stacked so highly against her. Jill's achievements were only a reflection of how well they performed their duties, and she wanted to make sure that they knew exactly how much she truly appreciated all of their efforts on her behalf. "I can honestly say that you brought me back from the brink of emotional death. You took the time to piece together a broken human being with a broken heart, mind, and soul. Your perseverance was the glue that held me together and kept me from breaking again. I shall never take for granted all the care you showered me with," she added just before she sealed the envelope. She left a bit of her heart between those folded sheets of paper, extremely grateful to the staff for making her progress their crusade and the return of her emotional and psychological health their goal.

The sun was shining brightly on the glorious morning at the end of March 1996, as a trembling Jill, a smile on her thin face and a heart full of hope, stepped out of her mother's car and entered her house. It had been a long time since that tragic day back in November the year before, when she had been whisked away by ambulance, not aware as to where or why she was being taken. She hadn't been aware of anything at all back then, a day that now felt like another lifetime to her. "It feels good to be back at home again, Mom. It has indeed been a long time," she told her mother with an equal dose of relief and fear. She was finally where she knew she truly belonged. She was home again.

CHAPTER 17

At first, being home alone most of the time frightened Jill, her state of mind on the fragile side still. Every corner of every room was a painful reminder of the extreme sadness that had nearly robbed her of her sanity and ultimately, her very life. What had started as a fairytale romance come true turned into a nightmare before she barely had the chance to start living it. Drew's death, which was never too far from her thoughts, was one of her deepest sorrows, but it hadn't ended there. As much as she tried to concentrate on the many joyful memories connected to their home, the sorrow and grief that she unfortunately experienced there overshadowed a grand part of those happy times. For days, she dwelled with the idea of selling the house and moving on, but upon lengthy reflective searching, she came to the wise conclusion that she simply wasn't strong enough, physically as well as emotionally, to undertake such a major task. Not quite yet anyway, she reasoned. DJ's room remained locked, and she had no intention of going in there any time in the future, if ever. As difficult as it was for her, she knew that if she was to survive and move forward, she had to always look ahead, never back. Before going to bed every night and upon getting up every morning, she recited the same insightful proverb, which had become her virtual lifeline of late. *Yesterday is gone, tomorrow is yet to come, so all we have is today. Live it as if it is your last.* It was so true, she reminded herself, for no one knew what the next day could bring. The Serenity Prayer became her mantra, one she lived faithfully by and recited whenever she felt weighed down by her pain, the wise meaning of the words something we all should learn to truly understand. There were indeed things in her life that she knew she would never be able to change, no matter how deeply she wished that she could; better save her energy for those things that she could. The events of the last eight months would help to guide her in distinguishing between what she could and couldn't change and, save for her recovery, this was the only positive thing to come out of so much misery. Accepting defeat was something that she had learned the hard way, even though she had fought it tooth and nail. The meaning behind the inspiring words had been capable of quite a bit of soul healing, and she quickly learned to lean on them for guidance whenever she felt the need to. In time, she would even learn to lean more and more on herself, but until then, she embraced the help they provided her with.

Slowly, she started to venture out, trying to recapture the person she once was, and to her amazement, it felt good to be among other people again. On her very first outing, she headed directly to Saint Lawrence Church, a place she had turned her back to on the day she found out that her little boy was going to die. She had only been there once since, and that had been during her father's funeral mass. She had done it out of respect for him, her family, and father Mancini, none of whom had the slightest hint that she had broken away from her religion a long time before. With small, tentative steps, she approached the altar she had known so well all her life. As she knelt on the first pew, her wobbly knees threatened to give out, so she leaned her small bottom against the seat behind her for added support. *Not this time,* she willed herself. *I will not allow my fears, my insecurities, to get in the way of what I must now overcome.* As she began to talk, she raised her gaze, forcing herself to look at the form of Jesus as he hung there, painfully nailed to the large cross. Her voice faltered at first, and she had to swallow hard in order to go on; no one was going to do that for her, not any longer! She was determined to accomplish what she had set out to do, regardless of how difficult it was to have to face up to what she had done. She was well aware that she had to make amends for her lack in judgment back in 1983, when she had allowed her desperation at the prospect of losing DJ to take complete control, to blend the lines between what was right and what was wrong. Everything in her life then had been overshadowed by the enormity of her heartache. The worst part though, was that she wasn't sure if she would have handled the situation any differently than she did unless she knew in advance that DJ was going to grow up to be a killer. She had a lot to be forgiven for.

All alone inside the blessedly empty church, she made her confession directly to God and his son, leaving nothing out, in spite of how excruciatingly difficult some of her candid admissions were to acknowledge. Saying them out loud was ten times harder than she had imagined, but that didn't stop her. No priest was required as she confessed her sins, for she felt she needed to talk directly to the Lord without any help from a third person. Coming straight from the heart, her words were so humble and sincere that they were absorbed by her surroundings, for she heard no lingering echo after each word was spoken. As the weight began to slowly lift from her heavy conscience, she found herself weeping tears of gratitude and relief. Having made her peace with her Lord and her faith, Jill apologized several times for having lost sight of her beliefs. She then went on to make a solemn vow to never allow anything or anyone to interfere with her faith again, a vow she had every intention of keeping for the remainder of her natural life.

At the time, Jill was not aware that her good friend, Father Mancini, had passed away while she was at Silver Hills. He had gone on to join Drew and her dad and was still probably delighting them with tales about his beloved village of San Clemente, in the hills of Eastern Italy. Because her condition was so precarious when Father Mancini had died, her mother and siblings had decided not to tell her anything about it. Since bad news travelled fast, they tried to delay delivering them for a little while longer, preferring to wait until the timing was right in order to let her know. They were sure that someday Jill would be able to plant her feet on solid ground once more, and that was the time when they would tell her.

Leaving Saint Lawrence Church with a much lighter conscience and outlook for the future, she drove directly to the Shelton Animal Shelter, the same placed from where she had adopted her beloved Pepper so many years before. Within minutes of arriving there, she had already fallen completely in love with a pair of big round brown eyes lost in compact field of soft fur. They belonged to the tiniest puppy she had ever seen in her entire life. She was not sure whether she was looking at a puppy or a kitten, not at first anyway. The two-month-old creature weighing less than one pound was a female that happened to be half Pomeranian and half Chihuahua. Her absurdly small face was no bigger than a plum and was easily overpowered by big brown eyes that seemed to observe everything with infinite curiosity. She was so little that she could easily fit inside Jill's shirt pocket. Her soft coating was of a very light shade of tan on her neck, torso, and tail and off-white on her precious tiny face, underbelly, and legs. Around her mouth the fur was dark gray, making her tiny snout appear even smaller. "She is so adorable," Jill squealed in pure fascination, her heart already won over by the vivacious little thing. "She looks more like a kitten than a puppy. Are you sure that she is really a dog?" She asked the animal control officer, cradling the bouncy ball of fur against her neck while being extra careful not to squeeze her too hard. The puppy, tail wagging at lightning speed, suddenly began to cover Jill's face with butterfly kisses, her small pink tongue busy tickling her future owner in her sheer happiness and enthusiasm. "For one so tiny, you sure have a lot of spunk, don't you, little girl?" Jill mused, unable to suppress her joy at the clear display of affection she was being showered with. That puppy was able to make her laugh more in a few minutes than she had in quite a long time, which made Jill's spirits soar as high as her love for the dog already had.

Stopping by the local pet shop on her way home, she expediently purchased every single thing she thought her new companion would need, the dog happily asleep inside her shoulder bag. She felt a rush of happiness wash over her while she was selecting the items because those purchases were not for herself but for someone else, someone that wanted and needed her almost as much as she wanted and needed this someone. The young man behind the counter didn't even realize that the puppy was sleeping inside the purse until Jill happened to place it on the countertop in order to get her wallet out. Unexpectedly, the little dog decided to make her presence known by stretching two tiny legs out of the purse. Caught by surprise, the amused clerk asked Jill if she could take the puppy out of her bag so that he could hold it. More than happy to show off her new friend, Jill lifted the still sleepy creature out of her bag, proud that the dog was hers and hers alone filling her heart. The clerk, Jimmy, couldn't get over how little the puppy really was, so small that she literally wobbled when she walked, tripping over her own miniature legs. She actually looked just like a walking tan-and-white pompom with a face on it.

On the way back to her car, Jill was approached by a passerby who, upon seeing the miniscule creature in her hand, literally stopped on his tracks, turned around, and asked her what kind of animal it was. When she told him that it was a dog, he shook his head in disbelief, saying that it looked more like a kitten to him, with ears so small that they really didn't belong on a dog's head. Before she realized what was happening, a small group of people had gathered around, and while the passerby asked to hold the little creature, the others looked in awe, asking her where she had gotten "the simply precious little thing." By the time she was finally able to reach her car, a good half hour had passed, but she didn't mind it at all. The little munchkin, back inside the safety of the purse, was hers to love, to care for, and to keep, and it felt really, really good. This time, the light at the end of the proverbial tunnel came in the form of a tiny eleven-ounce female puppy with an adorable face, a pair of absolutely captivatingly large brown eyes, and a disproportionally huge heart to boot. And all that goodness incredibly fit comfortably inside the palm of just one of Jill's hands.

Back at home, Jill gingerly lifted the puppy out of her purse, where she had fallen asleep again. Lethargic and groggy at first, the dog fell several times on the soft rug before she finally found some form of wobbly balance, and before long she was busily sniffing around her new home. Jill decided to name the puppy Lyla, and soon the sweet and cuddly creature became her tireless shadow. Following her absolutely everywhere she went, Lyla never seemed to get tired, her tiny legs struggling to keep up with her owner's much faster pace. Amazingly, albeit later than sooner, she always managed to somehow get where she wanted to go. From the start, the little dog was capable of doing wonders at lifting Jill's spirits, and she found herself laughing more during their first day together than she had in several months, going back to the time of her father's unexpected death. And then, after she had found all that incriminating evidence of her son's involvement in all those unsolved murders soon after, her days of laughing irrevocably came to an abrupt halt.

As she started to grow a little, Lyla's coloring became even more defined, the tan taking on a honeylike hue, and the off-white turning to a very light shade of cream. Gone was the dark fur around her little snout, replaced by a much lighter shade of gray. Her fluffy tail, in the true trademark of her Pomeranian heritage, was very furry and curled back toward her neck, which her owner found utterly charming. Her ears were very small, indeed resembling those of a kitten. The fur on her body though, was of medium length and most definitely nowhere as thick or long as that of a full-blooded Pomeranian. "She looks like that little dog on all those Taco Bell commercials, but mine had ear-reduction surgery and is wearing a mink coat," she was fond of telling everyone, pride swelling her huge heart to twice its normal size. Lyla continued to follow Jill everywhere, even to the bathroom, where she patiently sat on the navy blue rug while her best friend took a shower. The minute Jill stepped out of the tub though, the ears perked up and the curly tail began to move. The dog happily licked the drops of water still on her owner's wet ankles and feet, tickling Jill with her tiny rough tongue, tail wagging at a frantic speed by then. As she settled down to watch some TV, the sweet dog always nestled quietly right next to Jill's left thigh, happy to snuggle under the blanket with her loving owner.

Before long, Lyla had abandoned the lavish dog bed that Jill had bought for her and had placed at the bottom of hers, preferring instead to sneak under her owner's sheets. Her warm, soft little body was a source of immense comfort as she pressed herself against Jill's right thigh, a welcomed reassurance that she was really there for her. Indeed Jill didn't feel quite so alone anymore, for Lyla went to great lengths to show her how much she was loved, always happy just to see and be near her, and all that devotion didn't go unnoticed and was returned tenfold. Jill wasn't quite sure of who needed whom the most, but she knew for a fact that Lyla always gave much more than she ever received. "Thank you, little one," Jill softly told her companion before dozing off every night. "You have brought into my life a new kind of joy and selfless emotion, feelings that were missing from my heart for quite some time. I'll be forever grateful to you for having found your way into my heart and home, but above all else, for finding your way to me. I promise to never let you down, my precious one, for as long as we both live and beyond." And, as usual, Lyla responded to Jill's loving words by inching her little body even closer to hers, so close that Jill could literally feel the dog's rapid heartbeat through the fabric of her nightgown.

Life for Jill took on a new meaning since Lyla came into it. Her mother and siblings all breathed a collective sigh of relief as they noticed the positive changes in her personality and communication efforts. They called the two of them a match made in heaven. Slowly, the old Jill began to emerge from within, a little bit at a time. She was now clearly less depressed than when she was first released from Silver Hills a few weeks before. She even started to talk in terms of the future, which she hadn't done until then. She appeared to have come to terms with the fact that DJ still refused to see her, telling her family that she was sure that, deep down, he knew just how much she loved him and vice versa. That he remained very angry at her for turning him in was a fact that she had finally learned to live with and respect. As difficult as it was for her to be estranged from her only child, she was also fully aware that she would not have been able to live with herself had she acted any differently than she ultimately did. She couldn't have kept quiet while he continued his rampant path of death and destruction. Having him that mad at her was not what she expected or wished for, not in a million years, but it was far better than not being able to live with her own conscience. No matter what anyone said or thought, it was the lesser of two evils, and that had to be enough for her for now. Someone had to stop his reign of destruction and, unfortunately, there was no one else besides her that could have done that. In spite of the extremely high price she had paid by doing the right thing, not to mention the consequences her decision had unleashed upon herself, it was the only alternative left, albeit the hardest one as well. *Time heals all wounds*, she thought with nostalgia during her quiet times with Lyla, her hand absentmindedly caressing the dog's soft fur just as it had caressed DJ's blond curls when he was a little boy.

*　　*　　*

Sophia, who had only seen her grandson once since his arrest, tried on numerous occasions to see him again, but DJ had refused to see his grandmother thereafter. After trying a few more times without success she had, just like Jill, eventually stopped going to the prison altogether. DJ's constant and blatant rejections became simply too traumatic for her to handle. Visits from his uncles, Daniel and Nicholas, and from his Aunt Tara were all refused as well. His lame excuse as to why he didn't want to see them served to simply add unnecessary insult to injury. It was his claim that it was too painful for him to see his grandma, uncles, and aunt under such deplorable circumstances, and he just wanted to spare everyone any added stress and pain. After DJ's conviction, Eric and Marissa, who attempted to see their godson at least three times in the first week alone, were given basically the same washed-out message. Even Jack, who had become so close to DJ before his arrest, was turned away without seeing him either. DJ was either too ashamed to see any of them, or he just couldn't care less, and although his family and friends weren't really sure of which, they heavily leaned toward the second hypothesis. Although they all wanted to believe in the former, they had to consider the latter, for they simply didn't recognize the person he had become. All except Jill.

Because they couldn't believe a word DJ said, Daniel, Nicholas, and Tara were deeply disappointed in the young man they cared about with such passion since the day he was born. After he was arrested, they had met, just the three of them, to discuss their nephew's incarceration and possible conviction. They had purposely left their mother out of the meetings in order to spare her any further stress, for they knew that she was still reeling from their father's sudden death. After hours of back and forth discussion, often interrupted by outbursts of anger and frustration, many times preceded and followed by sobs and tears, all three of them ultimately came to the same sad conclusion about DJ and the whole ordeal. Unfortunately, the young man they had loved with all their heart was no longer around. And the worst part was that not once did he ever show an ounce of remorse over the fact that he had robbed six young girls of their lives. Since the DJ behind bars was incapable of feeling any remorse or sympathy for all the pain and destruction he caused to so many people, how could they still expect him to care about them? As part of his immediate family, they were caught between the deep love they still had for their nephew, the pity they felt for the shell of a human being he had become, and the enormous amount of anger and resentment they harbored about the crimes he had committed. There were so many victims of his cruelty, they acknowledged, unable to deny the truth. Their hearts went out to all he had killed and their loved ones. But their hearts also went out to their baby sister, for Jill was probably the biggest and most innocent victim of all.

They were willing to do anything in the world to help and protect her and continued to berate themselves for not having tried a lot harder when she spurned their attempts to come to her aid. She always declined their offers of support the few times she answered the phone, and during those brief conversations, she always begged them not to come to the house, asking them to simply give her a little more time to process it all. But they should have known better then to abide by her request to be left alone, for they all knew how much she loved her son and was hurting at the time. Feeling defeated and at a loss as to how to help and beyond crushed by her plight, they ended up simply taking the easy way out by acquiescing to her request, they later came to realize. Needless to say, when the news of her total nervous breakdown reached them, they felt crushed by the depth of their guilt. When she was admitted to Saint Vincent's hospital, they were told that she was probably not going to make it through the night but she did, and not only that night but every single one since. At Silver Hills, there wasn't even the slightest hint of recognition in her vacant eyes, no connection whatsoever with anyone or anything outside her lost mind. Her catatonic state was excruciatingly hard for her siblings to witness or accept. They felt a deep sense of hopelessness and helplessness when they were told that there was absolutely nothing they could do for Jill. But then, ever so slowly, they were blessed with a miracle that began unfolding right in front of their eyes as they faithfully took turns visiting her on a daily basis at Silver Hills. Her progress was so sporadic and slow that they often doubted if the minimal improvements they saw were real or simply wishful dreaming on their part. With the passing of time though, there was no denying the presence of a faint light of recognition that started to burn in her hauntingly sad eyes, a flame that continued to grow increasingly brighter with each passing week. The day when Jill was finally discharged from Silver Hills was a major victory for the Chandler family, a day that, for quite a long time, they seriously doubted they would ever live to see. Thanks to the combined efforts of several very knowledgeable and dedicated professionals and guided by the ever-present hands of God, they finally had their Jill back, battered and bruised, but still in one piece. DJ, on the other hand, was a different matter altogether, for although he appeared to be physically free of any battering or bruising, he was far from being intact. Something was definitely missing within, a thing we all referred to as a conscience or perhaps something simply known as a soul.

*   *   *

Drew's parents were not able to come back East when William had died so suddenly, but they sent the Chandlers an absolutely beautiful arrangement in the shape of a huge heart. It was completely made out of yellow roses and white baby's breath, which they remembered were Jill's favorite flower. Along with the arrangement, they sent a long and thoughtfully written condolence card that was read by every member of the family more than once or twice. They were, unfortunately, also unable to come to Connecticut during DJ's trial, mainly due to the fact that Deborah was very worried about her husband's frail condition. Raymond's poor health was on everyone's mind, and they feared that the stress of the proceedings might prove to be just too taxing and traumatic for him to bear. The elder Millners had not seen their grandson for nearly three years by then and missed him terribly but didn't think they could handle seeing him under such harsh conditions. When Jill was released from Silver Hills, however, they made a combined effort and managed to fly in from California. They needed to see with their own eyes that she was indeed all right.

Initially, they intended to stay for a total of two weeks, since Raymond's condition continued to deteriorate from day to day, but decided to extend their visit for an extra week. Upon reflecting on it, Deborah came to the sad realization that this was probably the last time their darling daughter-in-law would see Raymond alive. They were aware of the equally sad fact that DJ had repeatedly refused to see his own mother, no matter how often she made the trip to the prison. When they had received the news that Jill had become so ill herself, teetering on the brink of death, they had become inconsolable. The severity of her illness, both physically and mentally, still brought tears to their eyes whenever they thought about it. It crushed them to know how close they all came to losing her.

They were also aware that DJ had seen his maternal grandmother, Sophia, only once since his incarceration and that he declined all visits from his maternal uncles and aunt. Knowing how close the Chandler family had always been, the Millners' hearts went out to them, especially since they'd had no choice but to give up ever seeing him again. Still, they held on to their hope that DJ would not turn them away, especially since they had come from so far away to see him. He had always been a source of joy in their lives from the minute he was born, and they needed to see him at least one more time before they became too old and sick to travel, a day that, unfortunately, was fast approaching. Always practical, Deborah was never one to overlook things, so she wasn't about to ignore that sad but true fact as she grew older and wiser. Jill tried to prepare them as best as she could just in case her son refused to see them as well, which, unfortunately, was more of a reality than a possibility. Both of her in-laws, however, remained adamant in their decision to still give it a try. They felt that they owed DJ and themselves at least that much, reassuring her that while they were hoping for the best, they were fully prepared to face and accept the worst. Jill quickly offered to drive to the prison even though she knew very well that she wouldn't be going in with them, which was a reality that she had learned to live with. "I'll do some shopping while you enjoy your time with your grandson," she graciously added, and her in-laws were sincerely grateful and deeply relieved, since it instantly lifted the awkwardness out of the undeniably touchy and delicate situation.

Driving always had a calming effect on Jill, and she silently prayed that for once DJ would think of someone else besides himself. She could understand why he remained angry with her, for she had been the one who had turned him into the police. Truth be said though, he was the one who betrayed her love and trust each time he killed every one of those poor girls, but so be it. But why refuse to see those who had done nothing but love him, like her Mom and siblings, Jack, and even Eric and Marissa? She really hoped that he would do the right thing by agreeing to see his grandparents, for their sake as well as his own. With a worried heart, she sadly watched the elder and suddenly old and frail Millners slowly walk toward the prison's main gate.

The facility, impressive in its enormous size alone, was a real shock for those who saw it for the first time. It was probably built that way for exactly that purpose, an intimidating structure that hopefully would serve as a deterrent to those who were toying with the idea of breaking the law for whatever reason. If it was indeed successful in giving some of them second thoughts about whether or not they chose to follow a life of crime, no one knew for sure. The facility, however, certainly met its goal at intimidating the Millners and many like them. It was the building's overall coldness and sense of total isolation from the world outside its massive confinement that struck them the most. It managed to leave a scary, creepy, and uneasy sensation in its wake, an impression that lasted before, during, and for a long time after their visit was over with. But even if the impenetrable way in which the building was erected somehow failed to do so, the air of regimented discipline and total oblivion from the life the rest of society was free to enjoy, drove the point across without preamble. Add to it the seclusion that the thick concrete walls represented, and the point was indeed well taken, barbed wires and all. The heavy iron bars and even heavier iron gates were enough to scare even the bravest of souls, especially the unforgettable sound that they made when they slammed shut behind someone. Even if they were being closed only on a temporary basis, as was the case with Deborah and Raymond, those were the same gates that slammed behind every single inmate, day in and day out. It was indeed a powerful insight into what it meant to be locked up. The overall impression generated by the combination of all those factors was hopefully enough to get someone to reconsider before it became too late to undo the harm already done. It was a real shame that many would-be criminals didn't remember the fact that for every action, there was always a reaction and consequence. That reality, which actually applied to everyone in general, was much more poignant when attached to those with a criminal background, for punishment sooner or later would have to be faced. It was much easier to avoid temptation than to pay the price for choosing not to do so. Deborah couldn't help but dwell on the fact that, aside from the staff working there, only the most feared and violent offenders were housed behind these fortresslike walls. And their beloved grandson was one of them. They could never suspect that he was just about the worst of them all!

To their utter surprise, DJ agreed to see them right away the minute he was told who his visitors were. As he entered the visiting room, Deborah let out a sigh of relief to see that he appeared to be in excellent physical condition. And he was even more handsome than ever, if that was possible. He also seemed to have bulked up in prison, which he later explained was from the repetitive daily exercises he managed to do in the confinement of his cell. He greeted both of them with a wide captivating smile so much like their Drew. His hygiene was impeccable and that truly pleased his worried grandparents who didn't know what to expect and were more than a little apprehensive as to what they would see when the three of them came face-to-face. With a pang in her heart, Deborah quickly sensed that DJ's enthusiastic greeting was hollow, lacking real emotion. Even the charismatic smile he wore was a facade, and all the warmth that used to radiate from his beautiful blue eyes was no longer there. Although on the outside he had only gotten even better looking, inside he had gone away, even if he pretended to still be the old DJ.

Very politely, he asked them both how they were doing, attentively asking many questions about his Uncle Phillip, his Aunt Hannah, and the rest of their growing families with what appeared to be a mixture of curiosity, interest, and delight. He seemed to be quite eager to hear all they had to say, often laughing at his cousins' crazy antics, described in great detail by his beloved grandparents. But it was all a front anyway, and Deborah immediately felt it. Not once did he ask about his mother or her health, which hurt her deeply. He didn't mention any of the crimes he was found guilty of, acting as if he had been sent to summer camp instead of a maximum security prison. He showed no hint of remorse for what he had done or for the enormous amount of grief he had ultimately caused to so many innocent people, his own family included. His grandparents didn't ask either. They continued to exchange lighthearted conversation, happy to simply be there, near the grandchild they loved so much still in spite of what he was found guilty of. By no means did they expect to simply forget the pain he had caused, but they couldn't just turn off the deep affection they had for him either. It was all so complicated, but in their hearts, he remained their DJ, no matter how much that same love ended up hurting them on so many levels. Far sooner than they wished, the guard informed them that their visitation hour was over, and Deborah found it hard not to cry in front of her grandson. As DJ got up to say good-bye to his grandparents, he slowly bent down and placed a kiss on their cheek. Although his eyes remained on both of their faces, his kiss was delivered in a somewhat detached, if not mechanical and well-rehearsed manner, but one had to know the old DJ to notice the difference. He didn't even look back for one more glance at them either before he was escorted back to his cell. With a shaky hand, Deborah clutched her chest in a feeble attempt to protect her already wounded heart. DJ's obvious lack of real interest was like a well-sharpened knife that easily sliced through her soul, her love for him as strong and sincere as ever even though she doubted very much that it was even slightly reciprocated. Taking Raymond's frail hand in hers, she sadly walked beside her loving husband, fully aware that neither one of them would live long enough to ever see their beloved grandson again.

The trip back to Jill's house was a subdued one. Deborah made a point of telling her daughter-in-law that her son looked well and fit. For the news-starving mother, that morsel of news was like a drop of rain in the arid Sahara desert and barely touched the surface of her immense need to know how her only child was faring. Since no further information came forth, she had no choice but to be contented with that much for the time being. There were hundreds of questions that Jill would love to ask about DJ, but she knew her mother-in-law well; when she was ready to really talk about it, she would and not a minute sooner. Before long, the three of them settled into a quiet mood, chatting here and there just to break the awkward silence that hung around them during the long ride home. Both Raymond and Deborah were fully aware of what Jill was thinking as she drove, but neither felt comfortable talking about it inside the confinement of the car. They needed time to process it all before delving into the difficult matter feet first.

190

Back home, Jill headed straight to the kitchen to make a fresh pot of coffee just like her mother-in-law used to during their Saturday morning visits to their home in Trumbull. The major difference between then and now was that a contented little boy called DJ was no longer happily watching cartoons in the family room. *If only we could turn back the clock*, she silently wished once more, perhaps for the thousandth time already.

Sitting around the table in the warm and sunny kitchen, Deborah began to unwind, allowing her tense and achy body to relax. The sad expression on Jill's face was hard not to notice, the eagerness and hunger she tried to tone down shooting from her eyes like bloodied stars. Without a word, she pleaded with her mother-in-law to please say something more about the son she had not seen in so long–seven months to be precise. With a sigh, Deborah started to relate their visit with DJ in detail, leaving out only the fact that she felt no real connection coming from him anymore, no real love or interest on his part. If it wasn't for the fact that he still looked quite a bit like Drew, the Millners could almost say that this particular DJ wasn't even related to them. Of course they would never say that to Jill, but this DJ, whom they still loved with all their heart and soul, was simply a ghost of the old one as far as feelings and emotions were concerned. Wanting to appease Jill's need to know, Deborah decided, with God's forgiveness, to add quite a bit more to the story. How could a few little white lies hurt now? Besides, she wanted to bring some peace of mind to the young woman whom she loved like a daughter. She kindly went on tell Jill that DJ had inquired about his mother and how she was doing, asking them to please convey his message to her. "He also asked us to let you know that he is doing just fine and that you should not worry about him," Deborah added. Jill's eyes instantly filled with tears, and they became much brighter and happier than they had just a few seconds before. Giving her some time to compose herself, Deborah went on to say how DJ reiterated his love for his mother on more than one occasion. Carefully though, she reminded Jill not to get her hopes up too quickly because she didn't want to see her disappointed once more. Yes, DJ had said that he loved his mother, but he had also been implicitly firm and clear in his request that she not come to see him because he would continue to refuse to meet with her.

Jill's eyes, filled with tears, showed in detail how hard it was to hear that, a bolt of pain crossing her face and quickly shattering all the hopes she had been nursing for so long. Taking hold of her daughter-in-law's suddenly cold hands, Deborah took a deep breath before she resumed talking. "Jill, my darling," she tentatively proceeded with a voice that was slow but steady in spite of the sadness that had settled in her heart, "you can't continue to beat yourself up like this. You can't change the past, none of us can, you can only learn from it. You did nothing wrong, but I can't make you understand or accept that. Destiny dealt you a lousy hand, and yet you still managed to stay in the game. You can't assume responsibility for DJ's actions, and neither should you feel guilty for having turned him in. What else could you have done? Ignore all that you had just found out? As a mother, I feel your pain, but he left you no choice, did he? Every single one of those poor girls had a mother too, darling, never forget that! Besides, DJ chose to do what he did, but you had no choice in the matter, did you? You are a very intelligent woman, therefore I'm not going to mince words with you. DJ wasn't going to stop, not on his own anyway, because he was already hooked by then. Power is an extremely dangerous weapon, and overpowering those girls became like a drug to him. In time, it became more like a game, a toxic combination of wants and needs and with a massive dose of self-entitlement thrown in. After his arrest, I spent hours at the library reading about cases like his. I felt an overwhelming need to know what was happening and why my grandson felt the need to do what he did so that I could be of help to both of you. What I learned, unfortunately, was not what I had expected or wanted to. Suffice it to say, the most common denominator that I ended up finding in every case that I read was a destructive an unrelenting addiction to power and control above all else. Rape is not about sex, you know that! Whether you are ready to admit it to yourself or not, DJ was more than willing to sacrifice the lives of as many women as he felt was necessary to satisfy his increasing appetite for power and control. But once they taste it, that insatiable hunger, they usually get hooked on it for life. The question here is a simple one, honey; how many more girls were going to lose their lives before he was caught? How many more, Jill? We both know what the answer is, if we can put our love for DJ on pause for just a moment. How many more girls would he have killed until then? And what would that knowledge have done to you as a mother, sweetheart, as his mother? You have absolutely no idea how much Raymond and I, and the rest of the family, admire your courage and strength when it would have been easier to simply keep your findings to yourself. We wish that we were just half the person you are. Please, darling, it's about time you stop punishing yourself for your son's crimes. Most mothers in your place wouldn't have been able to do what you ultimately did. Our biggest sadness comes from the fact that our son didn't live long enough to continue to enjoy being married to you. We couldn't have asked for a better wife for Drew, even if we were to live our lives ten times over."

Upon hearing such comforting words, all Jill managed to say was a low, raspy thank you, which was barely heard above the thick sound of her choked-up tears. A weak but genuine smile suddenly appeared on her lips, conveying a lot more than all the words in a dictionary ever could, for she truly loved her in-laws and what they were trying to do. Inside though, her heart was torn, one half wanting to be able to really believe what Deborah had said, and the other half telling her she had absolutely no right to. *Oh, honey! If you only knew the whole truth as to why I still feel so guilty, I wonder what you would think about your darling daughter-in-law then. DJ didn't sin alone. He had plenty of help from me. I might not have had any way of knowing it at the time, but I certainly did my part. Amy, Samantha, how will I ever repair the harm that I have caused?* She didn't feel worthy of any forgiveness, much less praise, no matter how much she wished for it. Having both was out of the question regardless of all her good intentions and deeds since. She had committed the ultimate sin, only no one was aware of that terrible fact, but that did not negate her culpability in the horrible tragedy that started way before the body of the first victim was even found. Back in June of 1983–that was when the very first girl had died, a couple of weeks after DJ started coming home from school complaining of a headache. The fatal brain tumor was there to stay and DJ was going to die, and she could not lose her son. Then the "miracle," as they had all called it. No one knew the truth then, no one but her own guilty conscience, along with her forever condemned soul. But that truth could no longer be denied, only ignored and covered up for the time being. Denial would not make it go away.

Jill hated to see her in-laws leave, keenly aware that she probably would never see her father-in-law alive again, but she understood that their lives were now in California. She made sure to introduce Jack to them, telling them how supportive he had been during the trial and her long illness. Deborah and Raymond remembered him well from his days as the principal of the school where both Drew and Jill had worked, as well as how fond their son had been of his friend. Seeing how happy and relaxed Jill seemed when Jack was around made them feel a little better about having to leave again. Besides her dedicated family, she had Eric, Marissa, and their three children in her life. And then, along came Jack and Lyla, just at the right time respectively. Saying good-bye would be difficult, they knew, but they were genuinely grateful to see that Jill had so many people around besides the most adorable little puppy they had ever seen. Thank God their own children and grandchildren were waiting for them on the opposite side of the country, as glad to have them back as they would eventually feel about being back. But in the meantime, they would miss Jill so.

I'm going to miss them so much, Jill thought as she saw the relief written all over her father and mother-in-law's faces after reconnecting with Jack. But they had their kids and grandkids to go back to, and they were probably more than eager to see all of them again. Jill held on to the fact that Raymond and Deborah would be surrounded by their loving family as they grew older still. Their children and their families would love and look after them until their time to leave this world arrived, a time she hoped was a long way off but feared might not, especially for Raymond. Hugging them both close to her heart, she kissed their wrinkled faces with all the love she felt. And when the day came that she had to say good-bye to them at the airport once more, she managed to do so without shedding a single tear; there would be plenty of time for tears when Jack drove her back. Time and distance spared no one, she reflected with acceptance and resignation as her in-laws turned around one last time to look in her direction before disappearing from sight. Reaching for Jack's warm hand, she got ready to go home. Home and Lyla.

CHAPTER 18

It was now April and Jill, running some last minute errands that afternoon, stopped by the Big Y Supermarket, located in the nearby town of Monroe, in order to pick up some grocery items she was in need of. Suddenly, she spotted a familiar face heading her way. Due to the fact that she had been slightly nearsighted ever since she was a little girl, she wasn't able to clearly see the other person's face until she was only a few feet away. To her surprise and delight, the woman turned out to be none other than Rose, the kind nurse she had liked so much and who had gone out of her way to help her when she was a patient at Silver Hills. Feeling at little awkward for a moment, Jill was not quite sure how to proceed, but the friendly smile on Rose's face gave her the go ahead she was looking for. After sharing a warm embrace, the two young women chatted for a while, exchanging pieces and bits about their lives since they had last seen each other. Yes, Rose was still working at Silver Hills, a job she simply loved and was very proud of, and yes, Jill was doing remarkably well and had even gotten herself a little puppy that she simply adored. "Jack is fine, thank God, and so are my mother, brothers, and sisters. Nice of you to remember," she added, the smile never leaving her lips. The conversation flowed easily between the two women, who Jill had a feeling were pretty close in age. Way sooner than she wished for, the two were saying good-bye as they resumed running their errands for the day. About three weeks later, Jill stopped by the neighborhood Walgreen's pharmacy in order to pick up a few toiletries that were on special when, to her pleasant surprise, she bumped into Rose again. This time around though, she didn't wait for Rose to make the first move, approaching her with a broad grin that was instantly reciprocated, their affinity for one another clearly written on their faces. That led to quite a lot of amiable chatting before they once more found themselves having to part, still way too soon for them both. The truth was that they would have loved to continue their conversation for a little while longer even though neither one expressed their wishes out loud, fearful to sound too forward. The third encounter was almost inevitable, since they appeared to live in the same neighborhood, thus probably patronized some of the same establishments. June 6 started out sunny and warm from the get go, the perfect late spring kind of weather she loved so much. In the early afternoon, Jill decided to drive down to the Countryside cleaners, in the Huntington Center part of Shelton, in order to pick up some spring and summer items she had dropped off a few days earlier. As she was about to pay for them, she felt a gentle tap on her left shoulder. Slightly startled, she slowly turned around. The radiant smile that greeted her was so contagious that it caused her to automatically smile in return, a warm feeling enveloping her heart in a cloud of fondness and surprise. This time, however, instead of chatting in the aisles as they had done in the past, Rose found herself cordially inviting Jill to her nearby house for some "fresh brewed coffee and homemade cranberry-orange scones." "My specialty," she proudly added, her grin widening as she playfully winked at her newfound friend, the bond connecting them becoming more solid and precious with each word they exchanged. Jill, more than glad to accept the friendly invitation, agreed to follow Rose's car in her own as they headed out of the parking lot together. They travelled for less than ten minutes before they turned onto the street where Rose lived, a quiet neighborhood right off of Booth Hill Road and about eight blocks from where Jill's house was actually located. *What a small world!* she chuckled, an amused grin instantly spreading across her face, happy to know that Rose lived so close by.

The neat yellow Cape-Cod-style house was utterly charming and quite obviously well cared for. The perennial gardens were simply a feast for the eyes, awash in beautifully vibrant colors, most in full bloom already. Several hanging flower baskets lined the expansive front porch, adding more color to the house. To one side of the porch, a double swing gently swayed in the early June breeze, very inviting to anyone passing by, while a white wrought iron bistro set consisting of a small mosaic-topped round table and two high-backed chairs sat on the opposite side of the swing. With brightly colored cushions that matched the shades of the potted plants scattered around the large veranda, the decor made for a very welcoming overall feeling for those approaching the front door. "What a lovely porch," Jill exclaimed sincerely to no one in particular, her words simply reflecting what she was thinking out loud. Upon entering the house, she found herself in the middle of a cheerfully painted living room, the light green hue on the walls complementing the polished dark wood floors to perfection. A cozy and deep fireplace took up an entire corner of the generously sized room. As she headed to the kitchen to make the coffee, Rose kindly invited Jill to make herself at home. Looking around with genuine admiration, she continued to study the absolutely beautiful and impeccably decorated room. She spotted the picture of a smiling young man hugging an equally smiling Rose, with a precious little girl between the two of them, her shiny dark hair cascading over slim shoulders and framing a petite angelic face. Additional photographs showcased the same child in various stages of growth, all by herself in some and surrounded by several smiling people in others, including Rose. "What a beautiful family," Jill muttered to herself with a slight touch of envy in her voice. "I'm so happy for you, Rose," she added with sincerity, her words thick with longing. The couch in the ample living room was a huge, overstuffed, and inviting one, the kind that beckoned a person to simply let go and happily sink into its thick-cushioned luxury. Even the sage green and beige striped fabric covering the entire piece conveyed a sense of tranquility and serenity, a vibe that Jill picked up as soon as she first entered the house. She gladly accepted Rose's invitation and made herself at home, not once doubting the sincerity of her words. She indeed sat down, allowing herself to simply sink into its alluring softness with a contented sigh, a smile still on her satisfied face, almost purring like a well-fed cat on a sunny window sill. Rose soon appeared carrying a carved teak tray upon which she had placed two colorful coffee mugs next to matching sugar and cream bowls. A generous plate of heavenly-smelling scones occupied the center of the tray, two small plates of butter and raspberry jam to the side. "You never mentioned that you were married," Jill said with interest as she took the coffee mug being offered to her by the still smiling woman. Rose, however, waited until she was sitting down before answering her, seeming to take her time in the process of doing so. "I was," came the simple reply, "my husband died a long time ago, when our daughter was almost two years old." *Just like me*, Jill thought, at once filled with deep compassion and understanding. "He was killed in a car crash," she added, momentarily lost in her thoughts. *What a strange coincidence,* Jill reflected, her mind starting to wander at the candidly stated revelation. "From the kitchen I could hear several emergency vehicles, their sirens screaming as they rushed by. I had just gotten our daughter up and was preparing breakfast for the three of us as I had done so many times before, eagerly waiting for my husband to get home. Never in a million years could I have imagined that those wailing, frightening sirens were bringing those same vehicles to the scene of a horrific car accident just around the corner from us, on Daniels Farm Road to be precise. That was where my Matt lay gravely injured, near death. He never made it to the hospital because his injuries were so severe that he died in the ambulance on his way there." "Matt?" Jill asked, trying hard to ignore the suddenly raised hairs on the back of her neck, her heart beginning to perform somersaults inside her chest. "Yes, Matt," came the barely audible response as Rose took a deep breath to calm her heart. "My husband's name was Matthew. Matthew Brice Kingston. He was only twenty-seven years old when he died," she added with an effort, choking back the tears now forming behind her burning eyes, threatening to breakdown the wall she had so carefully erected around the excruciatingly painful memory of so long ago. A shiver ran down Jill's spine all of a sudden, shaking her to the core. Did she hear along the way, from someone she couldn't quite remember now, that another man had also died in the same accident that had killed Drew, or was her mind now simply playing cruel tricks on her for some unknown reason? Did someone else die on that day? Could it really have happened, and she had just buried that fact way deep in her subconscious as a means of protection from any added pain? She went on, continuing to question herself, her thoughts, of their own volition, wandering off to that tragic time in her life when she had lost her own husband. Rose's low voice, however, managed to bring her instantly back to the here and now as she resumed talking in a resigned tone. "I was told by someone at the time, I can't quite remember who, that the driver of the other car, unfortunately, hit a puddle and lost control of it. They collided so hard that the other car flipped over twice, landing on its roof. The other driver, poor man, apparently died instantly. Thank God his little boy, who was strapped in his car seat behind his dad, survived the crash with little more than minor injuries, and that was nothing short of a miracle. As bad as I felt for myself, my little girl, and Matt's family, I could not help but feel great compassion for the other man's loved ones, for I realized that those poor people were suffering in the exact same manner and going through the very same unimaginable heartache and pain that we were all going through at the time. In my mind, that made us all kindred spirits going through the exact same agony, regardless of the fact that we didn't even know one another. My pain was their pain and vice versa, if you can understand what I mean. Here I was, barely twenty-three years old and a widow already with a two-year-old little girl to bring up alone." Rose was so involved in telling the sad events that she didn't notice Jill's contrite expression or the fact that she had a stunned look on her face as she continued her painful and, at the same time, cathartic story. "Matt and I didn't get married until a few weeks after our baby was born. You see, I'm not originally from Connecticut. I moved here when I was nineteen years old. I was actually born and raised in Meadow Hills, a small rural town in Missouri. I come from a large farming family and am the second oldest of nine children, five boys and four girls. My mom and dad, Julia and Jonathan, had inherited the farm from my maternal grandparents, and we lived mainly from what we planted and raised, selling what we could spare to pay the bills. The kids ranged from twenty-one to four years of age when I first left, and their names are Josh, Caroline, Michael, Jason, Allie, Jeremy, Bruce, and Cassie, the baby of the family. Things were really tough at home, and money was always scarce, no matter how hard we all worked. I could see the worry in my parents' faces, not knowing whether or not they had enough money to pay all the bills at the end of each month, always struggling just to get by. That's why I immediately accepted a position as a live-in nanny for a well-to-do couple right here in Woodbridge. My mom and dad tried very hard to talk me out of leaving, but I wouldn't hear of it. I was nothing but a farming girl from a very small town with a population of less than two thousand habitants, and they were truly afraid that I wouldn't be able to do well in a much bigger place, but I felt that I had to at least try. Mr. Kessler was a local cardiologist who worked at Yale New Haven Hospital while also having a private practice in North Haven. Mrs. Kessler was a corporate lawyer and worked in North Haven as well. I was hired to care for their two young children, Stephanie, four, who was enrolled in preschool from eight thirty in the morning to four in the afternoon, and little Ryan, only two years old. Because their parents had such demanding and busy careers, I had to work Mondays thru Saturdays, with Sundays off to do as I pleased. Because I was trying to send as much money as I could to my family in Meadow Hills, there wasn't that much left over for entertainment. My favorite thing to do, which by the way, didn't cost me a single dime, was to window shop at the Milford Mall, making mental purchases of clothes that I knew I would never be able to afford. But it was a lot of fun nonetheless in my happy world of make believe. And that's where I first met my husband. I was strolling around the mall on a rainy Sunday afternoon when I spotted him, this really nice-looking guy coming toward me. He was carrying a few shopping bags at the time, and as he passed, by he politely smiled at me. Without realizing what I was doing, I stopped dead in my tracks and just stared at him. He was handsome all right, but it was his beautiful smile that captivated me as soon as I saw it. He continued on his way, but then, to my delight, he turned around and came right back, approaching me in either a shy or undecided way, I couldn't tell which. He hesitated before extending his hand for me to shake, an odd thing to do even back then, and introduced himself. We started to walk slowly side by side. I found myself stealing furtive glances at him and caught him doing the same thing to me. We were both awfully awkward at first. But soon I was no longer interested in looking at any of the store windows we were going by, preferring instead to steal furtive glances at him when I was not staring at the floor directly in front of me. I caught Matt doing the exact same thing. It was the beginning of October in 1972, and I remember it as clearly as if it were today! We hit it off right away and, in no time at all, became inseparable. We got along so well that, before I knew what hit me, I had fallen head over heels in love with him and was sure that he felt exactly the same way about me. I didn't worry much when I first missed my period almost a full year into our relationship, so secure was I about Matt and me. When I told Matt that I was pregnant though, his reaction was totally the opposite of what I had expected and hoped for. No misty eyes, no hugs, no reassurances about our future together, nothing. To my surprise, he got really upset and scared, saying that neither one of us was financially stable or emotionally ready to have a child. Abortion, I angrily told him, was out of the question for me, and deep down I truly feel that Matt thought the same way even though he didn't say so at the time. As my flat belly grew rounder, the pressure of an unwanted pregnancy put so much stress on our relationship that Matt ultimately broke up with me. I was devastated and felt totally betrayed by the father of my unborn baby, whom I loved with every fiber of my being. His family was not aware of any of it, but he didn't tell that fact until after our child was already born. During my pregnancy, however, I found myself deeply resentful toward them for what I wrongly perceived to be total lack of caring on their part. The child was, after all, their grandchild, whether they liked it or not for heaven's sake. They should have showed some interest, if not in me, at least in the child I was carrying, who was their grandchild whether they liked it or not, but I never heard from any of them. Perhaps I was too naïve, but I never saw any of it coming, not really, and was totally heartbroken over it. Fortunately, my employers allowed me to stay on as their nanny until about two weeks before my due date. Since I lived with them until then, I was able to save some money even though I continued to send half of my salary to my family all along. I rented a small one-bedroom apartment in Derby, one that luckily included all the utilities except for the telephone. I spent the last two weeks prior to going in for the delivery getting the place ready for my baby's arrival. Matt didn't even come to see us in the hospital after our little girl was born. I was very sad and hurt then, away from my parents and my siblings, but worse of all was the fact that I was away from the only man I had ever loved, and love still with all my heart to this day, the father of my precious newborn daughter. I had been home from the hospital for just about a couple of weeks when, totally out of the blue, he showed up at my doorstep, saying that he missed me like crazy and that he wanted for us to get back together again because he couldn't bear to live without me. When I placed our baby in his arms, he just melted. I never knew that a man could cry so much, for my father never did, not in front of me anyway. When I asked him why he was crying, he gently took my hands in his and candidly told me that he was crying for all the seconds we were apart, for everything he ended up missing because of his foolishness and lack of maturity, vowing never to leave my side again. We were married six weeks later," she added, a touch of longing in her voice. "Unfortunately for us, he died less than two years after, unable to keep his vow to never leave my side again," came the sadly heartbreaking remark. "What about your daughter? Is she in school right now?," Jill asked, hoping against hope that Rose would say yes, thus appeasing the sick and suffocating feeling that hovered over her like a menacing dark cloud and had ever since she first learned that her friend had lost her own husband in a car crash just like she did. The young woman's features, however, took on a pained expression, and her eyes reflected the intensity of her devastation, slicing right through Jill's decimated heart in an instant, her spine suddenly gone cold while her hands began to sweat. "My daughter died when she was nine years old," she answered in a hushed tone, now barely above a whisper. "What? How"?–was all that Jill managed to say, the knot in her stomach getting tighter and tighter, threatening to savagely sever her body in two. She found it almost impossible to even breathe when, suddenly, her burning eyes rested on an object that had been sitting in front of her all along–a pink, yellow, and white ceramic vase in the shape of a baby's bootie which she had failed to notice before, right there, on the mantle above the massive fireplace. Her eyes transfixed, Jill felt her body tumble into a deep black hole, the quick drop as frightful as the inevitable impact at the very bottom of it. Recalling the loss was so devastating to Rose that she had to pause for a moment in order to compose herself a bit before resuming her story once more. She was totally oblivious to the paleness that had suddenly assailed her friend's face as her eyes remained impaled on the delicate ceramic vase. "I still don't understand and can't believe it, no matter how many years have gone by," she went on in a grief-filled voice, the pained look never leaving her face. "One minute, Sam was riding on the swing hanging from that old oak tree in the backyard; back and forth, back and forth she rode, her innocent laughter filling my heart with joy and gratitude. 'I am flying high,' she chanted over and over again in that high-pitched voice of hers that I knew so well and had grown to love so much. The next minute, nothing but total silence. I patiently waited for her to burst through the kitchen door as she had done hundreds of times before, only this time she was taking way too long to come back inside," Rose stammered. Her voice, cracking under the weight of her pain, trailed off. "I ran outside to find out what was taking her so long and that's when I saw her little form just lying there, not moving at all. I had graduated from nursing school just two weeks before, and my skills were still not that sharp, but I don't believe any training in the world could ever prepare you for something as devastating as that. I cradled her fragile head carefully in my trembling hands, and even with my limited basic skills, the knowledge was, unfortunately for me, still there. I couldn't help but notice that her neck seemed to be at an awkward angle. She was not breathing, I noticed right away; I looked for a pulse but found none. I gently laid her head back on the grass again and ran back into the house as fast as I could to call 911. For some insane reason that I to this day can't comprehend, the operator failed to understand the urgency of my call, asking me really stupid and pointless questions that I simply didn't have the time or inclination to answer. I remember thinking, enraged, why is this woman wasting so much precious time that we clearly don't have when all I wanted, all that I really needed at the time, was for the damned paramedics to get there as soon as possible so that they could make my little girl well again?" Rose's usually soft voice, which had steadily risen as she continued to describe the traumatic events, suddenly got lower again as she resumed the story. "I now realize that deep down I must have known all along that it was already too late, that my precious little girl was already gone, but I simply couldn't acknowledge that sad fact. Not then and not now. No mother could, I'm sure. After a few minutes that for me seemed like hours, I heard the sirens as the ambulance rounded the corner and approached the house. A couple of paramedics quickly knelt by Sam's still body, roughly pushing me aside and out of their way, which made me quite furious. I had covered my daughter with a blanket, holding her little hands in mine to warm them up because they were getting increasingly cold with each passing minute. And now, these rude people were shoving me aside as if I was nothing but a nuisance or a curious bystander, upsetting me even more than I already was. Please, just concentrate on helping my child, I wanted to scream, my mind all over the place, not able to think rationally at the time, my limited professional experience totally out the window. To add insult to injury, they had the audacity to deny my request to ride in the back of the ambulance with my child, giving me what I thought was nothing more than some lame excuse back then. They said that they needed all the elbow room available in order to move around freely so that they could better help her, but I didn't buy their explanations at all, indignation clouding my already overcrowded mind. What they didn't understand, what they would never even begin to understand, was that I felt like I would never see my daughter alive again if I let her out of my sight. I now realize how irrational and unfair my behavior was, but at the time, it somehow made perfect sense to me. My daughter needed me, and these seemingly uncaring people were hell-bent on keeping me from being with her, and that was all I could think about. Anger, anguish, fury, fear all rolled up into a lead ball that struck me in the chest, knocking the wind right out of my lungs, my heart being trampled on by a truth that I could never come to terms with.

The coffee felt really soothing going down her throat as Rose paused for a minute before resuming her sad tale. Jill's wide eyes, unable to look away, remained on her face, her own expression one of pure agony and disbelief. "Driving behind the ambulance, I was nearly blinded by my own tears, but I was beyond caring by then. I don't even remember parking my car. Rushing inside the emergency room, ironically the same one I had gone to on the night I was in labor with my daughter nine years before, I was met by a nurse who told me that she was being examined by the ER physician as we spoke, a Dr. Colbert, if I recall correctly. As I waited for any news about her condition, I prayed to every saint that I could think of. I probably came up with the names of a few who didn't even exist, in my desperation to get as much help as I was sure my daughter was going to need to pull through. When the emergency room physician finally came out to talk to me, I sensed the truth even before he had a chance to open his mouth, and I silently shouted for him not to dare say what he was about to. His downcast eyes and somber expression told me what I already knew but tried so hard to deny. My little girl was already gone, just like that, in a split second." Rose's strained voice trailed off, the newly reopened wound starting to bleed all over again. Shaking, Jill feared that if she tried to stand up then, her legs would simply refuse to sustain the rest of her body. Unable to move a single muscle, she remained seated when all she wanted to do was to get up and run away as fast and as far as she could. She needed to run away and hide, from Rose, from the world, from herself, but most of all, from the cruel and cold truth staring her right in the face. The tragedy that she ultimately caused couldn't be denied now. With tears freely running down her cheeks, she searched her tormented mind for something, anything to say just to break the painful silence that had permeated the room. "Your daughter's name is . . . was Samantha?" she managed to ask in a shallow voice, one that hid the insurmountable desolation and guilt she felt. "Yes" came the simple reply, an enormous effort on Rose's part over the lump that had formed in her constricted throat. "Samantha Rose Kingston. Since my daughter and I both shared the same middle name, I asked all my relatives and friends to call me Rose in her honor after she died. My birth name, however, is Amy. My maiden name was Brennan. Amy Brennan. Amy Rose Brennan to be exact," she concluded, completely oblivious to the pallor that had further assailed Jill's face, which was now totally devoid of any color, her mouth open in a scream that never left her throat.

Blinking rapidly, Jill tried to clear her head, which was ready to explode. *It can't be*, she wanted to shout. *Please, dear God, don't let this be*, she begged repeatedly in her mind, unable to believe how much sorrow destiny could often times dish out. *But this is not just a cruel coincidence as I had so hoped it would be, is it*? she finally acquiesced, no longer able to deny the undeniable. *What have I done to this poor woman? What have I done to her innocent little girl? How could I have done all this to these kind people? And for what, I ask? What did I accomplish besides unspeakable acts of pain and human sacrifice?"* she agonized, her guilt quickly building up and turning into a full state of panic with each breath she took. Totally unaware of the turmoil her revelation had caused in Jill's head and heart, Rose continued to speak in that calm, controlled, and soft voice that Jill had grown to admire so much. "After Sam died, I felt completely and utterly lost, isolated, devastated. Life as I had known was over for me. First Matt, then Sam, it was all too much for me to handle. I wanted to run away somewhere, anywhere, away from everyone and everything, and never come back again. I thought about going back to my parents' home in Missouri, but how could I leave my Matthew and my Samantha behind? I was in such physical, emotional, and mental pain that I seriously contemplated ending my life once and for all, to go join Matt and Sam, where I needed to be and where I belonged, never to be separated again. But then, after a lot of soul-searching, I finally came to the realization that suicide wasn't the answer. It never is the answer nor should it ever be. I thought about Matt's parents who were also going through the pain of first losing their son and then their beloved grandchild. There were so many others who needed me, people who were probably hurting as much or even more than I was, for whatever reason, so I decided to put my grief to good use and not allow Sam's death to be in vain. That was the reason why I turned to psychiatric nursing as a career choice, a decision that turned out to ultimately be my very own salvation. You see, I wanted more than anything else to be of some comfort to my patients. I wanted to help them heal from what afflicted them, be the source of their affliction and torment an emotional, a physical, or a psychological one. In my sincere efforts, I ended up healing myself in the process as well without even realizing it. I concentrated so hard on my patients' needs and pain that, for a while anyway, I forgot about my own. I vividly remember the very first day I saw you, all alone, sitting on that chair by the tall window in the corner of the common room. You looked so fragile and lost and so, so sad. I was instantly drawn to you, you know? For some unknown reason to me at the time, I felt a connection to you that went way beyond any that I had ever experienced before or felt since. It was like a common link that I could not understand, let alone explain. The only thing that I knew and was sure of was that I was meant to help you somehow, but even stranger than that was the feeling that I, for some reason, needed you as much as you needed me. I made it my personal crusade to assist you as you crawled out of the bottomless pit you had fallen into, to be there as you started to emerge from the thick darkness that had swallowed you whole. I wanted to be by your side as you got started on your way to getting well again, just like it had happened to me. And now, I firmly believe that it was my own daughter, my little angel all along, who was guiding me by the hand to the one person she knew needed me more than anyone else at Silver Hills at the time, and that person was you, Jill. I will be forever grateful that our paths crossed when they did but even more grateful, given the circumstances, that things worked out as well as they did for you, my friend, as well as for me." Such kind and sincere words spoken by this gentle and caring woman were Jill's undoing. She quickly swallowed the last of her coffee, careful not to drop the mug as she returned it to the tray with shaking hands, leaving her scone untouched. She quickly came up with a plausible excuse and an apology about having forgotten a previous engagement she had made, hastily bid her hostess good-bye, and departed the house as quickly as her wobbly legs would carry her. She tried, with every ounce of strength she could still find in her beaten body, to remain composed and in an upright position, at least long enough to reach the privacy of her car. *Don't let me fall apart. I can't fall apart now. Please, not yet. Not until I'm all alone again,* she fervently prayed, not daring to look back at the poor woman she had hurt so deeply and for so long and who now considered her a good friend. "Oh, Amy, if you only knew the whole truth, what then? Would you still like me as much as you think you do?" The terrible outcome was as heavy on her heart as it was on her conscience. Her soul wasn't even in the equation, having ceased to matter many years before this devastating day.

*   *   *

Behind the wheel, Jill found it literally impossible to focus. Neither could she control the violent trembling that had taken over her entire body, her jumbled thoughts in such turmoil that she couldn't think or see straight. She fumbled with the car keys as she tried to insert them in the ignition, her face a mask of desperation and horror. As tears poured from her tormented eyes, she was finally able to start her car. She proceeded to slowly back out of Amy's driveway as the unsuspecting woman, completely unaware of the havoc her story had caused in her new friend's mind, waved at her with a smile on her beautiful face. While she was driving, Jill was forced to pull to the side of the road several times in order to compose herself before returning to the road, her mind on overdrive by then. The cold and clammy hands gripping the steering wheel refused her command to cease their infernal trembling, making it very difficult for her to safely maneuver the car, but she continued to drive anyway, aware only that she needed to keep on going, destination unknown. Totally oblivious as to where she was headed, she simply forged ahead turning left or right at will, with no clear purpose in mind and no direction to speak of. After a while, she found herself in the same park where she used to take DJ and Pepper on the weekends, during a much happier time, at time that now seemed over a hundred years ago. At the deserted park, she sat on the first bench she came across, totally immersed in her sorrow. Her erratic thoughts, running away from her, were nothing more than a jumble of images and events set in fast-forward mode. The sun remained warm even though it was almost five thirty in the afternoon by then. Lost in her thoughts, she wasn't aware of anything but the pounding of her heart and the heaviness upon her shoulders. With both of her arms resting limply against the back of the bench, she looked at nothing in particular, her eyes simply staring ahead. Suddenly she felt a hand firmly grip her right shoulder. Startled out of her stupor, she turned around and stared in disbelief at the young and handsome face of her tormentor, a face she had vowed to forget but had hoped she would not. The cold and calculating smile was the same, his eyes devoid of any trace of emotion, his demeanor even more cynical than she remembered. "*You!*" she hissed, unable to mask her disdain. "You despicable and evil creature, you bastard. What have you made me do?" she shouted in accusation, fury clearly detected in her harsh voice. "Me?" he answered casually, in a clearly mocking tone. "Nothing," he continued, drawing out the word as if savoring each individual syllable one at a time. "I made you do nothing, that's what I did. I merely made you a proposition. If I remember correctly, and I do, you were the one who chose to accept it, were you not?" The brutality of his words, compounded by the cruel truthfulness of their meaning, managed to deliver a final blow to her critically wounded soul. Defeated, Jill lowered her gaze, unable to tolerate his blatant scrutiny any longer. "Now," he droned on, addressing his defenseless prey once again, "if you are not happy with the bargain *you* made back then, I have a solution for you," he proceeded, accentuating the word *you*, which lingered in the air far longer than necessary. "And what would this so called solution be?" she asked, aware of the fear that was creeping back into her voice in spite of her efforts to keep it under control. "Very well, then. Very well indeed. I am willing to restore the life that *we* took so long ago, but in order for me to do so, you must forfeit your son's life this time. No other will do." He paused, allowing his words to fully reach their chosen target. "Again, I must remind you that it will be your choice and not mine, remember that. Are you now prepared to handle the consequences?" He asked, knowing that he had her exactly where he wanted her, cowered and cornered, with nowhere to turn. He had known this since that first afternoon when he had first laid eyes on her back in the summer of 1983, the clearly distraught young mother that was simply desperate to save the life of her dying nine-year-old son. During what she later acknowledged was a fatal encounter, she would have done absolutely anything he asked of her, just about anything. And now, thirteen years later, she finally realized that he had been sure of it even before they "bumped" into each other, making her tremble with the growing amount of anger his arrogant self-assurance provoked in her. How predictable mere mortals were, he mused, quite satisfied with himself and the power he exerted over most of them, if not all. But we should never be greedy, should we? His bargaining skills were second to none, but it was his uncanny ability to patiently wait until the time was just right in order to take action that clearly distinguished him from any other. He was always above superb, optimum being a superlative he carried out extremely well, and self-doubt something he knew absolutely nothing about. Although she was frightened to the core by the power she realized he possessed, Jill still refused to acknowledge the depth of her fear, for ultimately she hated him far more than she feared the truly odious and despicable creature he truly was. Her indignation and remorse quickly took over, infusing her with renewed courage that forced her to raise her eyes again. His ruthlessness, however, was more powerful than her certitude. He soon appeared to have Jill reduced to a pile of ashes once more. He was not one to back down and never had. An opportunist, he was well-versed on the weaknesses of humans, which was the narrow open door through which he sauntered in, taking what he wanted the most–their soul. This one time, though, he completely misinterpreted Jill's despise and remorse for weakness and was momentarily taken by surprise with the resolve he suddenly saw deep in her eyes. For once, she stared right back at him with unflinching determination, a strength she had never shown before. "*Do it!*" she answered in a curt and chilling tone, the simple reply resonating loudly in her ears as she lowered her gaze again. Jill was well aware that she was, once again, discarding the fundamental teachings of her faith and personal beliefs, but she failed to find any other way out once more. She felt that she had to at least try to, somehow, rectify some of the wrong she had unknowingly caused. The incredible amount of hurt and pain inflicted upon so many innocent and undeserving people was like a tempest of human suffering that had run rampant and for far too long already. It ended up becoming an all-consuming secret that left deep scars in her conscience, and she would never be able to complete the healing process unless she was able to heal two other people first. Again, Jill found herself at a dead end with only one solution for the dilemma she had unwillingly created. It was a predicament uncannily similar to the one she had to face when DJ was nine years old and dying. Back then, she had been given the chance to restore his life, and now it was Amy and Sam's turn. The ultimate price she would have to pay was steep and one she could never fathom she would ever contemplate, let alone agree to. But times had certainly changed, and circumstances dictated that she behave accordingly. After everything she had become aware of in the painful year since DJ's arrest, acting any differently would be an even bigger injustice. When she added to the facts already known what she had just found out from Rose, how could she simply refuse to at least repay for some of the kindness the long-suffering woman had showered upon her during and after her nervous breakdown? It was a price that she couldn't afford not to pay. The miracle she had been granted back in 1983 she now recoiled from. It had hit her with unrestrained viciousness on the day she found the silver metal box hidden under DJ's bed and finished her off when she found out that Rose was really Amy Brennan.

She so despised the evil creature standing in front of her, that she didn't trust herself to even look in his direction. She could probably shred him to pieces with her hate-guided bare hands, if not literally, at least in her mind. He was probably just gloating at what he must've perceived as a victory on his part, the odious beast, once again proving how weak she truly was with her gaze down like a gutless being. With a smug grin on his lips, he was probably just itching to rub her face in the fact that she was nothing more than a predictable mere human, no different than all the others before or since her, the sick and egotistical bastard! Given the chance, she would like nothing less than to slowly but viciously scratch his cold and calculating eyes right out of their sockets. By the time she had finally calmed down enough to look up again, the young man was gone, no detectable sign of his presence, let alone his existence, anywhere to be found.

CHAPTER 19

Life in a maximum security prison was extremely difficult to say the least, even for the hardest of criminals. For DJ, it was no different. One always slept with an eye open and a fist ready especially during the long hours of the night. Under the cover of total darkness, any undetected shadow could easily turn into one's foe. He was a confirmed coward and had been most of his life, one who never had the balls to raise a hand against another male. His "expertise" was saved only for those who were clearly much weaker than he was, those he was sure that he could easily control and dominate. Drew was very conscientious about avoiding conflict with his fellow inmates at any cost, keeping a low profile at all times. Not wanting to call any unnecessary attention to his persona, he preferred to fly under the radar whenever possible. He continually paid close attention to his surroundings, especially the whereabouts of the other incarcerated men around him, twenty-four hours a day, seven days a week, never letting his guard down. What he lacked in courage, he more than made up for in intellect and common sense, and like a cat, he always seemed to land on his feet. It had been an arduous challenge for him though, but he managed to remain ahead of the game called survival. Anyone could very well attach at least a hundred different adjectives to him, most of them of a negative and heartless nature, but not a single person could, nor should, ever doubt his exceptionally high level of intelligence. Always trying to ensure his safety above anything else, he was most concerned with the fact that in prison, his good looks served only to place him in greater danger. He was aware of the fact that they actually worked against him and not in his favor, as they had done all his life in the outside world from the time he was only a little boy. Amazingly, thus far, he had managed to elude trouble albeit he came very close to it on several occasions. He worked hard at maintaining a low profile when away from the relative security of his cell by conducting himself in a careful and reserved manner. More amazing than that though, was the fact that he had managed to avoid becoming another prisoner's "bitch." The term, which was widely used to describe an inmate who became the "property" of a more powerful inmate, was a common and well-known reality among men who had been incarcerated for prolonged periods of time. Being someone's "property" meant safety for the "bitch," but it also meant that they became sex slaves and errand boys for their "masters." The prisoners sexual needs didn't simply go away once they were locked up, so many had to make do with another male, even though most were not even close to being homosexuals. It had been that way since men first created the much larger prisons so prevalent nowadays, which housed prisoners by the thousands literally under one roof, albeit in individual cells. But if an inmate really wanted to gain access at another, sooner or later he would find a way, separate cells and all; it was only a matter of time, along with the right connections and opportunity. Either way, they always found the means to gain sexual gratification, one way or the other. It seemed beyond ironic and totally unjust that DJ, who had savagely violated six young women after killing them in a carefully orchestrated and cold fashion, had, thus far, so cleverly been able to avoid being sexually abused while behind bars. Being raped would at least give him a small taste of his own medicine, of the cruelty he inflicted while gaining so much pleasure from the atrocious crimes he carried out. How much pleasure would he take if he was the one being so brutally attacked? But his time would come, if there was any justice at all here on earth. "One can never be too careful around here," he scowled, feigning a false bravado that he had never known or possessed. At mealtimes, he sat alone, quickly glancing from side to side before finally sitting down. He ate his meals just as quickly, leaving promptly as soon as he was done, never lingering around afterwards. Very astute, he was well aware of the fact that many inmates had taken a profound dislike to him, to put it mildly, and he wasn't about to do anything stupid that would certainly only serve to stir up this hornet's nest that was now his permanent abode. Knowing full well that danger lurked in practically every corner, he followed an extremely regimented routine, which he performed on a daily basis whenever he was locked in his cell. The series of exercises aimed at keeping him in the best physical condition possible as well as maintaining his impressively muscular physique was achieved after countless hours of very specific exercises. Such dedication had paid off in a matter of weeks, strengthening every muscle in his trim body without the help of any exercise equipment whatsoever. "No bastard son of a bitch would dare to mess with me now, not in the shape that I am in," he gloated every chance he got, giving himself all the credit he felt he had duly earned. Because no one ever gave him the satisfaction of congratulating him for the success he had achieved, he gave himself the proverbial pat in the back every chance he got. "Those lousy sons of mother-fucking bitches," he silently cursed in his head, clenching his right fist in a controlled fit of anger that he was simply too coward to openly express and never would. He was on his way to return his food tray after having finished his 6:00 p.m. meal when his attention was suddenly drawn to shouts being exchanged by two burly men not far from where he stood. Before long, the two were engaged in a fierce fist fight that quickly escalated into a full-blown brawl. As testosterone levels rose, tempers suddenly flared up, and long-buried old grudges resurfaced in no time at all. Like wildfire, the fight spread totally out of control, involving an increasing number of other inmates and turning the cafeteria into a wrestling rink. Within seconds, several guards quickly moved in and desperately tried to disperse the unruly crowd by separating the fighting men, but no matter how fast they worked, they failed to gain any ground. In the pandemonium that ensued, more men joined in, some of them not even aware of why they were getting involved, fighting simply for the heck of it and more than eager to put some of the pent-up energy they had accumulated over time to good use. And nothing at all could beat the adrenalin rush of a good old-fashioned free-for-all cafeteria brawl for accomplishing that.

Drew was just about to place his tray on the conveyor belt that would carry it back to the kitchen to be cleared, when his eyes caught a shiny light being reflected off of some sort of metal object that was being held up high in the air. The raised arm holding the knife, which had been cleverly fashioned from the handle of a table spoon, came down swiftly and expertly, the knife embedding deeply into Drew's midleft chest, penetrating with ease through fabric and flesh. Blood immediately started to pour out of the ghastly wound in spurts, quickly turning the color of his jumpsuit into a bright mixture of orange and vivid red. DJ automatically tried to cover the hole with his right hand in a feeble attempt to stop the continuous flow of blood but managing only to have it easily slip between his trembling fingers and little else. As it continued to gush out, the blood formed what looked like a macabre, life-sucking five-fingered fountain. In the few minutes that it took for him to succumb to his mortal injury, he realized that death was fast approaching, and that realization filled him with waves of sheer vulnerability and unchecked terror. It was nothing short of a small dose of well-deserved poetic justice. For one who derived such sense of power, domination, and sexual pleasure from all those girls he tortured and killed, DJ felt nothing but common panic and fear in the short time preceding his own demise, just like his victims had. Unfortunately though, his ending came far too quickly and quietly amid the shouts and curses being exchanged among the fighting inmates that surrounded his body. It would certainly have been of some small consolation to the families of the young women he had so callously killed, to know that DJ's thoughts were so mundane and void of self-importance in the end, had they been privy of that bit of information. No bravery, no fanfare, no bragging whatsoever, nothing but common unadulterated fear. A fitting farewell to someone who had no heart, no conscience, no emotions, who didn't even had the decency to feel the slightest hint of remorse for the young girls he had killed. He had been so self-centered during his life that noble words such as remorse and forgiveness never entered his mind, for they had no place in his very selective vocabulary. As the guards continued to work hard at putting a stop to the violent conflict, DJ lay dying on the dirty cafeteria floor, the black and white vinyl tiles providing the perfect background for the deep red color of his blood. As it continued to pour out of his chest wound, it quickly spread around his mortally wounded body like a fittingly sinister halo, framing an equally sinister man.

No one seemed to notice the form lying on the ground as they continued to fight around him. Perhaps many of them did but simply chose not to, which was something no one would ever know for sure, and neither would any of them care to. But even if anyone had deemed that the correct thing to do was to come to his aid, it wouldn't have mattered anyway. DJ's fate had been sealed the second he entered the cafeteria that evening, for what he had no idea would be the last meal in his troubled, marred life, a life that would probably not be truly missed by any other person besides his long-suffering mother. Drew William Millner Jr., beloved son of the late Drew James and Jillian Elizabeth Millner, who came into the world on a night filled with love and joy and surrounded by a cozy blanket of promises, hopes, and dreams, left this same world all alone, deprived of what he came to value the most–his own sense of power and self-entitlement. Drew William Millner Jr., pure male beauty and perfection on the outside yet lacking the slightest semblance to a human being on the inside. A heart made of stone, a mind filled with evil thoughts and deeds and absolutely no soul to speak of.

*　　*　　*

Amy woke up startled when she felt the soft touch of a hand caressing the side of her face. The TV was still on, casting an eerie glow around the dark slender form standing directly in front of her. As she tried to focus, a sweet voice said, "Wake up, sleepy head." *That voice!* Amy shook her head, trying hard to identify the person who was talking to her, still not fully awake yet. It took her a while, but she finally found her voice. "Who are you? How did you get in?" The sun was setting on what had been a strange day. First, her friend Jill had left abruptly a little while before and without even tasting her scone. And now, some stranger had gained access into her home and was caressing her. "Who are you?" she repeated in a tentative low voice, totally confused by what was happening. As her eyes slowly adjusted to the darkness, she was finally able to partially see the smiling face only inches away from her own, silky dark hair falling below her shoulders and halfway down her back. Speaking a little louder this time, Amy slowly went on even though nothing made any sense to her at the moment. "Sam? Is that really you, Sam? Am I still dreaming?" she whispered, unwilling to break the spell. It was as wonderful as it was painful to see what her little girl would look like had she lived. "How I wish that this wasn't a dream, darling, yet I don't want to wake up," she said with a voice that was slightly higher this time. The form got even closer to where she sat so still that it appeared as if she had been sewn onto the couch's fabric. A hand softly touched the side of Amy's face again, lingering there for a few seconds before lovingly tucking a strand of chestnut hair behind her left ear with infinite tenderness. "Is that you, Sam?" she asked again. "Of course it's me, Mom! What a silly question to ask. Who else could it be but you daughter, you silly thing?" Jolted by hearing the voice, Amy rubbed her eyes, only then beginning to doubt whether that she was still sleeping or not. With the smiling face only inches from her own, she reached out, eager to touch her little girl but more than afraid she wouldn't be able to. Feeling the softness of her young skin under her trembling fingers, she suddenly recoiled, startled by the imaginable reality. "What's the matter, Mom? Are you all right?" Sam asked, her voice edged with concern at her mother's strange reaction the minute she touched her cheek. Not getting an answer, she continued, trying not to jump to any conclusions and not really worry until she had concrete reason to. After all, her mother had been deep asleep when she arrived and was probably still groggy from being awaken so quickly, especially when she was not expecting it. "You look like you have just seen a ghost, Mom, so pale and scared. I can guarantee you that I'm not a ghost, or at least I don't believe that I am. Not yet, anyway!" Sam went on with a laughing tone in her voice. Seeing that her mother's expression remained unbelievably pale and confused, she stopped her teasing altogether. Suddenly she started to grow very worried by the look of total confusion and surprise on her mother's usually happy and relaxed face. "You are starting to freak me out now. What's going on, Mom?" Sam asked, getting hold of her mother's cold and trembling hands with increasing apprehension. "Oh, Sam, my little Sam, can this possibly be you? I must be dreaming still, but if I am, please darling, don't you dare wake me up, I beg you, just don't wake me up. Not yet." "You are not making any sense, Mom. Snap out of it," Sam said, becoming more and more puzzled by her mother's clearly odd behavior. "I'm terribly sorry if I frightened you, I certainly didn't mean to. I rang the door bell several times, and when you didn't come to the door, I used my old key and let myself in. I knew you were at home because I peeked through the tiny windows on the garage door and saw your car in there. Dazed, Amy remained seated and completely unable to understand how her daughter could possibly be right there in front of her, all grown up, talking to her, *touching her. How can this possibly be! I really don't know what's really going on here! Will somebody please tell me what's going on here? Please . . .* Far too stunned to speak, she simply allowed her mind to drift back in time, to the day when her precious baby was born, so beautiful and so utterly perfect. Her head was perfectly round and covered with a soft coating of shiny dark hair, so much like her own. She had a tiny button nose and pouty pink lips, chubby little hands and feet that were so small they were simply adorable, both fitting comfortably inside her hand with plenty of room to spare. How someone so small could be so utterly perfect in every sense of the word was beyond imagining. She marveled at the tiny creature now looking at her, the same little one that had managed to swiftly and single-handedly steal her heart without even trying the minute she had been placed in her loving arms. She had never imagined such feelings even existed, incredible emotions that immediately overshadowed any other she had ever experienced before or since, making Matt's absence a little less painful to handle. Deep down though, she still held on to hope that he would, somehow, just show up at her door one day, making everything all right once more. "Oh, Matt, our little angel is so beautiful, even more so than I had imagined she would be. She looks a lot like you, sweetheart," Amy said to herself as she cradled little Samantha close to her chest and both fell into a peaceful and contented sleep.

After leaving the hospital, she got home by taxi, back to her nearly empty one-bedroom apartment in Derby. The small and barely furnished place was instantly taken over by the immense love she felt for her newborn daughter, every corner, every nook and cranny was filled to capacity with this newfound and unbelievably special feeling. The baby's crib, which she had proudly and painstakingly restored to its original beauty, was a lucky find from the Goodwill Store in Monroe and now stood in its place of honor, right next to Amy's rundown sleigh double bed in the sparsely furnished bedroom. An old rocker, its dark red fabric well-worn on the back and on the seat and armrests, sat by the single window in the relatively small room, patiently waiting to be put to good use. The equally modest living room was sparsely furnished as well and consisted mainly of a dark green high-backed couch, which was still in fairly good condition given the fact that it was well over ten years old by then. The sofa was another lucky Goodwill find, one that upon closer inspection revealed a solid wood frame still intact, although the upholstery had obviously seen better days. The velvety brocade material covering the piece had been meticulously cleaned by a grateful Amy, the ugly stains that had originally made it such a bargain to begin with no longer a noticeable problem at all. An odd-shaped end table, which had been perfectly painted in a soft beige color, sat on the right side of the couch with a pretty hurricane lamp–its flowery glass-dome shade perfectly matching the table neatly placed on top. A twenty-two-inch black-and-white television set was perched on a tall square bar stool, which was painted in the same beige color as the end table, making both pieces appear to actually be a set. Amy quickly learned that a can of good quality paint could literally work miracles on old mismatched pieces of second-hand furniture. She gladly took full advantage of this easy an inexpensive bit of knowledge, making sure she used every drop of paint she could squeeze out of that one single can. A dark green Formica kitchen table with two metal-framed and vinyl-covered chairs completed the contents of the small but spotless apartment. Although quite modest, it was very neat and comfortable, a cozy little home for Amy and little Sam, and for that she was truly grateful. Amy knew from experience how a few necessary items could really go a long way when your heart was filled with love and your tummy free of hunger pains. That was plenty for them, not only for the time being, but if it was meant to be, for as long as it took. Holding her precious infant in her arms as she gently rocked her to sleep with the help of the old, worn-out rocker, Amy felt undeniably lucky, no doubt the luckiest person on earth by far. No other woman had ever given birth to a baby as perfect and beautiful as her little Samantha, she was simply sure.

The first few days at home proved to be very challenging for Amy and Sam, with money being so scarce, but they had each other and that was enough for them. Besides, having been raised in a large but poor farming family had indeed been a very good foundation upon which Amy began to build their future on. She was well-adept at living a simple life, one that often did not include anything that was not absolutely necessary or essential to get by. She had learned at a very young age to differentiate between wanting something versus really needing it, a lesson she was glad to have been taught during all the hard times she experienced while growing up and which she continued to experience still. It was not that much of a problem for her now to go without, she realized with a mixture of pride and relief. Besides, the only things that really and truly mattered to Amy were the fact that she and her little girl were together, that they both had enough to eat, and that the bills were all paid in full and, most importantly, on time. She often thought about Matt, missing him immensely the few times she allowed herself to feel sorry for herself, but she tried very hard not to dwell too long on it or about the fact that he was no longer in her life and in the life of their precious daughter. "It is just you and me, baby, one for all and all for one."

Amy focused all her energy on Sam's every new move or sound, marveling at the incredible changes unfolding right before her eyes. How wonderful the miracle of being able to create a new life was, of bringing this new life into the world, and then having the enormous joy of seeing that same precious life evolve and progress. Every single day became a world of undiscovered surprises to find and celebrate together, bringing with it something new to rejoice about; whether it was big or small simply made no difference to Amy. Amazingly, no day was quite the same as the one before or the one yet to come, and Amy could hardly wait to find out what it was that ultimately made it so.

Before long, mother and daughter had settled into a quiet, peaceful, and comforting routine. Sam was an exceptionally calm and contented baby, one that was quite easy to care for. Their day usually started at around 6:00 a.m. and concluded with the baby's 10:00 p.m. feeding, after which she slept through the night from the get go. Amy had heard horror stories about extremely sleep-deprived parents and was truly grateful that Sam was such a little angel thus far. Being the second oldest of nine children, she also remembered how long it took for some of her younger siblings to actually sleep through the entire night. The fact that Sam had already started to sleep from her last feeding until daybreak without waking up in between was truly a miracle and a gift, one that was unusual indeed. Early on their second Saturday at home after leaving the hospital, Amy was marveling at the beauty of the warm and sunny late May morning when she was startled to hear the front doorbell ring. Since she hardly knew anyone and was not expecting any visitors, she felt a little reluctant to open the door. The caller, however, was quite persistent, continuing to press the doorbell repeatedly when she didn't come to the door. Finally relenting a little, she muttered under her breath that she might as well see who the person was. She had every intention of politely but firmly sending him or her expediently on their way as soon as she possibly could. She opened the door just a crack, the security chain still hooked, and froze in place, holding the deep breath that she had just inhaled. Amy was totally taken by surprise at the sight of Matt standing there, a sheepish smile on his lips and a miserable look on his gaunt face. Momentarily speechless, she unlatched the chain and moved aside, making a slight motion with her hand for him to come in. Suddenly all the old feelings she still felt for him came rushing in, a deluge of water on a parched canyon bed flooding her mind with a mixture of sorrow and hope. As if on cue, the baby woke up from her nap and started to cry, bringing Amy right back to the then and there. She timidly asked Matt if he wanted to see their child, and he quickly nodded yes, his eyes glued to her beloved face. He was suddenly unable to find his voice, partially due to the surprise of hearing the infant cry and partially because he was still very emotional about seeing Amy again after so many months apart. When she placed their tiny little girl in his arms, a grin quickly appeared on his drawn face, instantly bringing back some of the light that had clearly been missing from his misty and somber eyes. Matt never left that night, and they were married on a balmy Sunday afternoon on June 30, 1974, by a close family friend who happened to be a justice of the peace. The small and intimate ceremony took place in John and Barbara Kingston's modest but cozy living room, with his older brother, Stephen, and older sister, Linda, in attendance, their six-week-old daughter peacefully asleep in her loving grandmother's arms. The Kingston family, Amy quickly realized, was far richer in love than in money. They wished that they could give their son and new bride a far more fitting wedding but were very limited as to how much they could afford to financially contribute to the special occasion. What they lacked in the form of a lavish party, however, they more than made up in their happiness and pride for the young couple and their precious little girl. Barbara, well-known for her cooking and baking skills, had dedicated the entire previous day making the wedding cake, her surprise gift to the newlyweds. The beautiful heart shaped confection was a feast for the eyes, better than any that could have been made by even the most renowned bakeries in town. Made totally from scratch, the large chocolate cake with a fresh raspberry filling was covered with homemade white frosting and was masterfully decorated with small red roses and tiny green leaves. The intricate design culminated with a gorgeous bouquet of much larger red roses surrounding the delicate porcelain figurine of a smiling bride and groom. That very same ornament had decorated John and Barbara's wedding cake more than thirty years before, as well as six generations before that. Barbara intended to give to it to her son and new daughter-in-law as a wedding gift, hopefully to be passed on to the many generations to come, not because of its future monetary value but because of its sentimental one, a true family heirloom of the most loving kind to treasure. Following Linda's touching toast to her little brother and his wife, the giddy couple happily cut the cake, which they proudly shared with their loved ones. The intimate yet truly memorable occasion didn't leave a single dry eye among the small gathering, from beginning to end. After a while, the newly married couple collected their precious baby and headed home. "Someday," Matt said in a husky voice that was filled with emotion as he tenderly brought his bride's left hand to his lips, kissing the simple gold wedding band he had just placed on her ring finger, "I will give you the honeymoon that you truly deserve, my love. I promise you at least that." "It is not necessary," Amy managed to answer, her low voice laden with the immense love she felt around and inside her as she slowly looked from the handsome man sitting proudly beside her to their little angel fast asleep in her car seat. "I have just about everything that I ever wanted, wished for, and dreamed of right here right now," she said, her words coming straight from the heart. She thanked God for all she had already been blessed with, being totally sincere with her feelings and hopes for the future, a promising one now that they were finally together. All she truly wished for in life was to continue loving her husband and daughter, being allowed to grow old with him, in good times as well as bad ones. She was also looking forward to having many more children with Matt, brothers and sisters for their precious little Samantha as soon as their finances became more stable than they currently were. Very young still, they had plenty of time ahead to expand their family, she reasoned as she held her husband's right hand in both of hers, a look of pure contentment across her delicate face, her emerald green eyes filled with the gleam of love and happiness. And little Sam, who slept through the whole ride home, seemed to totally agree with her mommy and daddy. Endearing sighs and many other special noises that only small babies are able to make periodically escaped from her lips while she remained in her blissful state of deep sleep. Amy was filled with enormous warmth, pride, and peace, which all started and ended with two very special people–Mathew Brice Kingston and Samantha Rose Kingston.

Life was far from easy for the newly formed family, but somehow they still managed to scrape together enough money to put toward a down payment on a home of their own, a dream they both had ever since they had gotten married. The charming yellow Cape-Cod-style house with six modest but very spacious rooms was located in a child-friendly neighborhood in the Huntington section of Shelton, right off of Booth Hill Road. It was about thirty minutes from Matt's childhood home in Hamden, which they agreed was very convenient all the way around for the whole family. Before he met Amy, Matt had attended Gateway Community College in North Haven on a part-time basis. He did that while holding down a full-time job as an apprentice electrician in a small company owned and operated by his dad's older brother, his Uncle Ralph. He landed a job as an electrician at Saint Vincent's Hospital, in Bridgeport, from three in the afternoon until eleven thirty at night, glad and relieved to finally have full health and dental insurance for all three of them. He also took out a life insurance policy for added security should anything ever happen to him in the future, for no one really knew what the following day might possibly have in store for them. Although it was a hardship on their finances at the time, he felt very strongly that Amy and Sam needed some sort of protection should anything happen to him. He only wished that they could afford a better policy as well as another special one that included some form of full mortgage payment upon his death, but they were way too expensive for them to swing it just then. *Perhaps in a couple of years or so, we will be in a better financial place than we are currently*, he thought, *but for now, this is the best we can possibly do and still manage to pay all the bills on time.* He soon took a second job at night, from midnight to 7:00 a.m., working as a security guard in the nearby Trumbull Shopping Mall four times a week. He even managed to work an occasional Saturday or Sunday when asked to. He was very proud of the fact that he was able to keep Amy at home, caring for their daughter. He would often say to his clearly worried parents when they voiced their concern about the fact that he worked so many hours every week: "I know that I work hard, Mom, but I am totally happy, I really am. Please, stop worrying about me. We are all just fine, and I consider myself extremely lucky to have my little family and you guys by my side. I love you both with all my heart, and someday I'm going to make you all very proud of my success. My hard work will pay off big time and then you will worry no more, I promise! Just have faith in me, okay? Besides, I'm still very young, and there will be plenty of time for taking it easy once I get where I am headed, you'll see." With the extra income from his second job, he was able to cover all their usual expenses with more ease and even had some money left over for a few "luxuries" here and there. Their favorite thing to do was to go out on a "date" every so often. The evening would usually start with a quiet romantic dinner at the Olive Garden Restaurant, a very pleasant yet affordable Italian eatery in Milford were the food was always delicious and the portions very generous. The laid-back meal would be followed by catching a movie at the Crown Multiplex Theater in Trumbull, usually a "chick flick." Matt used to tease Amy even though he secretly enjoyed them almost as much as his wife did. The magical night usually culminated with them making love for hours in front of a roaring fire in the massive fireplace in their living room, their daughter safe and sound for the night at her grandparent's house. Matt was in fact on his way home from working an extra shift at the mall on that rainy, cold Monday morning in late April, when he was so tragically killed in that horrific car crash back in 1976. They had been married for less than two short years when he died, and with his sudden death, two of his promises ended up not being fulfilled; the first was to Amy, to grow old beside her, and never, ever leave, and the second to his parents, that someday he would be so successful that they would never again have to worry about him. Never and ever–two words so simple and desired yet so hard to attain or keep, even for the hardiest of humans, for in reality they simply did not exist. There is no ever or never, not really, only "for as long as we have, or for as long as we can." If Amy could only have Matt back, and for as long as she could, she thought with soul deep sadness, not yet aware, not at the time anyway, that her life was still full of surprises to come, some of them great in their simplicity, others massive in the intensity of their pain.

"Mom, please say something," Sam's anxious voice managed to cut through Amy's reverie, bringing her abruptly back to the present. Completely and utterly overwhelmed by the events quickly unfolding before her, all Amy managed to do was to tell her precious daughter how much she was loved, had always been loved, and would forever be loved. As she continued to repeat those words over and over, her thoughts drifted back in time once more. Sam, crawling at six months, her toothless smile as captivating as her emerald green eyes, and learning to walk a couple of weeks before her first birthday. The large whale-shaped ice cream cake, covered with bright pink and white frosting and tiny hot pink flowers had a large birthday candle showing a number one in the center. With her cherubic little face literally aglow with unrestrained happiness and with a bright pink birthday hat firmly placed on top of the small dark-haired head, she was being encouraged by everyone to blow out the lit candle. No matter how hard she tried though, all she managed to do was to make the flame sway back and forth without putting it out. "Blow it again, baby. You can do it, blow at it again," they all cheered her on. With great effort on her part and all the strength a one-year-old could muster, she finally succeeded in blowing the stubborn candle out, a grin of accomplishment and self-satisfaction reflected in her huge eyes. Everyone clapped then, with Sam clapping with her dimpled chubby hands faster than anyone else in the room. Her happiness was so innocent and contagious that, in a split second, it had cast a magical spell on all the people present as they gave up any pretenses of propriety and simply joined in. Gifts soon surrounded the overjoyed child, who tore up the wrapping paper with gusto, pieces of it flying everywhere before her parents finally stepped in to help her get to whatever was inside. Such a joyous time, Amy sighted in her forage into the past. Then, Matt's untimely death, and how it totally shattered their lives and those of his loved ones apart. Barbara Kingston, heart shredded to pieces by her son's death, still managed to find the strength to be there for Amy, her husband, and remaining children. She allowed herself to totally and completely fall apart only when she was all by herself and was sure that no one could hear her, which was usually in the shower. That was the only time when she gave in to her anguish. She knew how they all looked up to her for support and guidance, and she would not let anyone down, least of all Matt, her darling son, taken from them at the tender age of twenty-seven. "Oh, Matt. My sweet and loving Matt. Why did you have to go, son, when you were so happy and wanted here? You owe me a big one, Lord, for you picked one of my most precious flowers to plant in your garden. In your hands I now leave his care." His death shook both Amy and Sam to the core, with Sam not being able to understand why her daddy never came home from work anymore. Patiently, Amy tried to explain the reason to the inconsolable child. Somehow Matt's parents managed to gather enough money to fly Amy's mother and father in for the funeral, and that proved to be instrumental in appeasing the toddler at times, just long enough for Amy to recuperate a little herself from the devastating blow that Matt's death delivered to all of them. But she was soon right back by her child's side, with her motherly touch and so much tenderness that it slowly began to work its magic in mending Sam's broken heart. Her parents were supposed to stay for only two weeks but ended up prolonging their stay to well over two months. They were very reluctant to leave their child and grandchild again, knowing how much they needed them still, both emotionally and physically. Farming obligations and the rest of their kids' needs, however, forced them to return to Missouri filled with sadness and heavy hearts. With the proceeds from Matt's modest life insurance policy plus the money she received from the automobile insurance settlement, Amy was able to continue staying home with Sam. She had to be very careful and wise as to how, when, and where she spent the money down to the last cent, but fortunately, she somehow managed to keep the creditors at bay. She often went without in order to pay the house mortgage on time, but she made sure that she did everything she possibly could in order to hold on to the house that Matt had worked so hard to buy. It was there that they had shared so many special moments and all the inevitable concerns as they began to build their lives together as a family. It was in the same bedroom that she still occupied where Matt had slept beside her for the last time. Amy, who found out she was pregnant the week before Matt died, grieved even further when she began to bleed heavily two weeks after the funeral; the stress of the ordeal was simply too great for the developing fetus to endure. She felt cheated of an extra part of Matt in the form of the child she was carrying but lost, thus becoming even more thankful that she at least had Sam. The adorable little girl was very much like her dad in so many unexpected ways.

About two months after her husband's death, Amy applied for and was granted a student loan, which she used to enter nursing school on a part-time basis, a dream she had nurtured ever since she was a little girl herself on the small family farm in Meadow Hills. It took her much longer than the other students, a total of six arduous and dedicated years of studying nonstop, and quite often well into the night after Sam had gone to sleep, before she successfully completed her studies. She finally graduated with high honors from Saint Vincent's College of Nursing on May 22, 1983, two weeks before Sam's tragic swing accident. "Matt would be so proud of you," her in-laws said after she received her hard-earned diploma. Their hugs and words of praise and encouragement made the already emotional graduation ceremony more meaningful for her, and she thanked God for Barbara and John's love and support. Sam, beaming like a ray of sunshine, never left Amy's side, her little hand snuggly held by that of her extraordinary mother, the special bond between them palpable and more than clear for anyone to see. That incredible bond had grown over the course of many years, as mother and daughter became each other's best friend, united by something more profound than blood ties alone. They were indeed one for all and all for one.

The years between 1976, when Matt died, and 1979, which was the last year that Samantha stayed at home with her mother full time before starting school, were a period of healing for both mother and daughter. They were filled with trips to local parks, frequent visits with her in-laws, who simply adored their little granddaughter, scraped knees, falling baby's teeth, occasional nightmares that frightened the sweet little girl but were promptly soothed by her devoted mother, and lots of kisses in between. First day of kindergarten arrived way too soon for Amy as Samantha bravely waved good-bye to her mother, promising to be a very good girl and not cry at all after she left. It was a promise she had to work hard to keep but somehow managed to. She literally ran into her mother's open arms as the first day of school came to an end, her head brimming with all kinds of stories she could hardly wait to share. As the days turned into weeks, the praises started to arrive about Sam's endearing ways, along with her kindness toward her classmates and the staff at school. Reports of how well she was doing kept on coming as the weeks quickly turned into months. During the very first parent-teacher conference, Amy could hardly contain her pride as Sam's kindergarten teacher sung the little girl praise after praise. "Samantha is a very considerate, friendly, well-behaved, and well-adjusted student. She is always ready and willing to help her classmates, any and all who might need a little extra assistance, a smile always on her beautiful little face," Mrs. Connors reported to a proud, happy, and delighted Amy. "That's my girl!" Amy beamed, unable to contain her enthusiasm. As a reward for the excellent report Sam received, she decided to take her daughter out for a celebratory ice-cream Sunday right after the conference was over, followed by the movie of her choice. Sam was beyond happy, almost unable to sit still long enough to finish her treat. At the movie theater though, she sat very ladylike, a huge bucket of buttered popcorn between mother and child and an equally satisfied smile on both of their faces.

Sam was now playing in the backyard, swinging back and forth, higher and higher, her long dark hair following her small form like a protective blanket, her laughter mingling with the sound of birds singing their happy little summer tunes. Sam was now graduating from elementary school, her forest green cap and gown accentuating her petite and delicate face and thin frame, the color of the garment enhancing the color of her eyes, so alive and full of innocence, hope, and joy. *Wait just a minute!* Amy's mind shouted at once in total disarray. *How can this be if Sam never had the chance to graduate from elementary school because, unfortunately, she died three short weeks before finishing the third grade. What is going on here? Can someone tell me, for goodness sake? I must be losing my mind. Won't someone please be kind enough to tell me what is really going on? Have I gone insane?* Fearing that it was already too late and that she had indeed lost her mind, cold sweat and chills took over her body, and she closed her eyes trying to shut the world around her out as well. How else could she explain something that simply had no feasible explanation unless she had simply lost her faculties? Amy's thoughts, with a will of their own, unmercifully returned to the worst day in her entire life, surpassing even the horribly painful day when Matt, her darling husband and best friend, had died. That was the tragic day of her only child's swing accident. She could again clearly see her precious daughter soaring up in the air, laughing, chanting happily as only children seemed to be able to. Then, the eerie sound of silence, the loudest sound of all for any parent to hear, suddenly flooding her mind and unhinging her entire world. The unthinkable and overwhelming lack of noise, as if even the birds momentarily forgot how to sing their carefree melodies, was like a dull knife slowly sinking into Amy's chest in slow motion. She could see herself running outside, her heart rate racing totally out of control, held sky high by the sheer force of her fear. Her heart became agonizingly lodged in her constricted throat the very second she spotted her beloved little girl just lying there motionless, a small heap on the cool grass. As if in a trance, she clearly recalled every movement, every minute detail, thus being able to see herself exactly as it was back in 1983, quickly kneeling by her daughter's unmoving form. With a sick feeling threatening to overpower all of her other senses, she cradled her daughter's head gingerly in her shaking hands, fervently praying for her child to be all right. She was just about to lay Sam's head carefully down on the ground again so that she could run back inside the house to call 911, when suddenly, Sam opened her eyes and moaned, the best sound in the world for a frightened mother to hear at a moment like that. "I fell down, Mommy," she cried, sounding very small, scared, and fragile, all at the same time. "Are you okay, honey? Do you hurt anywhere?" Amy asked her daughter, trying hard not to panic, which would only serve to further upset the already frightened child. "I don't think so, but I got really scared when I slipped off the swing and was falling. Really, really scared, Mommy," Sam said in a trembling voice, looking at her mother with tear-soaked cheeks, so innocent and trusting. Her eyes never left her mother's, which were exactly the same color and shade as her own. "It is okay, my love, there is no need to be scared anymore. You are going to be just fine, you'll see," she added soothingly. "I am right here next to you, and I am, after all, a nurse, remember? You will have the honor of being my very first patient. I will take very good care of you, I promise. What do you think about that, sweetheart?" Amy said, scooping her daughter easily in her arms and carrying her precious little bundle safely inside, beyond glad to feel Sam's strong heartbeat through her cotton blouse, a sound that was pure music to Amy's ears.

Sam's first day of high school was a time of discovery for mother and daughter. Amy, who until then had not stopped to look at Samantha as her little girl still, was suddenly hit with the reality that her little girl had morphed into a truly beautiful young lady, one that was now on the verge of womanhood. A popular teen, her dynamic personality seemed to appeal to all who met her. She was an exceptionally good student, able to keep her grades much higher than average month after month. She made friends easily wherever she went and was well-liked by the "cool kids" and the "brainy crowd." After trying out for and successfully getting a spot on the Shelton High School cheerleading squad, Sam saw her popularity with her peers, both male and female, rise even more. She was a truly good soul, and as beautiful on the inside as she was on the outside, the kind of person that her friends seemed to gravitate to when they needed help or simply a shoulder to cry on. She wasn't, by any means, a saint, but she was easier to handle than most teens her age. She managed to escape some of the trappings that many of her classmates fell into, like problems with drugs, alcohol, cigarettes and pot smoking, casual sex, and so forth. She did, however, break curfew more than once, sneaking out to see a movie without her mother's permission. She also loved to window shop at the local mall, and that is where she could be found on those rare occasions when she did skip school. Indeed she had tried drinking with some of her friends but got so sick afterwards that she swore off the stuff for good. Although she smoked a couple of cigarettes, she didn't like them any better than alcohol. Showing incredible maturity for her age, she decided on her own that pot was something she wasn't even going to try, aware that it almost always led to the use of much heavier drugs. She wasn't about to do that to herself or her mother, she vowed, as usual thinking twice before acting. Having sex just for the heck of it or just because everyone else was doing it wasn't in her agenda either. When the right guy came along she would decide if premarital sex was for her or not, but until then, she decided to simply act fifteen and enjoy her youth to the max.

Since she was her own person and had a good head on her shoulders, she didn't fall victim to peer pressure, refusing to do anything that made her feel uncomfortable. When she turned sixteen, her mother gave her permission to sign up for driving lessons, which was every teenager's dream. Amy bought her daughter an older Chevrolet Grand Am after she passed her exam on her first try. The 1985 model had a burgundy-colored body with black bumpers and side protection strips. Even though the car was over five years old at the time, it had been very well-kept by the previous owners and didn't have a single scratch on its original shiny paint. The gray vinyl interior was in great condition as well, and Sam took pride in keeping it that way.

Not once during her daughter's four years of high school did Amy ever receive any major complaint from Sam's teachers. Very seldom was she aware that Sam had gotten into some sort of trouble, be it with her classmates or anyone else for that matter. She had prepared herself, as best as she could anyway, for the so called "terrible teen years" that she had heard so much about, and when the time came and went without any drastic changes in Sam's personality or behavior, she breathed a sigh of relief. She thanked Matt for watching over their child, knowing in her heart that he was certainly exerting his loving paternal influence over his little girl.

During her senior year, Sam started to date a very nice young man by the name of Mark Mitchell, who was three years older than she. They met when she attended her best friend, Ashley's, eighteenth birthday party. They were introduced to each other by David, Ashley's boyfriend of two years, and became an item from that night on. On the day of her prom, an occasion most high school girls dreamt about with equal doses of anticipation and apprehension, Sam looked absolutely stunning in a pale blue dress. Her shiny dark hair, reaching down past her tiny waist, made her eyes look even greener than ever on that particular afternoon. She was simply glowing with the sheer happiness of being young and in love. Mark, who was equally debonair in his elegant black tuxedo, carefully tried to pin the exquisite lavender orchid corsage to Sam's dress with trembling hands. His blue eyes were captivated by the beauty of her upturned face. About eight inches taller than Sam who proudly stood at a full five foot and four inches on a good day, he seemed to tower above her petite frame. *What a strikingly beautiful couple these two make,* a glowing Amy silently acknowledged, her heart overflowing with joy for her cherished daughter and her newly found mate. She remembered very well how wonderful and magical it felt like to be that young and that much in love, images of Matt's smiling and handsome face filling her with a mixture of gratitude and longing. She was glad that Sam and Mark had found each other as she continued to snap picture after picture of the ecstatic couple. It was almost impossible to capture the magic of that moment, but she certainly gave it her best shot. With their happiness lingering behind, she waved good-bye to the young couple as they left for the exciting evening ahead. She was caught by surprise when they turned around and winked at her, for it was exactly what Matt used to do all the time while they were dating and even more often after they were married. *You are here, aren't you, my love? Can you see what a beautiful and wonderful young woman we have created, sweetheart? She possesses only the best of you and me, darling, and in precisely the right amount and all in perfect harmony.* In spite of all the pain she had endured, Amy considered herself to be a very lucky woman. She had met and married the love of her life, and even though their union was very short-lived, it had been enough to last her a lifetime. Together they had found true love and had conceived their precious Samantha. Matt would always be alive for Amy and go on in the form of their incredibly kind child.

* * *

Mark graduated from the Police Academy on November 5, 1993, at the age of twenty-three and started to work as a Shelton police officer soon after. He knew that he wanted to be a cop ever since he was a little boy because he came from four generations of cops. His great-great-grandfather, Walter, had been in law enforcement at the turn of the twentieth century. His great-grandfather, Joseph, was also a police officer in the town of Trumbull from 1928 to 1964, retiring with the rank of lieutenant. His grandfather, Anthony, was a retired former chief of police in nearby Newtown, where he lived still. His father, Ron, worked as a detective in the town of Monroe, where Mark and his siblings were born and raised. Law enforcement was literally in his blood, he often told his mother, Carolyn, when she asked him why he wanted to become a cop. She often reminded her son that now she would have to worry about two of the most important men in her life instead of just about her husband. She was well aware of how often they placed their lives at risk every time they left the house, and that fact caused her a great deal of concern. She didn't rest until she heard the last one of them insert his key in the front door, a signal that they were all safe under one roof again. That was her signal that everything was all right and that she could finally fall asleep. "Thank God your younger brothers show no desire of becoming police officers, for I don't think I could handle it if they did. And your sister is still too young to really know what she wants to be when she grows up," Carolyn would often say, relief clearly detected in her resigned voice. His mother was right though, for neither Luke nor Jason had shown any interest whatsoever in careers that had anything to do with the police force. "Please, son, make sure that you are very careful when you are in uniform, but be just as careful when you are not. I only have one Mark, you know?" the concerned mother said whenever he was getting ready to go to work. "And honey, always remember these simple three words: I love you," she repeated every single time she kissed her eldest child good-bye, praying that the good Lord would bring her son back home safe and sound, just as she did with her husband, and had done for so many years with her father-in-law. She always left the front porch light on until every member of the household was accounted for, firmly believing that the light would guide each one of them safely back where they belonged. That porch light symbolized the beacon of her love for them, illuminating their paths directly to where she knew they would always be protected. That porch light would bring them home.

Sam started her freshman year at Southern Connecticut State University, located in New Haven, in the fall of 1993 as well, a couple of months before Mark's graduation. By the time she entered her junior year, the young couple had become engaged and were happily planning their upcoming wedding. The months leading up to the nuptials were quite hectic for Sam and Mark but were certainly no less hectic for their parents. Amy, who didn't have a traditional church wedding, wanted to go all out for her daughter. Due to her well-paying job as a registered nurse, she was financially stable, albeit far from being rich. She wished to give Sam the wedding of her dreams and had looked forward to that day since she was a little girl. As kind as ever, Sam always made a point of including her future mother-in-law every time she and her mother went looking for her wedding dress. Parading in front of them in more than a dozen gowns, she asked their honest opinion about each one. Once she had narrowed the selection down to two distinctively different styles, she seemed to hit a stalemate. Noticing her indecision, her wise mother-in-law told her to simply close her eyes and picture herself on her wedding day. "Now," Carolyn went on, "describe to us what you look like." "Like a fairytale princess," Sam answered, her voice dreamlike. "Then, honey, you have just made your choice, haven't you?" Carolyn said. Looking at both gowns, Sam knew exactly what her mother-in-law was talking about. By using simple logic, she had given Sam the guidance she was looking for while not making any suggestions one way or the other.

Because she knew that her mother and Mark's parents had insisted on equally sharing the final cost of the wedding, Sam tried to be extra careful when choosing, from the food to the favors and everything in between. Saying that he trusted her judgment, Mark sort of excluded himself from the decision making when things became too complicated for his simple taste. "What a coward you are, Officer Mitchell!" Sam said, seeing right true his lame excuse. It would be up to her to make sure that their parents didn't incur any more expenses than they had to. They worked hard for their money, and she didn't want to abuse their generosity. And now, checking the price tag on the gown she had chosen, Sam's heart fell to her feet, for it was way too expensive to even consider. Carolyn, who didn't miss the look of disappointment that momentarily crossed her face, pulled her aside and asked why she seemed to be having second thoughts. "Oh, I don't know about this dress. Perhaps I should look at some more before we buy it," Sam replied, her voice betraying her words as she spoke them. "What is it, darling? What seems to have worried you all of a sudden? You know that you can tell me, Sam" Carolyn went on, trying to reassure the young bride. Sam, who had started to call her mother-in-law "Mom" when she became engaged, looked at Carolyn with tear-filled eyes when she spoke again. "Well, Mom, I have this big dilemma in my hands. You see, there's this "little angel," the good Sam, on my left shoulder, always reminding me to be reasonable, to try keeping the costs down since you guys and my mother are so generously paying for everything. But then, there's this "little devil," the bad Sam, sitting on my right shoulder, telling me to go for it, since I'm only planning on getting married once. The two of them argue all the time, and I'm caught in the middle, not knowing what to do!" Seeming to be absorbing it all, Carolyn took a few seconds before addressing her son's future bride. "And who's winning, darling?" she finally asked, trying her best not to breakdown laughing over Sam's predicament. "The little devil in me is winning, Mom. By far . . . ," Sam replied, mortified, a look of consternation overpowering her delicate features. "So, go ahead, let the little devil win this one time. I'm sure that between your Mom and us, we'll be able to manage it. Tell that little angel of yours to take a break, okay?" Sensing nothing but sincerity in her mother-in-law's voice, Sam relaxed once more. The light of happiness was back in her eyes as she hugged her wedding dress.

To her surprise, the salesperson, who also happened to be the owner of the shop called The Modern Bride Boutique, offered her a twenty-five percent discount. What Sam didn't know was that she decided to do so at the last minute after she overheard what she had said to Carolyn. With the discount, the final cost of the gown ended up being less than any of the others she had tried on, putting a smile on everyone's face, including the owner's. In her nineteen years in the business, she had helped literally hundreds of brides, if not thousands, but none as radiant as the one that stood in front of her at the moment. She could've been dressed in rags and she still would make a very beautiful bride. Lucky groom, she thought as she said good-bye to the three of them.

When the happy day finally arrived, a smiling Samantha indeed looked like a fairytale princess. Her off-the-shoulder creation had long fitted sleeves and top, all beaded in intricate detail, and a full, wide skirt that further accentuated her insanely small waist. The detachable twelve-foot train was embellished with literally thousands of shiny beads and tiny white pearls, which matched the gown's top. The skirt was so well-made, with small bunches of beaded flowers all around that Sam could remove the long train anytime during the reception, and the dress would continue to be just as elegant from every conceivable angle. Her hair was gathered high on her head, a beaded tiara holding back a mass of long curls under her waist-length veil, a few loose tendrils framing her delicate face. Amy, herself a vision of pure elegance and grace, wore an absolutely stunning champagne-colored silk gown. The one-of-a-kind creation was designed and made especially for her by a gifted seamstress she happened to be friends with. The top of the dress was fitted to her still slim figure and adorned with a very delicate pattern highlighted with golden-colored beads of all shapes and sizes, which sparkled like thousands of little stars under the soft church lights. The full skirt, made out of several yards of silk chiffon, seemed to float in the air with each step she took.

The atmosphere was romantic and magical inside Saint Lawrence Church on the afternoon of the ceremony. The truly special occasion created the kind of ambiance that only weddings had the ability to. All eyes were fixed on both mother and daughter as the visibly emotional pair walked slowly down the aisle. The absence of the bride's father made quite a few guests shed some tears, especially those who had known Matt well and now missed him more than ever. He should have been the one walking beside his beautiful daughter, they all thought with sadness, knowing how a daughter's wedding was a day every father dreamed of and one that Matt unfortunately did not get a chance to enjoy. Thank God Amy was there to step in for him. At the altar, Mark could hardly believe the beauty of the woman walking toward him and who literally took his breath away. The second he saw her coming, all silk, tulle, and lace, his legs began to tremble, his knees threatening to buckle at the very sight of his gorgeous bride. *I am truly a lucky man*, he admitted with gratitude, *the luckiest one in the world for sure*!

As Mark took Sam's small shaky right hand in his left one, tears began to silently roll down Amy's face. She could feel Matt's presence there, right beside her, giving his blessing to the union between their little girl and her very special young man. As his mother-in-law took her place of honor on the second pew, directly behind the giggly bridesmaids and adorable flower girl, Mark whispered to Sam how truly beautiful she looked, meaning every word he spoke. It was a phrase he repeated often throughout the church ceremony and the fabulous reception that followed afterwards.

The newlyweds danced together for the very first time as husband and wife to the sound of "Grow Old Along With Me," a little known song they had first heard when it was dedicated to them by Mark's parents during their engagement party. The touching tune sung by Mary Chapin Carpenter was actually one of the last songs written by John

Lennon and which he recorded just a few days before he was killed in 1980. Even though it was never completely finished, John had recorded it anyway, just the way it was, and Mary Chapin Carpenter re-recorded and released it quite a few years later. The romantic song sent shivers up and down Amy's spine every time she heard it. She once again felt Matt's presence right next to her as the words of the sentimentally written song reminded her of the wish she had made twenty-one years before on her own wedding day. With great longing, she recalled how Matt had taken her left hand to his lips and kissed the simple gold wedding band he had just placed on her ring finger, the same one she now touched with such tenderness. She also recalled how he promised to never leave her, a promise that he wasn't able to fulfill. She had wanted nothing more than to be able to grow old along with him and their daughter, but that dream was shattered by his sudden death less than two years later. And then, along came this song . . .

The best man's toast, given by Mark's brother, Luke, was hilarious from beginning to end. He kept everyone in stitches, his anecdotes coming so naturally and so fast that the entire room erupted into laughter several times during his speech. In a clearly exaggerated manner, he described what it was really like growing up in the Mitchell household. The siblings' antics were already well-known to many but came as an extremely funny surprise to the remainder of the guests. The fact that all the males on their dad's side of the family were cops was the basis of merciless jokes, and Luke wasted no time teasing Mark, who was also a cop. He was also ruthless in his description of what it was like to go to a family reunion—meter maids, speeding tickets, and all. "We never know if or when Dad is going take out his handcuffs and use them on us. Being the son of a cop hasn't been easy, let me tell you. Dad waits for us to get home with a breathalyzer machine ready to go. We are always afraid that he is going to just nail our ass for one thing or another, even for something we are only thinking of doing, things like skipping school, taking a twenty-dollar bill from his wallet or peeing in the backyard." The uproar was so intense that many found themselves dabbing at their eyes or clutching their sides from laughing so hard and for so long. By contrast, the maid of honor, Ashley, who had been Sam's best friend since their first year of high school, had the opposite effect during her toast to the newlyweds. Her candid words had the room in complete silence, everyone touched with the sincerity they felt coming from the emotional young woman. Sam and Ashley, having both lost their dad as small children, had found each other as teenagers, two kindred spirits with a common bond, as she so poignantly described. They considered themselves more like sisters than friends, she added, looking at Sam's radiant face, crying and all. Although most guests had tears in their eyes, they were definitely tears of joy and not pity, joy for these two friends who grew up to be loving and decent adults in spite of the tremendous loss they had both suffered at a very early age. And the way they had turned out was mostly due, no doubt, to the unfailing strength and courage demonstrated by their surviving parent. As Ashley said the words, she looked at her own mother, then at Sam's mom, thanking them both with her eyes, for herself as well as for her best friend. Their mothers had indeed struggled but ultimately, and to their merit, had succeeded in raising two very well-adjusted and caring young women.

224

By the time she finished talking, she was in tears herself as she was being hugged by Sam, Amy, and her mother, Amanda.

When it came time for the father-daughter dance, Sam lovingly held her mother's hand as she escorted her to the center of the dance floor. She had kept her song choice a secret, wanting to truly pay tribute to the person who had sacrificed so much and worked so hard to raise her alone. "Wind Beneath My Wings," sang by Bette Midler, had just started and Amy already found it difficult not to cry. Sam, in a low voice that only her mother could hear, began singing the lyrics in Amy's ear, the words expressing everything she wanted to say but didn't know how. By the time the song ended, both were trying hard to suppress the tears that were hiding just beneath the surface, eyes burning by their urgent need to be shed. *Matt, darling, how I wish you were here in the physical sense, my love. It should have been you dancing with our daughter, not me. We should be having such a great time together, the three of us. I know that you are here in spirit, but I wish that I could see you one more time. Just one more time,* Amy thought as she slowly walked their daughter back to where her groom stood mesmerized. With a twitch in her heart, she silently paid tribute to the only man she had ever loved and continued to love to this day still. Matt would always remain her one and only love for the rest of her natural life.

The postcard Samantha and Mark sent her from their honeymoon in Aruba sat in a delicate golden filigree frame on the mantle above the fireplace. Next to it, a lovely ceramic vase in the shape of a baby's bootie often reminded Amy of the truly loving couple who had given it to her the day after her precious daughter was born. At the time, her wonderful roommate and spouse, having sensed that Amy was not only lonely but alone, had extended their open arms to her and little Sam. Although the beautiful bouquet of red roses, with a white rose in the center for the baby, had long dried, the thoughtful and comforting sentiment it represented was forever alive in her heart, the card attached to it safely put away in her daughter's baby album. That unexpected gesture of kindness from two people she had barely known but who were more than willing to show her how much they cared meant more to her than they would ever know, at a time when she had needed it the most. Unfortunately, with the passing of so many years, she could no longer remember their faces or last name, but the compassion they had shown then could never, and would never, be taken for granted or forgotten. Their act of compassion and understanding was a gift that she tried to pass along whenever she had the chance to.

"You drifted off again, Mom. What in God's name has you so distracted tonight, Amy Rose Kingston? Is there anything you are not telling me? You know that I'll find out sooner or later, so you better not keep anything from me," Sam said, her voice finally managing to bring Amy's thoughts back to the present again. *Is this really the present, or am I still asleep? Do I dare let myself believe that this is all real, or am I simply setting myself up for nothing but heartbreak?* she went on, afraid to believe it but even more afraid not to. Were her eyes deceiving her, or was her daughter really standing there in person, a mere few inches in front of her, all grown up already? When words failed her, Amy did the only thing she could think of. Slowly, she stood up on legs that seem made of rubber and quickly took the few steps that separated the two of them. With shaky arms that had been empty for so long, she gathered her precious daughter to her chest, her fierce hug telling her how much she was loved. She kept Sam within the circle of her embrace until her heartbeat slowed down to a more normal rate. When she finally found the strength to speak, Amy repeated what her embrace had tried to, her words so low that even she could hardly hear them. A puzzled look crossed Sam's face, momentarily rendering her speechless as well. Was there any reason for her mother's bizarre behavior? she silently asked. Swallowing hard, she resumed talking, her voice barely masking the concern mounting in her mind. "I know how much you love me, Mom. You have done nothing but love me for the past twenty-two years. I can assure you that I have never doubted that, not even for a single moment. Now, I have a very important question to ask you. Are you ready? Do you think you have any room left in that huge heart of yours to love one more?" Sam asked, a mischievous smile illuminating the beauty of her delicate features, a brighter-than-everf glow shining in her happy eyes. In her right hand, she held a home pregnancy test, the unmistakably bright pink line it displayed clearly visible across its tiny window. In her left hand, she held a second pregnancy test, the line across the tiny window as easily visible and as brightly pink as the first one. "Just to be sure, I did two pregnancy tests, and guess what, Mom? Mark and I are going to have a baby. Are you ready to become a grandmother?" With a strength she had no idea she was still capable of, Amy hugged her daughter so tightly that she feared she would break Sam in two. With both locked in a long-awaited and well-deserved embrace, Amy caressed her child's head with infinite tenderness, their hearts beating wildly with happiness, their erratic rhythm somehow in perfect unison once more. How could one explain a miracle to anyone, but better yet, why should one? Especially when it was a miracle of such magnitude? Why not simply remain eternally grateful for having received one instead of wasting precious time trying to understand how or why? After all, miracles did indeed happen, and for Amy, there was simply no question about it. She was holding her own in her loving arms right then and there. Yes, miracles definitely existed, even when you were not looking for or expecting one.

*   *   *

Mom was certainly acting strangely tonight, Sam reflected once she got behind the wheel, concern slightly creasing her forehead. "I have never seen her like this," she exclaimed out loud to no one but herself, "literally begging me not to go, not to leave her, as if she was afraid that I would simply vanish into thin air if I left her sight. I'll call her as soon as I get home, just to make sure that she's all right." Sam went on, carefully buckling her seatbelt. Before backing out of the long driveway, she wrestled with the idea of whether or not she should go back inside and spend a little more time with her clearly agitated mother. Usually a very rational and objective person, she finally decided that it would probably be better if she didn't make too much fuss about her mother's odd behavior in the long run. "Perhaps she had a bad dream while she dozed off, that's all. It happens to me at times, like when I have that horrible dream that I died a long time ago when I was only a child. Thank God I never shared those dreams with her. Then, for sure, she would not let me be away from her for a second!" Sam chuckled. Slowly, she began her short journey back home and was just about halfway there when she suddenly remembered that Mark would be working a double shift that night, the extra money a blessing now that they had a baby on the way. "That's what happens when you marry a cop! There is never one around when you need them," she teased, laughing at her own joke. Being all by herself most likely meant a quiet evening for her, perhaps watching one of her favorite movies on the VCR. And that would be *An Officer and a Gentleman*, no doubt, she chuckled again, amused by her fascination with the unforgettable story line. She knew the entire movie more than well and practically frame for frame, having seen it at least a dozen times already, if not twice that. And yet she never seemed to get tired of it. Her favorite part of all was the scene at the end of the film, when Richard Gere, absolutely dashing in his white naval uniform, carried a totally surprised and delighted Debra Winger in his strong arms, taking her forever away from her dull factory job, the same one she had dreamed of leaving behind for a very long time. The incredibly romantic ending never failed to nail her right in the heart. She had always loved a good tearjerker anyway, and this had to be one of the best she had ever seen. "You are such a sap for a sob story," Mark usually said when he caught her crying during one particular scene or another. "So I am and proud of it," she often retorted. "It is part of the package, sir. For better or worse, remember," she added with extra sassiness as they continued to tease each other back and forth until one of them mercifully gave up, and that someone was usually Mark. But, truth be said, there was a little secret as to why she loved *An Officer and a Gentleman* so much, and that was the fact that, like almost every woman in the country, she had a harmless crush on Richard Gere, whom she considered the sexiest man on the planet besides Mark, of course! Who could resist his charm and allure? And his handsome face and strong body were not to be overlooked either, she mused.

As she continued to drive, her mind shifted gears, and she began to reflect on all the sacrifices that her mother had to make in order to give her a good life and how well she had managed to accomplish that. She had to be a mother and a father to Sam and had excelled in both roles, never backing away from the challenge and responsibility of raising a toddler alone while, at the same time, trying to mend her own shattered heart. She could only imagine what her poor mother must have gone through, how much she must have suffered when her father died, so young and under such tragic circumstances. Her mother never entertained the thought of dating someone again when, as a more mature person, Sam had tried to encourage her to. "I am still in love with your dad, darling. There's no room in my heart for another man, and there'll never be. All I need now to go on is you, Sam," she would say each and every time she was asked, no sign of the slightest hesitation in sight. And true to her word, her mother who became a widow at the tender age of twenty-three never even looked at another man.

She knew that her father's picture, which her mother kept on her bedside table, was the last face she saw before falling asleep and the first thing she saw upon waking up. In the precious picture, the handsome young face with happy eyes and an even happier smile, managed to convey a lot without saying a word. Sam wished with all her heart that she had gotten to know her father better, her recollection of him fuzzy at best. The only thing she was still able to remember well was the sound of his laughter, very male while at the same time light and sweet, and the smell of his aftershave lotion. That's why she had given a bottle of Brut to Mark on their first Christmas as boyfriend and girlfriend. He continued to use it still, even though Sam didn't tell him why she had given it to him until after they were already married.

Her dad's family had been instrumental in helping to mold her into the kind of person she turned out to be, she acknowledged with gratitude. His older sister, Linda, was not only her favorite aunt but her godmother as well. She gave Sam a position she simply loved, as a preschool teacher at The Bears and Bees Nursery School, which was located right there in Huntington, a few minutes away from the newlyweds' house. Her aunt had started the now well-established business from scratch, often working long hours that ran well into the late evening hours. Sam fondly remembered spending most of her free time helping her out, feeling all grown-up as she did so. Her aunt's husband, Mike, was often there, landing a hand whenever possible, as were their three children–her cousins Rachel, Ryan, and Allie. It took a while, but The Bears and Bees finally succeeded and was now a well-known and respected nursery school, and Sam was very proud that she had been part of it from the ground up.

Before she had a chance to realize why, her thoughts veered away from her mother and her aunt to another mother, a very brave one indeed, called Jill Millner. She was the mother of the young serial killer who had been apprehended the year before, after a massive but failed manhunt. Unfortunately though, by then he had already raped and killed six vibrant and innocent young women, all in Fairfield and New Haven Counties. Sam reflected on the fact that the incredibly courageous mother had found the strength to turn her one and only child in to the police, admiration and sadness infusing into her heart. Mrs. Millner had done so after accidentally finding undeniable incriminating evidence of his involvement in the horrendous crimes inside a metal box hidden under his very own bed. On duty that afternoon, Mark had been the first police officer to enter the Millners' home on the day of Drew Millner's arrest. And it was also Mark who had handcuffed the stunned young man while reading him his Miranda rights. "I am so glad that the bastard is now behind bars where he belongs," Mark had said when he finally got home that night. "He won't be able to cause any further harm to anyone else, at least from this point on." He had been so shaken by the events surrounding the crimes, as well as those leading to Drew's capture, that he seemed unable to let go. She was so attuned to her husband's character and moods that she realized right away how upset he really was by what had transpired that day. Far too agitated to leave it behind, as he had always been able to until then, he definitely needed to talk about the incident still. "God only knows how many more girls he would have maimed and killed if his poor mother didn't have the courage to stop him. I shudder to think . . . We had absolutely no clues in any of the crimes except for the fact that they were all committed by the same sick son of a bitch. And that was only because the semen specimen he left behind matched in all six cases. It is just about impossible for anyone to even imagine what thoughts were going through his poor mother's head as she picked up the phone and summoned the police," he had carried on. Obviously having needed to purge himself of the horror and complexity of the disturbing and depraved case, he couldn't help but talk about the events that weighed heavy on his mind. Sam had been more than glad to listen to her husband and even more than willing to share some of his burden, if only for a little while. "When we got to the house, Mrs. Millner opened the front door without saying a word, but the expression on her face spoke volumes. She never looked us in the eye but simply stood aside to let us in. All her attention was riveted to her son's relaxed form as he watched TV, lying on the family room couch." Mark had stopped talking for a few seconds in order to collect his thoughts, and Sam had felt a strong urge to have her husband, who was nearly twice her size, climb on her lap so that she could try to sooth away some torment he had been subjected to. "What amazes me the most," he had added with a sigh, his voice barely audible and thick with emotion, "is that Mrs. Millner appeared not to have thought about herself at all or about what she was ultimately giving up as she dialed 911. I doubt it very much that she would have found the strength and courage to go through with it if she had. No parent would . . . I know that I probably wouldn't, not with my child anyway, and I'm a police officer, sworn to always uphold the law to the best of my ability. But the best of my ability, I'm almost certain, would not include turning my own son in," Mark had candidly admitted, his forehead dropped into the palms of his shaky hands. "I guess you can only be 100 percent sure of how you would handle a particular situation when you are confronted by it, otherwise it's pure speculation. But turning your own child in? Anyway, God only knows how many lives Mrs. Millner saved by doing what she found the guts to do and what most parents wouldn't," he had continued, crushed by the enormity of her personal sacrifice, his voice trailing off to a thin whisper.

He had been in the courtroom during the first few days of Drew's trial, but the sight of his mother quietly sitting there without moving at all had been too much for Mark to handle. She had kept staring at her son with eyes filled with a mixture of grief and guilt, the deep love she felt for her child written all over her contrite face breaking his heart in two. He had finally come to the conclusion that he needed to let the case go, or it would simply destroy him. He had returned to the courtroom on the day he was called to give testimony, but seeing Drew's aloof expression and demeanor while he testified had been enough to make him swear to never come back. And he never did.

Finding herself in her driveway, Sam wondered how the heck she managed to get there. She hadn't paid much attention to where she was going, since her mind had been somewhere else during the entire trip. She lovingly patted her slightly rounded belly while she waited for the garage door to go up. Totally in love with the precious life growing inside already, she shut the engine off and gave herself a few extra minutes before exiting the car. She was still deeply immersed in thoughts about her husband, her mother, her baby, and life in general.

Touching her abdomen again, she fondly recalled the moment just the day before, when she first told Mark about the good news. Upon finding out for sure that she was indeed pregnant, Sam had phoned her husband at work and invited him to an impromptu picnic lunch at their very own special spot, which was a private little park by a quiet lake in town. It was there that they had finally kissed, during their first real date after her best friend's eighteenth birthday party. When he got there, Mark had found a relaxed Sam sitting on a corner of a red-and-white checkered tablecloth, her head turned upward, toward the warm sun. Her eyes were hidden behind a pair of oversized dark glasses, which made her delicate face appear even smaller than it already was. In the center of the tablecloth sat a heart-shaped wicker basket that Sam had bought in early spring at the Christmas Tree Shop in Orange—"her favorite place on earth to browse in," she often said. As he bent down to kiss her, she had pulled him down beside her, pressing her head against his broad chest as she wrapped both of her arms tightly around his waist. "It is against the law to bribe a police officer, little missy. You can get yourself arrested for that," he teased, eliciting a hearty laugh from her. "I can think of far more pleasurable things I can get in trouble for, can't you?" she teased right back. "As a matter of fact, I have, if you must know," she had pressed on. Noticing his puzzled expression, she had continued, "Get into trouble, I mean. And for doing far more pleasurable things and with none other than with you, my dear Officer Mitchell!" He had looked even more puzzled then, but she had chosen to ignore it for the time being. They had eaten their light lunch while he told her about his morning. She had become suddenly quiet as he talked, he had noticed, even though she continued to pay close attention to his words. She had brought chocolate-covered strawberries for dessert, which she had placed in two individual glass bowls inside a larger container filled with ice. The colorful lids on the glass bowls were bright blue and bright pink, respectively. "Pick one," she had asked, a conspiring smile on her lips. "Why?" he had countered. "Is there a difference in the strawberries or in the chocolate between the two bowls?" he had asked, going along with whatever game she appeared to be playing. "Not really," she had answered back, her smile widening. "The difference is not in the contents of the bowls, silly. The real difference is in the lids. Pink or blue, honey, which one do you prefer? And don't you dare say both!" she had continued, her eyes slowly studying his handsome features. "It really doesn't matter to me, Sam. I don't get why you are asking me to choose, anyway. What are you hiding, babe?" he had asked, more puzzled than ever by her mysterious behavior. "Come on, stud. This is not a tricky question nor do you have to be a rocket scientist to answer it," she had teased her befuddled husband, "and it requires only a one word reply, I promise. So here we go again, darling. Pink or blue?" At first he still hadn't got it, but suddenly it became more than clear to him. His mouth wide open in disbelief, he had finally answered her with a question of his own. "A baby? Are we having a baby, Sam?" She had only nodded yes because she was too chocked up to speak. The momentary look of shock on Mark's face had been quickly replaced by one of infinite joy. In one swift movement, he had reached for his wife, his arms encircling her small frame. He had held her so tightly that for a moment she feared he had cracked a couple of her ribs in his enthusiasm.

The chocolate-covered strawberries had been quickly forgotten by the young lovers, so wrapped up were they in each other. Without missing a beat, they had immediately began making all kinds of plans for the arrival of the new life they had created. They had both agreed that they didn't want to know the sex of the baby until the actual birth, preferring to be surprised one way or the other. The truth was that it really didn't matter anyway whether it was a little boy or a little girl as long as the baby was born perfectly healthy. They had then proceeded to discuss everything about the pregnancy, Sam's health, decorating the nursery, so on and so forth. They wouldn't need a book of baby's names since they had already picked them. Ethan Bryce, if it was a boy, and Brianna Rose, if it was a girl. Before they had a chance to think about it, they had found themselves discussing school issues and even college tuitions, which caused them to crack with laughter at how quickly they had moved from pregnancy to college graduation, all in literally one single breath. "At this rate," Sam had teased, "we will have the baby married before it is even born, the poor little thing." Realizing how ridiculous they sounded, both had started to laugh so hard that tears began to stream from their eyes. "I think that we should just slow down and enjoy every moment," Mark had finally managed to say. "Before long, our baby will be here, sweetheart, and then we can make all the plans that we want," Sam had added as she kissed her husband with all the passion of a woman totally in love, their unborn child securely nestled between the two of them. "We better stop before it's too late. I don't want to have to arrest us both for indecent exposure!" Mark had teased as he gave his wife a passionate but guarded kiss.

The sound of the garage door slowly closing behind her car instantly startled Sam back to the present, the taste of their passionate kiss lingering on her lips still. She gave herself a few minutes longer, not in any hurry to enter the house. In a second, her thoughts went back to her husband, her mother, Mark's family, and the baby growing inside her. She could already picture their precious infant in her arms, her anxiety for the arrival growing stronger by the minute even though the pregnancy took them both by surprise. They had agreed to wait for a couple of years before trying to conceive, but God had other plans, it seemed. So much for their method of contraception, she laughed. Sam never felt luckier, already looking forward to the day when the baby started to move, which should be in another two months or so, give or take a few days. In the meantime, she would simply wait, she thought, as she finally felt ready to open the car door.

CHAPTER 20

JULY 1996

Jill approached the newly dug grave with slow, tentative steps. She knew that it was there where she should feel physically closest to her son, for his body laid lifeless a mere seven feet below where she was now standing, but it had the opposite effect on her. It was there that she felt his absence the most, his distance from her wider than the entire universe. She knelt on the cool loose dirt, completely mindless of the small stones that dug painfully into her bare knees. She placed the massive bouquet of flowers she was carrying gently on the grave, by the headstone. The amazing arrangement consisted of twenty-two beautiful deep royal blue roses, one for each of DJ's short years on earth, and two large yellow roses in the center of the blue ones, one from his father and the other from her. She began to talk to her son in a low, husky voice, a voice punctuated by a string of muffled sobs that she tried hard to control. "Oh, Drew! My son, I'm still trying hard to find a reason for the way you acted, for doing all those horrible things, but I come up empty-handed every single time, darling. I wreck my brain in my endless quest to understand what it was that motivated you to stray, yet I simply cannot. Was it because you were in the car with your father on the morning he was killed? Did that tragic accident scar you for life, son? Or was it because of the brain tumor that 'miraculously' disappeared when you were only nine years old?" Jill had to pause for a while before she found her voice again, her eyes burning from the mounting tears that begged to be released. "Could that episode in your life have triggered some unknown change in your thinking capacity, possibly rendering you unable to control your emotions, to apparently so carelessly disregard the sanctity of life, human or otherwise? Coldness and callousness are terms that I would never have used to describe you, yet that is precisely what I constantly hear when your name is mentioned. I often wonder if, because I felt so bad about the fact that you lost your father at such an early age, I might have unknowingly tried to compensate you for all that you had gone through already. Did I overindulge you, sweetheart, irrevocably spoiling you in my eagerness to make up to you for your devastating and tragic loss?

Did I, DJ? Did I do you far more harm than good, son? I literally torture myself at times, thinking about all that you have done, the harm and pain you have caused, not only to your poor victims and their loved ones, but also to our family as well. No one escaped the wrath of your actions, least of all the six young girls whose lives you took," Jill murmured, her voice heavy under the weight of the guilt she felt. "People now refer to you as being a monster, a bad seed. I want you to know that I will never believe that, son. Never . . . I knew you better than anyone and in ways that nobody else did. To me, your loving mother, you will always be my precious son, my little angel with broken wings, as broken as the wings of all those poor little creatures that crossed your tortured path when you were growing up. So much misery, so much pain . . . And I fear that I'll forever wonder why. Why, DJ? I could have helped you, you know? Why didn't you confide in me, son? You know that I would have done anything for you, my love. I wish that you could have told me back then what it was that tormented you so. If I only knew . . ." With her head bowed and her shoulders slumped by the depth of her sorrow, she continued to talk to DJ, stopping to kiss the flowers on the ground as tenderly as if they were her son.

With her hands tightly clasped to her chest, Jill finally allowed the tears to come, and they fell in quick succession on the soft dirt. "Son, please forgive me for what I had no choice but do. Here I kneel, my heart shattered into a million pieces, asking you to forgive me as I have asked God Almighty to forgive you. We are both sinners, DJ, you and I, but somehow, someday, after we are both held accountable for all of our sins, I hope that we can finally be reunited again, together for all eternity–you, my darling, darling son, your father, and me. I love you so very much, DJ, and miss you more than you will ever know. I love you so."

Jill went on speaking slowly and softly, her voice often cracking with all the emotion she felt, telling her son all the things that she didn't get a chance to say while he was behind bars. How she wished that DJ had not banned her from his life after he went to prison. There was so much she wanted to explain and share with him, and the time had come to do just that. She continued to talk to him until everything she wanted and needed to say was finally said. Suddenly, she became aware that the sun was beginning to set already. Against her will, she realized that she would have to leave soon. She still wanted to visit her husband's grave before she left the cemetery that afternoon. A beautiful bouquet of yellow roses sat on the passenger seat, and she would lovingly carry them to where her Drew was buried a little for over twenty long years now. She would gently place the flowers on the grass that now covered the dirt, leaving a piece of her heart behind as she did so. Someday, she had already requested of her mother and siblings, she wanted to also be buried at Gate of Heaven Cemetery so that she could be near her husband and son. She felt great relief when they all agreed to honor her wishes. No other place would do. Unbeknownst to her, her mother had already bought a large plot, one that would accommodate all three of them, and had made all the arrangements necessary to move Drew and DJ's bodies upon Jill's death. Sophia felt it was the least she could do for the daughter who had brought her nothing but pride and joy and who had already suffered enough to last ten lifetimes. Thank God she now had Jack by her side, for she knew what a good man he really was. Besides loving Jill deeply, Sophia felt that Jack truly understood her. He gave her all the room to grieve for her husband and son when she felt the need to without withholding his affection and support. That fact alone told her everything she needed to know about his character and good heart.

Sobbing now, Jill bent her head down, kissing the cool ground covering her son's body several times before she proceeded to kiss the cold flat stone at the top of the grave. She promised to return as often as she possibly could, to spend more time with her beloved child. With a sigh, she turned her back to DJ's final resting place and with great effort, walked back to her car, reluctant to leave him. It was extremely painful to have to leave a loved one behind. She remembered it more than well from when Drew had died so suddenly and the devastation that his loss left in its wake after most of the initial shock wore off. Then, her father's heart attack, once again so totally unexpected and hard to overcome, a death no child ever quite recovered from no matter how young or old the parent was. And then her only child, her beloved and sorely missed DJ, forever gone as well. It was indeed a very traumatic time for her, and she tried to draw strength from deep within herself, from a well that she hoped would not dry up anytime soon.

The late afternoon sun, as it streamed through the lush foliage of the tall thick trees that surrounded the cemetery grounds, reflected off of the dark green marble headstone, casting eerie shadows upon the letters that were painstakingly carved by clearly patient and professional hands. The inscription, beautiful in its simplicity, read:

Drew William Millner Jr. (DJ)   Forever in my loving heart
Good night, moon!
Born 05-14-1974   Died 06-06-1996

*   *   *

The handsome young man appeared to be in absolutely no hurry to get wherever he was headed. With both hands deep in his pockets, he casually looked from one side to the other, feigning an interest he had never known nor wanted to. He seemed to have no care in the world as he leisurely strolled down the nearly dark and deserted streets at sundown, destination unknown. He whistled a light tune, breaking into the well-rehearsed cold and cynical smile he had mastered to perfection over the centuries, the same smile that never reached his cunning eyes. Every one of his measured steps was calculated with infinite precision, never rushed or unsure, bringing him closer and closer to someone, anyone, somewhere, anywhere, in need of his services and assistance, which he was always willing to oblige with courtesy, certainty, and speed. His was a mission that transcended time and place, an eternal search that knew no end.

*   *   *

Lyla waited patiently for her owner to come home from wherever it was that she went as she laid quietly by the door that lead directly to the garage, between the kitchen and the laundry room. Her adorable little face rested on top of the sweater Jill wore all day yesterday, the very same one she had absentmindedly dropped on the floor when she was placing some dirty clothes in the hamper earlier that morning. For the time being, the little dog's curled-up tail remained as motionless as the rest of her tiny relaxed body, but all that complacency was about to change soon. Somehow, she sensed Jill's car make the turn from Mohegan Road onto Rydell Drive, and in an instant, that same tail started to wag with joy and anticipation, going into overdrive as she heard the double garage door finally going up. Loving bright brown eyes immediately questioned Jill as to where she had been all day long, even though it had actually been just slightly over two hours since they last saw each other. It took a few minutes of petting and caressing before the overjoyed animal agreed to stop her enthusiastic homecoming salute, but eventually she became satisfied enough to slowly calm down. "It is so nice and comforting to know that you are here, at home, waiting for me, little one, always happy to see me no matter what!" Lyla's tiny ears perked up when she heard Jill's voice, and the euphoria started all over again, causing her to laugh for the first time that afternoon. Jill decided that a leisurely paced walk would do them both a world of good, since she felt as restless as her companion probably did. A couple of hours later and feeling much less tense than before, Jill returned home, preparing a simple sandwich for her dinner after giving a treat to her little friend. After she finished eating, they both headed to the family room where Lyla, snuggling right next to Jill, quietly fell asleep as her owner settled into her cozy recliner to watch some TV before they both retired for the night. Bedtime was by far their favorite time of the day, and they always followed a routine that was most satisfying and comforting for both of them. Lyla couldn't wait to be picked up and placed on top of the large bed, quickly disappearing under the covers the minute she got there. Her warm and soft body, as she gently pushed against her owner's right thigh, provided Jill with the serenity and peace of mind that she had come to rely on in order to quietly fall asleep. The tiny creature would probably never know how truly grateful Jill was for her existence, presence, and companionship, all of which were an irreplaceable source of comfort to her especially now that DJ was gone and with the house way too big for one person alone. Although Jack came over several times a week, Jill continued to hold off on marrying him, and he seemed to understand why, saying that being with her without the sanctity of marriage was much better than not being with her at all.

For quite some time, Jill had continued to struggle with the idea of selling the house and moving into a much smaller place, but there were too many memories inside her home, most of which she wouldn't trade for anything in the world. It was here where she had shared her heart and body with Drew who, besides being her husband, was her lover, soul mate, and best friend all in one. It was on that very same bed that she now shared with Lyla that her son was conceived. It was in this very same room that Drew slept beside her for the last time before he was so tragically killed. DJ's nursery, which she had so lovingly painted and decorated during the months preceding his birth, remained as it was twenty-two years before–a haven of green, yellow, and blue that brought her nothing but peace and all the good thoughts invariably associated with conceiving and then giving birth to him. She didn't remember much about the catastrophic two months she spent wasting away, a total recluse in her own bedroom, and that was actually a merciful blessing for her. DJ's bedroom had been sealed, and she had absolutely no intention of reopening the room or the wounds that were inflicted upon her mind and soul in there anytime soon and most probably never. After much soul searching and rivers of tears, she finally realized that home was the place where her heart truly was, and this was it. You couldn't escape your past, no matter how hard you sometimes wanted to, and as a result, you had only two paths to choose from–leave in denial or face the truth. Having lived in denial for such a long time, Jill wanted nothing but the truth, and the best way to accomplish that was by learning from times gone by, mistakes and all, and to continue to move ahead with the highest quality of life that you could possibly attain. To that extent, Lyla had, without any doubt, been her lifeline, her salvation, besides her renewed faith in God and in her religious beliefs. The love that she shared with her precious companion was as natural and essential to Jill as breathing, their devotion and dedication to each other much more comforting than anything else in her life for sure, even slightly ahead of her love for Jack. "Am I really worthy of your love, little one?" Jill said in a loving voice that was so low, she wasn't quite sure that the dog had heard her. As if capable of fully understanding the question she was just asked, which she most certainly did, Lyla inched as close as she possibly could to her owner, softly licking Jill's nightgown as if kissing her in affirmation, which she most certainly was. The simplest pleasures in life were by far the most meaningful of all, Jill reminded herself, the constant ache in her heart a little duller each time she looked at Lyla's kind and innocent little face. She found herself totally immersed in the adoration she always saw in the depths of those amazingly beautiful brown eyes. Jill could almost swear that she was now seeing the hint of a smile come across the dog's happy little face, or was it simply a mere reflection of her own?

EPILOGUE

(1997)

As the silver sedan expertly maneuvered through the dark and deserted streets of Derby, Connecticut, the driver, Mark Mitchell, touched the left side of his wife's face ever so gently with the back of his right hand. The streets had been plowed, he noticed with a great deal of gratitude and relief after what seemed to be endless hours of steady snowfall that managed to deposit, at the very least, about twenty inches of the white stuff on the ground before it finally moved on. *This is, after all, good old New England, and we happen to be smack in the middle of January*, he begrudgingly conceded. After years of being a police officer, he had gotten used to driving under all types of conditions, but nothing could ever beat freshly plowed and well sanded roads especially when you were on a very important mission, and this was, without a doubt, his most crucial mission of his life. Far into her labor, a clearly uncomfortable Samantha still managed to give her attentive husband a radiant smile. She simply loved it when he stroked her cheek like he just did a few seconds before; she wished that he did not have to pay such attention to his driving so that he could continue to touch her like that. If he was at all nervous, he certainly didn't show it, she mused, unable to stop glimpses of panic-stricken, clumsy, and utterly frantic fathers-to-be from slipping in and out of her head. The stereotypical images caused her to laugh out loud in spite of the severe contractions that had taken over her body for quite some time now. Puzzled by his wife's sudden attack of laughter, especially given the fact that she was clearly in a great deal of pain, he was about to ask her about it when the entrance to the emergency room at Griffin Hospital appeared to their right, causing a sudden shift in his train of thought. Mark stopped the car in front of the double glass doors and quickly walked over to the passenger side. As he was about to bend down and gently help his wife to her feet, a yellow taxi carefully drove up the entrance and proceeded to park right next to the Mitchell's car. A young woman, obviously quite far advanced in her pregnancy, slowly got out of the cab and then reached into the backseat, from where she retrieved a small overnight bag. Her face showed only a hint of the unbearable pain she was going through at the moment, the frown suddenly appearing on her beautiful face causing her lips to purse into a very thin line. Without uttering a single sound, she carefully started to walk toward the emergency room, her long blonde hair trailing behind her. As she was about to enter the hospital, she briefly looked at the Mitchells and smiled. For a few seconds, Sam felt herself start to shiver from head to toe, suddenly breaking into a cold sweat, a fact that truly unnerved her for some unknown reason. Instinctively, she reached for Mark's hand for reassurance, finding great comfort in its warmth as it encased her icy cold one, giving her a great sense of protection and security. Amazingly, as quickly as it came, the uneasy feeling suddenly disappeared, but she held onto her husband's hand still. Mark remained behind to give the clerk the information necessary for Sam's admission, while his wife was being wheeled directly into the labor and delivery unit. In the next cubicle, the young blonde girl was busy answering the questions posed to her by the sympathetic clerk, stopping quite often in order not to scream as another contraction threatened to split her body in two. As he looked up at the white wall right in front of him, he spotted a massive clock hanging there, slightly above the clerk's bent head. He chuckled out loud as he realized that it had stopped working nearly a half hour earlier and nobody had noticed. It was probably around the same time they had finally arrived at the hospital, for he was sure that it was now quite a bit later than *3:45:18 a.m.*

THE END

GROW OLD ALONG WITH ME

Grow old along with me the best is yet to be,
When our time has come, we will be as one,
God bless our love, God bless our love.

Grow old along with me, two branches of one tree,
Face the setting sun, when the day is done,
God bless our love, God bless our love.

Spending our lives together, man and wife together,
World without end, world without end,

Grow old along with me, whatever fate decrees,
We will see it through, for our love is true,
God bless our love, God bless our love.

This song was written by the late John Lennon in 1980 shortly before he was killed. It
was rerecorded in 1995 by Mary Chapin Carpenter.

Get Published, Inc!
Thorofare, NJ 08086
14 May, 2010
BA2010134